# Need

Nik Cohn was brought up in Derry, Northern Ireland.
His books include *Awopbopaloobop Alopbamboom*,
*I am Still the Greatest Says Johnny Angelo*, *Ball the Wall*
and *The Heart of the World*. He also wrote the story
that gave rise to *Saturday Night Fever* and collaborated
on *Rock Dreams* with artist Guy Peellaert.
He now lives in Shelter Island, New York
and Adara, County Donegal.

# NEED

## NIK COHN

Minerva

**A Minerva Paperback**
NEED

First published in Great Britain 1996
by Martin Secker & Warburg Limited
This Minerva edition published 1997

Random House UK Limited
20 Vauxhall Bridge Road, London SW1V 2SA

Random House Australia (Pty) Limited
20 Alfred Street, Milsons Point, Sydney,
New South Wales 2061, Australia

Random House New Zealand Limited
18 Poland Road, Glenfield, Auckland 10, New Zealand

Random House South Africa (Pty) Limited
Endulini, 5a Jubilee Road, Parktown 2193, South Africa

Random House UK Limited Reg. No. 954009

Reprinted 1997

A CIP catalogue record for this book
is available from the British Library
ISBN 0 7493 8675 4

Phototypeset in Sabon
Printed and bound in Great Britain
by Cox & Wyman Ltd, Reading, Berkshire

*For Vera and Norman Cohn;*
*and, of course,*
*for Michaela.*

# First

What Willie saw was a fat white woman.

She stepped out of Ferdousine's Zoo with a pearl-grey bird on her wrist, some kind of cockatoo or parakeet, and stood exposed on the sidewalk, her big body all pinks and creams in a flowered cotton dress cut straight up and down like a shift or maybe a converted bedsheet with armholes hacked out. It was hardly even daylight.

Apart from Willie D and Anna Crow double-parked by a fire hydrant in his red Spyder, the block was deserted. There was only heat and a guttering trash-fire, the smell of burnt rubber.

And the bird began to sport.

It flirted the air with wings outspread, did a back-flip, drifted as if hang-gliding. Then dropped like a stone to the kerb, playing dead. Then whirled back up again, flurrying. Its plume was a pale yellow cut with cinnamon, it had a vivid orange patch on either cheek, and when it fluttered, its wing feathers flashed hidden colours, not only pearl but shades of bracken and butter.

From where Willie watched, the flowers on the woman's dress looked like marigolds, or maybe some strain of daisy. There was a gap in her front teeth when she laughed, and the bird nuzzled at her hair, pecked lightly at her cheek. They

3

looked like lovers then, and the woman played the bird like a ball on a rubber band. Flipped it off her left shoulder and caught it on her right knee. Trapped it under one bricklayer's arm and held it struggling, squawking. Bumped its beak with her nose in a kiss.

Lank wisps of hair, gunmetal-grey, clung sweaty to her neck. When she raised her hand to brush them away, she caught sight of Willie D inside his Spyder.

The pied-pearl bird was nestled between her breasts, and her heavy legs were bare. Posed with one foot flat and the other raised on tiptoe, half sprung from its fluffy blue mule, she looked at Willie head on, and seemed to see him clean through.

It was as if she saw nothing. As if there was nothing to see. The bird, impatient for more play, kept tugging at her dress. Absent-minded, the woman brushed it off like lint, and stepped back inside the Zoo, out of sight.

Anna Crow's hand was creeping in Willie's groin. It was a sly sneaking hand, a dirty girl's hand, with bitten fingernails painted black. Willie had no use for it.

The way that woman had looked him through.

When the bird tugged at her dress, the flowered shift had been pulled taut across her thighs, the bloat of her belly. 'Who's the blowfish?' Willie said.

'Kate Root, I can't abide her. She has the room under mine, we're more or less cohabitors, but she never hardly speaks or gives me the time of day, just whips that beady eye on me like some kind of basilisk I think it is and gives me The Look, unclean, malign, I heard she was a witch one time.'

When she shifted her legs, the backs of her thighs blew farts against the black leather seat. 'Come to bed,' she said.

'Don't cheapen yourself,' said Willie. 'It ages you.'

4

It was as if he'd been stripped. Like one of those sick dreams in childhood where you get caught naked in class or the schoolyard. On reflex he took a quick look down himself, checking for stains or wrinkles, and that's when he saw what they'd done to his shoes.

Murdered them, that's what.

His olive-green wing tips in butter-soft suede by Manzio, hand-stitched, Cuban-heeled, with ostrich trim and retro-Valmenon tonguing. Only yesterday morning he had brushed them out with a new monofilament wire comb from Beddoes & Wine; stroked and pampered them till their coats had glistened like thoroughbreds on the muscle. Now they were dead meat.

Somebody had wasted them, execution-style. Their uppers had been smeared with oil and ashes, and their tongues cut out at the roots. They'd never known what hit them.

What kind of pervert would do such a thing? And how come he'd got away clean? The last time Willie could picture seeing them alive, the shoes had been propped on the brass rail at Sheherazade, not a smudge or speck on either one. So they must have been hit at Chez Stadium. Sometime while he was in conference, or Anna was yakking in his ear, rabbit rabbit, he couldn't hear himself think. In that dim back room like a windowless cell, you could barely see your own hands in there. Never mind some torpedo, slipsliding at your feet like a crawling snake.

Willie's stomach heaved, he could have had an accident right there. But you didn't destroy him that easy, and he put out Anna Crow at the fire hydrant instead, he drove.

Exactly speaking, the Spyder wasn't his. Bernice had given him a year's lease on it for his last birthday. A reward for turning twenty, plus a going-away present at the same time, before she'd headed out to marry her phony French marquis

5

or viscount or whatever, Count De Pennies they'd used to call him; who ran the fat farm in Rancho Mirage. Now the lease was down to its last three weeks. Eighteen days more, and Willie would be fresh out of car.

And Regina was no help. If only she'd listened to reason, not all those slanders and lies, that street-dirt scandalizing. If only she hadn't had her locks changed, and trapped his collected shoes inside, all twenty-eight pairs.

So: no wheels, no shoes, and no ready cash. Up in the South Bronx near Yankee Stadium, right off the Major Deegan Expressway, Pacquito Console owned a topless car-wash that was a potential goldmine, guaranteed, anyone could see that, only right now it was underfinanced, and Pacquito was touting for investors. Ten grand would buy ten per cent. To date Willie had squirrelled away almost half. But he couldn't touch that. Of course not. It was like his dowry.

That left only the change in his pockets. Fourteen bucks and jangle. Which wouldn't afford a gangrened sneaker.

Driving east through Central Park, he hit the rocker switch on the console, and the Spyder went into its programmed ballet. The side windows slid down, the quarter windows tucked back into the top, the clasps at the head of the windshield unlatched, the rear deck opened like a clamshell, and the folding steel top rose to tuck away behind the rear seat. Twenty seconds flat, and the coupe was converted to a missile, 320 horse, 24 value, twin-turbo.

Some crazy in Sheep Meadow had set fire to his own hair. Or maybe it was just a wig.

The thing about a topless carwash, all right, so it was not his dream exactly, but at least it was equity. What Deacon Landry called a commencement; Step One on the path to a balanced investment portfolio, and what was wrong with

6

that? Why would Anna Crow roll her eyes and make that honking noise like a strangled goose? She called it laughing. And why did every bitch who'd been to finishing school graduate with blocked sinuses? Was it some kind of diploma?

Fourteen dollars and change.

When the first sunlight hit the Midtown roofs the clock on a mirrored tower said 6.49, then 91°. A commencement, that was all. *You have to shit before you can crawl*. His Cousin Humberto had told him that.

Though Willie D felt no heat, he closed up the Spyder against the tightening streets. Put all those rods and pistons to work, shutting him in. Most days it made him feel like the boy in the bubble, immune. Not this day.

Across the Brooklyn Bridge he hung a right, passed into a white tunnel. First thing he saw when he got inside, the fat lady flipped a pied-pearl bird off her left shoulder, caught it on her right knee. Bumped its beak with her nose in a kiss.

This city certainly was full of ugly people.

Was it just imagination, or could he smell corruption? Hard to tell with all these fires and the reek of burnt rubber everywhere. When he hit the Belt Parkway he could see a pall of smoke like toxic yellow smog overhanging Manhattan. It was that kind of summer. A season of fat white women, and murdered shoes.

Footwear had always been his friend. Far back as he could remember, there had been an instinctive bond. Not that he sold other garments short. Whatever touched him, be it shirts, pants, even sweaters, became some part of him. Still his feeling for shoes went above and beyond. More than just apparel, they were his silent partners. His driving wheels, that steered him right.

Like any other love, they had brought grief. Persecution even. The year he turned fourteen, his Aunt Guadalupe, who

7

loved him best, had bought him a pair of Brunswick Glides, ice-blue with a shine that outdazzled the sun. The first day he wore them to Holy Martyrs the schoolyard was swept away. Paralysed with envy. You could feel the malice rise up shimmering in waves like heat off the concrete and tar, but nobody moved. Not at first. Not till he'd put his feet up on a litter bin, first the left, then the right, to inspect them for dust. He saw himself reflected, he was gorgeous. If there was one instant in his life when he knew for certain that he was special, set apart, that was it. Then Sister Teresa came by. Breathing hard and furious like always with her man's red hands outspread, the spatulate fingers flattened and scarred. And she'd caught Willie dreaming; lost. So she reached out and touched his nose, held it a moment between a thumb and bare forefinger, and she snapped it like a twig. To save him from perfection, she said.

'Jesus wept,' said Willie D in his Spyder now, thinking money, thinking stone cold cash. He was parked in Brighton Beach, in Little Odessa beneath the train tracks that ran twenty foot overhead, the El, where all the people and their faces and their signs were Russian, and when he went upstairs inside a room with yellow floorboards, Ivana was eating a tuna-melt sandwich. 'This man,' she said. 'He wanted to watch me swallow soup.'

Version Girl, he called her. A raised and reddened scar like a wire necklace ran round the base of her neck where a surgeon had cut her for thyroid, and all she did was tell tales. 'He gave me a Franklin to sit in the back of his car and let him voyeur me drink hot and sour. Some kind of Russian, he looked like a moulting bear. Smelled like one, too. Kept the soup in this metal canister like an urn or Chinese thermos with snakes and fire-tongue dragons painted on it, and inside it was scalding. One sip and my lips burned

8

up, I thought I like to died. I mean, I was screaming like *Oh my God*. But the man never said or stirred. Just kept flopping more twenties on me, pushing them down my top. Man had a touch like scar tissue. So I sipped again. He held the canister up over my face and started to tipping it, slow. And what was weird, by the fourth, or maybe the fifth swallow, I'd forgot to feel a thing. It was like I'd rubbed coke on my teeth and gums, inside my throat. I couldn't hurt and I couldn't taste. There was soup running over my chin and neck, all down my chest, and the Russian, he started to lick it off. Kept one of his fat fingers held against my throat, pressing tight against the pulse, so he could feel it kick back, each time a new mouthful went down. I thought he'd maybe strangle me. Thought I'd ought to start screaming. But he never even squeezed. Just kept on feeding me soup, more soup, till I'd drank the canister dry.'

As she remembered, she stripped. Pink spandex hotpants and a halter top, shiny black thighboots, and she searched herself for damage. 'Believe it, I was a mess,' she said. 'Hot sour was in my hair, soaked through my pants. So I started to fix my lipstick, and the fat bear Russian, what does he do then, he only bursts out sobbing. Kissing my hands, he wouldn't stop. *I'm loving you*, he kept on saying and saying.'

'They blew my shoes away,' Willie said.

'*I'm loving you*,' Ivana said. Rolling back her lower lip, she studied its reflection in her compact mirror, a constellation of livid purple circles ringed in white. 'What kind of statement was that?'

The El ran right past the window and, every time a train roared through, the whole room shook. Behind the drawn blinds, the walls were papered with a duck-hunting scene, green and yellow on faded teal – one duck flying high, two more lurking in tall reeds, and the hunter in his rowboat with his gun across his knees, a globular man puffed up like a gorged tick with ear-muffs and a walrus moustache.

A splash of white filmed the hunter's left eye. It might have been a flaw in the printing process, but what it looked like was a cast. 'What do I do now?' Willie asked.

'MSG brings me out in hives.'

'Go barefoot through the streets?'

'Then all my glands swell up, I look like a frog.'

'Wrap my feet in rags?'

'Or not a frog exactly. More like a salamander.'

Stripped, she dropped to her haunches and started to burrow for her drugs behind a skirting board. The angle that she squatted, doubled over with her butt stuck in the air, Willie could see in a single stretched bowbend from the pucker of her asshole to the back of her long neck where the dyed pink hair turned into fuzz soft as goosedown and the ends of her scar failed to meet.

Beneath the pillow on the metal-frame bed were two soup-sodden twenties, a ten and some singles. 'Impervious to fire,' said Ivana, shooting up, and Willie D walked out into Little Odessa.

Along the dark channel beneath the El the morning papers were printed in Cyrillic, and the sidewalk stands sold *pirogis* and *kvass*. Even in this heat, the men lounging in shop doorways favoured woollen shirts, thick scratchy socks, double-breasted suits with wide lapels. Inside the Yalta Café, old women with headscarves spooned jam into glasses of lemon tea. And all of them saw the ruined shoes. The oil and ashes, the tongueless mouths; there never was such disgrace.

Each train pounding overhead set off its own shower of sparks. A peck of pigeons, burned, whirled up into Willie's eyes. Behind the drumming of their wings, he saw the pearl-coloured bird drop like a stone, playing dead.

Now he started to get mad.

Which wasn't his style. Ask anyone he did business with, Deacon Landry, Mouse Williams, whoever, they'd tell you he was a gentleman. Taste and class, the good life, he believed in the finer things. But that didn't make him a pushover. No way the contract called for him to stand still and take it while some old douche-bag and her bird made a monkey out of him. Staring through him like shit on the half-shell, it wasn't right. No respect.

Inside the Spyder, which was his office, there were seats in soft Corinthian leather to bolster his back and nestle his buns, book-tapes to ease his mind. Before she changed the locks Regina had bought him a self-help library. *The Road Less Travelled*, and *Chicken Soup for the Soul*, and *Release the Prisoner: Your Secret Self and You*. He didn't follow the words, but the sound of the voices soothed him, they made a change from Rap.

One sentence he did recall. In *Release the Prisoner*, he thought it was: 'In times of stress, repeat to yourself: THOU ART THE LION GOD.'

He tried it out for size; it didn't sound as hot. Along the Coney Island projects, when he wheeled back towards the city, some of last night's fires were still burning. Fourteen dollars and change, plus two twenties, a ten and some singles. Say seventy bucks total. You couldn't buy a Gucci loafer or wing-tip Oxford for that. So there was no help for it. Though he'd sworn to himself he wouldn't, not ever again, he went to see Mrs Muhle.

Her apartment overlooking the East River was all shiny steel and glass, and she was baking zucchini bread. Flour whitened her hair, her flushed cheeks. When she saw Willie's shoes, all she said was: 'You poor boy. Oh, you poor, poor boy.'

She was a woman with no clothes underneath her clothes. Every movement she made, even raising her hand to touch his cheek, sent loose flesh rolling and flopping, spilling over like tumbled pups. 'I have made a significant salad,' she said. 'Mediterranean chicken *aux herbes*.'

When she recited the recipe, she made it sound like erotic verse. 'One medium-size yellow onion, peeled and quartered. Two carrots, peeled and chopped,' she sighed, and began to unbutton his shirt. 'One leek, white part only, cleaned and sliced.'

'I need a century,' Willie said.

'One teaspoon dried thyme, one bay leaf, six parsley sprigs, twelve black peppercorns, four cloves. Salt, to taste.' Her touch was damp, slightly oily, like her bread. 'Three whole chicken breasts, about three pounds. One-third cup virgin olive oil, two teaspoons dried oregano, two tablespoons drained capers, and one cup of imported olives, Niçoise preferred.' Then her mouth was on him, suckling. 'The juice of a fresh lemon,' she said.

Through the plate-glass window on the terrace, he saw the pied-pearl bird again, fluttering with wings outspread. It did a back-flip, drifted as if hang-gliding. The fat white woman looked at him head on. 'Eight cherry tomatoes, halved. A quarter pound green beans,' said Mrs Muhle. But Willie D had been there, and gone.

All afternoon he drove and drove without direction, set adrift in alien neighbourhoods, Flatbush, Crown Heights, Bed-Stuy, where no one knew his face or name, till he came to a park with a snot-green lake where you could paddle with bare feet, and there he stayed among children pushing model boats and old women feeding the ducks, waiting for the light to soften and fade, the evening to come and protect him.

12

At dusk in the West Village he left the Spyder idling outside a boutique with a moron name. A Shoe Like It, some kind of play on words.

The fragrance of footloose shoes inside was gamy, lush, abandoned. The girl that served him, the name printed on her breast was Mariella, and she said she came from the Philippines. Somewhere like Cerveza, it sounded like, but Willie couldn't tell for sure, her voice was so low and she swallowed her words. When she bent her head to tend to him, her hair was a long black veil that hid both her hands and his feet.

She had the gentlest touch. Her fingers moving on his ankles, then his insteps, felt like whispers in the dark, and her hair smelled of horse shampoo.

Roberta Gold's smell.

His Freshman year, it must have been. The year she'd sat at the desk in front of his. American History or maybe Algebra. The only girls he had smelled before were his Cousin Humberto's castoffs, and all of them had wigs or processes, or they slavered their hair with abusive substances. With all the garbage they sprayed on, you couldn't ever tell their real scent from bottled. But Roberta Gold, you knew without asking, she was all her own work. She wore her hair styled thick and tangled on top, cropped close against her cheeks, with one side flipped up in a curl like a crescent moon, and the texture was kind of coarse. You knew without thinking that her pussy was a Brillo pad. But the hair on her head, ash blonde, was only fuzzy; a dense fur.

It wasn't that she was pretty. The moment she turned round she was just another Jewish princess with braces and zits, a shape like a fire hydrant. Only her hair signified, the way she smelled like a horse, and the tiny sweet spot like a bud exposed at the crown, dead white.

13

From where Willie sat, he could number each blanched strand where it sprouted from that bud's opened pores. All he'd needed to do was reach out and pluck.

He never had.

Or rub them the wrong way. Make the hairs stand up stiff like hackles or the nap on a cat's back. Or bury both hands to the wrist, and scratch till he got satisfied.

Never.

His erection in A Shoe Like It was not so shy. It bobbed against Mariella's cheekbone, the shell of her ear. Still she did not cease to minister. The dead shoes were laid to rest in a plain white box, nothing ostentatious. Muzak played, and cool air soothed his soles. Looking down through the dark cascades of Mariella's hair, he glimpsed virgin armadillo.

What was that line Mouse Williams used? 'Good shoes talk, great shoes walk.' Willie D had never rightly known what he meant till now. When the armadillo's mouth kissed his heel, and he felt himself slide under, his left foot swallowed whole. And then the right, slick like oil, sweet as Tupelo honey. And when they raised him up of their own volition, twin powers greater than he could control. When they walked him outdoors and away for free, and Mariella never moved.

The streets were night now, and everything starting over. In the Spyder, rolling uptown, the metal brightness of noon seemed days ago, all its messages false alarms. Willie felt drained, out of blood, but pacified. Armadillos swaddled his feet, and the rest of him lay at rest. *Null's the void.* Sandman Ames had told him that. Or was it Warren White?

Sheherazade's dim blue light burned halfway along a neon block on Eighth Avenue, squeezed between a pawnshop and a porno house, two floors above a noodle shop.

14

Upstairs behind a beaded curtain was a room tricked out with anchors, fishing nets and Greek travel posters left over from when the club had been the Taverna Phaedra. Anna Crow drank brandy at a bar festooned with bazoukis and orange ceramic lobsters.

She stood in a dancer's pose, left foot angled out, tight belly thrusting. Below the frizz of her wild hennaed hair, her face showed chalky white. 'My love, my heart,' she said.

'Pernod and blackcurrant,' said Willie D.

Anna was not dressed so much as costumed in a long black Edwardian dress with lace frills down the front, a red shawl, and Spanish combs in her hair. 'Guess what you'll never guess,' she said. 'I got a job.'

'With a twist,' said Willie.

'One of those Verse-o-Grams. All I have to do is go where I'm sent and no questions asked on people's birthdays, anniversaries, at Xmas or Easter dressed to order and recite their favourite poems, say *Trees* or *Blowin' in the Wind*, *The Lake Isle of Innisfree* on St Patrick's Day, some speech from Shakespeare even, who knows? Like today for instance there was this Irishman whose wife died, she was a Gogarty, and I had to go to Downey's, where all his buddies were drinking and singing and weeping buckets except for him, he sat over a ginger ale with his face like a well-kept grave, but whose fault was that, not mine, it was a sweet poem anyway.'

In a spotlit circle that served as a stage a woman in see-through underwear did a belly dance for one table of Japanese tourists, another of drunken sailors. '*I will live in Ringsend*,' said Anna Crow, and stiffened her spine, '*with a red-headed whore and the fanlight gone in where it lights the hall door, and listen each night for her querulous shout as she streels in and the pubs empty out.* Funny word, *streels*, where was I? *Pubs empty out*, that's right. *To soothe that*

15

*wild breast with my old-fangled songs till she feels it redressed from inordinate wrongs, imagined outrageous preposterous wrongs, till peace at last comes shall be all I will do.* Now listen. *Where the little lamp blooms like a rose in the stew, and up the back garden the sound comes to me,* and here's the bit I like *comes to me* right here *of the lapsing unsoilable whispering sea,* I don't know what it's meant to mean exactly, *unsoilable sea,* but it sounds sort of noble and sad, don't you think? I do.'

Willie never should have come here.

He'd known it up-front. Every time he saw her it got his nerve-ends disordered. *Yakety-yak, don't come back,* whose poem was that? And humping her was worse. All angles and bones where no bones should be, black nails ripping at his butt. 'Tomorrow it's Coleridge,' she said. '*The Rime of the Ancient Mariner,* a stag party for the Sons of Neptune, I get to go as a mermaid, and flash my tits, my bazookas, my heavenly spheres.'

'What tits?'

'I hope you die screaming.' Her breath when she kissed him was rank, half-starved. Fucking mermaid was right. Or it would have been, only Deacon Landry had told him once that Men of Power never used foul language, not even in their sleep, it sapped their strength.

The woman belly-dancing detached her bra and threw it across the spotlights. It landed askew on one of the drunk sailors and clung to his ear, white strap dangling. Each time that Willie drew his toes in like claws, then slowly released them, he could feel the armadillos move with him, their soft bodies rippling and slithering in rhythm, sinuous as snakes.

Looking out towards the anchors and fishing nets, he watched the dancer's breasts rolling lazy like buoys at low tide, and fingered the unspent banknotes tucked in his hip pocket. 'THOU ART THE LION GOD,' he thought, took one sip at his drink, and instantly his stomach turned, his mouth was flooded with bile.

That bird. That fat white woman. 'Who does the bitch think she is?' cried Willie D.

The year she was seventeen, a senior at Mrs Sweetwater's in Charleston, there were days she danced ballet in a high white room under two chandeliers; and nights, moonlighting, she danced on King Street bartops in a red garter and G-string, and at spring break she drove home to Savannah in the Mustang her father gave her for not marrying the bass player with Easy Greasy.

Her father then was Chief Wigwam, he manufactured toys and novelties, Red Indian knick-knacks like rubber tomahawks and feathered weather-bonnets, buffalo-head bronzes and flaming spears, inflatable squaws complete with sex parts, his family called him Arnold, and they lived in a Spanish-style mansion called Camp Pocahontas, hard by Bonaventure Cemetery.

A pinch-mouth man he was, stiff as one of his own wooden Indians, though he wore feathers and warpaint for the St Patrick's Day parade and solid plastic peace-pipes for a living, ate animal crackers for his breakfast, still he called his daughter a whore. Which was a lie, she ran a little wild was all.

Still it was one thing, and then it was another thing, throwing up on Monsignor Bayliss, driving the Bentley into the swimming pool, sniffing coke with the hired help, nothing more than rites of passage really, but Chief Wigwam took it personally, he said it was like to kill him, and so it did, right in the middle of lunch, he was eating alphabet soup and suddenly turned purple, rose halfway out of his chair, 'You have to be kidding,' he said, and fell dead as he'd lived, face-down in his soup where Anna found him, fresh home from Mrs Sweetwater's, you wouldn't believe the guilt.

Such a start it gave her, even after the funeral and all she couldn't seem to settle, let alone go back to Charleston, she didn't even want to dance, only moped around Camp Pocahontas with its turrets and colonnades, vine-draped balconies, English maze and Chinese pagoda, which was how one day by the boating pond with all the azaleas in bloom she met a boy called Chase trying to float a canoe. And this boy, he was half-naked, just shorts and sneakers with earth-brown hair down past his shoulders and his flesh the same burnt brown, not tan but burnished like something wild, maybe dangerous. 'Nice day,' said Anna, and the boy looked back at her across the glittering pond, blinking sweat out of his eyes, his face smeared black with ashes or grease. 'Nice enough,' he said, and Anna was lost.

In those days, of course, she was loveliness itself, a race-horse all sinew and nerve, long dancer's muscles and her ass so pert, so spry she could carry a full cup of Earl Grey tea on its shelf and never spill a drop. Hardly even a drop.

In the middle of the pond on a rock was the concrete pagoda where Chief Wigwam had stored the feathers for his headdresses in a massive copper vat bigger than most houses. So they paddled their canoe, they eloped. Inside the pagoda was a balcony with a wrought-iron railing that circled maybe twenty foot above the vat full of feathers and when you looked down it was like drowning in colours, every bright shade in creation. But Chase didn't look, did not even glance, just put one hand on the rail and vaulted off into space, spinning down all arms and legs into the copper maw, feathers flew up in a fountain, the vat's sides roared like the noise-maker backstage in *Macbeth* at Mrs Sweetwater's during the witches' sabbath, and still he went down, rolling tumbling on his belly, on his back, on his fool head, sucked in deeper and deeper as if magnetized till he was socketed snug, enwombed you'd say if you were that way inclined, and everything resettled except for one green feather, halfway between chartreuse and aquamarine, that drifted on high, wafted right into Anna's hand.

What could she do? What choice did she have? Climbing up on the railing, she dived herself, a jack-knife with tuck, 2.5 degree of difficulty, with such perfect form that she made not a splash when she went under, she just went down down down and did not come up.

Not for days, weeks, months. There must have been moments when they surfaced for food or bodily functions, there had to be, but she had no memory of that, no sense of anything outside the vat where time had no function, nothing did, except for the great banks of feathers floating and drifting, then swirling in slow swelling waves, in all of their savage colours with all those savage names, carnelian and gamboge, plumbago and azulene, heliotrope curcumine miloro, indigo malachite verdigris prune. And even today after thirteen years, there were some mornings when Anna passed through Ferdousine's Zoo on her way to work, when Kate Root was feeding the birds and some caique or painted bunting began to strut and spread its wings, luxuriate, then she had to bite her hands, count to ten, not to fall on it bodily and rip out the brilliance in her bare hands, rub it into her face, her belly, her cunt, for all those times she'd twined herself on him like a standing tree, dark and dangerous, and

20

Chase when he spunked, he cried out in tongues, *Alas, alas the great city*, he said.

It had seemed an odd thing to mention.

Or maybe not. The way of the world these days, maybe it was just common sense. This very evening, coming out of Downey's after the wake, her passage had been blocked by two boys, they hardly looked old enough to jerk off, intoning through a megaphone, *And I stood upon the sands of the sea, and saw a beast rise up out of the sea, having seven heads and ten horns, and upon his horns ten crowns, and upon his heads the name of Blasphemy*: 'What could their mothers be thinking of?' Anna said.

But Willie made no reply. He hardly ever did. Nights like this she wondered why he bothered showing up. When he couldn't seem to abide her, could hardly tolerate her kiss or even touch. Just stood there like a parking meter waiting to be fed, and what did she do, like an idiot of course she fed him. Kept reaching out and babbling, *guess what you'll never guess*, it was so sick. Gushing like a flushed john, or the lapsing unsoilable sea, and all for what? A handful of gimme, a mouthful of much obliged.

When he wasn't even her style.

That's what she kept forgetting. That she was a dancer, and a dancer was an athlete, and an athlete belonged with other athletes. Weightlifters and jocks were her speed, prize-fighters, truck-drivers even, great slabs of meat with abs and glutes and pecs, deltoid development. Men with loose sloppy grins and red hands that picked her up bodily, could toss her like a cow-chip. Dumb animals, that only knew one dumb-animal thing. Not this halfhand runt that thought he was Kid Signify, Man of Power, when he was only . . .

. . . beautiful, she guessed.

Well, agreed. But lovely like a girl, a maiden, a fucking

*damsel* for God's sake, with those almond-slanted odalisque's eyes wet and sticky as molasses, and the olive flesh that glinted pale blue and green by her bedside light so that he looked amphibian, a fishboy, and even his dick hermaphrodite almost, slithering and sly, serpentine.

But his hair. That was the item she couldn't slide past, *the gaoler of her soul*, whose poem was that? Midnight-black and racehorse-sleek, silk when she ran it through her fingers, cotton candy when she puffed it high in a pompadour, black wings when she lost herself, 'Who does the bitch think she is?' Willie said.

'Which bitch?'

'The blowfish. The bag with the bird.'

'What about her?'

'Who does she think she is?'

'I never asked,' said Anna Crow. 'She wouldn't tell me if I did.'

'So how come you said she was a witch?'

'Just something I heard, don't ask me where, or maybe I made it up, I probably did, the way she looks at you on the stairs, never blinking, that white moon face with no more expression than Monterey Jack, could you blame me?'

The drunk sailor with tasselled bra dangling from his ear like a crooked lampshade pinched the fat dancer's ass on his way through to the men's room or rather Pointers as the sign said at Sheherazade, the women's said Setters, that was the kind of place this was, and Anna squealed extra loud to change the subject. Because if there was one topic she certainly did not intend to waste her night discussing, that topic was certainly Kate Root, the old bat, *the bag with the bird*, she must remember that.

Six nights a week she danced in this dump herself, she was Zenaide from Zonguldak, the Turkish Typhoon, but this

22

was her night off, she didn't know what she was doing here. 'Fly me to the moon,' she said. 'Failing that, Chez Stadium.'

It was their place. A dingy dark haven of leatherette and naugahyde, with clouds of nylon butterflies glued to the lowering ceiling, their spread wings bright with glitterdust, and every time your waitress brought you a fresh drink, a shower of sparkle shook loose, gold and blue, that drifted down like dandruff to settle on your shoulders, in your glass.

The men that gathered here had names and games out of some bad thriller, Mouse Williams and Sandman Ames, Deacon Landry, Warren White, Willie called them entrepreneurs, but Anna knew what that meant, panders with pretensions was all. The style of older men who were not riper, simply older. New Jacks past their sell-by dates, festooned with gold chains and bracelets, and the hostess dressed up in tights and tails, her name was Shanda Lear.

The word, she guessed, was *louche*.

In Charleston that time she'd danced in a revue at the Low Country called *Louche Lips Sink Ships* and the Citadel cadets charged the stage in a flying wedge, she thought they'd tear her limb from limb, 'I could use a kiss,' she said. 'Anna wants a little kiss.'

'About the carwash . . .' said Willie D.

'Just fucking hold me would do.'

'What I was thinking, it needs an angle, some kind of tease, to make it stand out. Maybe dressing the girls up like flowers and when the water hits them the petals fall off.'

'What kind of flowers?'

'I thought roses would be nice. Pink and yellow roses in layers. But then I thought, the cost. So what about lilies? And change the name to fit? Call it Tyger's Topless Carwash. Spelled "y" for a touch of class. Then the girls could be Tyger's Lilies.'

'Love it,' said Anna. 'Just love it to death.'

The way Chez Stadium was lit, there was only one weak bulb per booth, hardly more than a nightlight shaped like an ice-cream cone and painted rose-madder, the colour of the Painted Desert at Sunset in a Forties postcard, and its glimmer fell slanting across Willie's temple, directly onto the bridge of his broken nose where it thickened, where there was a faint reddish welt shaped like an arrowhead.

Of all of him it was the fragment that Anna craved most, the flaw that completed him. Across the booth while Willie droned on about Tyger Lilies and how every man had to start some place, even giants began with baby-steps, like Lincoln splitting rails and Elvis driving a truck, Berry Gordy was an auto-worker, even Deacon Landry had been a messenger once, she could hardly follow the words for aching, the hunger to touch it, squeeze it dry.

The arrowhead was upside down, pointing up. When Shanda Lear brought Willie's Pernod and blackcurrant, her wig dislodged a speck of glitterdust that landed on the arrow's tip, clung there like a gilded snowflake.

It looked just like a scab.

And scabs were Anna's passion. Squeezing blackheads was good, sucking the poison out of bee stings was better, but scabs were best. Those years she was married to Padgett when he shucked oysters, he'd used to come home nights with his money hand a jigsaw of nicks, whittles, slashes, and she preyed on him like a buzzard, no band-aid could keep her off, curses neither, it was love.

'Warren White raised gerbils on Staten Island, Mouse Williams licked stamps,' Willie said, and he knocked back his drink in one, a sudden rush of alcohol that raised his body-heat. His cheeks and throat flushed, his nose likewise, causing the speck of glitterdust to melt, fuse with the arrow-

24

head beneath, and the red welt seemed to swell and harden as Anna watched. Not that she was that way inclined, of course, but still and all she was human, and girls would be boys sometimes in Mrs Sweetwater's dorms, they couldn't help themselves, nor could she. So her fingers snaked out of their own accord and felt the swollen nubbin, no bigger than a gnat, 'Pardon me,' Anna said, she heard herself say. 'You have a clit on your nose.'

Willie didn't hit her. All he did was look in her face. Examine the skin that was thirty-three, well, call it twenty-nine, but already too taut across the cheekbones, she knew, too slack around the mouth, too many blue veins too close to the surface, any day one would burst, and then where would she be? Not with Willie D, that's for sure. Not trapped in those black sticky eyes and his stillness that was not really stillness at all, more a furious containment: 'Sandman Ames sold enemas door to door,' he said.

Uptown somewhere in the Barrio there was a cockfight scheduled. Deacon Landry had a bird showing, so did Warren White. When they left Chez Stadium for the pit, Willie followed behind.

All the way up inside the red Spyder he never spoke, just kept pushing the rocker switch, making all the windows go up and down, the roof retract and swing back, while a voice on the tape-deck with sugared plums in its mouth intoned an ode to empowerment, and Anna mended her mouth. 'Would you look at those fires! Oh God, I never saw the like,' she said, but that was a lie, one year she'd been in Detroit for Devil's Night when the whole city burned like a tinderbox, two hundred fires at once, three hundred, four, in lumber yards and abandoned buildings, slum properties the landlords had torched for the insurance, warehouses and factories, shelters, it was a holocaust, and the beauty took your breath away.

The cockpit was set up in a disused gymnasium behind the Kanawah Political Club, the pit surrounded by rough wooden walls and five rows of bleachers so steep you seemed to look straight down on the birds as they warred.

At three in the morning when Willie streeled in, Anna two steps behind, a Tulsa Red was fighting a Butcher Boy. The moment their handlers unloosed the cocks they flew straight at each other and met in the middle air, the steel gaffs like spurs flashing on the stumps of their legs. For a few seconds they were merged in a tangle of feathers and bloodied plumes, indivisible, then the Red was on top, the Butcher Boy was falling spinning on his back, one of the Red's gaffs had pierced his right eye, he was dead before he hit the ground.

'Cordova's Red wins. Nineteen seconds of the third pitting,' the referee declaimed. The bleachers were a green wash of banknotes, somebody threw a bottle against a wall, the explosion sounded like a petrol bomb going off, and in the pit the Red pecked idly at the Butcher Boy's draggled head, crowed his victory.

In Savannah when she was a schoolgirl cockfights had been for crackers and niggers, they did not occur on Victory Drive. Anna nibbled at her black nails for comfort. Deacon Landry was watching her. 'Popped your cherry?' he asked, not unkind, a coffee-coloured man with a diamond pinkie ring and a porkpie hat, one eye squinted against invisible smoke. Perched on his wrist preening was the cock of his dreams.

His name was Diablo. He was a Landry Grey, a strain that Deacon had spent a dozen years refining. His chest and shawl were a shade of granite, the tips of his long wings were

26

vermilion like flame, so were his thighs and head feathers, and his high curving tail gleamed peacock blue. His beak was lemon, his feet and legs bright orange. 'This bird is a bird no bird can beat. No bird alive,' Deacon Landry said.

'Did you have him blessed?' Willie asked.

'I went to the Babalawo, he was gone from home.'

'You should have him blessed.'

'I know it,' Deacon said. 'The man was gone.'

Tossing his head back and crowing aloud in Anna's face, the cock beat his wings together. 'I could bless him. I'd be happy and proud,' she said. 'I bring good luck, the best, I always have done, I blessed the Georgia Bulldogs once and they won eleven straight, it's just a knack, I guess.'

'Is that a fact?'

'You could look it up.'

Inside the gym full of embrocation and smoke the air was so dense she couldn't seem to catch her breath, she felt her face flushed and those red blotches that sprouted on her cheeks like consumption spots, she put her hand on Willie D's elbow for support but he was flaunting his left profile. Beneath the brim of Deacon Landry's porkpie hat, the squinting eyes tightened, measured her. But she blessed the bird anyway, '*Gesundheit*,' she said. With all her heart, and welcome to it. And Diablo understood, she knew he did. The way he looked at her with his bright yellow eye rimmed in black so proud and clear, you couldn't mistake a thing like that, you purely couldn't.

Sitting in the bleachers waiting for Diablo's fight and staring down into the pit it was like sitting inside a drum with the banknotes flashing from hand to hand, the bottle passing in brown-paper sacks, the feet pounding like thunder on the wooden boards, the heat, the halitosis air, the men sweating and the men cursing, the men praying to God, and Willie D

27

still talking and talking about his carwash, equity, a balanced portfolio, until she thought her head would split for silent screaming, and her eyes skittered sideways. Then she saw his new shoes, gentle Jesus, what *were* those things? Road kill?

The cock that Diablo was matched against was a Palmetto Muff, a scarfaced streetwise character with a dismissive eye, you could tell he thought he was God's own gift, and the instant that he was let loose he turned into a blur of motion, shuffling and showing off like Muhammad Ali, no Cassius Clay, darting forward and back with flurrying wings, raining sharp short blows with either gaff, too fast for Diablo to counter.

From the way Diablo foundered Anna thought he might be sick, and who could blame him if he was? Right before the first pitting Deacon Landry had blown cigar smoke in his eyes, not even a proper Havana, but something foul from a packet like White Owl or El Producto, it was a calculated insult, though Willie D said it was just to make him fighting mad, still he did not look furious, only befuddled. That beautiful cock all peacock-blue and granite and flame, with its proud head born to kingship, she couldn't hardly bear it. To watch him plod and blunder with no direction, while around him and above him the Palmetto Muff whirled and capered, spun in circles, leaped high in the air, slashing one gaff to the breast, another to the throat, a third to the skull itself. Until Diablo's comb, which had been such a rich deep red, turned a watery pink and his plumes were masked by blood. Yet he kept on coming regardless, dead game, lashing out at shadows like a blind thing. But the Muff just stared at him with that cold sneering eye and skipped away, let him fight himself out, then rose up sheer as a cliff-face and drove a gaff into his spine, deep, deep, pinning him to the pit,

28

paralysed, and his beak formed one last peck, he yawned, he died.

When Deacon picked him up and carried him away, his long neck hung down limp, his head banged against the bleacher steps. 'Some blessing,' Willie said.

It was Broadway before she stopped grieving. Inside the Spyder some man's voice with sugared plums in his mouth did not stop droning. She couldn't make out on the words, but they carried that sound of patient weariness as if addressing a retard that only those bone-dense themselves used. *'Till peace at last comes shall be all I will do,'* Anna said. So they came to Ferdousine's Zoo.

A nightlight was still on in Kate Root's room.

Double parked by the fire hydrant like *déjà vu* all over again, Anna found herself with hands clamped in armpits, they felt like they'd been scalded. 'If not a witch, what?' Willie asked.

'God knows, I don't.'

'She has to eat. She didn't get that size by starving.'

'Oh, that,' Anna said. 'She looks after the Zoo for old Ferdousine, feeds the animals and cleans them, keeps them decent, I suppose. Then she cuts hair sometimes in the back room, I never tried her myself.'

'Is that all?'

'I think she was in a circus once. Or was it burlesque? Some kind of act with knives.'

'What kind of knives?'

But Anna wasn't there any more, she was halfway across the street sleepwalking, she stumbled staggering through the doorway and down the passage, up the narrow steep stairway, sixteen steps past Kate's door, past Ferdousine's, then fourteen steps more to her own.

Across the landing was the room where poor Godwin had

used to live with his mixed metaphors, and upstairs in the attic of course was Crouch, and when she stooped to fumble her key in the lock, Willie was standing behind her, he put his mouth on her neck.

What was strange, he never would come here before. In the two months since she had first caught him watching himself read the *Wall Street Journal* in the back-bar mirror at Sweeney's, she'd fucked him in doorways and back seats and movies, at mass, on turf and in the slop; every place, in fact, but bed, her own cot with the broken-back mattress and the sheets that wouldn't wash clean, always came out a greyish yellow like powdered eggs, she'd never fucked him there.

Not until this night when she was already spent, hardly even needed him, but took him anyway, what choice did she have? By firelight her room was a dim purple like a bruise, she closed her eyes against it and Willie, they would only have upset her, and grappling her hands deep in his hair like a mane she rode and rode till she got done, she came sleeping.

By the time she woke it was daylight and Kate Root was busy in the Zoo. There was the sound of flat feet flapping on the boards, the squeak of cages sliding open and shut, birdsong, snake-hiss, the background buzz of *Good Day, New York*. Anna's neck and shoulders when she rolled over on her back were rigid, outraged, and her clenched hand jarred Willie's chin. His eyes were open wide. So was his mouth. 'What kind of knives?' he asked.

As Kate was standing on a stool with one arm upraised, feeding rape and millet to a white-fronted Amazon, she chanced to glance out through the transom and saw that the red car was back.

It looked reckless.

It looked the kind of car that a woman if she was just a girl with trim ankles and legs up to here in a little black dress could gun down the highway with her hair blowing free at a hundred miles an hour and when she needed gas she'd slam on the brakes at a country crossroads, fishtailing in a cloud of red dust, the boys on the porch all staring with their mouths ajar as she opened the door, extruded one tanned leg and looked up at them over her dark glasses, saying 'Please, I'm lost,' with a lick of her lips and a languorous sigh, 'Please, could one of you big strong men please help me?'

*Little black dress, my fat ass.*

The Zoo was a miniature jungle filled with snakes and tropical birds. Ferdousine, not liking to think of himself as a man who kept creatures in cages, had tried to camouflage the steel bars by cultivating a mail-order rainforest. Lianas and wandering jews swarmed the walls, the aisles were a maze of macarangas, and three parakeets sat in a ficus tree, their feathers glinting scarlet and bronze through the dark, dripping leaves.

Even in this dead heat, 94° by the clock outside the Chemical Bank, gas heaters glowed from every corner. The walls oozed sweat, the floorboards squelched. Kate, dispensing softbill pellets, dripped tallow like a candle.

She'd been in a foul mood all morning, since yesterday morning to tell the truth, a martyr to gas, and the style of gas that she hated worst. The kind that just sort of festered, never gathered to a proper fullness, where you could belch it loose but hung around for days, turning everything to acid. *Better an empty house than an unwelcome tenant.* Or maybe that was farts.

She wasn't in training any more. There was a time years back when gas like this had been her life partner, but that was before the Zoo. For ten years almost she'd had no visions and told no lies, felt virtually no pain. Just fed the beasts, cleaned their cages, and kept her mind on the Soaps. The only worry she allowed herself was *Days of Our Lives* – why Roman was siding with Marlena over Sami dating Alan, and how come Lucas had been arrested for murdering Curtis while Billie seemed to be in the clear, even though Curtis' ghost had taunted Billie during an intimate moment with Bo.

The basic trouble with Billie, any fool could see, was that she was besotted. How any woman so outwardly smart, with sloe eyes and glossy marshmallow lips like hers, could be such a fool to herself was past all understanding. It made Kate want to slap her sometimes. But what would be the use? A woman like that was somehow fated. You could talk sense to her till the cows turned blue, she just couldn't help herself.

This last business with Bo was absolutely the worst. So all right, he looked good in tight pants and his eyes burned like molten coals, he was still a two-timing snake, not worthy to lick Billie's boots. And meanwhile, face it, Billie wasn't getting any younger. What about her future? That's what haunted Kate.

Some mornings, like yesterday, she'd wake herself up with the worry. Even when she was out on the sidewalk with Pearl, giving the bird its morning constitutional, she couldn't help fretting. Her thoughts had been so snarled, she'd forgot to protect herself. Just turned her head without thinking and saw the red car by the hydrant. Anna Crow, and that Hispanic hoodlum she was hung up on, the one who looked like Prince or Glyph or whatever he called himself. Nice hair he had, still he wasn't her cup of tea. How could he be, when the boy she saw in him was only six years old?

That boy had bare legs in khaki shorts and a Menudo T-shirt, his hair was cropped convict-short, he rode a blue tricycle up and down the corridors of a dark labyrinthine apartment. Dustsheets covered most of the furniture, and there were heavy velvet curtains the colour of fallen chestnuts, kept drawn though it was a bright day outdoors. In the central room, beneath a corniced ceiling, two women sat at a card-table, one old and shaking in a wheelchair, the other dressed as a nurse. They didn't talk, just slapped cards on the green-baize table. Assorted cats were under their feet, on the dustsheets, crawling the velvet drapes. The child, abandoning his tricycle, began to stalk them. When he cornered one, a Persian, it slashed him across the cheek. And Kate got gas.

It was the embarrassment more than anything. That had been her curse all along. When she'd lived in the Ansonia, back in the days when she did visions for a living, she'd been surrounded by other psychics, the whole building was crawling with them. Spiritualists and paranormals, telepathists and psychokinesists, table-rappers, trance-writers, Tarot-readers and crystal-ball merchants, the works. And what a shower they were. Most of them, anyway. A few were not so bad, just earning a crust as best they could. But the rest of them, sweet suffering Mary! The way they preened, the airs they gave themselves. All those darkened rooms and unearthly voices, the jargon, the cant. Emanations and auras, psychic frequencies. The Gift.

Some gift.

What was it, after all? When you cut away the props and poses and verbiage, when you got right down to cases? Just seeing stuff. A bunch of snapshots. And most of those snaps bad news, at that. Not a thing to brag about. The opposite, if anything.

She remembered Madame Vronsky, who'd had visions for over sixty years, not a bad old skate in her way, if she did smell like last week's mackerel, saying to her one time: 'The Fifth Dimension, my dear,' she'd said. 'It's not all it's cracked up to be.'

And Madame V was someone who'd always seen good fortune, sudden windfalls, tall dark strangers, puppy dogs. While Kate herself saw nothing but wreckage.

That was the key, the clincher. If only she had been the breed of seer who sometimes saw happy endings, she might have endured. But some malignant fate had cast her as a mortician. Every time she received a picture, another soul went down the toilet. Strokes and seizures, abandonments, bankruptcies, serial slaughters – the graveyards were full of Kate Root Specials. Death sentences at thirty bucks a shot, tips optional.

If not for Ferdousine, she might still be trapped. Or pushing up daisies, more like. The first time she'd come across him, in fact, she had been running from the image of a ballerina shortly to lose a leg in a skiing accident. The Ansonia and all its works so oppressed her, she felt like going out the window. Which was not her style. So she went to watch cricket instead.

That game had always been a refuge. Fred Root, her great-uncle, had bowled for England back in the Twenties, and there had been a summer when she was fourteen when she stayed with him above the corner sweetshop he ran in Wol-verhampton, some dirty grey town in the Midlands. He was an old man then, dying of a bad heart, *a dicky ticker*, and he only half-filled his clothes. Still his hands were massive. She hadn't been exactly petite herself, even then. But Fred Root's fingers had swallowed hers like a snake vanishing a school of pink mice. And their feel, scaly smooth, had been like a snakeskin too.

When he'd had a few beers taken, he'd hold up his right hand to the light, his bowling hand, and bite the fingertips, the way a gold-prospector might test a nugget. '191,598,' he'd say. The number of balls he'd sent down in his first-class career. 'Thirty-three English summers, and not a single half-volley,' he'd say, and drink his own health. A maudlin old tosspot. She'd loved that man.

In his back garden with the lobelias and foxgloves and sweet williams in their tidy beds, all those bland English blooms, he had taught her the in-swinger, the leg-break, the googly. Those were not skills you ever forgot. So instead of slashing her wrists in the Ansonia, she'd ridden the Broadway Local to the Bronx and watched the West Indians playing in Van Cortlandt Park.

Ferdousine was sitting in the next deckchair. A dapper little party he looked, but hopelessly out of place and time even then, done up as an English gentleman on a country-house weekend, all tweeds and brogues and rough woollen socks, and talking down his nose in the accents of a prewar public schoolboy, vowels drawled, hard consonants spat out like grape pips.

All of this sat oddly with his dark and sallow flesh, his yellowed eyes and hawk's nose like the Mahdi in *Gordon of Khartoum*. The first remarks Kate dared risk, he responded curtly, as if she intruded. *La-di-da*, she thought, and she was just gathering up her things to move on when a soaring cover-drive came their way, a shot bound straight for the parking lot, except that she reached up her free hand, plucked it clean like a cherry.

'Fred Root was my great-uncle,' she said.

'A very great bowler,' Ferdousine replied. 'A very great bowler indeed.'

1931, when Fred Root was senior pro for Worcestershire, perhaps a little past his prime but still a force, Ferdousine's father had been chargé d'affaires at the Persian Embassy, and Ferdousine himself a day boy, cricket-crazed, at Westminster. 'Was it fun?' Kate asked.

'Not precisely,' he said. But not so brusquely this time, merely answering the question. He told her about the Embassy, court ritual under the Shah, and how to tie a bow-tie. Fastidious, dry as dust, he was everything she'd been looking for.

They'd sat like companions till close of play, and later on gone to an English tearoom in Greenwich Village, where they ate potted shrimps and fish-paste, rock buns, sherry trifle.

It was the food of childhood. Kate's mother had used to make English spreads each year for Charley Root's birthday. She'd hated them then, and they tasted worse now, but she wolfed them down anyhow. An exorcism, it felt like. And Ferdousine gorged right along with her, mouthful for vile mouthful, while he told her tales of Westminster. 'I was the tame wog in a nest of crypto-fascists,' he said. 'Once they forced an entire suet pudding down my throat.'

'Hot or cold?'

'Tepid.'

Kate could not picture this. What was more, she knew she never would. In Ferdousine, at last, she had met someone who cast no shadow.

He seemed to have no needs. No desires beyond cream cakes and meringues. No begging puppydog eyes or hands clutching at her sleeve, imploring her for certainty. Humans in their hungers, they were the curse of the industry. The curse of existence, really. It got so she couldn't stand to hear that word. *I need, you need, they need* – it made her want to scream. But she didn't, of course. She wouldn't get paid if she did.

But what a relief its absence brought. With Ferdousine, she was absolved from strain; from having to see a damn thing. Maybe that was why she forgot herself. Or maybe she was simply drunk on tipsy-cake. Whichever, she lost all sense of self-censorship, she told him about Charley Root.

Give him credit, the man never blinked. Never even broke the rhythm of his chewing. Only heard her out with his dark head cocked sideways, his yellow eyes like a curious bird, and the first time she stopped for breath, he asked her quietly, 'Did you ever hear tell of one Katerina Rhute? By any manner of chance?'

So that was that.

He knew the entire saga, chapter and verse. Truth to tell, he was better informed than Kate herself. Making sense out of things that made no sense was his life's work, he said, munching a sausage roll; he had created a whole library from his findings. Forty years' accumulation of clippings and cuttings, bound up in red morocco. Spinning suns and burning moons, stigmatics, flying nuns. Rains of toads, and bleeding statues, exploding whales and poltergeists, the works. And Katerina Rhute, of course.

Elbow-deep in Dundee cake, they didn't stop stuffing until the tearoom shut; and the next Sunday they met again at Van Cortlandt Park. All summer they watched cricket, and bloated up on cream teas. When fall came, ending the season, it had seemed only natural for Kate to abandon the Ansonia, cross Broadway to the Zoo. She had no children, no true country. None of Ferdousine's lodgers did. They were their own children, she supposed, and his house their nation.

Nine years, eight months, fourteen days.

How had they been? *Come see, commissar*, as Fred root used to say. She could have done without the gas heaters and the fake rainforest. On the other hand, the routine kept her lulled. The twice-daily repetitions of feeding and cleaning, the chirpings and rustlings and hissings, the smells, the steam heat – top them off with *Days of Our Lives*, and she had her own brand of Prozac.

No fuss, no fandango. She had grown slow and stout in this place; in this place, she'd learned not to see a thing. Every so often, somebody who remembered her from the Ansonia would track her down and try to pump her about their cheating lover, their dying mother, whatever. But she'd learned how to cope with those. Feed them a face like a boot, a smile like a ticket dispenser. Then back to the horn-billed conure, and the yellow-blotch salamander.

Until this boy. In his silly red car.

It was the blatancy that floored her. For a stranger to come to her home and expose himself like that, flash her in the open street – if this had been the *New York Post* or tabloid TV, she'd have said she felt violated.

Violated and dirty. Just sickened. Every time she moved,

took a turn around the jungle, the gas stabbed her again, jackknifing her, and she had to go feed snakes to straighten up.

Their cages sat in a bower of ferns and orchids. The scent of the orchids like embalming fluid, when combined with the brackish reek of snakeshit, never failed to soothe her. Sweat ran sluggish on her belly, her thighs, and she treated the California whipsnake, *masticophis lateralis*, to a bonus mouse.

This was her favourite snake. A lot of reptiles she could take or leave, they were no more than furniture. But the whipsnake was a picture – black on top, with a cream-coloured belly and one orange stripe along each flank, a coral-pink underside to its tail, anal divided, smooth dorsal scales. Waiting on the mouse, he held his flat broad skull cocked sideways like Ferdousine, his yellow-rimmed eye glinting like a brass Woolworth's ring.

That oversized eye was the charm, the reason Kate had named him Whip. Other snakes had beady eyes, evil eyes, hungry eyes. Only his seemed ironic, removed. When all around him rattled and hissed, he would barely stir, just let his tongue flick out. Then his eye, though it had no lid, would seem to droop, grow heavy. A film like a translucent caul would blur its black pupil, and the yellow rings quivered, as if with private laughter.

It was a lounge-lizard look. Glutted on mouse, Whip wore it now. A tango started playing in the room overhead, *Hernando's Hideaway*, and there were sounds of shuffling, two sets of footsteps on a hardened floor, one shambling and uncertain, the other light and flitting. Anna Crow was giving Ferdousine his dancing lesson.

At the tango's lurch and judder, Kate's stomach heaved, and all the prisoned gas burst from her at once. The eruption

39

was so violent, she ducked her head in self-defence, slapped her hand palm-flat against her guts to bind them. '*Regina Angelorum*,' she said. Anna Crow's boy was crossing Broadway with his hands in his pockets. Then he took out his right hand, held it up to the air, a gesture almost like a blessing.

And Kate saw knives.

Harvey McBurnettes, she'd know them anywhere. They were the same blades that Charley Root had always used. Stainless steel bowie-knives, ten inches long, with elegant curved blades sharpened at both edges, a heavy brass crossguard, a black leather grip. He used to call them his Susie Qs.

In the years they'd spent touring, he kept them in his bedside table with his cuff links and his pomade. They lived inside their own teak box lined with crushed velvet, midnight blue, and when Charley Root let them out before the show, the tips of their blades were oily, malicious, like the eyes of a Sonoran Shovelnose, *chionactis palarostris*.

By this time Charley Root no longer played the clubs and theatres, he travelled with a tent show, barnstorming through the Florida Panhandle. He drank too much Rebel Yell, and his hand had started to shake. It was so bad that his wife, Kate's own mother, had lost her nerve. The moment she was strapped into place and saw the first knife flash in Charley's gloved fist, she'd lose control of her bladder, it ruined the whole performance. So she'd had to leave the act, and Kate took her place.

She was eleven going on twelve, born in the East Texas pinewoods, schooled in Arkansas and Louisiana, presently residing in Fruitville, a few miles out of Sarasota, where Charley Root had rented a ranch-style bungalow. When they weren't touring, Kate had not a thing to do after dark but sit on the porch swing, counting fireflies. A big-boned girl even then, *strapping* was the kindly word. A hundred and fifty pounds, rock-solid and full of sap, too full for her own good. She didn't fear a living thing, or dead. Certainly not a fistful of oiled knives.

She was a Bird of Paradise, after all.

On stage, she performed dressed up in feathers, every colour of the rainbow, and when the band played *Cherokee*, and the knives started flying, those feathers were cut away in sections, limb by limb, till she stood revealed. In the flesh. Well, not quite the flesh. A bodystocking, or a flesh-tinted leotard. But the glare of the spotlight was so fierce, nobody in the audience could tell for sure. What was really her, and what was lies.

The Bird of Paradise wasn't the only gimmick that Charley Root used. Not only did he throw at feathers, he threw masked. Not only was he masked, his target was pinned to a rotating backboard. And not only did this board rotate, it varied speeds, quickening as each knife hit home, till it wound up spinning like a top, seemed hardly more than a blur.

All those back roads, all the jerkwater towns. Dade City and Destin, Trilby, Yalaha, Frostproof, through Manatee County, Polk County and Hardee too, clear out to Winter Haven. Mulberry that night when a man in plaids jumped up on stage, ripping out Kate's feathers in great handfuls, till Charley Root with his last knife pinned his hand against the spinning backboard, neat as a mounted butterfly. Or Boca Grande when the act was over, and she stepped away from the board to take her bow, only to hear laughter instead of wolf whistles, wheeling to see that the knives, instead of voluptuous beauty, had traced the outline of a hunchback dwarf.

41

Or Tarpon Springs.

Half a mile outside city limits, there was a patch of scrub field out back of Little Ollie's O-Boy Eats, with a dye-works across the highway, and a wallow of pigs rooting in the trough of a creek. The cracks in the walls of the trailer sucked in mixed smells of coal tar, burning grease and pigswill, and Charley Root's corset sat out on his dressing table.

He was a pendulous man with bleeding gums and piles, loose flesh hanging over his jewelled belt, but at night he mutated himself, turned into a masked avenger, the second coming of Lash Larue. The spurred black thighboots and the black cowboy shirt with the pearl buttons, the black pants too tight in the crotch, and the rhinestones on the cat burglar's black mask. The pomade and powder, the Limes de Buras cologne. The black gloves like a second skin. Last of all, the teeth.

This was a sacred rite, each step performed just so, and always in the exact same order. Except in Tarpon Springs, a town full of Greeks, where the ritual went crashing.

Everything was copasetic till Charley came to the teeth. But the moment he reached for his upper plate, the pigs began to racket, and the sudden uproar caused his hand to jerk. The plate was knocked flying to the floor, and its bonding broke. Molars and bicuspids scattered every which way, and Charley had to get down on his hands and knees, scrabbling under the vanity with his rump thrust high. Sausage-skinned in black leather, it looked overripe, fit to burst; and Kate began to laugh. Sprawled across her bed, half in and half out of her feathers, she caught the giggles and couldn't stop.

Charley Root turned to curse her. But his back was stiff, or his corset caught him wrong. Whichever, he got stuck halfway. And there he remained, frozen in her memory, looking back across one shoulder like a coquette surprised at her bath, some old tart run to flab, with his fallen cheeks all pancake and rouge, his lips painted cherry pink.

He'd wanted to hurt her then; she knew that. He could have killed her, but there was no time. The Susie Qs were glinting sly and greasy in their crushed-velvet beds, pigs kept blundering against the trailer walls, and *Goodbye Cruel World* was playing inside the tent. It was showtime.

Pitched in Ollie O'Boy's parking lot, the tent was barely quarter full. When the curtain was pulled back and the Bird of Paradise revealed, all gold and crimson and midnight-blue, Kate didn't hear one hand clapping.

Most nights, once the board had begun to rotate, she saw nothing more. Only felt the blades kissing cool and sleek, the jolt as they bit home. The first two or three always made her feel sexy. After that she mostly drifted. Thought of Elvis, or silk stockings, or getting her hair permed. But this night felt odd, she couldn't let go. Even when she was spun at speed, her vision refused to blur. Through the hot pink nimbus of the arc lights she saw the knives fanned in Charley Root's gloved left hand, then plucked one by one with his right. Each blade as it was raised above his shoulder, when his arm reared back before the throw, appeared to her frozen in close-up. She could see the long sweeping curve below, the clipped top, and each of the embossed waves, or were they ferns? They flew towards her lazily, showing off. Made sucking sounds as they slipped by. Each blade slower, more ostentatious than the one before.

The last knife came slowest of all, seemed almost to stop in mid-flight. As if it was caught in two minds, couldn't quite decide whether to stick her or pass her by.

It was an awkward situation. Spreadeagled, she felt the spinning board pocked and scratchy against her back, the iron bands that strapped down her arms and legs, and saw

43

Charley Root poised to take his bow. Masked but toothless, with his shirt-buttons straining and white coins of corset peeking through, he started to strip off his black gloves. Still *Cherokee* played on, and the knife's point, dangling, turned hazy-blue like smoke.

The taste in her mouth then was acrid, she felt as if she'd hit an air pocket and was falling weightless. She clamped her teeth against a rush of nausea, shut her eyes, and as she did so she caught a glimpse, somewhere out beyond the knife's edge, of a city street in daylight.

She saw a line of low wooden buildings in the rain, a bar, a hardware store, and some kind of medical shop, a plate-glass window filled with crutches and neck-braces, surgical trusses, all manner of miracle cures.

It was like looking into a diorama: a girl stood leaning against the glass, eating french fries out of a paper bag in a plastic raincoat with no stockings and no hat against the wet, just the morning paper on her head, held open at the Classifieds. She kept glancing at her watch, waiting on a bus, but she didn't seem impatient, merely curious. When the bus arrived, she placed one foot in a white orthopaedic shoe on the bottom step, then she must have sensed she was being watched, somehow spied on, because she looked back across her turned shoulder, the same coy pose that Charley Root had struck when he was scrabbling for his teeth under the vanity, only the girl's face beneath the evening paper was not rouged or raddled, it was suffused with light.

In that instant, the shock of recognition had whipped at Kate's eyes like a lash; she'd shouted out. But her cry made no sound. The only noise was the fat thwack of the Susie Q on the board behind her left ear, and a drizzle of applause, as she fell out of consciousness.

How could that be? To be strapped to a board in Tarpon

Springs, yet watching a girl in an open street, both at the same moment? Long afterwards, Kate had tried to describe it to Fred Root. *Don't be so bloody silly,* he'd said, and she had tried not to be, but there were moments like now when she couldn't help herself. Bloody silliness was her nature, the fashion she had been created.

So she got gas. So sharp and evil, it almost knocked her to her knees. By the time she settled, it was almost time for *Days of Our Lives.*

In yesterday's episode, Stefano had learned from Celeste that Tony was pretending to be blind in order to trap John and Kristen, and Sami and Lucas joined forces to break up Austin and Carrie. Bo, meanwhile, refused to believe Billie's claim that Gina was being brainwashed. So Billie, crushed, had returned Bo's ring.

But Kate could not concentrate. When Bo stole a kiss from Gina, the dirty dog, she felt no sense of betrayal. No sense of anything, in fact. All she could think of was a small boy on a blue tricycle, velvet drapes and Persian cats, and Tarpon Springs, and the teeth, the pigs, the knives, the girl waiting at the bus stop, and when the girl had turned her head. And Kate couldn't cope. Too much had come at her too fast, too fierce. Panic swept across her, she felt sickened. Stumbling through the jungle to Pearl's cage, she opened its gate wide. Opened the door to the Zoo as well, and gestured for her to fly away. But the fool bird refused to oblige. Instead of grabbing its freedom, all it did was flutter feebly in circles, bang its head on the walls and the ceiling, singe its wings on one of the gas heaters, and wind up tangled in a Virginia creeper, head-down and thrashing.

This was no kind of life.

No kind of life at all. Kate couldn't stay here and watch, not one moment more. So she left the bird to live or die, it could suit itself. She didn't even stop to lock the door, just walked out on Broadway in her housecoat and fluffy mules, and started swimming upstream. Past the OTB and La Perla *botanica*, past the Nu-U juice bar, Regan's funeral parlour, and Blanco y Negro, and the Chemical Bank where the clock now read 101°, until she found herself almost at Sweeney's, where she paused to catch her breath, she took a look around.

A child lay in the street.

At lunchtime John Joe Maguire sat in Sweeney's, drinking a Bud on draught. They had strange beer in this far country, cat's piss was the fact of the matter, but the bar was cool and dark, and there was a story on the TV about a girl being brainwashed, a man who was pretending to be blind.

It was only his third day in the city, his feet were not under him yet. At Christmas, when Juice Shovlin came home to Scath, red-faced and gleaming in a hired Daimler, buying drinks all around in Tigh Neachtain's, the man had scattered his business cards like confetti. *The Shovlin Group, Property and Pride*, the cards read. 'You must come up and see me sometime,' said Juice.

'I'll do that,' said John Joe.

'Good man yourself,' said Juice, and handed him a cigar in an aluminium tube, not some squitty little Hamlet or Whiff, but a torpedo thick and long as the dirty drawings in Tigh Neachtain's outhouse where John Joe was sick later on.

His mother was still living then, propped up in her bed at Uncle Frank's with her chocolates and Mills & Boon romances. But the morning after her funeral, he came down to breakfast late, with his suitcase already packed.

'If you're off to America the day, you'll be wanting a good breakfast,' said Uncle Frank.

47

'I'm not hungry.'

'Could you not face a rasher?' his Auntie Phyllis asked. 'Or a slice of blood sausage even?'

'I couldn't.'

'Why couldn't you? It's paid for,' said Uncle Frank, poring over the football pages. It was raining out, Cousin Declan was pulling on his boots by the kitchen door. 'I'd say Down would take some beating,' Cousin Declan said.

'I'd say they would,' said Uncle Frank.

The Shovlin Group had offices on Park Avenue, thirty-one floors up. When Juice Shovlin caught sight of John Joe and his suitcase, he burst out laughing. 'The Great Maguire,' he said. 'What the feck brings you here?'

'You said I must come.'

'Well, feck me rigid,' said Juice.

For the two days and nights since then John Joe had put up at a YMCA. He couldn't get much rest for the strange men jumping into his bed and out again at every hour, no food would stay on his stomach, and the heat had him sandbagged. But was he downhearted? He was not. Juice Shovlin had promised him a managerial position, he was due to start work this afternoon. Just time to clean his glass, and he walked out in the street.

For a moment the heat and white glare blinded him. When his vision cleared, a child was at his feet.

A young boy, seven or eight years old, lying on his side like a sleeper, with his feet on the sidewalk, his head lolling down off the kerb, and one hand stretched out in the light, its fingers loosely curled, as if soliciting alms.

From Sweeney's doorway you could only see one eye, and that was shut. John Joe's first thought was, *This child has gone to meet his maker. He is in a better place*; his second was to pass by. He was a stranger here himself, after all, and the street was full of other people. Any one among them could stop and mind. Only none of them did.

At least the child had shade. He was lying close by the rear wheel of a parked delivery van, almost under it in fact, a few yards away from the Blanco y Negro bodega. In the heat-haze above him, two men in blue coveralls were handing down crates of Boar's Head ham and baloney, and sliding them across the sidewalk on a metal conveyor-belt, down into the chill of the cellar. The owner of Blanco y Negro, studying the receipts, massaged a bright red apple on his sleeve and did not stop saying Shit. One of the men in coveralls showed him where to sign. Saying Shit louder, he threw down his apple untouched, and it started to roll down the street, then hit a rut and veered off at an angle until it arrived at the kerb, where it came to rest against the boy's body, cushioned in the crook behind his bare knees.

John Joe picked it up.

He took one bite, sweet but tasteless, mushy, and put the rest in his back pocket for safekeeping. Then he was squatting on his haunches, fumbling at the child's throat. It was his duty.

He found no pulse. Then again, he had no notion where to look for one. The flesh beneath his fingers felt cool, not cold, and when he pressed down, testing the collarbone, the breast, no trace of blood came away. Still the child made no stir or sound.

'Give him air. Let him breathe,' some man said. John Joe moved his thumb and forefinger against the child's lips, tried to prise the teeth open, but they would not part. His fingers felt clammy as slugs, obscene. When he lifted the shut eyelid, the orb was milky white. 'Kid can't breathe,' some other man said. 'Why don't you let the kid fuckin' breathe?'

All John Joe felt then was guilt. He saw his own crouched

49

shape, the child unmoving beneath his hand. *Not in front of all these people*, he thought. As if he'd struck down the boy himself. As perhaps he had. He laid his head against the boy's chest and listened, he strained, but all he could hear was the lurching of his own heart. Then he wanted to shake this boy, to slap him, he wanted to hurt him some way. But that was not feasible. *Not here*, he thought. *Not now.*

Next door to the Blanco y Negro, two men in suits were watching from inside a funeral parlour. The men in coveralls were watching, too, and the man who had thrown down his apple; an old lady in a walking frame, and her black nurse; three teenage girls in hotpants and halter tops; some man, some other man; and one large woman in a floral housecoat.

When this large woman knelt down beside the child's head, John Joe heard her grunt, could hear her stays creak. 'Don't be so bloody silly,' the woman said.

And the child got up. Rose like a whistled greyhound, in one smooth motion, and turned his face to the light. His opened eyes were hazel with golden flecks, but they didn't seem to see John Joe, or the large woman either. In the door of Blanco y Negro another woman was standing, shouting. A dark woman who cried out in a tongue that John Joe didn't understand, and on her fingers were clusters of rings, ruby red and emerald, that clutched the child, and bore him away.

Left alone with the woman whose stays creaked, John Joe fished the red apple from his back pocket and took another chomp, but it was no use, there was still no savour, no tang. 'Why waste your money? You might as well chew cotton wool,' the woman said. 'Or sugared woodpulp, why not?'

His first impression had been that she was fat, even gross, but now that he looked again, she only seemed hefty, a country woman's built. Strong, dimpled arms and a broad-boned pink face all freckles, pudding-basin grey hair, beads of sweat on a full upper lip, green eyes, and a gap between her front teeth. In the street's white glare, her skin looked rosy and roughened, as though she'd been rudely scrubbed at an outdoor tap on a raw morning. *A butter churner*, John Joe thought.

Those green eyes now looked him up and down, a steady and measuring stare he did not enjoy one bit. 'You'd be better off with a carrot. Help you see in the dark,' the woman said. 'If you'd care to see in the dark, that it.'

'I wouldn't mind.'

'Good. That's good.' But her mind had upped and walked away, he could sense that. Fumbling in the pocket of her housecoat, she found a half-smoked Camel. 'My bird got loose. She's stuck in the Virginia creeper,' the woman said.

An odd voice she had, dead flat, uninflected, that grated like stripped gears from too many smokes, an accent that wasn't English but put John Joe in mind of that country none the less, the tourists who pass through Kilmullen in season from Birmingham, Coventry and such. 'Were you ever in Leamington Spa?' he asked, but she gave no sign that she heard him, just linked his arm, though his apple was only half-eaten, and started to walk him down the block. Her big legs were bare, her blue slippers were out at the toes. 'The name is Kate,' she said. 'You may call me Miss Root.'

The place they came to shocked him. He'd been expecting a spinster's tidy room and a budgie, not to tumble into the Amazon, plunged with no word of warning inside a world of serpents and lizards, man-eating plants by the look of them, and fantastical birds straight out of a Tarzan book, parakeets and conures and hawk-headed caiques, all trilling and whooping to beat the band, with their eyes bright, bright, through the dark and dripping leaves.

51

A pied-pearl bird sat on the counter, staring at the blank screen of a portable TV. When it caught sight of Miss Root, it flew to her shoulder, started pecking at her hair and cheeks.

'Yon bird is trapped in no creeper,' said John Joe.

'But he was,' said Miss Root. 'Oh, he was.'

That seemed small excuse. The day was wearing on, time was flushing. 'Juice Shovlin's expecting me,' said John Joe.

'How would you like to earn ten bucks?'

'I am already in work.'

'Ten bucks for nothing. Almost nothing.'

'Night-manager at a warehouse.'

'So make it twenty.'

Fair play to her, it was money for old farts. All he was required to do was make a few passes with a broom, trim a few obstreperous vines, while Miss Root smoked Camels and watched TV with her bird.

The man that was pretending to be blind saw a murder, the woman who was being brainwashed ran screaming off a roof. When John Joe looked up from his chores, Miss Root was studying him again with her flat green eyes, a piercing the like he hadn't felt since Mrs Connolly in Chemistry, that style she'd had of pinning you like something on a slide, as if to say: *Your flies may not be undone as we speak, boy, but they will be, oh yes, they will.*

The heat in this room was hellfire. The gas heaters had bars like rows of ginger teeth, and the floorboards squelched like swamp wherever John Joe moved. 'I'm finished. All done,' he said.

'What you need is a haircut,' Miss Root told him then.

Along one wall there was a heavy velvet curtain, with a separate chamber on the other side. A salon, you might say, or simply a barbershop. Washbasin, mirror and old-fashioned barber's chair were grouped beneath a ceiling fan, and on the wall opposite hung a rotating pole.

'I had a trim only Friday but,' John Joe said.

'Just a smidgen off the top,' said Miss Root. 'A quick snip around the ears.'

What was her point? Timmy Mallory, *Tonsorial Artist*, had given him a short-back-and-sides in Glenties the morning of his mother's funeral. Timmy called it his Alcatraz Special, guaranteed good for a calendar month. And meanwhile Juice Shovlin sat waiting, thirty-one floors above Park Avenue, in his good suit and clean white shirt and a powdered roll of flesh on his neck shiny pink as bubble gum where the collar squeezed too tight. There was no reason to stay here, no probable cause in creation. 'A decent shave at least,' said Miss Root, and John Joe climbed into the barber's chair, he bowed his head in submission.

The ceiling fan purred steadily, uselessly; no breath of air stirred below. Up close, Miss Root smelled of animal cages and sawdust, Camels, carbolic soap, and her fingers on John Joe's face did not feel like any woman's. Impersonal, brusque, they slapped lather on him like a plasterer spackling an outhouse wall. At each stroke, a fresh fall of cigarette ash scattered on his forehead, his eyelids. Then he heard a razor stropping, and a pillow that might be breasts softly cradled the back of his skull.

The shape of this room was a long narrow funnel like a shooting gallery, with a barred window at the far end instead of tin ducks floating past. The window faced onto a red-brick wall, and the windowsill was strewn with cups, used teabags, half a packet of highland shortbread. John Joe did his best to freeze this frame, not let it go. But there was no use. Under Miss Root's hands he had no will, no self. Through the drifts of ash he felt his flesh turned and reshaped at whim. The straight-edged razor carved him a new set of cheekbones, a firmer chin and stronger jaw.

Behind the velvet curtain, some animal moaned in its sleep. 'Would that be a monkey?' he asked.

'Not on your life. Filthy beasts,' said Miss Root, and slapped a steam-hot towel on him, blistering, blinding him. Then there was only the sound of her breathing in, breathing out, and the fitful creaking of her stays, a tugboat riding at anchor.

In this darkness John Joe felt the next thing to nothing. 'Da had a monkey one time,' he said.

At Duchess Gardens, that was, when he was seven and they lived at the top of four flights of stairs above a padlocked green garden. There was one room in bright light, where his mother played the radio; another room, huddled and dark, was his own. A long thin corridor like a tunnel, like a rope dropped down a black well, led off someplace else. John Joe did not walk along it.

His mother's name was Bernadette, she had blue-black hair and blue-black eyes. He could not picture how her face looked then, just the wild morning sprawl of her hair on the pillows when he crept in bed beside her, the sun and sleep warm in the crook of her neck, the Victor Sylvester quick-steps playing soft on the bedside table, and the pink cardigan she wore as a bedjacket, its shaggy wool matted with the sugared smells of the night before. Lager and lime, rose-water soap, Jasmine Blossom perfume – Da despised these smells; he said they made a woman cheap. But Da, on these slow mornings, was not around.

Where was he? Doing road-work, driving his taxi, swilling tea in Tiny Doyle's. He was a prizefighter, a warrior, a man with thick purpled lips and a splayed nose, scars on both cheekbones, scars above and around both eyes. When he

fought, his name was announced as Kid Ojeah, but Bernadette called him Moses.

Inside the house he hardly spoke and, when he did, he
spoke funny. He used to rise before daybreak, put on his
clothes in the dark. When the front door creaked open, there
was a moment's silence. Da would start to whistle, trilling
light and fluttery like a nightbird. *Stop! In the Name of Love*,
he whistled, and danced down the stairs to the street.

One time, though, he had come inside John Joe's room,
and carried him off in his boxing robe, red satin embossed
with gold lettering, saying: KID OJEAH, THE LAGOS
LAMBASTER.

It was a raw morning near Christmas, the green garden
was black, and a black taxi stood parked at the corner. John
Joe sat by himself in the back seat, the satin robe felt slimy-
cold, his bare feet dangled in air. Whistling and laughing, Da
drove them through empty streets beneath high lamps. Fog
turned the light sulphurous, the streets seemed full of holes.
'I want my bed,' said John Joe.

'You can't have it,' said Da.

Across the pavement was a plate-glass window bright with
Christmas decorations; behind it was Tiny Doyle's. Wreathed
in steam, white men and black men in bomber jackets sat
eating egg, sausage and chips, drinking mugs of sweet tea.
When they saw Kid Ojeah in the doorway, they shouted out
his name like praise.

A life-size Santa Claus drove his sleigh and reindeer across
one wall. Fairy lights and iridescent balls, strings of tinsel
and paper chains made rainbows through the room.

'Who's this?' one man cried, pointing out John Joe.

'This is the Champ,' said Da.

Paraded on his father's shoulders, he was spun round the
room on high. The black men and white men shouted words

55

he did not know, and a woman frying bacon grabbed at his thigh, made kissing sounds through bright orange lips. 'Big head, big balls,' the woman said. Then they were through the back door, alone in a walled yard. A brindled mongrel bitch lay sleeping in dirty straw. When they passed by she opened one eye.

Across the yard another door led inside a chapel. The door was heavy oak, the chapel high-ceilinged and bitter cold. A boxing ring was set up beneath a stained-glass window that showed St George slaying the Dragon. One man skipped rope, another shadow-boxed. The morning light on the stained glass turned St George's sword to flaming gold.

Taking John Joe by the hand, Da led him on bare feet across the chapel floor. Beside a row of metal lockers a sofa sagged against one wall, its guts spilling down through the springs. Sprawled on the sofa was a fat man in a slouch hat and army greatcoat, eating peanuts. 'This man here, Tiny Doyle, he is your best uncle, sit on him,' said Da, placing John Joe with care on the fat man's chest. The man did not speak or stir, just spat shells. 'My own son needs must see me fight,' said Da, and walked through a ragged curtain into a locker room.

The man who re-emerged two minutes later wore high white boots with tassels, white trunks inscribed KO. When he struck a fighter's stance, fists clenched, one of his front teeth flashed gold. 'Look upon this man,' he said. 'Is he not great?' With his weight resting on the ball of his right foot, he flexed and posed, swivelling slowly through a half-circle, his back a drawn bow, his calf and thigh muscles ropes, his biceps bulging like twin mouths stuffed full of gobstoppers. 'What man born of woman could beat this man?' he cried. 'What creature of God's creation?'

'Jimmy Partridge,' said Tiny Doyle. 'Knocked you kicking inside three rounds.'

'I was sick that night. Indispose.'

'Arthur Crufts. Big Boy Williams. Lester Digges.'

'Sick, I tell you.'

'Tony Majors. Stoker Watts.'

'Sick,' said Da. 'Sick, sick.'

Across the chapel the skipping rope snapped and whirred, feet scuffled on canvas, the two men training snorted and gasped. 'Wrap me,' said Da, reaching out his hands for bandaging. 'Make me strong.'

'Fucking Ada,' said Tiny Doyle.

What came next? A black stranger leaping and whirling across the chapel floor, spinning through bars of shadow and strips of light, the tassels dancing on his boots, his arms pistoning in crimson gloves, a leather helmet like a cage, silver spray flying backwards, a gold sword on fire.

By the time they reached home John Joe was burning hot, ice cold. His mother at the top of the steep stairs stood waiting with her hair undone, her nails not painted.

'We took a ride,' said Da. 'Two men, two men.'

'In his bare feet,' said Bernadette.

'He had my robe. He knew no cold,' Kid Ojeah said, a laughing man. But his wife, with her long nails unsheathed, raked her hand across his cheek, made him bleed.

'You stupid damn gorilla. You ignorant ape,' she said, and threw John Joe in the bath.

The water was so hot, the shock made him cry. Submerged all at once, he struggled and thrashed to rise up but his mother held him pinned, refused to let him surface. Only when he submitted did she leave him go free. Her hands in lazy circles soaped his chest. 'Shut your eyes,' she said, and

57

he shut his eyes. 'You're safe,' his mother said, and he flooded the bath with piss.

Da was gone when he got out.

All that was left was the flat and his mother's room, her radio playing, her warm morning bed. There was something wrong with his chest, something weak that made him struggle for breath. His mother blamed Tiny Doyle, and kept John Joe home from school. In a tight square of brightness by her window she read him stories, taught him words by rote. 'Amber. Amble. Ambulance,' she said. Together they danced foxtrots and slow waltzes, they danced Irish jigs. On the wall by his mother's bed, next to the crucifix, were coloured pictures of cocker spaniels and toy poodles, red setters, terriers. 'Ambush. Amen,' she said. At her dressing table she brushed out her blue-black hair, a hundred strokes with the left hand, a hundred strokes with the right. She drank vodka and orange, she chewed peppermints; she sprayed her flesh with Almond Temptation Plus. *Secret Unguents of the Orient*, the plastic bottle read. Tame dogs on leashes walked in the green gardens below. 'I want one,' said John Joe.

'Amends.'

'A brindle bitch.'

'Amity. Amour,' his mother said. 'Amuck.'

On his birthday, instead of a dog, his presents were a picture book called *Saints: Adventures in Courage*, a snowglobe showing Calvary, and a pair of rabbit slippers. After dark he lay in his mother's bed and watched her dress up.

She clothed herself for a ballroom: peachblossom-pink silk drawers with matching uplift bra, starched white petticoats, a backless gown of alice blue. When she twirled on stiletto heels, the petticoat and gown flared out in a fan, displaying

58

her legs to the hip. 'Not so bad for an old maid,' she said. Bending low across the unmade bed, she kissed John Joe's eyes and throat and hair. Her bare shoulder against his cheek felt sleepy warm like fur. 'Dance with me,' she said.

'I will not,' said Da.

He stood in the doorway, black on black, with a ring-tailed monkey perched on his shoulder. It wore a red velvet jacket trimmed in gold, it shivered with cold, its face was grey and wizened like an old man's. 'I fought in Leamington Spa, eight rounds with Houston McBee,' said Kid Ojeah. 'I was invincible.'

'Out of my house,' said Bernadette.

'Still they rob me blind, the referee is a highwayman, I haul back in my dressing room for quittance. But Tiny Doyle, ace manager, will trade no money to me. Not a shilling, not a pence, not one tin farthing for hire. All he harvest me is this worthless monkey. For honour, he claim. For shame, say I.'

'I'll call the police.'

'You will not.'

When Da came close, his face was whittled and slashed like razor-stropped leather, his swollen eyes were red crescent moons. 'You're drunk,' said Bernadette.

'I am,' said Da. 'Drunk as a pale horse, drunk as a drunk cock. Drunk as any father may be.'

Outside in the street where rain slanted against the high lamps, he covered them, all three, with a black rain-slicker, a night watchman's cape. The monkey, shut up in darkness, began to whimper and riot. It stank of rot and urine, some stale sickness; it nipped at John Joe with sharp teeth. 'Free we be,' said Da, removing the cape, and then they were inside a clothing store, a basement lit orange and blue, where a man in a skullcap sat reading *True Detective*. The picture on the cover showed a half-naked blonde in terror, a hand with a blood-dripping knife. 'My own son requires apparel,' said Da. 'Same size like myself will suffice.'

The song he whistled next was *Walk on By*. The melody line spun and flickered, the monkey's teeth chattered, John Joe walked sloshing through puddles in shoes seven sizes too large. Heavy wedges of newspaper bound his feet, and all his clothes were held up by safety pins, yet he was shaped like a scaled-down man; a warrior.

They walked by side streets and mews through Notting Hill, behind Paddington. At a pub called Bonaparte's Retreat, where John Joe ate crisps, Da drank bitter. 'King Napoleon died in Elba, Kid Ojeah deceased in Leamington Spa,' he said. 'No more punching bag for peanuts. No more ape monkeys for honour. No more.'

Down in the depths of the watchman's cape was a whisky flask, which he suckled and passed to John Joe, but John Joe would not drink. Then his father was enraged. 'You take for your sick mother. You don't glean one true thing,' he said. 'How you make me waste for shame.'

Later they came into a neighbourhood of railway sidings, looming sheds, idled carriages and freight cars. Halfway across a bridge, high above the Paddington tracks, Da stopped short and scooped John Joe in his arms, bear-hugged him close and fierce.

'You don't take my drink, take my monkey,' he said.

'It smells.'

'All things smell. That is the game.'

Down below, invisible for the wet, goods trains shunted, coupled, broke apart. Drawing the monkey from its shelter, Da placed it on the bridge's iron parapet. Its fur was drenched, its velvet jacket ripped and fouled. Its old man's grey face peered up questioning, then a sudden squall made it scream. Scrabbling for purchase, it went skittering across the slick iron, teetered on the brink. 'Honour,' said Da, and gave it a push.

But that had been another land. Here in New York, in this new world, hot pincers pulled hairs out of John Joe's nostrils, a lemon-scented spray splashed his cheeks. Barnabas, the monkey was called. 'Dirty-minded perverts,' said Miss Root. 'All they're good for is jerking off.'

'Barney for short,' said John Joe.

'I wouldn't sully my shop.'

When the steam towel was peeled from his face, John Joe felt dispossessed. He was not a manner of man who trusted much to remembering, especially the past, but under cover of darkness it had seemed no harm. The moment he was stripped and thrown back in the light, though, everything felt wrong. The spinning stripes of the barber's pole dizzied him, the worn red-leather seat itched his nates, the enamel arms were slimy and cringing under his palms. When he reached up to feel his face, its planes and bones sat strangely to his touch. 'One shave, ten bucks, plus tax, plus tip, let's say twenty and call it quits,' he heard Miss Root muttering, and he tried to get up, but his legs were no use.

Three days with no compass – the long journey from Scath to Manhattan, bus and train and plane, and Juice Shovlin in a tight white collar, no sleep, no food that would stay down, this heat, and his bed swarmed by strangers at the YMCA – the entire parcel rose up at him swirling, hit him one left hook to the solar plexus, and he fell down out of his standing.

Miss Root's freckles when she bent close were a shifting field of sandflies. A single strand of tobacco had lodged in the gap between her front teeth. She kept trying to suck it free but it wouldn't budge. 'Bed,' she said.

'I have to go.'

'You can have poor Godwin's room.'

'Juice Shovlin's expecting me.'

'I hope you don't mind stained sheets.'

Grains of birdseed stuck to her hair, and the beads of sweat on her upper lip were fat and full as raindrops on a wire. 'Mind your step, there's a loose runner here somewhere,' she said. Her slippers on the stairs flapped at every step, her housecoat hung shapelessly as sacking. From below she looked like an old woman toiling. But when she turned her head, and John Joe saw the green cat's eyes, the strand of tobacco still stuck in the gapped front teeth, the face belonged to a schoolgirl. Then he was in a square room with no furnishings, just a mattress on a bedstead by another barred window. Miss Root switched on the light, but the bulb blew out. 'Never mind,' she said. 'It is an evil generation that asks for a sign.' And she shut him in the dark.

# Second

*D*rowning not waving, Stevie Smith wrote that, and wasn't it the truth? Splash, splash, glug, glug. Only this morning Verse-o-Gram had called her about a gig down in the Washington meat market doing Sylvia Plath and *Lesbos* for a sisterhood bond-in at the Clit Club, and Anna was thrilled, she reverenced that woman, always had done since her days at Shalimar after Chase had had his accident and that nice Dr Bone, instead of asking about her father, used to read her the Ariel poems. But what to wear? Verse-o-Gram's wardrobe for London in the Sixties was strictly miniskirts and white Courrège boots *à la* Twiggy, which hardly seemed the thing, but then again, what was? The only snaps she'd ever seen of Sylvia were black-and-whites, bundled up against the English weather in somebody's back garden, all nerves and wool. So miniskirt and Mod boots it was, and a mousy fringe wig that felt like Fuller brushes, never mind, the sisterhood seemed to lap it up, *Now I am silent, hate up to my neck, thick, thick* and *O vase of acid, it is love you are full of,* nobody said Boo.

Cash on the barrelhead, quick curtsey out the door, *I say I may be back. You know what lies are for,* and afterwards she had gone walking in the meat market. It was just finishing for the day, the trucks rolling out on Little West 12th beneath the disused El, the men in their bloodstained white coats heaving the last sides of beef across the cracked sidewalks, the steel shutters crashing down like scrims on Green Turtle Products and Royale Veal, Spartan Meats and Adolph Kusy's Pork Specials that had the best slogan, *We have the Meat and the Motion*, just the best, and the smells of sawdust, pickling brine, frozen slaughter everywhere, it made her feel sort of dreamy, coming so soon after Sylvia and *that night the moon dragged its blood bag*, it made her want her bed.

So she was standing on the corner across from the Liberty Inn where all the transvestite hookers took their johns, still in her miniskirt and boots trying to flag down a taxi, when up walked this gentleman of colour, two hundred pounds if he was an ounce, in midnight-blue hotpants and a matching wig, a love-charm bracelet dangling from one ankle, who spoke to her in a little-girl lisp. 'You got my pitch, bitch,' he said.

Another time and another place she might have laughed it off, *What an amusing misunderstanding! How frightfully delicious!*, but in the mouth of this man on this corner at this certain moment with the Clit Club and all those dead cows on meathooks behind her back it paralysed her almost. 'I don't want to hurt you. I can hurt you,' the man said, and what was the most galling thing, he didn't even sound hostile, only airing an infomercial, as one impersonator to another.

Praise the Lord, a gypsy cab pulled up in a cloud of dust and whisked her away before she could get herself in deeper, but changing scenes didn't change the film. Even when she was back home at the Zoo inside her room where she paid to stay safe there was still the mirror like fucking George Washington who could not tell a fucking lie, *a man that don't lie got nothing to say*, Waycross Martin used to say, but that was not the point, where was she? Oh, where was she?

In front of the mirror, mother-naked except for her Sylvia wig flopping in her eyes like a dead rabbit, Cape Cadaveral with bangs at thirty-three and the fruits of too many fasts, too many diet pills, too many IVs and stomach pumps, too many dance classes and not enough dance, a plucked chicken saying, 'I don't want to hurt you, I can hurt you,' but it sounded real weak, to be perfectly brutally frank, it sounded like nothing on earth.

Don't start her to talking, she might tell everything she knew. In bed, chafing and fretting under the off-white sheet, she took a look out the window across the roofs towards the Hudson River and saw a shower of sparks, but she was not in the mood; in fact she wasn't even there but back at Shalimar where she'd hardly felt a thing, sedated from asshole to eyeball the way she was, in that clean white room and those clean white corridors, and on her balcony at night with the frogs all croaking in chorus, the cicadas likewise, a night-choir, while she memorized the poems that nice Dr Bone had given her, Henry Vaughan and John Clare, Elizabeth Bishop, and Hopkins of course, *O let them be left, wildness and wet*, and *The Ballad of Rudolph Reed*, how did that go, *I am not hungry for berries, I am not hungry for bread*, that's right, *But hungry hungry for a house Where at night a man in bed*, at Shalimar she had slept so good, *May never hear the plaster Stir as if in pain*, yes, *May never hear the roaches Falling like fat rain*, at Shalimar she had slept.

When she woke it was darkness, she felt like a dead cow herself, and when she glanced through the window her voice of its own accord said *Uh-oh*, just like that, *uh-oh*. Then she was up and out across the landing, blundering in at poor Godwin's door, forgetting in her hurry that Godwin was long gone, not even startled to find another man's body in his

67

place, only hoping it was breathing or at least not stiff. 'Excuse, please,' Anna said. 'I don't like to intrude, honestly I don't, but I was sleeping, well, not really sleeping, more drowsing, sort of dreaming, you know the way you do, when I chanced to look up at Kate Root's Japanese garden, at least that's what she calls it, a waste of space if you ask me, she'd be better off quilting or knitting some baby a nice pair of socks, anyway I looked up and of course I might be wrong, I often am, but I think the roof's on fire.'

The man in the dark said nothing, only wrestled down the front of his white shirt to cover his underpants with one hand while reaching for his jeans with the other. 'Of course by rights I should tell Crouch, it's his responsibility after all, but what would be the use, he wouldn't lift a finger, couldn't give a flying fuck, drunk again if not worse, so I took the liberty, though I hate to wake any man, still it's better than burning alive, the name is Crow, Anna Crow, and who may I ask are you?'

'John Joe Maguire of Scaith-na-Tairbhe.'

'Never heard of it.'

'Three miles and a half from Croaghnaleaba, almost five from Lergynascaragh,' said John Joe. By the hall light his legs looked bony and inadequate, skimbleshanks, as he struggled with his jeans, and midway down his left thigh was a dark raised weal more or less in the shape of a bird with outspread wings and its throat upflung. 'Lordamercy, what's that?' Anna said.

'A birthmark only. I've had it my whole life.'

'Looks like a duck, no, a swan.'

'What about the roof's on fire?'

'A black swan,' Anna said. Squatting by the bedside she scratched at the weal with her black nails, making sure that it didn't come off, while her bottled red hair in the dimness glinted chestnut and roan, cinnabar, hellebore. 'The mark of the beast,' she said. 'Just fancy that.'

Outside on the landing there was a ladder to the attic, where a man rolled up in a blanket lay mumbling, a man the colour of baked clay. 'Don't mind if I do,' he said, seeing Anna, and put in his teeth.

'God curse you and castrate you, we could all have been pot roast in our beds by now and you still up here pig-happy, dreaming of free lunch.'

'I thank you kindly,' said Crouch.

In one corner was a sculpture of Marilyn Monroe with her dress raised to show her panties, and beyond a window looking onto the roof garden littered with dwarf pines, concrete deer, pots of lobelia and portulaca, a papier-mâché pagoda, and a wrought-iron brazier belching flames.

From inside Crouch's attic these flames seemed to leap high and wild against the night sky, but when John Joe clambered out for a closer look there was only cardboard, scrap paper, a charred pair of sneakers, one dead sparrow.

'So piss on it, why don't you?' Anna said.

When the fire had sputtered and turned to smoke, she led him back down the ladder inside her own room, which looked more like a junkshop than any lady's boudoir, stuffed to overflowing as it was with gewgaws and bibelots, old postcards and stuffed animals, Burmese scarves, Chinese slippers, ivory spice-pots from Nagaland, Claddagh rings, *fin de siècle* shoe-lasts for Parisian courtesans, gilt mirrors, vetivert-scented candles, Venetian fans, and many, many pictures of Anna Crow – as a cheerleader, as a Playboy bunny, in G-string and panties, in cherry-pink voile, in harem pants and veil, and almost lifesize in *Swan Lake*, languidly expiring at Mrs Sweetwater's. 'Just turned seventeen, a slip of a girl, a Georgia peach, a royal pain, *Vain as the leaf upon the stream and fickle as a changeful dream,* Sir Walter Scott, that stale fart, I never could abide him,' she said. 'But still and all, seventeen.'

In this room the light was murky but strong enough for her to see John Joe whole – a sulphurous-looking party somewhere in his thirties, scant and spindling, with his hair cropped convict-short, dabs of toilet paper stuck all over his chops, he must have butchered himself shaving. And something wrong with his right eye. The lid drooped half-shut, the muscles of the cheek were rigid, and the skin around the eye itself looked raw. 'Heavens to Betsy,' Anna said. 'What happened to your peeper?'

'It was an accident.'

'Of course it was.' As always in confusion, she assumed the position, her left foot angled out, knees braced, sway-backed. 'Besides, you can hardly see it, you'd never hardly notice,' she said. 'Almost hardly at all.'

'I had this frog.'

'No need to explain, no need at all, me and my big mouth with the foot in it, but it was the black swan, you see, it threw me for a loop. Not of course that that's an excuse, only still.'

'I used to jump him for pennies.'

'Good for you,' Anna said. And she meant it, she really did. Though she'd scarcely met this man, he might be an axe murderer or some brain-dead New Ager for all she knew, there was something about him that soothed her. The pink circle around his eye made him look like a panda, well, no, not a panda exactly, more of a mongrel, a mutt. Which she'd always had a weakness for, a soft spot, and why the fuck not? Mutts didn't snap and bite every time you moved, they had manners, they were grateful for scraps, they knew how

70

to shut up and adore. 'You seem a nice boy, harmless,' she said. 'Did you ever tend bar?'

'At Pansy Keane's wedding just.'

'Well, not to worry, we all have to start somewhere. I was thinking they might need a man in the place I dance, a dump but the drinks are free and you'd get to see my bazooms.'

But John Joe, she knew, could see those right now, tax-free, framed by the loose V of her lounging pyjamas where they dangled tubular, half-ripe. 'My boyfriend thinks I'm beautiful, my boyfriend drives a Spyder, my boyfriend has a magic flute,' Anna said, singsong. 'I love that boy to death.' Opposite her picture as the dying swan was an Art Nouveau mirror adorned with nymphs and Ganymedes that she used to brush the blue shadows from under her eyes, the feverish patches like TB stigmata from her cheeks. '*Spend all you have on loveliness*, don't make me laugh,' she said. Her long sprung foot, turned out in reflection, was ropy with sinews, swollen veins. 'What age am I?'

'I'd say twenty-nine.'

'Marry me,' Anna said. 'You might as well.'

At Sheherazade the smell of incense was strong, the smell of Lysol stronger. Bani Badpa, proprietor of record, sat drinking ouzo and glooming over his losses. 'This is John Joe Maguire, he works for you,' Anna said. 'You owe him forty dollars.'

'I am a dead man,' said Bani Badpa.

The storage space that Anna called her dressing room was out behind the kitchens, its shelves were full of canned chickpeas and roach motels, soiled tablecloths, sweetmeats, Raid.

One wall was covered with step-charts from *Belly or Bust*, mapping out the moves for the Cairo Snap, the Floating Veil, the Anatolian Shimmy, and a cyclostyled quotation from

Serena, stuck to the wall with spirit gum, reading *Glide in innocence. Endure with age. Untiringly seduce the world*, and through that wall came the sound of someone flushing a toilet that wouldn't flush and swearing tonelessly, *Khar Kosseh, Khar Kosseh*. 'Last year when I worked here first I was Xanthia, wine-red rose of the Aegean, this year I am Zenaide from Zonguldak, veiled houri, and the john still doesn't work,' Anna said. 'Then again, what does? My last husband sold sand, tons and tons of the stuff, enough to floor a desert, but Hurricane Hugo blew it all to hell and gone, nothing left but bar bills and blisters. So what could I do? I caught a Greyhound north. Sought solace, and found Ma Root.'

Midway across the storage space was a length of cord strung between two nails and draped with chiffon scarves to form a makeshift screen, and behind it she got changed. 'You want to hear a dumb story? I had this boy, his name was Chase, we lived in a vat full of feathers and everything was aces. But then, come Christmas, I took it in my mind to put on my clothes and go to church, though I knew I shouldn't, still I did. St John the Baptist's for midnight mass, all us Crows are Romans, of course, though I've heard there are other religions, I've even seen them on TV. So down on my knees I knelt and prayed and sang till I was hoarse, *Silent Night, Holy Night* I sang, then I fled. Rushed back to the vat of feathers and dived right in, home again, but when I hit bottom you know what I found? Another woman's falsies.'

Through the wall came sounds of hammering and wrenching, a strong man in his passion beating on a metal pipe. *Khar Kosseh*, the man's voice kept saying and saying, 'Iranians, they never know when to quit, enough's enough, like Ferdousine, the old goat, with his two left feet and wandering hands, just look at my poor toes black and blue, my ass pinched purple, and his touch, lordamercy, icy-cold like death and taxes or frozen lobster claws, I could eat them till I throw up, just scrumptious, where was I?' Anna said.

'In the vat. Full of feathers.'

'With another woman's foam, that's right. And Chase was not even there, I found him in the yard trimming hedges in khaki ducks and an alligator shirt, doused in English Leather, and I knew I'd lost him, gone forever, so what choice did I have, I took a Chief Wigwam bow-and-arrow and shot him through the heart, well, I would have done, but I missed my aim and hit his throat instead.'

'Was he hurt?'

'Not a whit. He just died.'

In the hallway Bani Badpa was kicking tin cans, banging on locked doors. 'Two minutes,' he said.

'*Khar Kosseh*,' Anna replied. 'The whole thing was just so unfair. I mean, I barely touched him, only pinked his Adam's apple, no more than a pin-prick, one bubble of blood; then I drove myself up to Charleston, stayed drunk two weeks on King Street, stole a gun, and by the time I made bail he'd croaked.'

'Thirty seconds.'

'Rust on the tin arrow was all. Blood poisoning, *caries sphacelus*, he was gone.'

A flourish of Mid-Eastern music sounded, drifting through the kitchens, and Anna when she pushed aside the screen of chiffon scarves stood posed against the shelves of chickpeas and Turkish Delight and Raid, in gold sandals and a turquoise veil, a shimmering lamé skirt slit to the hip, a jewelled headband enclosing a black-lacquer wig, sequins spangled in her bra, green glass like an emerald eye stuck in her navel.

In the mirror she was a dark girl, plump and sleekit, with

her flesh oiled to gleaming olive. 'I told you it was a dumb story,' she said.

Sheherazade at midnight was not filled to overflow, only fourteen men to watch her dance, and eight of those Bani Badpa's relations. Still, the patch of dancefloor that served as a stage went black, a drum roll sounded, and a disembodied voice like treacle or a blocked john declaimed, 'Bani Badpa Productions in collaboration with world-famed Sheherazade are proudly to present for the first time anywhere *Innocence Caged*, written and directed by Bani Badpa, his whole creation. This unique work is picturing an innocent maiden imprisoned by a much wicked vizier, although her love is already plight to a farming boy of her village. However, the vizier will not release her from succumbation to his lustful whim. In her cell alone with her griefly thoughts, now the maiden seeks escape in dreams. As performed tonight exclusively for your delectation of delight exclusively by international award-winning *danseuse orientale*, the ZEN-ZATIONAL ZENAIDE!!!'

So here went nothing in a turquoise veil, trapped in a caged circle with a dim spot for moonlight and the faint throbbing of a darbuka on the soundtrack. She could never think what to do with herself, just waggle her fingers she guessed, and act griefly. Bani Badpa's programme notes called for 'sybilant sighs like stirring wind' which was simple enough, kindly pass the dill pickles, but when it came to making her 'roseful bosom jib', her mouth 'gap with lunging', she was flummoxed, what did he take her for? Or no, don't answer that. Not after today and the Liberty Inn. When that TV hooker had put his hand on her and spun her round to see her face, the puzzled look in his eyes as if to say *I know men, I know women, I know men's that's women, but what in the name of fish and fowl is this?* With the heat so hot

74

you couldn't breathe, and those men all bloodstains on their white coats, and *Lesbos* running not rhyming through her like distemper, *I am packing the hard potatoes like good clothes, I am packing the babies, I am packing the sick cats*, what could a girl say?

Not a whole fucking lot.

Not when the darbuka gathered speed, the oud began to wail, and the prisoned maiden had to stir herself 'like a wakeful snake awaking', rising up in ripples, her belly quivering like jello and flashing light from its emerald eye. Offering up her hips while bending her spine slowly backwards in one smooth arch till her wig touched the dungeon floor. Lordamercy, the rush of blood to her head, she almost blacked out, but she didn't have the time. The kemenche had started shrieking like a thing possessed, the oud was going bananas, and now Zenzational Zenaide was zooming to her big finish, 'then a crazed madness enters in', where the maiden flung herself at the bars, and the bars flung her back, and she flung herself again, and again, 'flickersome like a firefly she whorls within the cruelest cage, O woe! The tender flesh of the pulchrous girl is torn by vile bonds infernal'. Until at last she was knocked to her knees, her dreams of freedom dashed, her lovely head bowed in defeat, while the music fluttered softly with broken wings, the kemenche with a last shriek perished, and the maiden was back where she'd started, take her out the oven, she was done.

Not much applause, none, in fact. By the time the house lights were raised Bani Badpa's relations were sitting around the kitchen drinking Wild Irish Rose, and the other marks had all gone home to bed, where Anna would be herself if she'd had a flyspeck of sense. Leaving only John Joe Maguire, plunked like a wooden Indian behind the bar with the bouzoukis and the ceramic lobsters in a red cutaway jacket, a stained bow-tie to match.

And Willie D.

Drinking something dark and sinister in a yachting blazer by Ralph Lauren, navy-blue double-breasted with anchors embossed on the brass buttons for the look that says salt, says spray, and a face on him like thunder. '*Mi corazon*, what ails you?' Anna asked.

'Gash got my cash,' said Willie.

Ill, it was ill.

You gave your trust, and this was the thanks you got. You showed a little compassion, and the bitches took it for weakness, they rolled you and used you for tampons.

When he thought of the first time he'd seen her, working the beat outside the Lincoln Tunnel in the rain and driving sleet, her and her sorry-ass friend, any other man would have kept right on going. Any man in his sane mind would have said *It's none of my business, I don't need the grief*. But he'd always been a sucker for losers. Mouse Williams said it was his Achilles heel, his fatal flaw, but he couldn't help himself. So he'd pulled his El Dorado over to the kerb, right in the mouth of the tunnel, the pit. *You just won the lottery*, he told her. *Climb in, and bring your needle friend with you*.

She was called Trish then, and her friend was Sammi Jo; they came from some dump in Jersey. Just another pair of channel swimmers hooking for their habit. Snuffling and scratching the whole way downtown; they called it flu, and he was such a boy scout then, he didn't even laugh.

The truth was, he'd spoiled them. He took them into his home, cleaned them up, gave them methadone and fresh underwear, changed their names to Ivana and Marla turned them into sisters, bought them fancy clothes and the finest in shoes, taught them how to eat asparagus, introduced them around town, got them connected with Men of Power, Sandman Ames and Patsy O, even Deacon Landry, the world of movers and shakers, and all for why? Because he cared, that's why. And because he had a vision. In the split-second it took to drive past them at Lincoln Tunnel, he'd caught a flash of something live, a spark, and the coldness wasn't in him to let that spark get snuffed out.

Cut right down to the bone and what he'd done, he'd put his faith in the human heart, and if that was considered a sin then pardon him to hell. So he should have known better. Agreed. But he was the way he was. And even today, after everything he'd suffered, he wasn't ashamed of it. When Marla took up with that jumped-up bricklayer from Queens, he didn't even ask for his investment back, just wrote it off to education. But Ivana? This one was bitter. She was the one he'd spotted first, the one he'd always felt closest to. The Alpha dog, the one he couldn't afford to lose. Because, if he did, he lost part of himself.

Forty-eight hundred bucks, to be exact.

He'd kept it stashed inside the room in Brighton Beach, rolled up in the hollow leg of her metal-frame bed, where the duck hunter with the cast could keep his eye on it. Not that he was superstitious. On the contrary. *Flipflop*, as the Deacon would say. People thought if you were Rican, every move you made was altars and ashes and drinking chicken's blood, you couldn't pick your nose without consulting the Babalawo. Which was the furthest thing from the truth. That stuff meant nothing to him. But casts, those were different. Their power had been laboratory proved, it was a known scientific fact. Any doctor could tell you.

That room had been his snug harbour, it seemed as safe as any bank. Safer, face it, with Patsy O back in town. Any time he made a score, he'd wait his time till Ivana was working or nodding, and pump the roll. Building patiently till the nut hit ten grand, and he could move on Tyger's Topless.

He'd had a dream. Now the dream had turned into Pedigree Chum. And whose doing was that? No prizes for guessing. Ever since the fat white woman had whipped her eye on him, his pants had been turned upside down.

It was like he had been coldcocked. Or hit by some curse, who knew? Maybe Anna Crow like a stopped clock was right for once, and this Kate Root really was some witch. Any way you cut it, she was bad news. One moment he had been cruising, in total control. The next, everything was mess. The murdered shoes, and that bird trailing him round town. And then, of course, the knives.

The moment Anna mentioned them, he had known them for a sign. *Some kind of act with knives*, she'd said, and he flashed an image of the fat woman in white tights and a whalebone corset. She looked just like those sepia photographs he'd found that time in the attic when he was in Sixth Grade.

He'd used to look over them on rainy days and days when he went lost. One of the women was strapped flat on her back to a white stallion with flaring nostrils and flying mane. Adah Isaacs Menken, he could still remember her name. She wore tights so close to flesh you had to strain your eyes to see she wasn't nude. And strain he had. With moth-eaten clothes and broken-down prams and mildewed books all around, dust up his nose and in his eyes, rain driving at the skylight, his kid sisters raising Cain in their bedroom down below, and all these hot bitches, dead a hundred years, with their chunky thighs, wasp waists, and their tits fat like that, balloons, the nipples would put your eye out.

He hadn't thought of the pictures in years. Adah Isaacs Menken, *Mazeppa*. And Evelyn Nesbit, *Poor Butterfly*. And Lillian Russell, the Jersey Lily. But now that it had snuck back in his mind, he couldn't flush it loose. All the time he was humping Anna, his mind had seen only Kate Root, a middle linebacker with tits, and the knives buzzing round her like bees. Not a pretty sight, you'd say. But it got him so hard, he hurt.

The way he felt then, he had no will of his own left, no mastery. As though he'd been kidnapped somehow. Like he was stolen property.

With a bone that wouldn't die.

All day afterwards, he'd been forced to move through the city with his hands folded in his lap. He couldn't think straight, couldn't catch his breath for the burn. Blue-ball murder, it was; such an agony he'd almost paid a visit to Tia Guadalupe and copped one of those Elegguas he didn't believe in. Anything at all to ease him, reverse the curse.

After dark he dropped by Chez Stadium, had cocktails with Deacon Landry and the rest. For a heartbeat he was almost tempted to confide in him, that's how far and deep he was gone. But what was he going to tell them? *Dear Abby, there is this tub of lard whitemeat with a bird, fifty if she's a day, who took one look at me, now all I can picture is her getting knives thrown at her head, and I'm so hard you could hang Old Glory from me, what remedy would you suggest?* He fancied not.

So he sat silent, suffering, while the rest of the table swapped toasts and bull, and Mouse Williams told this story about a freak his Uncle Cyrille had sent him from Hotlanta, Ruby Redd her name was. How she'd come into his room in her travelling coat with not a stitch underneath, twirling and pirouetting round the floor like some bright young

Bambi at the cotillion ball, saying 'What do you think? Am I not beautiful?' And Mouse he'd just stared at her, that graveyard look he had, and said, 'Beautiful?' he'd told her, 'It ain't beauty till the blind man smile.'

*The blind man smile* – for Willie, it was like hitting a switch. One line out of darkness, and suddenly he could see his way clear. To be exorcised from the knives, he needed knives of his own. And he knew just the blind man to provide them.

He left without laughing, drove out to Coney Island. But his dick still gave him no peace. Shooting pains raked his groin, his balls, so evil he couldn't steer right. No way he was fit to deal with any blind man in this condition. So he took a sidebar to Brighton Beach, down the tunnel beneath the El, past the Russian news-stands and the *kvass* stalls, and called on Ivana for relief. Only to find she was gone.

As if she'd never been. Her clothes and wigs and make-up, her drugs and works, even the smell of her was wiped out. And so was Willie's nest egg.

She hadn't even troubled to cover her tracks. The metal-frame bed was slashed and trashed, its hollow leg swinging loose like a broken crutch. Inside, where the cash should have been, there was now just a puddle of hot-sour soup.

How could she do this thing? She had covered up the cast, that's how. Forty-nine duck hunters in rowboats were repeated on the wallpaper, with their walrus moustaches and their rifles across their knees, and each of them now sported an eyepatch, kelly-green, coloured in with Magic Marker.

So this was grief.

Anna Crow had told him a story once about this boy she shot who'd died, of course he hadn't believed a word, but he didn't like to show bad manners, so he asked her how she'd felt, and all Anna said was, 'Old.' Which had made no sense to him at the time, hardly anything she said ever did, but now the word came back on him, repeated like a Sabrett's frank. And his dick went limp.

Not just limp, but lost. As though he had been plunged into icy water, or a swimming pool filled with starving piranhas. So shrivelled he was, he could have thrown up for shame. But that was not feasible. Men of Power, when they were cornered, were at their most dangerous. Muhammad Ali had been like that, Richard Nixon as well. And Willie was from the same school. Never mind the blood, just give him one more round, and he'd get equalized.

Time to visit Anna Crow.

When he walked into Sheherazade, she was doing her dumb number in the cage, and there was a new man the colour of jaundice behind the bar. He looked like someone had whacked his eye with a branding-iron, his mama probably, but Willie in his condition could not be bothered to ask.

He was so deep in shock, he couldn't remember the name of his drink of choice, or even how it tasted. Something dark and sweet and sticky, that was the most he could conjure up, so he wound up drinking cognac with Welch's grape juice, which tasted good, not as good as the drink he'd forgot the name of, but what did it matter now? When the gash had got his cash, and gone.

He thought it in numbness, not rage. Then he heard that he'd said it out loud. Which was an embarrassment. Even blindsided and whiplashed, he wasn't so scrambled that he wanted his business made public. Deacon Landry and them would rotissomat his ass. All in fun, of course, and the spirit of good fellowship. Still, he'd rather not, thanks but no thanks. So he kept his mouth filled with grape juice, and left her hand to do the talking, stroking and stirring down south, though what did it win her tonight? Not a ripple. Not a twitch.

The way she clung on him then, you'd think it was her house had burned, not his. Her make-up where she'd sweated had formed rills and eddies, a cocoa-washed sandbank at the pit of her throat, it looked like Rockaway Beach at low tide. 'I thought you were never coming. I thought you wouldn't come,' she said. 'Why such a tragic face?'

'Death in the family.'

Anna asked nothing more, just drank down her brandy, then placed his hand with spread fingers over her heart. 'How much do you love me?' Willie asked her, nuzzling her ear.

'How deep is the ocean? How high is the sky?'

'Fifty bucks?'

'Say forty, and go fuck yourself.'

No breath of air stirred in the street, the smoke rose up straight. Where the Spyder sat parked, a man was shouting through a megaphone, he looked like a corn-fed college boy from Iowa or Idaho, one of those places that you never thought really existed till it jumped up flapping in your face. '*For the great day of his wrath is come, and who shall be able to stand?*' he cried.

Willie D wouldn't dignify him with an answer.

Driving back across the East River to Brooklyn he punched up one of Regina's self-help tapes. *Water Thoughts* it was called, some New Age Muzak symphonette. As a rule he couldn't stand that faggot puke, but this was no night for as a rule. The quiet lapping of the synthesizer, its ceaseless circular spinning, he felt as if he was floating weightless in a vat of maple syrup. There was no damage here, and no appetite. Nothing as rude as hurt.

83

Maybe she was a dyke.

That would explain a lot. Well, of course. The way she'd fallen apart after Marla took off, all her zap and pizzazz run to seed, not a sign of that first spark he'd seen in her. Just laying around the apartment all day scratching and yawning, no wonder her johns took a hike, and he'd had to move her out of Manhattan, stick her away in Brighton Beach with the Russians, who didn't know any better.

A clit-nuzzler.

He hadn't stood a chance. Nobody would have, not even Deacon Landry. No power on earth could have kept her in line, or stopped her from ripping him off. It was no weakness on his part. *Flipflop*, in fact. The more man he was, the worse she was bound to betray him. That was the nature of the beast.

Just write it down as an Act of God. Or a work-related injury, better yet. A badge of honour. But who would have thought it? The girl kept a picture of Jon Bon Jovi in her closet, she even took it with her when she ran. *Go figure skate*, as Anna Crow said. The Muzak oozing from the floor speakers kept licking at his feet, creeping slowly up his legs, warm and sticky. When he looked down, his new shoes, his brand new armadillos, were looking up. *It ain't beauty till the blind man smile*. That was one true statement.

He knew Coney Island from way back. The summer he was rising ten, it was the season that Billy Martin came back one more time as Yankee manager, the Eurythmics cut *Sweet Dreams*, and Angie Crane, her father ran numbers, took him down in the boiler room. She wore panties sewed with purple hearts, there was a mole on her hip that looked like a tadpole, she smelled of melting tar, and his Uncle Sanchez died.

They were never close or anything, Willie was just living in his house and he was an old man sinking, a rattle-sack

84

who spoke no word of English, only sucked his gums and remembered back in his village, the dances and weddings and wakes. He used to sit propped up in an overstuffed armchair with broken springs and blown blue roses for a pattern, reading *El Diario* and half-smoking, half-chewing on Rob Roy cigars till they were pulp. The most revolting thing you ever saw. Dog-slobber and mush, and that's how he died, halfway through the box-scores. Laid down the paper, gave one cough, and he croaked.

When his mouth fell open, the cigar fell out, he'd hardly begun to work on it, and it rolled underneath the piano, where Willie sat and watched.

The night of the wake, the kitchen was stuffed full of people with greasy hands and greasy mouths eating *pastellilos* and *arroz con grandules*, they looked like one body with forty heads, and he took shelter in the front parlour where Uncle Sanchez was laid out in a pine coffin ringed by scented candles and screw the Health Codes, he was safe home in Banos de Coamo by now.

It was Willie's first stiff, the stench of calla lilies and incense mixed with embalming fluid almost made him throw up, but he raised up on tiptoes instead, and draped himself jack-knifed over the coffin's edge. Only Uncle Sanchez wasn't inside; some stranger was in his place. A man made of yellow wax with dyed black hair brushed across his bald skull; blood-red lips like Dracula's, curled back from a set of store-bought pearly-whites never stained by cigar smoke; and no eyes.

Or his eyes were covered by silver dollars. And Willie needed to see underneath. When he reached down to explore, the silver dollars felt lukewarm, a little slimy, against the ball of his thumb, but the eyelids beneath felt cool and dry, something like the texture of black grapeskins.

Just a sliver of eyeball showed, cloudy yellow, at the lower rim of the socket, and if you wanted to see the pupil whole, you had to peel back the lid like peeling a raw shrimp. A creature that Willie could never tolerate. So he hung there on the coffin, the silver dollars curled in his palm. Some drunk was singing *Dias y Noches Perdidas* in the kitchen, then a man's voice spoke behind his back, 'How about them Yankees?' it said.

His Cousin Humberto. The biggest man that Willie had ever been in one room with. A hardcore bodybuilder, baked bright orange by the tanning lamp, with wild horses tattoed on his shoulders and arms, and every time he flexed, the horses swished their tails, started running.

He had a pocket radio with him, and he sat himself down in Uncle Sanchez' armchair to listen to the ballgame. The springs twanged and popped, the candles flickered but didn't go out. It was the bottom of the eight, and the Orioles were leading 3–2, with the Yankees coming to bat. But Cousin Humberto was no way dismayed. 'They don't die. Every time you think they're nailed, that's when they rise up ripping,' he said, dragging on a cigar, and Willie lit up his own, the mangled stub he'd picked up underneath the piano, they smoked together in silence.

Not a word, just Humberto cracking his knuckles and the far murmur of the ballgame, with the yellow wax stretched in his box and the reek of embalming fluid in Willie's eyes, on his hands, underneath his nails, the two silver dollars tucked safe in his cuff, and Nettles homered to right, an upper-deck shot, scoring Randolph and Don Baylor, Righetti took the win, Goose Gossage got the save.

So he was a man then, and three days later, when Aunt Sanchez had her dispersal sale, Cousin Humberto took him for the summer, brought him to Coney Island where Hum-

86

berto worked as a whip on the Wall of Death and lived with his girlfriend Oceana on Surf Avenue, third-floor front in a fall-down apartment house filled with mutations: a lizardskin boy; a red-bearded lady; a goat-hoofed man; twins with X-ray eyes.

All of these and many others were the property of Mr Sy Stein, who ran a chain of sideshows called Stein's Amazements on the boardwalk and in the alleys. A man got up like Buffalo Bill in cavalry boots with silver spurs, deerskin fringe jacket, a goatee and waxed moustaches and shoulder-length silver hair. And outsize black shades as well. Because the man was blind.

From his window Willie could see the whole carnival laid out, the Big Dipper and the Tilter Whirl, the shooting galleries and girlie shows, the gypsy fortune-tellers, the Tunnel of Love, the House of Mirth, Bluebeard's Castle, all the lights and colours and flashing neon, and they were glamour in his mind. But he wasn't allowed to go walking, he had to stay cooped up all summer in Mr Stein's building with Bones the living skeleton and Stretcho the human pretzel; and Marvin Dobbs whose face was carved down the middle as if with an axe, leaving him two foreheads, two noses, two mouths; and Abigail Alicia, the World's Most Illustrated Woman, who was covered every inch in biblical scenes, Noah's Ark marching two by two up her spine, Lazarus rising on one thigh and the walls of Jericho tumbling on the other, Lucifer cast out of her navel, Moses sermonizing above her mount. Between her breasts the tattoo read *My beloved is gone down into his garden, to the beds of spices*, but over the cleft of her ass when she turned her back to scratch it said: *By the rivers of Babylon, there we sat down, yea, we wept, we remembered Zion.*

All over the house there were women hungry to feed him.

87

Some gave him cookies, some candies, some cake. Even Oceana gave him Snickers and let him watch her in her bath, the woman had nipples like baby's thumbs.

The room where Oceana lived with his Cousin Humberto was set up like a gym with barbells and exercise machines, and when Humberto came home from whipping on the Wall of Death, he lifted weights in bikini shorts, his shaved body all oiled and greased, the Yankees on the radio, and the wild horses rearing and plunging, careening out of control. Some nights he'd gentle them and stroke their manes, let them nuzzle his hand, and others he'd ride them straight into walls, it all depended on what pills he'd took, and how Reggie Jackson did.

After he was gone a snail's trail of suntan lotion marked every place he'd passed, and Oceana sat drinking tea in an old bathrobe, sewing sequins on padded bathing suits for the Traverse Triplets, while Abel Bonder threw knives at the wall.

This man had a withered right hand. According to Oceana he had been a star years back, one of the biggest names in the business, but he'd had an accident or something, anyway his hand was ruined, and now he had to relearn his trade, teach himself to throw lefty. A squit of a man always in a fresh-pressed black suit and black tie, black shoes shined to mirrors, he looked like a mortician, and all day long he threw knives in different patterns, a fan, a pyramid, sometimes a heart. But the blades never seemed to fly right. Instead of hitting the target solid, they fluttered and scrabbled, dying quails, with the radio tuned to *Make-Believe Ballroom*, all these sappy old songs like one great sigh, *Mona Lisa* and *Deep Purple* and *Stardust*, and Willie sitting in the window, stuck.

On the table next to him was a bottle of Spanish brandy with a picture of a courtyard in old Seville, a red lantern in an orange tree, a young gypsy girl with a fan and combs in her hair sipping from a crystal goblet, and a masked caballero in a swirling cape leaning over her, proffering a blood-red rose.

There must have been a gimmick or maybe fluorescent paint in the label, some trick like that. At any rate, when Oceana got to drinking and the liquor level fell, the whole courtyard lit up, the lantern glowed, the gypsy's fan seemed to flicker and dance, the red rose turned to flame.

And Able Bonder handed Willie his knives. Showed him how to hold them, how to sight and aim. *A natural*, Abel Bonder called him. Then the man went out for a walk and didn't come back alive. The knives were orphaned.

By rights they should have been Willie's, that's what the deceased would have wished, but Mr Stein took them in lieu of rent. Just because he was the man he was. A blinded jackdaw who hoarded every souvenir he could lay hands on, the bearded lady's shavings, flakes and scabs from the lizardskin boy, he plain couldn't bear to be parted. So he garnished Abel Bonder's blades, and locked them in his safe, and soon the season ended.

Marvin Dobbs and Abigail Alicia transferred to Florida, Oceana took a job at Nathan's. Then nobody drank from the Spanish brandy, the courtyard didn't light up, the red rose didn't turn to flame. Left alone, Willie sat at a window smeared and blurred with suntan oil, looking down at the abandoned rides, the rows of steel-shuttered sideshows. Thinking of Abel Bonder, and of Abel Bonder's knives, the knives that should have been his. Till his Aunt Rosario came to fetch him, and Coney Island ended.

He'd hardly been back since. Just driven past on his way to Brighton Beach, hurtling through the war zones. But this night he parked, and burrowed into the few alleys that were still active. Murals of Madonna and Snoop Doggy Dogg were surrounded by boarded windows, the scrunch of broken glass underfoot, and the sign on the chained door of Stein's Amazements read TWO-HEADED MAN CLOSED FOR RENOVATION.

Mr Stein himself sat drinking peppermint schnapps in the bar next door, still dressed as Buffalo Bill except for the cavalry boots. His feet, grotesquely swollen, were now housed in bedroom slippers with the toes cut out, and stray drops of schnapps clung to the goatee, the waxed moustaches.

The view down the bar onto the Boardwalk was framed like an oversize TV screen. As Willie watched, an unending stream of musclemen in bodysuits drifted past, and old shuffling Jews with *yarmulkes*, and girls in their summer skins, Italian men in Bermuda shorts and socks, Russian women in tents, Kate Root in white tights and corsets, Ivana dyke-naked, duck hunters with green eyepatches.

Mr Stein kept his shades turned towards the light, his mouth half-open in a leering blind man's smile, but at the sound of money, twin twenties slapped on the bar behind him, he swivelled his head. 'Who goes there?' he asked, startled, when Willie came close. One long tress of silver hair had worked lose from under his Stetson, dangled across his cheek like an unravelled vine. 'Don't hurt me,' cried Mr Stein.

The din, this unending bedlam, how was she supposed to function? Between the birds racketing in the Zoo, and *Little Brown Jug* booming overhead, Ferdousine's feet numb-fumbling on the hardwood floor, and that moron in the street with his megaphone announcing the Last Days, *And I heard a great voice out of the temple saying to the seven angels, Go your ways, and pour out the vials of the wrath of God upon the earth*, how could she keep her mind on Billie and Bo?

Worse, the TV was on the blink. A 14-inch Zenith, black-and-white, she'd had it forever, and now it was letting her down. Every time that Billie raised her voice, she turned to snow. And she was raising her voice a lot. Which was only human; her whole future was on the line. Considering all she'd been through, the incest and the drug addiction and the porn films, not to mention getting arrested for Curtis' murder, it was inspiring how far she'd come already. But were her troubles really done? Would Bo ever get over Hope? Or would there always be this shadow?

Finding him lounging in Hope's bra and panties was not a good sign, you couldn't pretend it was. 'Hand the scumbag his hat,' Kate said, and that boy with the shiny red car walked in.

He came half-strutting, half-gliding, in soot-black, torero

pants by Yohji Yamamoto and a shot-silk amethyst shirt, carrying a leather case that he set on the counter next to Pearl where she perched staring at the blizzard on the screen.

'I heard you know knives,' he said.

'Anna Crow,' said Kate. 'I'll slaughter that slut.'

Without the camouflage of his car, the boyfriend looked exactly that, a boy, a sneaking schoolboy. Wilfredo Diliberto, he said his name was, but she could call him Wilfred. His voice, which was soft, almost whispery, lagged a hint behind the beat. This gave it a slyness, a slither of insinuation, as if everything he said concealed a subtext and most of his words meant their opposites. 'I never was around knives before, they always seemed so dangerous,' he said. 'But maybe you could teach me. Show me a thing, or two.'

'Not a chance.'

'A few easy moves, that's all.'

His stare as he spoke was sideways, a slanted look of teasing. But when he stood close Kate could see the pulses jump in his throat, at his temple, and she saw him crouched in an attic, looking at dirty pictures, it was just disgusting.

The taste in the back of her throat then was Ollie's O-Boy Eats – chili corndogs, flapjacks, spoilt milk – and she covered her mouth with *Soap Digest*.

'I could pay,' said Wilfred.

'Don't,' said Kate. 'Please don't.'

When Billie soul-kissed Bo, her nose job crinkled and twitched like a hungry rabbit. The trouble with lips like hers, in one shot you looked like a goddess of love, and the next like The Little Engine That Could. 'At least let me show you my equipment,' said Wilfred. 'That couldn't hurt; how could it hurt? To sneak a peek at a blade?'

The leather case on the counter was distressed wine-red morocco, bruised and scuffed at the corners, and the knives

92

inside when he exposed them to light were blotched with rust, their points dulled. But the lush sweep of their curve was lovely still. Lying couched in crushed purple velvet, they looked like church.

Harvey McBurnettes.

What could she do? Not a thing. Just pretend she hadn't noticed, turn away. Climb upon a stool, and busy herself with a bird. 'Of course they need shining up, a little spit and polish,' the boy was saying. 'A touch of TLC, and they'll be born again.'

'Get out of my zoo,' said Kate.

It came out forcibly but not strident, by no means a shriek. Merely an instruction as she returned to floor level, and pressed one hand against his chest, palm flat, fingers up, a Stop sign. One sustained backwards thrust then, and Kate had shunted him through the door, out into the street.

Without his box of knives he looked lost, a lost child. 'You'll be sorry,' he said.

She already was. When she came back to the counter *Days of Our Lives* had ended she didn't know where, leaving her adrift, without bearings. Some days she would have consoled herself with *Guiding Light* or *As the World Turns*, which came on next, but she had no heart for either one. She couldn't settle to a thing, not the soaps or the birds' evening feed, not even a Camel. All she wanted was out of here. But that would have given the boy too much honour. To cut and run in panic, a headless chicken, that would not be becoming.

She was stuck then, immured with a flock of birds, a nest of serpents and their accumulated shit, what Ferdousine called the *fruit of their feculent visitations*. Their din and their stink, and the heat, this ceaseless swelter. As a rule she barely noticed it, took it as a given. Today she felt it throttle her.

93

*Limp as last week's lettuce*, that had been Fred Root's saying. But he had been speaking of English summer, sizzling at seventy. The day he took her to the cricket, a Saturday league game behind Bellamy's Brewery. The two of them sitting in uncut grass that smelled of brown ale and barley wine, drinking sweet milky tea out of a thermos, him with his Gold Flakes, her with her Space Blasters, and the brewery sign across the field, *Bellamy's Beer Cures What Ales You*. 'Hot as Hades,' Fred Root said, a word she had not heard before. Looking past his nodding head she saw the crimson ball rise high, turn into a red-winged bird.

Sick fancies.

She needed a day away, that was all. Or even an afternoon at Van Cortlandt Park in a deck chair, keeping score. Or she could have used a trip upstate to those thirty-five acres near Glens Falls, the acres she'd never got around yet to visiting, though she'd owned them fifteen years, must be. Since way back in the Ansonia era, at any rate, when Prince Claessen had come to her and she hadn't known if she should call him Your Highness or simply Sire. She'd got herself all flustered, till it turned out that Prince was not a title, only his father's conceit, and the man himself trained racehorses.

Which was certainly a switch. Kate was forever plagued by horse players seeking winners. All voyants were, they couldn't have paid their rent otherwise. But a trainer, that was a twist. And a trainer in luck, what's more. Jaipur Johnnie had already won the Wood Memorial for him, and the Travers up at Saratoga, and was favoured in the Great Suburban. Horse of the Year seemed a near certainty, and then millions in breeding fees. Plus the man had a dazzling wife, a partner he'd trust with his life, a family who adored him. His existence seemed so blessed, it terrified him. So he came to Kate, to have her search for a flaw.

94

One look at him, of course, and she'd found it. She saw his wife run off with his brother, Jaipur Johnnie break a leg, his partner busted for embezzlement, his family turn to jackals, and Prince himself dead, a suicide, his pistol in his mouth. But she didn't tell him that, not in so many words; it wouldn't have been good for business. She merely advised him to watch his step around guns, and have a nice day. But the man was not so simple, he smelled a rat. Started asking questions and wouldn't stop. The more she stalled, the deeper he probed. When his session was finished, he booked another, and another. Soon he couldn't move without her. *What guns?* he kept on asking. *Pistols*, she told him at last, and he paid her bill, went home. Added a brief codicil to his will, then walked into Jaipur Johnnie's stall and let himself be kicked to death. Anything to cheat the trigger. Leaving Kate the thirty-five acres near Glens Falls, plus a gelding named Baloney Breath. *For services rendered*, the codicil said.

Take it in the spirit intended, Ferdousine had told her. But she'd never been clear what spirit that might be, so the farm and nag had gone unused. Baloney Breath, at last hearing, was still alive and kicking. Kate thought of him with distant distaste.

Not today, though. On this afternoon she'd have tramped the length of the New York State Thruway for one good ooze of slop between her toes, a single whiff of horseshit hot and strong. And that was a danger signal. When a woman her age, who didn't know grass from green shag, started pining for Mother Nature, it might be time to speed the friendly bullet. *Ladies of equinoctal years*, Ferdousine called them. You never could trust these old boilers.

Besides, how could she take a powder? When she knew that the Zoo was history without her, would fall apart the moment she wasn't around? After all, be honest, who else

95

…ed to preserve it? Crouch? Maguire? Ferdousine
…ell, who, then? The burden was hers, and hers

…out Maguire, but what use to pretend? The first
moment she had laid eyes on him, she thought that he might
come in handy; the second, she knew he never would. *Nincompoop* was a fine word, *jobbernowl* another. Still he
seemed to belong in this place somehow. He went with the
colour scheme, all ninety-nine shades of it. Once in, it had
seemed unthinkable to boot him out. And then, in certain
lights, he seemed familiar. Something about his posture, the
set of his head maybe. But no, she couldn't define it, she was
probably dead wrong. Most likely he was simply one more
stray off the streets. Another ball and chain.

*Terribilis est locus iste . . .*

Some creature was moving behind the ferns. It couldn't be
a bird, the eyes weren't bright enough, it had to be a customer. A rare sighting in these dog days, the heat mostly held
them at bay. The hottest July on record, so Ferdousine said,
with the worst fires and the most heart attacks. But this
character seemed to thrive on it. A stout party in beard and
baggies, guts cascading out of a Lollapalooza sweatshirt, he
carried a can of King Cobra, breathed its fumes all over the
zebra-tailed lizard and the Mojave rattlesnake. 'A hundred
three in the shade, they're dropping like flies out there,' he
said, and poked a fat finger through the bars of a sleeping
garter snake, *thamnophis cyrtopsis*. 'Is this one poisonous?'

'Deadly,' said Kate, and blew a smoke ring. 'He rubs his
venom on his cage, one touch and you're fishbait.'

*Terribilis est locus iste hic domus Dei . . .*

Left alone, she turned back to the TV. A bleeding man in
a white bedrobe was pushing a nurse into an empty elevator
shaft, his rubber gloves were around her throat, she was

96

screaming but no sound came out. *General Hospital*, Kate thought. Was it really that late? *Hic domus Dei et porta coeli.*

On the counter next to Pearl, who was snoring standing up, the red morocco box stood open, the rusted knives glowed dimly in their crushed velvet beds. She knew they were no use to her. No good could come of them, she should sling them straight into the garbage. But it was beyond her power. She could no more resist them than a nest full of chocolate truffles. With nobody to see, not a soul to know or tell. Her fingers curled like talons. Hovered over one blade, then another, then settled on a third. Prised it free, handle first, and weighed it in the palm of her hand. Felt its balance, the harmony of its parts. Pressed its dulled point into the ball of her thumb, it was as blunt as a rubber nipple. Dangled it and let it swing, a pendulum, a censer.

Its grey gleam in the Zoo's darkness was fat and cynical as any whipsnake's eye. At the butt of the haft the last owner had scratched his initials. They were grown blurred and faint with age, Kate had to strain to make them out. *AB*, she read at last. Abel Bonder. Then her hand had slipped, and she was bleeding, and Pearl would not stop squawking.

'Have a macaroon,' said Ferdousine.

'A dizzy spell,' said Kate.

'Or a slice of Melba toast.'

They were in Ferdousine's sitting room. Each afternoon he took high tea here, framed by a stage-set that masqueraded as a scholar's den. 'A buttered scone,' he said, his voice still stuck in prewar Westminster, all drawled vowels and spat consonants, and a sniff before each phrase, as if savouring its scent. 'A cucumber sandwich,' he said. 'Or perhaps a potted shrimp.'

It was not an act that age had improved. Across the years

his dryness had turned dusty, his nicety gone to fuss. He kept on fiddling with the details – a high-winged starch collar here, a pair of gold-rimmed pince-nez there – but the pose of Persian sage as English gentleman seemed more and more untenable. The phrase that Kate used to herself, *he didn't ring true*. But she had no heart to tell him that. Besides, it was too late. At his age, what other part would he have time to master?

At least the props were solid – the high, strait windows, the parquet floor, the antique silk rug from Shushtar, the Spy cricket prints and the scenes from Farsi myth, all slaughter and sex. Heavy oak bookcases were lined with reference books, from *The Book of Thoth* to *Magic of Abra-Melin the Mage*; custom-built pine cabinets spilled over with files. An A–Z of miracles and their mediums: Conchita Gonzalez of Garabandal, and Joseph of Copertino, Marija of Medjugorje, Padre Pio, the weeping statue of Syracuse. Stuff that bored Kate stiff, yet she felt comfort here, it was always easy to drowse.

All she'd ever asked was not to see. And in this room she felt blindfold, secure. So she stuffed herself with pork pies and luncheon meats, while Ferdousine sucked at a *sohan*, a large flat disc of caramel with squashed pistachios that his cousin sent him from Isfahan. It made a noise like a bird's bones breaking as he nibbled, quick pecking bites just so.

'And this young man, John Joseph I believe the name is,' said Ferdousine, sniffing. 'What might be your intentions there?'

'To make a man out of him,' Kate replied.

'Heh heh.' He still carried his head cocked sideways, but the curious bird's eyes were not yellow now, they were a dishwater grey. 'To make a man,' he said, and sniffed again. 'Heh heh.'

The project that he was presently engaged on involved a Magdalena Santos of Alajuela, Costa Rica, just twelve years old, who'd been surprised by the Devil in her bath, and had then flown backwards with so much force that she smashed clean through the bath-house wall, hurtled across the back yard and out into the road, narrowly missing a passing truck and finally coming to rest against the steps of the local *cantina*, bruised and shaken but otherwise undamaged, still holding tight to her bar of soap.

On Ferdousine's working table was a small mountain of press cuttings, scraps of letters, numbered stickers for cross-reference, and foolscap sheets of yellow notepaper handwritten in purple ink like a brasserie menu. A hooded light fell on his hands blotched with liver spots, his fingers clawed by arthritis. 'A most remarkable simulacrum,' he said. 'An eidolon without parallel.'

'Pass the jam tarts,' said Kate.

'One thinks of Charmaine Dupont of Maine, perhaps of Isabella Moffo.' But she was no longer listening, no amount of jam tarts could bribe her. All this slicing and dicing, these boneyard speculations, it wasn't decent. *It is an evil generation that asks for a sign.* Who had she told that to?

She must have been eating too fast, her head had started to throb. Maybe closing her eyes would ease her. Then again, maybe not. The sneaking schoolboy had been bad enough, his box of knives worse. But Abel Bonder? That was past toleration.

*Whispering Death*, that was how he'd been billed. On stage his movements had been so restrained, so understated, that the knives seemed to glide self-propelled, and when they hit the board, you hardly heard a sound. Just a hiss, a muffled sigh, like a fish slipping into boiling water.

The season she'd known him, it was the year after Tarpon

Springs. Charley Root had retired by then, no promoter would hire him any more, and they were living above a bakeshop in Palmetto. Kate's mother was dying in the back room.

Kate had not known her well, they'd never talked much. While she was still working, she had seemed no more than one of Charley Root's appendages, a figure in some other room, crossing herself at mirrors, drenching her own feathers at the sight of knives. But now that she was bedridden, she seemed to hog the whole apartment. The murmur of her prayers, the sicksweet reek of candles and blown flowers from the altar she kept in her room – you couldn't catch your breath for sanctity.

Charley Root himself could not stand to stop indoors. He ran a book out of his garage, greyhounds and jai alai mostly, and soused on Rebel Yell. When other knife-throwers came through town, they used to stay in Kate's room, she'd have to sleep on a Laz-E-Boy downstairs.

Knife-throwing was a figure of speech. *Impalement* was the technical term, the word preferred by the pros, though Kate liked *blading* better, it sounded more sporting somehow. She had recently turned twelve, all freckles and teeth-braces, with a flat English drone that she'd picked up from Charley Root, an infection she couldn't kick. But Abel Bonder seemed not to mind. He used to stand in the doorway, filing his fingernails, and watching her watch TV. A lean and whittled man – *blade-thin*, Charley Root used to say for a laugh – in a black suit and black patent shoes.

He had the loveliest hands. Not a whole lot of wingspan, but long and slender with tapered, girl's fingers, and the moons of his nails a faint ghostly blue. A symptom of heart disease, Kate had heard, but how could that be true? If he'd had a heart, Charley Root would not have reverenced him.

Would never have made him a present of his own knives. Not his Harvey McBurnettes.

Elvis was on the Steve Allen Show, the Jimmy Dorsey Show. But with Abel Bonder watching her, and Charley Root glugging Rebel Yell, and her mother's dying smell in the back room, Kate couldn't cream undisturbed. So she took refuge in the bakeshop downstairs.

*Pasquale Brito's Sweet Tooth*. A sallow-face man with a smoker's cough, a smile like cracked glass, you'd never have guessed he had so much yeast in him. Or icing sugar, either. But he was the finest master-baker in the Panhandle. Plaited loaves and sourdough hearts, wedding breads all cinnamon and wild honey. And his pies. Sweet suffering mother of us all, those pies! Strawberry and rhubarb, frangipani, four-and-twenty blackbirds, mud and moon. Every sugared thing under the sun. *Beignets* and brioches, *cannoli, pain perdu,* bullfrogs, marzipan logs, *pinocatte alla perugina* and *cornetti con panna montate* and *biscotti di novara*. And *ma'amouls*. Of course, his orange-blossom *ma'amouls*.

They were his speciality; had won prizes from Kissimmee to St Pete. Little tartlets no bigger than your thumb, stuffed with almonds, walnuts, pistachios and dates, and slathered over with a white cream made of rose-water and pulverized Bois de Panama, Pasquale Brito called it *naatiffe*. He'd got the recipe from his Syrian girlfriend, a nurse built like a Mack truck, used to come see him every afternoon late when surgery got out, and they'd retire to his kitchen. Leaving Kate in charge of the bakeshop. Up to her tits in meringues.

On this certain afternoon, with thick soupy rain outdoors and the bakery windows all steam, she had sat reading *Heartbeat* or *Teen Flame*, she couldn't swear which, and when she glanced up, Abel Bonder was standing in the doorway, eating Shoofly Pie.

He looked like a black sun. Or some kind of reckoning. Stood watching in his black suit and tie, his black shoes shined to wing-tip mirrors, and all he did, he breathed in. Sucked up the smells of damp bread like a poultice still warm from the oven, the rain's steam seeping, and the day's last batch of fresh pies oozing sap on the pine counter, its wood stained dark with their juices. Hung there straight and still with his pinched gravedigger's face turned half-sideways, raised at a slight angle, he made Kate think of some white-stick blind man groping for light, and she laughed. Because she was embarrassed, was all. Flushed and sweated as she was, crab-coloured, she thought, a freckled crab, and her mouth crucified by braces. Still, she laughed. And Abel Bonder handled her. He put his blade hand on her breast, and he threw her on her back. Drove her down legs-kicking in the *ma'amouls*, slithering and sliding through the Bois de Panama. Pile-drove her so hard that she flew right off the counter, scrambling and flailing, she skinned her elbows, her knees, she didn't care, she was out the door and running free, and that was all of Whispering Death.

But not all of his baggage. On the next afternoon Kate was walking home from school with Maria and Bobbie Jane, they were her best friends, and they were passing McMurdo's Hardware when she spotted a ratty ginger toupee, sitting lost on the windowsill.

All day, ever since early Mass, she had been feeling dizzy, untethered, as if nothing was in its right place. So when she saw this hairpiece, she didn't walk on the way she should, she stopped and picked it up. A most malignant object, normally she wouldn't have touched it with Charley Root, but some sick spirit was on her, this day she could not stay her hand.

What she remembered best about McMurdo's window,

there was a pair of stainless steel fire tongs, and at the instant her hand touched the toupee, these tongs blazed with light. At first flash she thought it was a Susie Q, but she was wrong, this was no knife glinting, it was only the girl from Tarpon Springs, the one in the plastic raincoat. The exact same girl, no doubt of that. Except that she wasn't wearing her raincoat this time. It was summer in Palmetto, the sun was bright and fierce. So the girl was dressed in pedal-pushers and shorts, a halter-top.

Lounging in McMurdo's doorway for shade, she was licking on an ice-cream cone, it looked like Rocky Road, with her white shoulders and midriff bare, and her long bare legs so gorgeous, no words could begin to describe. Then she turned her head, saw the wig like a dead ginger kitten in Kate's hand, and the toupee burst into flame.

At least she thought it did. She could have sworn. But when she came back to herself, Maria and Bobbie Jane said nothing about any rug, denied all knowledge. Which was strange, to say the least. Because Kate had felt her hand burn, her whole palm seared where she'd cupped the plate. The pain had been so fierce and true, she kept the wound bandaged till Labor Day.

No fun in that heat. But Abel Bonder had worse. Drunk in his hotel room in Tampa, he got his hand snagged in an electric toaster, cooked it to a crisp, and the hand shrivelled up, there was no blade extant that it could hold or throw in his life again.

1958. July.

Almost forty years gone by, and still she could not face a *ma'amoul*; she guessed she never would. And now the asshole was back. Fouling the Zoo, messing with Pearl, intruding on Billie and Bo. Even inside this room, she couldn't push him back.

'Have some fruitcake,' said Ferdousine.

'Glacé cherries. They give you cancer.'

'I was not aware of that.'

'I saw it on *Geraldo*,' said Kate. 'They kill you dead.'

No place left, it seemed, that she could rest secure. When she looked down to brush the stray crumbs from her lap, she heard a muffled rippling below, something rubbery and squished, a creaking like some leaky tug rocking at anchor before a storm. It was her girdle, and it was no use, it held nothing at bay. The birds were racketing and screeching in the Zoo downstairs, the snakes were hissing for their tea, the apocalypse preachers in the street were still ranting about the beast with seven heads and on each head the name of blasphemy, and somebody was crashing and blundering on the stairs, something was kicking at the door. 'Could I tempt you to broach a rock bun?' said Ferdousine. His old man's hairless skull looked indecently exposed. 'What would you say to a treacle tart?'

*Terribilis est locus iste . . .*

Some one or thing was falling.

He had been jumping frogs for pennies with Juice Shovlin, and his frog had kept winning. The frog was called Alan Rudkin after the fighter, and like the fighter he was undersized, not quite balanced right. One of his front legs was malformed, causing him to stagger and sometimes keel over on landing. Juice Shovlin kept calling foul, claiming he was drunk or doped, but such was not the truth of it, he was simply a born champion, he had a champion's battling heart.

On this afternoon Rudkin had won five straight rounds in a breeze, never raised a sweat. Four pennies sat beside John Joe's mark, but Juice Shovlin wouldn't come across with the fifth, he was a bad loser. 'You have that frog jazzed to the eyeballs,' he said. Even in those years he was big for his age and red, with wet red lips, that's why they called him Juice. 'Fecking chancer, fecking cheat,' he said. 'I should have your guts for fecking garters.'

They were playing in the road outside the national school and it came on to snow, so they ran home. When they reached the Shovlins' gate, Juice spat on John Joe's shoes, a fat gob like a white worm. 'Wait here till I fetch you your penny. Your fecking blood money,' he said, and ran away indoors.

The snow came harder then, and it brought on the dusk.

Rudkin was taking little hops by the roadside, just to keep in practice. Then Juice Shovlin was running back, carrying a copper pan held out before him at arm's length. His knuckles were clenched tight round the handle, red and raw, and the copper pan was full of boiling milk. Without breaking stride, he scooped up Rudkin and threw him in. The milk seethed and bubbled. 'Here's what I owe you,' Juice Shovlin said, and his red knuckles flicked, the pan turned over, Rudkin flew out sprawling on a thin white sheet. It glimmered in the dusk, this hissing sheet, and flew into John Joe's face. Then he was stretched on the ground, a coin was in his mouth.

What he remembered was not pain, not then, but the Brasso taste of the penny, the velvety taste of the snow, the bile-bitter taste of black mud. Then a thin sour smell like piss gone cold. He lay five weeks in his mother's room, in the hollowed curve of her bed like a boat, his head bound up in dock leaves. 'How much does it hurt?' his mother asked.

'How much is it meant to?' he said.

Rising ten he must have been, his second winter in Scath, the winter his Uncle Frank bought the colour TV, and his Cousin Niall played half-back for Donegal, and his mother, when John Joe vacated her bed, set up house in it herself.

The sickness that ailed her had no name. 'My trouble,' was all she called it, and the only cure was rest. On good days she might take a turn around the kitchen garden or sit at her window embroidering. Certain Saturday nights she'd feel strong enough in herself to go dancing at the Hollywood Ballroom. But the payback was always deadly, she'd be prostrated for days. Dr McGill brought her red pills and pink and green. They sat in rows on her bedside table; they were no help. In the evenings John Joe carried up her tea on a tray, fish fingers or a ham salad, tinned peaches with processed milk, but the effort of chewing overstrained her, she could only manage the yellow cling peaches that took no work, slithered down all by themselves.

Together they listened to records; foxtrots, quicksteps, paso dobles. When the rhythms got too vivid, her breathing hurt and she had to rest. Propped up like an effigy in her fluffy pink bedjacket, she sucked on Black Magics to calm herself, or sipped that dyed-orange drink with the funny smell. She said it put the roses in her cheeks, dabbing perfume behind her ears and in the hollow of her throat, sometimes Jasmine Blossom, sometimes Almond Temptation Plus, while John Joe read to her aloud.

The books came twice a month in the travelling library that stopped outside the schoolhouse. Barbara Cartland, Virginia Holt, Georgette Heyer. And *Rebecca*; of course, *Rebecca*. They had ploughed through that so many times, whole passages were stuck to him verbatim, he never could prise them loose: *There was Manderley, our Manderley, secretive and silent as it had always been, the grey stone shining in the moonlight of my dream, the mullioned windows reflecting the green lawns and the terrace. Time could not wreck the perfect symmetry of those walls, nor the site itself, a jewel in the hollow of the hand.*

His second winter only. The day they'd reached Kilmullen first it had been Fair Day, the Diamond was wedged so solid with livestock that the bus couldn't force a way through, and they were set down between three sheep and a heifer. It was raining, a thin damp that seemed to seep, not fall, and roped animals swarmed the gutters. In the alley between Chique Fashions and the Eureka Cinema they passed a cow lowing for its lost calf. That was the most awful sound.

It was the middle of the afternoon, but the street lights

were already turned on. They glowed like foglamps through the mist, merging men and beasts into a shapeless black mass, impervious to the wet. Amber strips of light gleamed from the pubs, an old man reeling fell down at their feet. Taking John Joe's hand, his mother snatched him inside the Hotel Regina, where she had once worked as a chambermaid.

This was a place of darkness – oak panelling stained the colour of brown Windsor soup, stuffed owls in cases and the *Death of Robert Emmet* in oils looking down on holed linoleum. Drinking men were lined three-deep along a dark mahogany bar, trading flesh under a dead TV, their gumboots clogged with mud and their sodden coats steaming.

One of them, a hawk-faced man with avid blue eyes and a hooked nose, had five yellow teeth in his head. 'This is your Granpa Maguire, say hullo to your Granpa Maguire,' said Bernadette, and the man turned his head to look. To see this yellow boy with a runny nose, his free hand clutched at his crotch. 'God's curse on me,' said his grandfather. 'I should have died before.'

In Scath itself, up the gap, there were eight houses lived in, twenty-seven abandoned, the schoolhouse, a ruined chapel, three standing stones, a megalithic tomb, and forty-one souls. Every house had its own dog; only the Maguires had none. Uncle Frank, sometime away in England, had gone allergic.

He had owned two betting shops in Burton-on-Trent, he'd married a woman who drank dry sherry, and when she died, he came home rich with two working sons. Team-handed, they built a square concrete house like a white barracks with plate-glass windows and indoor plumbing, and moved Granpa Maguire down the hill from the cottage where six generations had lived and farmed on nineteen acres cleft from rock and mountain bog.

In that dogless house Bernadette was given the upstairs back bedroom and John Joe the closet below the stairs. From his mother's window you could look out on a grove of rowan and beech, and the Shovlins' new piggery with its sterilized metal pens beyond. '*Manderley, our Manderley*,' he read, and read again.

Downstairs in the kitchen where the family fed there were glossy framed pictures of Pope John XXIII and the Kennedy brothers. Granpa Maguire and Uncle Frank and Cousin Declan and Cousin Niall and Auntie Phyllis that wasn't really his aunt at all ate off white plates with pale-blue rims, but John Joe's plate was speckled like a soiled brown egg. 'To save confusion in the washing-up. To save fuss and bother,' Auntie Phyllis explained.

It was understandable so. In Scath there were many who would not have fed in the same room with John Joe, many more who would have locked him away from sight. Dermot Blaney, that mooncalf boy, was kept shackled to his bed; at nights you could hear him howling. But the Maguires only saved fuss and bother. In the hour of their affliction, they suffered disgrace without complaint. 'We are rightly punished so,' said Granpa Maguire. 'Though we cannot guess our sin, yet we welcome our correction.'

If only John Joe would agree to eat his blood pudding. If he would just swallow it down and thankful, no bitter word would be spoken. But in his pride he refused to submit. Ever since Juice Shovlin told him that the casing was made of used French letters, wrapped round swine guts and maggots, he thought himself too grand.

The portraits of fallen heroes looked down on him where he sat in front of his speckled plate, faced by one slice of white blood pudding, one black. 'John Fitzgerald Kennedy,' said Uncle Frank. 'That was a godly man.'

'A child of grace,' said Granpa Maguire.

'A man that ate blood pudding any time it crossed his plate and welcome, you'd hear not a word or belch.'

'A man that knew the word Gratitude.'

'I'd say he was,' said Granpa Maguire.

Picking up the frying pan off the stovetop, Cousin Declan circuited the table and poured fresh grease sizzling on each plate. Where it hit John Joe's puddings, the grease bubbled up like raw sores. 'A man that died a martyr with his head blown off,' Cousin Declan said. 'Brains and matter all over the shop.'

When John Joe cut up the puddings into bites they made fourteen cubes on his plate, and he forked them inside his mouth one by one, filled his cheeks till he could feel them bulge out, elastic as rubber balls. 'And his fair bride beside him,' said Auntie Phyllis. 'And her in her nice, laundered suit.'

'Not laundered for long,' said Uncle Frank. 'Not when yer man's head had landed in her lap, and the blood pouring off him in buckets.'

'Like a geyser,' said Granpa Maguire.

'Like a pig with its throat slit,' said Uncle Frank.

And the puddings blew up. They flew like a black curse and then a white curse from John Joe's stuffed mouth. Fourteen neatly cubed turds on the laid table. 'I'd say that would be a hard way to go,' Auntie Phyllis said.

'I'd say it would,' said Granpa Maguire.

Up the hill in the abandoned cottage the thatch was gone through, the windows were all knocked out, but the fire still sat laid and primed, and unraked ashes still bedded the hearth.

Scaith-na-Tairbhe the hillside was called, the Shelter of the Bull, where years ago St Conall himself had sought refuge from a storm. Rods of lightning like spears had pursued the saint across the moors, striking closer with each shaft, and the only refuge the saint could see was a fastness in the rocks. This fastness was home to a murderous white bull that could turn any man to chaff with one blast from his nostrils. The hillside was scattered with scorched flesh, bleached bones, but St Conall had no fear. Raising high his pilgrim's staff, he knocked once upon the rocks and was transformed into running water. Then the white bull, thirsting, drank deep of him and a great gladness coursed through the beast. With one heave of its massive shoulders it overthrew the domain, rocks, glen and all, and channelled the stream into a haven, out of the lightning's path. When St Conall returned to his own body, he found himself in a grove of rowan and beech with the white bull stretched sleeping at his feet, as peaceable as a fireside mutt.

That was the tale told, at least. And the running stream still ran, flowing into the Shovlins' cesspit. But John Joe had no white bull dreaming, all he had was a male stoat called Winstone with one ear missing and a crushed paw that he'd found half-killed behind a sack of Banner seed.

At first sight of John Joe the stoat had hauled itself onto his hind legs with front paws clawed, a fighter's pose. One of his eyes was damaged even worse than John Joe's, the fur above it ripped out in tufts, the eye itself filled with blood. Brambles barbed the torn fur, and where whiskers should have been, only broken stubs were left. Still the stoat bared his fangs, ripe to scrap again.

Standing there with his snout oozing gore he had looked just deadly, a warrior fit for Kid Ojeah or any other hard man. When John Joe strayed too close, the stoat drove him back with a spew of musk from its rear end, a smell like rotted mothballs. So he sat by the unraked fire and worked his jaws on a caramel chew, and in due time the stoat subsided as well, went back to licking its wounds. It was Saturday morning, there was no school. They were silent partners, so.

Winstone was a champion's name. A featherweight; a Welshman from Merthyr Tydfil, slender and sleek as any stoat might be, beautiful in motion. W. Barrington Dalby on the radio said he had an educated left hand. But he was fatally flawed, he had no power. Time and again he'd fight Vincente Salvidar for the world title, and Salvidar would give him a pasting. Still nothing could daunt his fighter's heart. As soon as he was healed, he'd be back for one more shot.

But the stoat healed clumsily. His ripped pelt grew back in tufts, his bad paw was permanently twisted. Worse than Rudkin, he was. Hunting rabbits he pitched and ricocheted, a helter-skelter blur of limbs, like a four-legged Keystone Cop. Afterwards, mud-caked and dripping blood, he would shamble back inside the cottage, sink down, spent, in the yellowed nest of old *Donegal Democrats* he had built beside the fire, and dispatch his prey with rigid jaws, flinching at each bite, as if breaking in dentures.

The travelling library fetched a dog-eared paperback titled *Ferrets and Other Fancies* by Finbar O Riain. It said that the stoat in other lands was called an ermine, *mustela erminea*, a class of overblown weasel, but in Irish it was an *easog*. Sixteen inches from point of snout to tip of tail, it was faster than any man born of woman, could squeeze through the narrowest of crevices and chinks, and climb the most inaccessible tree, swinging over and under its branches at jet speed. A hunter of deadliness nonpareil, its piercing eyes endowed it with radar vision, while its rounded ears half-buried in fur could detect the faintest creak in crisp dry leaves or flirt in the wind. 'Then speedily comes the quietus,' wrote Finbar O Riain. 'A *coup de grâce* to the nape of the neck, the long sharp canines or fangs drilling upwards through the prey's cranium directly into the brain. This leads to fast death indeed.'

Other gifts noted were an aptitude for acrobatics, also a clairvoyant foreknowledge of fire and flood, impending drought. 'Due to its telepathic potency, the *easog* is viewed with awe, nay dread,' the article finished up. 'It is a species apart, noble, dignified and incorruptible.'

The stone floor of the cottage was carpeted with bird droppings and rotted newsprint. Under the holed thatch where loosestrife bloomed, *dead men's fingers* they called it, John Joe gorged on Sam Spudz crisps in the sunburst packet, and Red Hots that sizzled his lips and made his mouth pucker like a wet willie, while Winstone polished off two field mice, a hooded owl. Then they walked the hills, they scaled the high rocks behind Scaith-na-Tairbhe. They were the Lone Ranger and Tonto, they were masked marauders, they were one-eyed jacks. They were wounded warriors both.

Whin bushes tore at John Joe's legs, fieldspar stained his clothes. From the cliffs above Malinbeg he watched the bald wet dogsheads of the seals tossed like black caps on the tide. Across a swirling channel was Inishconnell and its fallen-down church, the burial ground riotous with wild garlic and purslane, easy for the picking. If they reached that place, they could rest safe. Winstone would catch birds and fish for feed, John Joe would teach him how to jump frogs, and they'd never be caught unawares by fire and flood, they would always see drought coming.

The only problem, stoats shrank from the touch of salt water. At the lap of the waves Winstone hissed and snarled, spat like a scalded cat. John Joe, to show him the way, waded three steps in the channel, and was suddenly sucked thigh-deep. Something white and live grappled at his knee. Seen through-water it looked like a link of white blood sausage. Or maybe it was a woman's arm, plump and pampered. Whirling on the tide, he cried out for help. But Winstone kept backing away. He must have heard the dread in John Joe's cry, smelled the funk. There was no honour in those. So he hid himself in the gorse.

In the night John Joe woke up in his blankets sweating. Barefoot in his pyjamas he snuck out of the closet and up the hill to the back cottage but Winstone was not gathered there. Not a pile of chewed bones spoke of him. Not even a dried bloodstain was left.

The night was still and warm, choked with scent. In the ash grove behind the cottage, St Conall's stream ran glittering in moonlight. John Joe knelt down to bathe his hot face. When he looked into the water, the reflection was full of stoats.

They walked upright on their hind legs, moved in single file, a crocodile of a dozen or more. Their leader carried a small female, dead and stiff, balanced crosswise in its mouth, while the others formed its cortège. The moon turned their white fronts to silver, their dark furred heads looked like monks' cowls. Treading stately, treading slow, the procession passed in silence through the grove and over the freshwater stream, into the shelter of the bull, and disappeared.

Winstone, limping, walked fifth in line.

And John Joe himself? On this morning in Ferdousine's Zoo, he washed himself at the bathroom sink, still breathing the odours of those stale sheets, the bedpans, the Almond Temptation Plus. *When I awoke the next morning, just after six o'clock, and got up and went to the window there was a foggy dew upon the grass like frost . . . Here at Mander-*

*ley a new day was starting*. Outside the door, there were noises of shuffling and bludgeoning, a rhythmless jarring.

Some one or thing was falling.

When he looked downstairs he saw a large indefinite shape wrapped in a lime-green sheet and slung over a man's shoulder in a fireman's lift.

'Gangway,' said Crouch. 'Death coming down.'

Even doubled over and stumbling, he seemed possessed of grace, an innate elegance. But the lime-green sheet had fallen away to reveal a naked foot, a shapely calf. 'Cold and getting colder as we speak,' said Crouch. 'Every body has its day.'

'Not on my stairs, it doesn't,' said Miss Root, emerging from Ferdousine's room, and gave him a straight-arm shot with the heel of her hand, sent both man and his burden spinning.

Outdoors on the street Anna Crow posed in a leotard and leg warmers, her whiteness made starker by sunlight and her wild hair more flaming. Extending one leg horizontally against the wall of Nature's Nurture, the health-food store next door, she flexed her calves and palpated her thighs, groaning softly at each thrust. 'Ferdousine, that freak,' she said. 'Ballroom dancer my succulent asshole. Lascivious old coffin more like it, *is it not strange that desire should so long outlive performance*, Henry Fourth or maybe Fifth, every bone in my body aches with pushing him off me like an octopus or triffid, the more fingers you cut off at the pass the more he sprouts, you wouldn't believe the state of my butt, what's yellow and black and screams?'

'The name of blasphemy,' said Crouch.

He and John Joe stood loitering on the sidewalk with the green sheet slung between them like a hammock, Crouch at the head and John Joe at the feet. 'So you two have met, I see,' Anna said, and she gripped Crouch by his arm, turned

115

mock-conspirator. 'A man of mystery, our Maguire,' she said, stage-whispering. 'He has this birthmark on his thigh, a raised weal like a cattle-brand, it shows a black swan.'

'You shit me.'

'With spread wings,' Anna said. 'And throat upflung.'

*Natty* was the word that John Joe formed, seeing Crouch by daylight for the first time. Even clothed in coveralls and a shower cap, there was something in his motions, the delicacy with which he tucked a dangling arm back beneath its sheet, that made you think of a song-and-dance man, a shuffler in a vested suit with gold watch and fob, a brown derby. 'That a fact?' he said.

'Botch me with cellulites if I tell a lie.'

When Crouch walked on, John Joe was forced to follow, it was his duty. Patches of damp had soaked through the green sheet, staining it a mucoid yellow, and John Joe's hands were coated in brackish ooze. Nothing in the job description had prepared him for this. *Feel free to be my prisoner* was all Miss Root had said. Not one word spoken about death coming down.

By the time they had trundled across Broadway and arrived in Riverside Park, he felt greasy as melting wax. But Crouch had stayed bone-dry. Pausing at a fire hydrant, he laid his burden down with a dull splat, a soft wet cracking. 'This is no righteous way. There is no glory here,' he said, and turned the hydrant loose. 'A job of work, that's all it is.'

At the water's gush the green sheet was flooded, swept aside. Underneath was the statue of Marilyn Monroe.

In Crouch's attic the night before she'd looked sculpted from wood but in the park by the river she was revealed as pulp. Her colours were running, flesh and fabric churned together to a dark slime. Whole sections of the torso had already decomposed; eyes, nostrils and mouth were merged in a single maw. And at bottom of this quag, peeping through in slivers and eyes, was a shining field of styrofoam, the colour of bubblegum.

'*Whereby the world that then was, being overflowed by water, perished*,' said Crouch, and hit Marilyn with the hydrant's full spate, obliterating all trace of her, her face and limbs, her panties, even the soft golden down that covered her inner thighs, till all that remained was a scrubbed pink mannequin.

Again they moved on, John Joe and Crouch, climbing high above the river till they reached a steel grate like a manhole that Crouch raised and slid inside, pulling the mannequin in behind him. A flight of steep stone steps led down into the dark. Some were broken, some missing altogether. Icy wetness brushed at John Joe's cheeks and throat. He grabbed a rusted pipe to save himself from falling, the pipe came away in his hands, and when he touched bottom he was in a disused railroad tunnel, with a bonfire glowing redly in the distance, barely bright enough to steer by.

'*For the day of his great wrath is come*,' some stranger said in the dark.

'*And who shall be able to stand?*' Crouch answered.

All that showed of the stranger at first were eyes. Then a figure detached itself from the blackness and worked its way towards them. As John Joe's sight began to adjust he made out the glint of the tracks, and the tunnel's walls with a rash of little alcoves hollowed out in its bricks. People were sitting and lying in these, people watching. 'I brought the new model,' said Crouch, and he thrust the mannequin towards the stranger's bosom. But that man did not seem to notice, he was busy staring at John Joe's bad eye. 'What man is this?' he demanded.

'He bears the mark,' said Crouch.

Backlit by the bonfire down the tracks, the man's shape ringed in fire showed one huge globe for his body, a smaller globe for his skull. Twenty stone or more he must be, John Joe reckoned, three hundred pounds let's say, wearing something swaddling that almost passed in the dimness for a monk's robes but turned out to be a schoolmaster's gown, its wide sleeves ripped and draggling. 'Is this true?' the man asked.

'It's only a birthmark, sure.'

'Weal or wale, it's all the same. Do you tote the brand? Are you printed with the trademark?'

John Joe had no idea. Furthermore, this class of talk did not sit well in his ear. For preference, he would have chosen to climb back up the stone steps where he'd come from, but he couldn't locate them in the weeping walls. All he could see were bricks, and eyes, and the stranger's head thrust forward against the light like a buffalo's, that seemed to spring with no neck or nonsense direct from the great darkness of his chest.

Midnight purple, topped by a knitted wool cap, this head looked a black hothouse grape ripe to bursting. But the voice that came from it was high-pitched, almost girlish. 'The name is Master Maitland, the fiery flood approaches,' this voice said. '*In the which the heavens shall pass away with a great noise, and the elements shall melt with fervent heat, the earth also and the works that are therein shall be burned up.*'

There'd been a man years ago in Dunkineely, that arsehole of nowhere, who had used to state matters along the same lines. A most intemperate speaker, John Joe had always found him, too full of himself by half. A bit of a tosser, if truth be known. And this Master Maitland seemed cut from the like cloth.

Lightly and politely, to cause no offence, John Joe began

118

to back away, but the man had his arm firmly hooked, he could not shift. 'Only those of us that are freed souls, they alone may rise exempt,' the Master said. 'When the flaming tide arrives at their toes, they alone are raised on high, given wings, and what becomes of them then?'

'I wouldn't care to venture an opinion.'

'They turn into black swans.'

# Third

Third

One month had passed. It was the end of August now, but the heat did not let up. Willie D had another dream he could not remember. Then he was between sleeping and waking, and he was dying again on Kate Root's leg, just like he'd died in Ferdousine's Zoo.

Her left leg, lower.

She was standing on a stool, reaching over her head to feed a bird, and Willie was watching the swell of her calf. It was surprisingly shapely. Big but firm and strongly made, the rising slab of its muscle still springy. Its flesh was layered like two coats of paint, lush cream underneath, a coarse glaze like pink stucco on top, and there wasn't a trace of hairiness, not even a shaved stubble. Except in one small patch of white, right above her anklebone. Some old scar that had lost its pigment, he guessed, with three long and limber hairs, reddish-gold, that sprouted from the open pores like reeds. And Willie was caught up by craving. To blow on them, soft, soft. To make them riffle and sway.

He couldn't do that, of course; she would be bound to notice. So he forced himself to start climbing. He scaled the roughened red shale of her shin, then tackled the lazy outward curve like a kite's wing above. But these spaces seemed immense. There was no oxygen, no place to rest. By the time he reached the roll of fat behind her knee, with its foolish

123

crease that had no function, no possible point, he felt like a rock-climber without pick or crampons, clinging to a greased ledge by his fingernails, slipping away through his sweat and hers till the last of his strength failed him, and he tumbled through air.

Same thing happened every time. Night after night, the same sleepless dream. Then he'd rise up under sweat-soaked sheets, throw off their ropes and choking knots, and try to work out, one more once, this thing that had happened to him.

He didn't know where to start.

That whole day with the knives had been anarchy. A series of blind jumps with no rhyme or reason. All he could say for sure, it had begun with Pacquito Console in Crotona Park. They were in conference re the carwash, and Pacquito was arguing against the tygers. 'Mermaids would be more apropos,' he said. 'Carwash, water, sea, mermaids, it's more conceptually evolved.'

'Tygers are more dynamic.'

'But mermaids work for scale,' Pacquito said, and Willie felt too cheapened to dispute him. He was looking over Pacquito's bald head at the wall calendar in his office, Tremont Tool & Die, and Miss July was dressed or undressed as a pirate. He saw that she had an eye-patch; he needed air. So then he was on the Major Deegan headed south, and two redneck mothers in a Dodge pick-up with a bumper sticker saying *God, Guns and Guts Made America – Let's Keep All Three* kept cutting him off.

The driver rolled his window down and started to yelling language, dissing the Spyder, and Billy Ray Cyrus was on the radio. *Achy Breaky Heart*, Willie loathed and despised that tune. So he took his pistol and shot the asshole's tyre out.

Or was *asshole* language? Borderline, he guessed. A judgment call.

And he didn't even like guns.

Not that they bothered him or anything, they just didn't suit his clothes. If it wasn't for respect, he wouldn't even carry. As it was, he used one of Deacon Landry's pieces, a stainless-steel Walther PPK-S. That was James Bond's gun of choice, it had history on its side. Still you couldn't say it pleasured him. It was a tool, nothing more.

A tool he never should have exposed, not in the morning rush hour, leave alone put to work. It wasn't politics, he knew that. Not his style at all.

But then, what *was* his style these days? He no longer knew for sure. Every move he made felt foreign to him, he couldn't trust himself for a minute.

In the world according to Deacon Landry, the one absolute was control. You had to give off certainty, or you were dead meat. And these bitches, of course, could scent the lack in a nanosecond. That's how come Ivana had raised up her nerve to rip him off. From the moment that Kate Root nailed him, his smell must have changed, his taste as well. Sour milk, sloppy gravy; weak shit. So Ivana was freed to betray him. Use him with impunity. All of it was the fat woman's fault.

The only thing he knew to do was face her down. Confront her in her own lair, and force her to turn him loose. Sliding down off the Major Deegan, he put away his firearms, set his mind on repose. *Water Thoughts. Release the Prisoner.* Then he was in Ferdousine's Zoo, and Abel Bonder's knives were under his arm, tucked up tidily in their beds.

The moment he was inside, he knew he'd made a mistake. He hadn't programmed his moves, had failed to prepare himself. He'd thought he would walk in whistling, flash the knives, maybe throw a couple, and walk out again. Then

Kate Root would know him for who he really was. Stop looking at him funny, leave off bugging him, and he'd be shot of her. End of story.

Simple. Except that it wasn't. For one thing, he hadn't figured on the Zoo itself. Pets were not toys that fell inside his territory. Old women, fags and families had them, and he was none of those. So he was not trained to handle them. When suddenly they surrounded him, he had no defence.

The stench alone knocked him sideways. Looking round, all he saw were birds and snakes, a lot of plants, but what he smelled were cats, the same rancid reek that used to fill the old Jew lady's apartment on Fifth Avenue when his mother was a nurse who played cards with her and he rode his blue tricycle up and down the corridors. 'I heard you know knives,' he heard himself say, but his voice didn't come out right, he sounded womanish. 'Anna Crow, I'll slaughter the slut,' the woman replied, but she didn't look at him, she was too busy watching TV.

Some soap. The garbage on daytime TV, he wouldn't stoop to soil his brain, and those black-and-white Zeniths anyhow, you couldn't see squat for snow. 'I never was around knives before, they always seemed so dangerous,' he was saying now, like some pantywaist, a pillow-biter; he was mortified. But at least this time Kate Root looked up. At least she showed him her face.

It wasn't so old.

Hardly old at all, in fact. Once his eyes had adjusted and he could see past the pudding-bowl grey hair and not a trace of make-up, she looked almost unused.

What had he been expecting? Lines and wrinkles, drastic damage. But there was only a faint tracery around her eyes and mouth like the painted cracks on those ornamental Russian eggs they sold underneath the El in Brighton Beach, and the rest of her was freckles; she could have been some kid.

Her green eyes were childish, too. They didn't angle or slide, just looked straight past him at something outdoors. 'At least let me show you my equipment,' Willie said, not so much like a flit this time, more like some used-car salesman kissing ass. But Kate Root refused to look, she turned her back. Climbed on the stool that led to her bird, and shut him out, leaving him to roam the aisles.

He tried to track down those cats, their stink was eating him alive, but he couldn't find them anywhere. In the end he came full circle, and that was when he saw it: the white patch on Kate Root's leg; the three reddish hairs.

Just one blow. One little puff.

A sigh would do.

Then he was outside the Zoo. And now a month had gone by. The summer, this burning season, was almost done, but still this craving rode his back. This monkey he could not spank.

His business was in shambles. He must have visited with Pacquito Console a dozen times or more, and a dozen times he'd lost the thread, forgotten what brought him there or why he was meant to care anyway. Tygers, mermaids, topless gerbils – let somebody else decide. The lease was up on the Spyder, and the rent was past due in Brighton Beach, and his left shoe pinched; the armadillo was raw and fraying at the heel. And the plain truth was, he didn't give a toss, a flying fish. None of this was his concern.

Twenty-eight pairs of shoes were sitting in Regina's closet. Hi-tops and wingtips, loafers and Oxfords, Roscoe de Llama lizardskins, Havana flats by Miami Mort Amity, two-tone Berkeley Musser suedes and steel-heeled Kahlil marengos, green-olive canvas Piccozis, Just A Gigolo co-respondents, black-and-tan fantasies, burnt-almond Lamourettes. Everything beneath the sun but tassels, you wouldn't catch him castrated in those. All he had to do was give Patsy O a call, and he'd have the whole collection back in a New York minute. But he just couldn't seem to find the dime.

There were nights when he had no stomach for Chez Stadium even, couldn't look the Deacon in the eye, and, as for Anna Crow, he couldn't conceive how he'd ever stood to stand her, never mind feed her sex. *Deep down, you really don't like women*, she kept telling him now. Which was a bare-faced lie. Women, cars, shoes, he liked them all fine. But Pacquito Console's word was correct: right now, they were not apropos.

Most nights these days he stayed to himself in Brighton Beach, holed up in the room beside the El. Tried to catch a doze between trains. Or catch a dream, to be exact.

Time was, dreams had been his speciality. When he was a child, he couldn't seem to lay down without popping one. He used to dream so profuse and vivid, his mother kept *The Success Dream Book* by Prof. De Herbert always handy at his bedside, so that they could work out the meanings the minute he woke, and the messages wouldn't get lost. Even now he could recite the book's equations by heart. 'ABDOMEN: a sure sign of flattery. GOULASH: you will suffer from indigestion in the not far distant future. JELLYFISH: you will cause trouble on account of a slip of your tongue. LONGSHOREMAN: you will be caught stealing by your employer. Nevertheless, you will not be punished. PARACHUTE: you are a lion-hearted person, and for this reason you are going to succeed in all your undertakings. SLAUGHTERHOUSE: you will succeed in obtaining your wishes. TWIST MOUTH: you are being scandled by your neighbours. UKELELE: you will become a great sportsman as the years roll on.'

After each image came its matching number in bold type, to help turn it into money. Many times, when a Lottery drawing was due, a wolf pack of aunts and nieces under Tia Guadalupe would sit up howling in the next room, waiting on him to dream a PALACE, dream a YARD, dream WRAPPING PAPER, and if he came across, they gave him trinkets or candies, even dollars sometimes.

He had been lord of his manor then, a household name in his own household. If not for Bombo Garcia, he could have written himself a free ticket.

The man was some breed of cousin. A semi-pro ballplayer, played rightfield with the Piscataway Pirates. He had the God-given tools to go to the top, he had everything it takes but desire. Pick any baseball cliché you like, he fitted it. He didn't hit homers but moonshots, he had a rifle for an arm, and trying to throw a fastball past him was like trying to throw a lamb chop past a starving wolf. Major-league scouts would come to watch him play and go home drooling. All he needed was work, and he could have been the next Roberto Clemente. But work was not Bombo's speed. He was too busy with the babes, too hungover half the time, and the other half he was sleeping. So you could write his epitaph, right there: *He had the biggest dick in Piscataway, but no ass to push it with*.

Babes and the booze he could have survived, but sleep was the death of him. There never was such a slugger for slumber. Man slept in the showers, in the batting cage, on the bench. He even nodded off in rightfield, dozing under lazy flyballs.

Scratch Johnson, his manager, kept trying to give him wake-up calls. *You can't play this game on snooze control. You have to give it 110 per cent, like your back's to the wall, every day's for all the marbles, there's no tomorrow. You gotta believe*, he said. *You have to have a dream*. All that good stuff. But Bombo Garcia didn't know from dreams, he only knew sleep.

In the end the Pirates ran out of patience and pillows. When they caught him sawing logs in the manager's office, right in the middle of the seventh-inning stretch, they kicked his butt in the street. So Bombo went on a six-day drunk. He rambled halfway across Jersey and back, Trenton to Asbury Park, Teaneck to East Orange, and then he showed up at Willie's house with his raggedy ass hanging out of his pants, a breath like kerosene. Mumbling how he had to have a dream, he'd never make it otherwise. And Willie's mother, like an idiot, fell for it. *Dreams? We got a million of 'em*, she said. *Come in and rest your bones.*

Bombo, of course, was not the man that needed to be asked twice. Before Willie's mother could get the door half-open, he was up the stairs and into bed, knocking out the Zs in triplicate.

Willie's bedroom was right next door, there was only a plywood wall no thicker than a screen or a membrane almost between them, and he was trying to get some sleep. With so much pressure on him, between Prof. De Herbert and his relations waiting on him for numbers, he could never get his proper rest, he could not sleep for dreaming. A few minutes' doze, then he'd cough up his dream like some Speak Your Weight machine, and the rest of the night he'd spend staring at the walls, with an endless tickertape, ASPARAGUS, DIPHTHERIA, LOBSTERS, ROOSTER, TURPENTINE, VOMIT, ZIGZAG, spooling through his sleep-starved brain.

So anyhow, cut to the chase. He couldn't swear to what happened next, not in so many words, he had to take Tia Guadalupe's word. But it seemed like he was trying to sleep on one side of the screen, and Bombo Garcia was trying to have a dream on the other, and somehow screwy they must have got confused, half-unconscious as they were, curled back to back like Siamese twins. By some freak their spirit-spines must have fused and their chemistries swapped places. At any rate, when Willie woke again it was the day after tomorrow, he'd slept for thirty-two hours. And afterwards, he never could remember another dream, not to save his life. While Bombo, he had all the dreams he could handle. But they didn't concern the Yankees or the Orioles, they only showed him a dry cleaner's in Canarsie with a crack house in the basement.

Or that was the tale handed down. The gospel according to Tia Guadalupe. Which explained why Willie now, stretched on his bed in Brighton Beach, had a dream he couldn't remember, and then he was between sleeping and waking, dying on Kate Root's leg.

When the next train plundered through and set the bed's brass frame to shuddering, he sat up straight and dreamless to find himself surrounded by the forty-nine duck hunters with their walrus moustaches and green eye-patches, their forty-nine guns that didn't shoot, and one sentence stood plain as a thought-bubble in his mind: *I am not my self*.

Course he wasn't.

His true self would not put up with this. Would never have stood still to be used and abused, thrown away like a broken toy. Not unless the fix was in.

Take a look at the story straight on, as if this had all happened to a stranger, some other body entirely, and see how it printed out. A man of power at his age, a blowfish at Kate Root's – the only way the set-up made sense, there had to be another force at work. Why else would he be brought to his knees? Howling at the moon for three red hairs?

Possession was an ugly word.

But sexy, just the same. The moment it spelled itself, he felt renewed. Blotting out the duck hunters, he put on a pair of dove-grey flannels, an absinthe cambric shirt. He brushed and creamed and oiled the armadillos, then he brushed and creamed and oiled them some more.

Tia Guadalupe lived in Morrisania, five floors up in the last tenement still occupied on a block of gutted shells. The walls were so rotted you could look clear through, there were holes like open wounds, but Guadalupe's own apartment was kept immaculate, a Santeria shrine.

Though she wasn't connected to Willie by blood, she had been *madrina* to his mother and his aunts, she seemed like family. An outsized woman of maybe seventy, painted bright as a Dutch doll, in a plain white dress that flowed like robes. When she saw him at the door, her first glance was at his feet, coated in dust and nameless crud from his subway ride, and her second glance scoured the street below. 'What happened to the Spyder?' she asked.

'Possession is an ugly word.'

'Repossession's uglier.' Still she let him inside her hallway, where candles burned and one cabinet was filled with her Warriors and Eleggua, another with the otanes of Babalu-Aye, and she brought him a glass of dusty water, she placed her hot fingers on his wrist. 'A full sack of woe,' she said, and lit a cigar, a White Owl. 'What is it you want?'

'A hair.'

Next to Willie's foot was a drum draped with necklaces of corn that spilled loosely across an altar made from a pair of baby shoes, a model car, a set of maracas, and a cluster of wooden axes, red and white in honour of

Chango, god of lightning. 'Male, female or other?' Tia Guadalupe asked.

'A lady of a certain age.'

'Head, pubic, underarm or excess?'

'A leg.'

'Money, sickness or love?'

'523,' said Willie D. 'A hunger.'

He told her everything then, the Zoo, the knives, the birds and snakes, the black-and-white Zenith, the three reddish hairs, and Tia Guadalupe heard him without comment, only moved when he was done. Puffing at her cigar, she dipped inside a wooden chest and brought forth a miniature bottle of rum, a brown-paper sack filled with smoked fish, dried possum and popcorn. 'Where's the problem?' she asked.

'Left shin. Two inches above the ankle, maybe two and a half,' Willie said, and Tia Guadalupe lifted the hem of her white dress. Raised it coyly like the flap of a tent to reveal monumental legs swathed in black hairs as thick as a pelt, and she snipped off three with the kitchen scissors, she dropped them in a plastic bag. 'You should never have let the Spyder go,' she said, puffing deep. 'How do you travel without it?'

'Flat feet.'

'982,' said Tia Guadalupe, and she pushed him out on the stairway, she started to close the door. 'A sign of cowardice.'

Penetrating the Zoo was easy. Anna Crow in a moment of false hope had given him a key. All he had to do was wait till Kate Root's reading light went out upstairs, and prowl.

Stealing by flashlight from the hallway through the barber-shop and the crushed-velvet curtain into the menagerie, his only enemies were the smell and the graveyard silence. Instead of creeping he'd have liked to kick out, raise an uproar. Anything to break the stillness.

His torch tracked the rows of masked cages, the climbing jungles, the aisles crawling with unnameable growths. At any moment an anaconda might uncoil from the darkness with flashing tongue, or some man-eating plant clutch at his throat. Well, they might do. But the only creature awake seemed to be one snake, and that was safely caged.

*California Whipsnake*, its label said. A glitzy-looking character, black with flashes of pink and orange, and a yellow-rimmed eye that measured Willie calmly, seemed to find him somehow amusing.

Kate Root had looked at him the same way. Contemplating the whipsnake, Willie saw the woman – her gapped front teeth and her freckles, her wide flat forehead that carried no lines, her green eyes with their steady gaze as if she was studying fate or flying fish behind your back, as if she held some secret she wasn't telling, no money or angle would tempt her.

A conspirator's look.

That was it. The look of privileged data. What was it the FBI agents always said in movies? *Classified information, We are not at liberty to divulge*. And her snake was down with the same jive. Its blinkless gaze withered him and ranked him, sucked out what was left of his resolve.

Still, he couldn't run. Having broken and entered, he had no choice but to see the job through. Groping and fumbling among the roots of a ficus tree, he found soft soil that parted at his touch and he buried the bottle of rum, the sack of popcorn, possum and fish. 'An offering to Osain,' Tia Guadalupe had called them. If they didn't fix Kate Root, at least they would give her pause for thought. An awkward hour or two, and maybe a migraine headache. Vomiting and evil cramps at her monthlies, too, or was she past those? Hard to tell. Crouching, he spat on Osain's feast in its shallow grave for luck, and began to cover it over. The damp earth felt like ooze, malign; the choke of darkness was a rope. His nerve failing him, he scrambled away from the burial site, banged his skull on a sheeted cage. The sound it made was a muffled chime like a funeral bell. Whirling from it, he saw the whipsnake laughing.

Well, not exactly laughing. More like snickering. But mocking him anyway. His clumsiness and his panic, the dread that had brought him here. 982: FALLEN ARCHES: *a sign of cowardice*. And that was the plain fact. Chickenshit; some squeaming girl. To go in terror of three lousy hairs. To let them shrivel and burn him like this, drag him down into ignorance. Humblemumbling like a peasant, some toothless old woman from El Pajuil. When those hairs should have been a challenge, not a threat. A trial of strength. Like a Holy Grail, or whatever. Instead of running from them, or plotting to destroy them, he should have faced them head-on. Blown on them when he had the chance. Or anything else he desired. Sucked them, bitten them, chewed them up and spat them out. Be possessed by them, yes, if that's what it took.

Would that have killed him?

Hardly. For a beat, in his self-disgust, he almost went back to Osain's grave and dug him up again. But the thought of that black slime running on his hands forbade him. What he needed was to get back to Brighton Beach, lay himself down flat on his brass bed beside the El, and try to steal back some of Bombo Garcia's sleep. When he surfaced, he would face the hairs fresh. Be strong to master them. Flirt them, or tease them, or make them stand rigid and tense. Or bend them back, doubled over, corn sheaves before a storm. With their long stalks curved and graceful. Three swans' necks waiting to be severed. Bowed helpless beneath the blade. A guillotine. Or a Harvey McBurnette.

These vampires of today, they had it all too easy. In Kate Root's youth the undead life had been one long heartache. If it wasn't a crucifix it was garlic; if not dawn, a stake through the heart. But these days, it seemed to her, the damned were a bunch of pampered prima donnas, worse than baseball players. Power, glamour, *la vie en rose* – the world was their oyster. And did they appreciate it? In a pig's ear. Nothing but moan, moan, moan, from first page to last. She hadn't the patience. No, really she hadn't. The paperback flopped from her hand, she stubbed out her Camel on its spine, and settled herself to sleep.

She was a career insomniac, four hours in a night was a banquet to her, but in her middle years she'd devised a routine that sometimes helped. When all else failed, she'd play cricket with Fred Root in his back garden.

Kate batted, he bowled. They used a tennis ball and a dustbin for the wicket, and she'd watch him run in from the lobelia beds, or shamble in rather, a big, ungainly, brick-faced man in baggy flannels and suspenders, his great feet in carpet slippers pointed outwards as he waddled like Charlie Chaplin. *Plates of meat*, he'd called them, but they looked more like frogman's flippers to her. Flap, flap, double-flap, they went, and her focus moved to his right hand. He held the ball between his second and third fingers, beef sausages, they seemed. In the moment of release, his little finger flicked sideways, he flipped his wrist. The scuffed grey tennis ball swung down and in upon her, then kicked upwards, knifing straight for her chest and throat. Bodyline, that was called. She didn't try to smite it, what would be the point? Broken windows were six and out. Her only ambition was not to be hit or hurt. To play the ball down safely. Lay it motionless at the feet of the sweet williams. One dead ball.

Normally it took a couple of overs before she was lulled. But this night the vampires in their vanity had left her drained. Already by the third delivery she felt herself easing away, and the bat handle began to slip through her fingers, when she heard something moving downstairs.

A random and somnolent scuffling, it sounded like a snake sleepwalking. Maybe one of the blind Texans; Maguire must have left its cage unlocked. God's gift to boghopping, you couldn't trust him to wipe a parakeet's ass. Not that a parakeet needed its ass wiped, of course. But you couldn't have trusted him if it did.

Stumbling down the stairs with a stun-gun in her hand and her dressing gown untied, her hair all in her eyes, she had almost reached bottom before it occurred to her that this might not be a snake; it sounded more like a thief in the night.

For a moment common sense almost got the best of her. But only for a moment. Then a giddiness possessed her, and she burst through the velvet curtain; she took three paces through the room, brandishing the stun-gun like Excalibur.

What was she playing at? She was being a supervixen. The style of desperado in movies who shouted *Freeze!* and *Up against the wall, motherfucker!*, slapping heads and kicking tails, reducing the bad guys to jello. If the intruder had made one wrong move, she would have pulped him. With pleasure.

138

But he didn't stir. Caught in the act, bending low above the cash register with his sticky hand in the till, he did not have the decency to stick his hands up. He didn't even look startled, certainly not terrified. Just stared at the dressing gown slipping her shoulders, and her shape inside her pink nightie with the sky-blue periwinkles at the neck, or were they forget-me-nots? And her legs, her bare legs, exposed to above the knee. And her feet not even in their mules, she hadn't had the time. And her breasts.

He could see her nipples.

How could he miss them? Whenever she was overheated, at all agitated, they popped right up. Dark and swollen they'd look, absolutely depraved.

Her first reflex was to grab at the errant edges of her gown, pull them shut. Her second was to put away the gun before it hurt someone. And as she laid the gun on the counter, she saw the thief's hands. They were not full of banknotes, or even the back copies of *Soap Digest* she kept stashed in the cheque compartment. In fact, they held nothing at all. But she knew what he had sought, even so. She knew just what he'd been after.

Wilfredo Whoever; Anna Crow's pet delinquent.

Of course, she knew. How could she not? With the boy's eyes still on her under his nice hair, all blurred and smeary they looked, and dreadful in their hunger.

Something broke in her then. Though he had caused her only turmoil, had turned her life to sewage, she could not stand those eyes on her. Anger went from her. So did contempt. 'You poor sap,' said Kate.

'It was just . . .' Wilfredo began, but she had no time to hear his excuses or explanations or any other whines. Already she was bustling around behind the counter, kicking aside sacks of birdseed and dried rape, opening the safe concealed by the poster of Billie and Bo. 'Tomorrow night. Seven o'clock,' she said, handing him Abel Bonder's knives in their red-leather case, and she flushed him from the Zoo a second time.

She was beat.

Upstairs, though safe in her bed again, she couldn't stop twitching. Her room was a cell, twelve foot square, and painted flat white. Its only artwork hung crooked, a hand-painted photo of Fred Root, the blown-up frontispiece from his autobiography, *A Cricket Pro's Lot*, which showed a man with a face like forty miles of bad road, smirking lopsidedly through a hard-scrabble of seams and potholes and ruts. At Worcester in 1926, the very first day of summer, he had ripped out Australia's heart in a morning, then polished off a beefsteak, a complete veal pie and four bottles of light ale for lunch. But he brought her no help now.

She couldn't be bothered to straighten him even. All that registered on these walls were their smudges and scars, a landscape so bleak that she snapped out her nightlight, risked the dark for preference.

Immensity. In which swam a boychild tucked into a foetal curl, his spine pressed against a plywood screen. In the next room a wax model of a man's corpse lay surrounded by plastic lilies, watched over by an illustrated woman. A bottle of brandy sat on a table by an open window that looked out across a funfair to an elevated railroad and a bedroom full of ducks. Or no, not ducks. On second look they were fighting cocks with steel spurs on their legs. One of the spurs pierced an eye. A single drop of blood appeared, and that was when Kate switched her light back on, saw herself in her bedside mirror: a fright, flushed and sweating, her hair a total disgrace.

But desired.

An object of passion.

She didn't know why this boy wanted her, and she didn't care to speculate. Wilfredo, Wilfredo . . . Diliberto, that was it. *But she could call him Wilfred.* With his slant eyes and tiny feet, his olive skin the tint of a lizard's underbelly. She couldn't guess what his game might be. But she knew the smell of need.

It made a change, at least. During these last years she had felt like an invisible woman. Men didn't notice her, other women did not compete. Some little trollop like Anna Crow would give her one glance as she passed, then dismiss her. Spinster, old maid. *A single lady of equinoctal years.* As if she had no sex. As if, deepest down, she didn't exist.

Anna as in anathema, Crow as in carrion, what gave her the right? A couple of failed marriages, a dose of clap, a few dozen or a hundred one-night stands? Kate herself had been engaged eight times.

Never married, that was true. But affianced, betrothed or otherwise plighted eight times, in five cities and three states, to accredited suitors from all walks and stations of life. A pastry chef, an oculist, a fallen priest, a steeldriving man, a trombonist, an ambulance chaser, a barber, a pawnbroker. All of them had loved her, or that was the word they'd used. And she had liked all of them in return.

In the long run, of course, it couldn't ever work. Sooner or later they'd find out who she was and what she did, exactly what her history had been, and then the jig was up. Either they lost their nerve. Or, what was worse, much harder to endure, they turned into acolytes. Psychic groupies, forever harping at her for instant visions like so much Reddi-whip, till she couldn't stand it, she had to blow them off.

*The Fifth Dimension? It's not all it's cracked up to be* – Madame Vronsky had got that one right. For a certainty, it played hell with your orgasms. Though she'd heard that executioners had the same trouble. Swings and roundabouts, she supposed. The grass was always greener.

But so much blether. Such a carry-on and commotion just because she had sight. A knack that wasn't her doing, that she could not even control.

It made her pillow hot on both sides.

It made her wish she'd been a shopgirl or some waitress, free to jump out of her window any night she felt the urge, head for the nearest dance hall and pick up any stranger that caught the light, pull him out in the back alley. Or a cocktail lounge would do. With one of those blue neon signs, the champagne glass and bubbles. Or a bowling alley, even.

That was the only sex she had ever wet-dreamed about. In her teens, when she was in Jeanerette, she'd used to sneak out the back door between visions and hitch a ride on Highway 90. There was a place in New Iberia, the Club Why Not, she'd heard was Babylon on the half-shell. But Charley Root had always caught up to her, and dragged her home intact. Or an approximation thereof, as Ferdousine would say. No mindless abandon for Katy. No such fucking luck.

The year that *Rubber Ball* was a hit.

Bobby Vee, or was it Bobby Vinton? And now it was Snoop Doggy Dogg. And she had rolls of fat behind her knees. Still and all, she was desired.

It almost felt a pity that she didn't desire him back. Wilfredo Diliberto. Little Wilfred. It almost seemed a loss. But what was a girl supposed to do? She didn't find him attractive. He didn't ring her chimes. Did anyone still say that? *Not the cream in my coffee, not the cherry on my sundae. Not the sour cream on my baked potato.* No, he wasn't. *Not, not, not.*

In the morning, though, she woke to find herself back to

twitching. The early sunlight slanting across the white walls stained them arsenic yellow, turned Fred Root's crooked grin into a homicidal leer. How could she have slept with his picture at that sick angle? More to the point, how could she have lain awake and thought such thoughts without throwing up? *Not the sour cream on my baked potato. But what was a girl supposed to do?* Give herself an enema, if she could still find the right hole.

All her senses felt overturned, her nerve endings exposed and raw, the way that ex-junkies described when they told you their cold-turkey stories if you didn't get away from them in time. No extra layers of skin left, no protection. Every sound a fingernail scraped on a blackboard, and every touch another bruise.

The weight was the worst. The gross tonnage of the past. She felt stuffed to bursting with it, bloated like a rotting fish. At the window she tested for shifting breezes, but there were none. Smoke didn't drift, loose papers on the street were not stirred. Not a thing that Kate could see moved.

It was a day for a bonfire.

She laboured, huffing, on the stairs, her nightie rode her like a hairshirt. And meeting Anna Crow didn't help. Especially an Anna Crow wearing a long trailing robe of azure velvet, a blonde wig curling down her back and silk daisies garlanded in her hair, silk daisies in bracelets at either wrist. 'Ophelia?' Kate asked.

'*La Belle Dame sans Merci.*'

'*Oh what can oil thee, knight-at-arms, alone and feebly squeaking?* I did that at school, it stunk. Miss Etheridge in the Ninth Grade, she wore silk stockings. Real silk. Married a stoker in the merchant marine, but he sank.'

'How *triste*,' Anna said. She looked nervous, and Kate couldn't blame her, dressed up like a mobile florist's with that belt of moulting marigolds round her waist. 'That's my fragrant zone,' she explained. 'You know, *I made her a garland for her head, and bracelets too, and fragrant zone; She look'd at me as she did love, and made sweet moan.'*

*'She took me to her elfine grot.'*

'Yes, I know, sickening, but that's Verse-o-Gram for you; ours not to critique what they write, ours just to be white and recite,' Anna said. She made to edge past Kate, and they brushed arms. For a beat Kate saw her in a wheelchair, swaddled in blankets, being pushed by a uniformed nurse down a white corridor. Then she was on these stairs again, practising her droop. '*The sedge is wither'd from the lake, And no birds sing,*' she said, and passed on like death going down.

A nasty turn, but Kate was not entirely shocked. From the moment she'd wakened, she had suspected as much. That creeping in her fingertips, the buzzing in her ears – she knew the symptoms all too well. In the Ansonia, they'd been her living.

No place to run, no use to hide. And besides, she had need of kindling. So she walked without knocking into Ferdousine's sitting room, where he sat eating his breakfast. *Patum pepperium*, it looked like. Melba toast and burnt Seville marmalade, and the cricket scores in the English papers. 'I need my files,' Kate said.

The man did not protest. Only regarded her with his head cocked sideways as ever, his bird's eyes intrigued but not alarmed. He wiped his fingers clean on a starched napkin, one by one. Held them up to the light for inspection, and he was eighteen again. A Westminster schoolboy on vacation, standing on a latticed balcony that looked like a set in a Sabu movie, *The Thief of Baghdad* or some such, looking down into an inner courtyard lit by oil lamps.

Inside this courtyard there was great feasting. A wedding party, it seemed, with musicians and jugglers and acrobats. All the guests were loosely robed, the men in djellabas and the women in chadors, but Ferdousine himself, watching from above, was dressed in Oxford bags, a Fair Isle sweater, a cravat.

There was a woman with him. A faceless and shapeless bundle swathed in black, leaning over the balcony with her *shalwar kameez* flipped up to expose her naked buttocks. Round and fatted as Dutch cheeses they looked, but pocked and flabby, gone to pulp. Not an appetising prospect, Kate thought, but Ferdousine didn't seem to mind. On the contrary, he squeezed and pinched them with relish.

The woman had no reaction. Seemed oblivious to everything but the wedding feast in the courtyard below, a scene straight out of an ad for Turkish delight, all flickering oil lamps and inlaid marble: the guests in their robes reclining on peacock-patterned cushions, the violinists strolling among the pomegranate trees, the belly dancers and tumblers, the aghound with his hennaed beard and long painted fingernails like talons chanting prayers beside the goldfish pool, the groom drinking arak from a silver goblet, the veiled bride in her jewelled headdress, and the peacocks, of course, peacocks out the kazoo.

Beside the pool marriage gifts were heaped on ornate teak tables – a silken quilt made of a thousand pieces, brass and copper drinking vessels, lapis lazuli plates – and the faceless woman in the balcony above kept leaning out further and further into space, straining to catch a closer look, till it looked as if she must overbalance at any moment, flutter down like a great black bird shot out of a tree.

A magician stood directly beneath her, and began to coax a kingfisher through a velvet hoop no bigger than a curtain ring. The kingfisher seemed to have no bones, no substance, and the magician fed it through a sequence of shrinking circles, first the bleached eye socket of a skull, then the neck of a wine bottle, finally the entrance to his own ear, which swallowed the bird without trace, and, as it disappeared, Ferdousine gave the woman's buttocks a slap, plunged himself into her rear. Took the road less travelled, and Kate nearly choked.

The dirty bastard; the filthy swine. In the street a man with a megaphone was shouting *Seal up those things which the seven thunders uttered, and write them not*, while Ferdousine nibbled at his melba toast. 'Have some burnt marmalade,' he said.

'Just my files will do,' Kate snapped, and when he failed to move she fetched them herself. Three bulging manilla folders, cross-referenced and classified, complete with bibliography, she carried them up to the roof above poor Godwin's room where she kept her garden.

Sheltered in a suntrap, and peopled by concrete deer, this garden bore carrots and onions and squash, green tomatoes propped on curtain rods, rows of flaccid broad beans. Wild flowers tangled with herbs, and weeds ran riot everywhere. Alehoof and comfrey, skullcap and creeping jenny. When Kate stepped out among them, melted tar sucked at her feet like quicksand.

Vandals had molested the wrought-iron brazier where she burned dead leaves. It reeked of stale piss and lighter fluid, and a sparrow lay decomposing in a bed of charred rubber. But this sacrilege only hardened her resolve. Grabbing paper from the files in random fistfuls, she started thrusting it and hurling it into the brazier's gut, pounding on the pile to make it lay flat, cursing at it when it went astray. Newsprint stories, publicity flyers, wire pictures. Treatises and pamphlets. The manuscript of a Ph.D thesis in German. Glossy magazines in Italian, Spanish, Greek. And boxes full of souvenirs. Katerina Rhute key rings and wallets and barrettes, Katerina Rhute prayer books, model Katerina Rhutes in first-communion dresses. Rubber-stamped autographs, and *I Bear Witness* scented candles. Katerina Rhute decals and buttons. Deodorant and mouthwash. Bubblegum.

*A* was for Amarillo.

Lot of cows in Amarillo. Back in 1959, cows and churches was all she wrote, and Charley Root had set up shop in a store-front chapel, born again as Brother Karl Rhute. Her mother had done the Christian thing by then, and Palmetto was tired of them. Between kited cheques and rival bookies who wanted him kneecapped, Charley Root had run out of real estate. So they'd saddled the hound and ridden. Tallahassee and Port St Joe and Pensacola, Mobile and Biloxi, Pass Christian, Zachary and Opelousas, Nachitoches and Nacogdoches, Waxahachie and Cisco, Sweetwater and Lubbock, till Amarillo seemed the only place left. Especially when Charley Root caught sight of its skyline all spires and crosses, and the sinners picking their way through the cowchips with their billfolds hanging out. Right then, he tossed his Racing Form in the trash, and found the Lord.

He'd been sliding that way anyhow. Ever since the night in Tarpon Springs, in fact. Not that Kate had told him the details; she never was a blabbermouth. But Charley always had a nose for an angle. Somehow he'd caught a whiff of money. So he kept his beady eye on her, and when she got embroiled with the ginger toupee at McMurdo's Hardware, came home with her hand in bandages, he knew he was in luck.

It must have seemed like a last-minute reprieve. Like being handed a brand-new ticket. Abel Bonder had his knives, God had his wife, and now he could trade in the name of Rhute, which spelled like a touch of class, not a goddamn rutabaga.

In Amarillo, when he wasn't tied up healing, he stuck on Kate like rice on ice. There was a city park with a boating lake, Buddy Holly Park, where she liked to cycle after school, and Karl Rhute would peddle right behind, his breath like an exhaust pipe, belching sour-mash toxics down her neck.

Late afternoons there was a crap game behind a boathouse, where she would be bribed with ice-cream, sometimes Rocky Road, sometimes chocolate mint chip, while Karl on his knees prayed to his new friend up top for seven the hard way. There was a baseball cage and miniature golf, there were rowboats on the lake. And Kate saw the girl for the third time.

It was late spring, the April sun was sinking across the lake, and she came trotting across the baseball field in blue-jeans and a sweatshirt, playing with a beach ball. Flipping and sporting it in the air, showing off. Doing tricks like rolling it down her back, then bumping it with her tailbone and catching it on her heel. Or making the ball bounce fast, faster, fastest, till its stripes became a blur, a spinning sun like a top on the girl's shoulder, then on her bowed neck, then on the back of her stretching hand.

The faster the ball whirled, the faster she ran behind it. Flying past the boathouse and the dice game, she hardly had time to glance in Kate's eyes. Just one flash, and she was past, skimming over the grass in radiance towards the lake's edge, into the flame of the setting sun, and when she reached the water, she neither seemed to dive or float above it, she simply blended with it, she vanished, ball and all. Leaving Kate to stare at the space she had left. To stare into the sun, which did not burn her eyes – she didn't even feel it. Standing unaware as her ice-cream melted and dripped down her skirt,

148

until even Karl Rhute noticed, and he shouted at her to shape up. 'What are you playing at?' he yelled, and Kate's voice answered without permission, as if a stranger spoke through her: '*Sancta Virgo Virginum*,' it said.

So the jig was up, her cover blown. Karl Rhute carried her home semiconscious, fed her a cup of hot chocolate, then he was on the phone to the *Clarion*, who sent along a cub reporter. 'MIRACLE AT BUDDY HOLLY?' the headline next morning read. Page 5, column 3; not much more than a filler. But Karl Rhute had caught a glimpse of Zion, and he was a pit bull, no power could shake him loose.

Kate herself was mortified. The girl had come to her in good faith, as a free gift. Even to talk of her seemed a betrayal, the worst kind of spiritual boasting. To turn her into cash seemed mortal sin.

Oddly enough, the girl herself seemed to take no offence. Far from leaving in a huff, she even chose to appear more often. Her visitations came weekly, then almost daily. Soon she was Kate's best friend.

A dog came too, a stray mutt that the girl had picked up somewhere in her travels, part terrier and part border collie, his other parts God knows what. One ear up and the other down, black coat spotted with white, and an irregular white circle like a melted monocle round his left eye, which gave him a quizzical look. The girl left him in Kate's care, and Kate named him Pompey, she couldn't say why.

Charley Root tried to run the mongrel off, he was a man who loathed and despised all dogs. Filthy, slobbering pests, he thought them; the love of them was a disease. Still, he was in no position to argue. Needing Katerina, he couldn't afford to anger Kate. So Pompey was housed and fed, an animal of no breeding, no brain, no quality whatever, except for eagerness. His face with its one cocked ear never lost its vigilance, even in sleep. He had been created to wait, and serve, nothing more. The girl came to see him every weekend.

By now the press called her the Amarillo Virgin, but that was not how she seemed to Kate. There was nothing motherly about her, you would never have thought that she had a child. In age, she might have been Kate's big sister, but that wasn't right either; she didn't act bossy or sarcastic the way big sisters did. If anything, she was most like a hall monitor in school, the sort you'd have a crush to die for, gracious and serene, a little bit distant in the nature of things but infinitely patient.

When they could no longer meet publicly without being hounded by the press, she came to Kate in private, in her bedroom or the back yard, frequently in her bath. Sometimes she brought a chocolate bar or a sucker; once, a ham and Swiss sandwich on rye. Often she seemed weary, maybe worn by too much travel. And always there was a vague sense of melancholy, though she never thought to complain. A yearning, Kate thought. A feeling of loss.

Maybe she had been unlucky in love.

Maybe she had grown up in a village or on a farm, and one day a smooth operator had come calling. A travelling salesman, say, or even a criminal on the run. Who had won the girl's heart, and they had run off together; they'd driven by night like Bonnie and Clyde, living on love and their wits, till one day the Law caught up with them and her lover died in a hail of bullets, they'd filled him full of lead, leaving the girl to wander on alone, haunted by his memory, a fugitive all her days.

It was just a thought, of course.

But it seemed to fit. That would explain the restless way the girl sat, never quite in repose, perched on a windowsill or tree stump or even the toilet seat, she had no false pride, with her face half-turned from the light as if listening, as if she was forever waiting, though nothing ever arrived.

Nothing except for tourists, that is. With Karl Rhute's stoking, what had started as a squib on page five of the *Clarion* soon turned into a cult. TV crews started gathering outside the garden fence, and writers from the national press. An article appeared in *Newsweek*, and a Hollywood agent with a toothbrush moustache threw pebbles at her window, his name was Irvin Lipschitz. Tour buses unloaded the convinced and the merely curious, and Karl Rhute set up a concession stand: T-shirts and postcards, Katerinaburgers on a sesame-seed bun. A pop-up picturebook was published, there was talk of a record deal. Billy Graham sent a Christmas card.

By global standards it was small potatoes. Nothing you could compare with Conchita of Garabandal's cult in the Sixties, or the spiritual Disneyland that Marija of Medjugorje would spawn in the Eighties, three million pilgrims in a year. Katerina at her peak was good for one busload of trippers per day, perhaps five thousand bucks a week. Chickenfeed, really. But not to Karl Rhute.

Nor to the Church, which determined to shut his playhouse down. A Monsignor Beebe travelled up from Dallas, a reed-thin man with a huge head, puffy and purplish round the jowls, he looked like a blood clot on a stick, and he brandished a black book called *False Apparitions*. Afterwards, scientists with white coats put her through a battery of tests, electroencephalographs and electro-oculographs, and many raps across the kneecap with a rubber hammer. And all of them together agreed that she was fraudulent, a brazen imposter. There was no Amarillo Virgin, there was nothing. 'Evil is an absence,' said Monsignor Beebe.

Kate could have told him that for free. The girl she knew

was not the type they were looking for at all. According to *False Apparitions*, the Virgin was a lady in long white robes who never showed her feet and was indescribably beautiful, her conversation all beatitudes. But this girl wore sneakers or stack-heeled boots, you had to assume that she had feet underneath, and she spoke a bare minimum, seemed happier to listen. Hard to know what she was really thinking, but reverence and fuss made her tense, that was obvious, while stories helped her relax. 'Call me Mary,' she said, and seemed happiest when Kate spoke of Elvis.

Sometimes she showed herself to the trippers as they hung over the garden fence, snapping instant photos. It didn't seem to bother her, she'd only shrug and smile; and the light from her eyes then was blinding. Kate would put up a hand to shield her own sight from its dazzle, and all the trippers would start to scream, *Look at the sun! Oh my God, look at the sun!*

Later on, they'd claim to have seen the Amarillo Virgin for themselves, a footless lady in white robes, beautiful beyond words. If Kate could have seen with their eyes, Monsignor Beebe might have left her in peace. But she couldn't, and she could hardly lie. 'The Virgin has no feet, has no feet, has no feet,' the Monsignor kept insisting. 'Mary does,' she kept replying. And so she was cast into darkness.

When the Amarillo Report was released, a writer called Steinwood from the *Washington Post* followed close behind, a man who put Kate in mind of a centaur and wanted to know where the money had went. Every dollar that Karl Rhute charged was meant to go towards building a shrine in Buddy Holly Park. Instead of which he now drove a pink Cadillac and owned a poolhall outside Odessa, a cathouse in San Angelo. So Steinwood wrote his story, and the IRS came calling. Katerina was excommunicated, Mary took a vacation, Pompey went to the pound. And Karl Rhute changed names again.

That should have been the end; it wasn't. For two more years, Charley Root traipsed her round the south-west, working her in shorter and shorter seasons, ten days in Tatum, a weekend in Flagstaff, a matinee in Almagordo, till the string was played out.

The girl didn't seem to blame her even then; leastways, she never said so. She just visited more rarely, and for shorter spans. Even when she was present she seemed distracted. Perhaps she was missing Pompey.

Kate was turned fifteen, everything had changed. Trawling Louisiana that fall, they stopped in St Martinville. There was a child's swing in the motel yard, strung between two locust trees. She rode it at dusk, and the girl came to her one last time, talked with her a space, then she faded in air, she was gone.

Nothing left of Mary now but cheap souvenirs and trash. Three files filled with junk on a New York roof. A front page from the *Clarion* headlined AMARILLO VIRGIN EXPOSED kept trying to cling to Kate's dressing gown, only she wouldn't let it, she hurtled it down into the brazier with all the rest, and set it blazing. Poured out the miniatures of rum that she had found in the Zoo overnight, strange fruit that ficus trees bore in the summer season, and she tossed a half-smoked Camel.

The sudden whoosh of flame, a dragon's breath, made her stumble backwards, turn her head. The morning's heat was up now, the city sweltering again. Up and down the block, and all over the neighbourhood, fires were burning on roofs just like hers. It made Kate feel she belonged, that she was a part of the community, and she raised her eyes to the sun, it hung in yellow haze like one more fire. Like a circus hoop for terriers to jump through. Or the cricket ball she'd seen that time with Fred Root in the field behind the brewery. *Bellamy's Beer, Good For What Ales You*. Sitting in the long grass that smelled of barley wine, drinking sweet milky tea, when the ball rose high, turned into a red-winged bird.

When that ball had swooped again to split her nose like a ripe plum, she hadn't felt a thing. *Now then*, Fred Root had said, bribing her not to cry with a Space Blaster. It was her favourite candy, a long tube of caramel shaped like a rocket with lemon powder inside, coated with a thin shell of chocolate, and when you bit through that shell, a rush of fizzy lemon flew out, Fred Root called it sherbert, but it felt more like battery acid. So tart it made her eyes water, and the water mingled with the blood from her burst nose, she was a mess. *Now then, now then*, the old man kept saying helplessly, and she wanted to comfort him. *It was the light*, she said.

*It always is*, Fred Root replied.

O f course there was no shadow of doubt in his mind where his duty lay. Juice Shovlin was his friend, and more than friend, his sponsor. If not for the warmth of his invitation that lunchtime at Tigh Neachtain's, John Joe might never have travelled to America in his own lifetime. He could easily have rotted his days to death in Scath, and not once strutted the wider stage.

That was the great truth to bear in mind. There were a power of forces in this city to lead any man astray, all classes of seductions, but he had an obligation. After all, it was Juice who'd made him what he was.

When first he was brought to Scath Uncle Frank didn't care for him to be seen alive, so he was not sent to school. Then the social worker rode her bike into the yard, and the next week he was togged out in blazer and knee-socks, packed off down the road to that grey stone building with the high windows where it was so cold that he couldn't grip his pen, the purple ink spilled and blotted his tablets, and the teacher called him Gunga Din.

In that season, he was seen fit for monkey nuts only. Stout Mackeson used to bellow like a gorilla when he passed, make his mouth go all bulging like the chimps in the ads for PG Tips and dangle his arms so the knuckles brushed the ground and circle John Joe with his eyes crossed. It was a trial.

And Juice Shovlin had rescued him. He was in the year above, already a star. Not a scholar born, but a great athlete in his own right. Handball, football, hurling, he was a master of all Gaelic games, destined to play for Donegal if injury didn't ruin him. A laughing loud boy, cock of the walk he was always, and so full of sap you could fill a bucket with his drippings like they did with the rubber trees in tropic lands, he would have made a fresh set of tyres for every bike and tractor in Kilmullen. A terrible temper on him when he was crossed, nobody could deny it. Cuchulain likewise had been no stranger to rage.

For a term he never gave John Joe a look, then on the last day at lunchbreak he walked up without a blink, laughing and sporting with his gang, Peter Tookey, Jocko Conlon, Bar McBride and all, and clapped him on his shoulder, man to man. 'What's it like to be a nigger? Is it dark in there?' he asked.

'At night just,' said John Joe.

'Good man yourself,' said Juice with another clap on the shoulder, and a laugh that would topple a barn, and John Joe was under his protection ever since.

Night and day was the change. Instead of an outcast, he was included in every game and outing. *The Great Maguire*, Juice Shovlin named him, for what cause he couldn't tell, and at each word John Joe spoke, there was a fresh round of laughs.

He was a mascot then. Another style of monkey on a stick, and this brought its hardships also. When his eye was burned, there was a time that he thought he'd do better alone. But where was the force in holding a grudge? *No use crying over spilt milk*. Juice Shovlin said so himself.

And what were the alternatives besides? Blood pudding for breakfast, his mother's romances after tea. These years

156

she'd moved on to Maeve Binchy and *Light a Penny Candle*. *'Johnny was annoyed that he hadn't been invited to the wedding, but Elizabeth was cool and firm. It was tempting, very tempting to take him with her. The handsome Johnny Stone would steal the show, he would be proof that little shy Elizabeth White had done well in the world. He would be so charming too,'* John Joe read, while Bernadette worked through another box of Black Magic. 'Hector Wall,' she said, popping an orange creme. 'The only man I ever loved.'

'What about Da?'

'Hector could be so charming, he drove a Humber Supreme, I danced with him at the Kilburn Palais. The paso doble and the tango, and the Viennese waltz on the night I wore my organdy gown, alice-blue, with a white silk orchid for my corsage. We fit like gloves, little shy Bernadette Maguire and handsome Hector Wall, I thought we'd be partners for ever. Only Hector had a weakness, it broke my heart.'

'What class of weakness?'

'The love that dare not speak its name in public toilets, and the day it all came out in court, your father in his taxi was the darkie who drove me home.'

A few of those orange cremes went a long way on a full stomach, especially after onions. With Juice Shovlin as his mentor, at least he was entitled to have his skull crushed like an eggshell on a football field or later stand loafing against a wall in the Hollywood Ballroom on Saturday nights, watching Ann-Marie Tully's crackers when she twirled jiving and her skirts flew up. Or Eithne Ward's were almost as shapely. Though they only giggled when he asked them to dance, it took Juice to persuade them, and even then they'd run away screaming when the All-Stars struck up a smoocher, they wouldn't slow-dance for the world, not even on a dare. So that afterwards John Joe would need to peddle his Rudge up and over the gap in all weathers to Gilooley's knocking shop in Killybegs. Else he might have committed a violence.

It was Juice Shovlin's word as well that brought him his job at Muldoon's. 'Money for old rope,' Juice said, and it was the truth. All he had to do was stand around inside a big metal drum with slick walls like the Wheel of Death at Bundoran, dressed in rubber from head to foot, coveralls and thighboots, long gloves past his elbows, and a shower cap, watching a load of dead fish get translated into fertilizer.

He stood on a platform over the drum's belly, feeding fish guts and fish bodies into a great rotating screw that pulped them all to paste. After a few weeks he felt so at home he didn't notice the fish even, just the spiralling screw, expanding and contracting. 'The insatiable maw,' Juice called it in his office upstairs with the brass nameplate on his desk and the leatherette swivel chair. 'The cunt of creation.'

But it wasn't cunt that John Joe saw, it was the other, and filthy at that. The stench of fish would never wash off him. Soaping and scouring only muffled the stink, overlaid it with a film of saccharin that quickly faded, leaving him three parts catfood, only one part man.

He thought that Ann-Marie Tully and Eithne Ward would never stop gagging. Then Briege came along, and she savoured him like stout.

She was a research assistant up from Trinity, Dublin, on a grant. Collecting folk myths or some such for *Roinn na neacha neamhbeo agus nithe nach bhfuil ann*, the Department of Unalive Beings and Things Without Existence, and strutting her stuff half-naked at 2001 Odyssey in Ballybofey, she hadn't as much on her back as would stuff a crutch.

Come the morning after the night before, she had informed Juice Shovlin that she was in the market for local colour. So when John Joe came off his shift, there she was waiting in the road outside Muldoon's. '*Buachaill buí*. Yellow boy,' she said.

It was his first kiss in daylight. To be fair, it was his first kiss for free at all. In her Civic driving to her room, she put her fat pink tongue in his mouth outside Davenish Memorial Marble. '*An de bheoibh nó de mhairbh thú?*' she asked. 'Are you of the living or the dead?'

'I'd say living.'

'So kiss me deadly,' said Briege.

Plump as an otter she was, and slippery too, sliding through his fingers wherever he touched. On his back he learned that she was not a researcher really, she was really a journalist, her first love was TV, what she really wanted to do was make documentaries and go to the States, she really felt she belonged there, it was her spiritual home, and she really loved Marvin Gaye, didn't he? Well, he would of course. Gulping in great lungfuls of him like a fish-glue elixir at each thrust down, rolling her eyes at each slow drag back. 'And James Brown, too,' she said, subsiding on his chest. As she stilled, the gulps shrank to sips. 'And Jimi Hendrix, of course,' she said, and slept.

In the night, though, she woke up writhing. 'I'm too high-strung. If I don't do my Yoga I flip,' she said. John Joe brushed away her tears that felt and smelled like cod-liver oil. 'Too sensitive,' she said, and jumping still naked from her bed, she did a Starburst on the rug.

Her legs flew up over her shoulders and twined behind her neck, her puppy-fat chin rested on her crotch. Then the whole force of her body was gathered into her anus. Tiny currents began to spread outwards through her buttocks, through her belly and trunk, spreading faster and wider, more intense at each spasm, till it seemed she must fly apart. But she didn't. At the moment of dissolution the spasms

159

softened, the circles began to close again. Until no other muscle, no nerve of her moved, just that one bud pulsing. 'You should try it yourself,' she said. 'Put hair on your chest.' Then she was back to Dublin, safe home.

All of this John Joe took in his stride, he'd read the like in dirty books. Only one question nagged and dismayed him: why would he love Marvin Gaye?

When he asked Juice Shovlin, and Juice explained, he was banjaxed. All his life he had been called nigger, darkie, coon, but he'd never thought that made him black. Not properly. Blacks were people you saw on the TV news rioting in South Africa or starving some other place, or else in shoot-em-ups at the Eureka, *Shaft* and *Superfly* and *Uptown Saturday Night*, living the life of Larry up in Harlem, fancy cars and big hats and girls in tight red dresses, all classes of artillery. In the films they seemed to have great gas altogether, but those men couldn't be him, he was not of their race whatever.

Or was he? Maybe he had missed the point. *Black*. Maybe there was something here had escaped him. *To be black*. What was the meaning of this?

The only black he had met in person, Da, was not around to tell him. Besides, that man would be bound to be biased. Given hindsight he wished he had wriggled loose and tried to pin Briege down, not let her escape in a Starburst. She could have set him straight in a jiffy. Or told him a good book to read. As it was, he hadn't a clue.

Still didn't. Since he'd fallen to earth in New York, he felt his own skin as false colours. Blacks passing on the street spoke to him in code, assuming a connection, but he lacked the key. *I'm chilling* and *you be illing* and *he's down with that*, and who was this Momma person, what evil could she have done them? He would have liked to question Crouch.

Ask him, man to man, *Is it dark in there?* But he didn't like to presume.

And now the roof was on fire again.

At first he'd thought it was an illusion, the power of suggestion, because Mr Ferdousine was playing *Smoke Gets in Your Eyes* upstairs for his dancing lesson. Then a streamer of burning newspaper fell flapping and flailing to the ground like a winged bird at the Zoo's door where he was watering the wandering jew. O VIRGIN EXPOSED, the remains of the headline read.

For a trice, his impulse was to run upstairs and start battling the flames. But no, he would not be exploited. Let someone else go piss on them this time; firefighting was not his hire.

He had more than enough on his plate as it was. Another day, another duty, so it seemed. Imagine Juice Shovlin, thirty-one floors up above Park Avenue, waiting and waiting to no avail. But how was John Joe to get away? When Miss Root needed him in the Zoo; and Anna Crow needed him to run errands, needed him to serve; and Bani Badpa needed him for a night barman. And the Black Swans, of course, they had their needs as well. Those people depended on him.

Since that first time in the tunnel, he'd come to see them in a better light. Master Maitland, on fuller acquaintance, had proved no bad sort, although a mite intemperate. He had known great sadness in his life; you had to remember that. Try to see things through the Master's own eyes, and there was much a toiling man could learn.

As for the Swans themselves, they lived in a space they had named Mount Tabor, though it was located deep underground, five levels below Grand Central Station.

According to Crouch, there were hundreds, even thousands of citizens who existed in a like manner, scattered in tunnels and sealed chambers throughout the subway system. Some were homeless and some criminals, some not right in the head, but most were only refugees from daylight. The guards and journalists called them Mole People; that was incorrect. They were subterraneans just.

There had been such dwellers for many years, maybe for decades. Nobody had paid them mind till recently, when some lady from a university had written a book. Now magazine writers and TV crews were following her trail. The subway guards had started to polish their shoes and spruce their hair, hoping for a moment's stardom. What was not so pleasing, they had also started to oil their guns.

To reach Mount Tabor this day John Joe passed through the subway stile onto the platform for the Times Square shuttle and simply kept walking.

The tracks led him into blackness. When the trains came roaring down upon him, he hugged the walls, hiding his face till danger passed and he could find the secret vent that took him down deeper, crawling on his belly through a steel tube that brought him into an echoing chamber.

Just like in the tunnel beneath Riverside Park, the first time he'd met Master Maitland, he didn't see faces or bodies here, only eyes. For a long space, he walked a high ledge above abandoned tracks, picking his way past sleeping bags and mattresses and piles of human excrement; then he descended a rusted iron stairway that ended in naked rock-face; and finally he swung himself down by a cable, hand under hand, to a last tunnel that brought him home.

As good as any spy film it felt when he stopped halfway down this tunnel, tapped with his keys on a metal steampipe and received two taps in reply. A door swung open in the rockface, and he had reached Mount Tabor.

Twenty-three Black Swans and eleven of their children

were grouped around a concrete clearing lit by two gas lanterns, some eating Egg McMuffins and others sipping Coke. Two women were hanging up laundry, a man was fixing a leaky waterbed. 'You're late,' said Master Maitland.

'The Severe Macaw took sick. A dose of the French Moult.'

'Ananias,' the Master said. His shoulders hunched and rocked in anger, and the great bull's head that rose straight out of his monstrous chest seemed lowered to charge. '*And there were lightnings, and voices, and thunderings,*' he cried in his high girl's voice. But as quickly as his rage had flared, it withered. '*And an earthquake,*' he sighed. '*And a great hail.*'

He had found and built this shelter by himself, two years ago at Pentecost. Or found it again, to be exact, for he had known of the place's existence long ago. Before he was the Master, he had been plain Luscious Maitland, employee of the Manhattan Transport Authority (MTA), who mapped the subways for his living.

The way that John Joe had heard the story from Crouch, Luscious Maitland had once been a rising star in that authority, freely tipped for high honours, until an efficiency expert named Randall Gurdler was turned loose on his department. A smiling smooth man with a furled silk handkerchief in his breast pocket and the smell of violets on his breath, this expert had uncovered certain irregularities, financial in their nature. In truth, it was all a misunderstanding, a foolish mistake, but Gurdler refused to accept this. Instead, he had twisted the facts to his own unclean purposes, using them as building blocks to further his career, which vaulted him ever upwards, from efficiency expert to publicity officer, spokesman to comptroller, and finally to President of the entire MTA. While Luscious Maitland lay caged in jail. Three years in Attica, and Crouch had been his cellmate.

Another man in his position might have been crushed, his spirit shattered, but Maitland was not the fall-down kind. Instead of brooding on his wrongs, he sought the reasons that lay behind them. Studied his Bible day by day, and by night he read another book. *The Deaths of Joachim*, this second book was called, and in its pages at last he saw the truth clear. His fall had been no accident. Nor was Randall Gurdler a casual interloper. The entire story had been foretold.

In his cell a vision came to him by night of Gurdler in a telephone booth, dialling a number with eight digits, and those digits spelled 666-BEAST. At that moment the scales fell from Maitland's eyes and he saw that violet-breathed hypocrite in his true created nature, with his body like unto a leopard, and his feet as the feet of a bear, and his mouth as the mouth of a lion. Then he saw the smiling head wounded to the death, and that deadly wound healed, and he knew that the Antichrist was alive and well in Jay Street, Brooklyn, at the offices of the MTA.

The thing that puzzled him at first in this revelation was the function of the subways. Why had Gurdler chosen them as his battleground? What could be their hidden power? Then he bethought him of the fiery flood to come when Babylon falls, that great city, because she made all nations drink of the wine of her wrath of her fornication. And everything made sense. By infiltrating the MTA, Gurdler had positioned himself at the heart and core of the city's nervous system. At the moment ordained, he needed only to throw a switch, and the tracks would be consumed by flame, a holocaust that would burst from underground, from deep within the belly of the Beast, and devour the metropolis above, exterminating all sinning creatures in a torrent of fire; a flood.

What could be simpler or more devastating? With Luscious Maitland safely confined, the one man with the nerve and knowledge to face Gurdler down, who could hope to deflect his aim? The guards and even the warder laughed when informed, the mayor never answered his letters. The only man alive who would listen was Crouch, and he was given no choice.

Crouch at that time was a tap-dancer by profession, a forger by trade. Artwork had always been his forte, and he had decorated their cell with many paintings. Under Maitland's influence, he now drew a figure on a throne, his face like unto jasper and sardine stone, with a rainbow around the throne, in sight like an emerald. And another figure in the midst of seven candlesticks, clothed in a rough garment down to his feet and girt about the paps with a golden thong. And horses with the heads of lions and tails like scorpions, and their riders like angels of the bottomless pit had breast-plates of jacinth, and of brimstone. *You told my story. You are my eyes*, Master Maitland said. *My own eyes a flame of fire.*

The first day he was released, the Master returned to the subways that had been his life, scouring the labyrinth beneath them for sanctuary. Crouch thought him crazy to go house-hunting there, so close to the Beast's own lair. But that was simply because Crouch did not know Physics. Couldn't grasp the simple fact that a flame flies upwards, and the safest place to shelter is directly beneath its source. When the doomed and damned city overhead was blazing, freed souls five levels down would merely be pleasantly warmed, snug as bugs. And when flame turned to flood, no sweat, they would turn to black swans, and fly.

By the time that Crouch himself was paroled, he found the Master surrounded by twenty-four elders and their families.

Some had been subterraneans when he found them, others had been awaiting a sign. One had been a nurse, and one a schoolteacher. There was a plumber and a short-order cook, an electrician and a whore. All the necessities of life, you'd say, except for Art, and that was where Crouch came in.

By the wayside one day, fallen off a truck, he chanced on a job lot of mannequins. They had been created in the images of supermodels and Hollywood icons; he turned them into prophecies. Cindy Crawford and Elle Macpherson and Madonna were transformed into three unclean spirits like frogs come out of the mouth of the dragon, and out of the mouth of the beast, and out of the mouth of the false prophet. Ava Gardner became a mighty angel come down from heaven, clothed with a cloud. And to Brigitte Bardot were given two wings of a great eagle, that she might fly into the wilderness.

These apparitions lined Mount Tabor now when John Joe stood mumbling in his lateness, and Black Swans watched smirking. Of the original twenty-four, all were still present save three, who had wandered off or perhaps been hijacked by the transit police, Randall Gurdler's men.

That was the one great danger in this place – the squads of licensed thugs who swarmed the tunnels some nights with drawn guns, rounding up crack addicts, thieves and freed souls without distinction, breaking heads. Sometimes they sprayed gunfire without even aiming, blasting at rats and anything else that moved. Jerzy Polacki, the plumber, had lost a thumb that way. Marvella Crabtree had lost her son.

Though that murder had tried them sorely, their faith had endured, and even strengthened. The Boniface brothers, Brulant and Toussaint, had requisitioned a few rifles. Luther Pratt and Joe Easter had added six Beretta 9-mils, 92F, plus a couple dozen snub-nosed .38s, and Burdette Merryweather had chipped in an Uzi. Mount Tabor, which had started as an asylum, was become a citadel: *New Jerusalem*, Master Maitland said.

Still and all, John Joe felt easy here. Not so much when the Master called him Ananias, maybe, but as a rule he felt right in his element. And not because of Randall Gurdler and the Beast and 666, that sounded a load of bollix. But who could tell for certain sure? In any case, he wasn't bothered. What he liked about this spot, citadel or no, was that it felt like a social club, and he was a welcome member.

More than welcome, honoured. From the first time Crouch had brought him along, and made him display his birthmark, he had been the special guest artiste round here. Though anyone with half an eye could see that was no swan, more like a rook if anything, you'd have thought he was bold Robert Emmet reborn. Any class of treat that crossed his mind, a cup of tea, a ginger biscuit, love, it was his on a dumbwaiter, help yourself.

Another kind of mascot.

Well he knew that, of course; he wasn't blind. At least this time there was no mockery to it, he wasn't made a freak. A quirk among other quirks only, and where was the damage in that?

Besides, if he was a mascot, he was also a sign. *A patent portent*, the Master called him. As advertised and foretold in *The Deaths of Joachim*.

That volume was the Swans' holy book. A battered volume wrapped in canvas sacking, it told a martyr's tale.

According to its text, Joachim was born a slave in 1522. Mulatto son of a Venetian trader, a bastard born in Tunis, he had been raised at the court of a local potentate, where he'd showed an aptitude for languages and music, and in due course had been sold to another trader, this time a

Genoese, who brought him back to Italy. His master dying suddenly, he had then commenced to wander through Europe, sometimes working as a farmhand or day-labourer, sometimes begging, or making music in the streets.

His musical talents were many, he played the pipes and stringed instruments and a form of xylophone, but his greatest love was the drum, and it was as a drummer that he earned his keep in Würzburg, playing daily in the city's central square, while another North African, a one-legged beggar named Emico, accompanied him on the fife.

The winter of 1545 was bitter hard, and the two musicians almost starved. A great storm swept through the city, freezing all living things. Joachim and Emico huddled against the blizzard in the doorway of Würzburg's cathedral and prepared themselves to die. At the storm's height, however, just as Joachim was lapsing into unconsciousness, the Virgin appeared to him.

She was wearing white robes, and surrounded by a heavenly radiance, but her feet were bound in a supplicant's rags, and her message was austere. She spoke to him of the fiery flood to come, and the black swans who would survive it, and she told him what his own role must be. Instead of using his drum to make people dance, he was to employ it as the instrument of God. And this he promptly did. Rising out of his stupor, he found that the storm had quite abated, and his hunger with it. Entirely restored, he strapped on his drum and began to march through the sleeping town, spreading the pure Word.

Many citizens abused him and showered him with ordure, while others laughed him to scorn. Only one, an apostate priest named Nikolaus, recognized the truth of his vision. Together they formed the original Brethren of Black Swans, and established their own Mount Tabor in a dye-works.

Day after day Joachim toured the cities and the countryside, drumming the Last Days, and gradually followers gathered to him. Shepherds and mill hands and unemployed workers, migrants and beggars, they rallied to his call, and waited for the flood of flame to strike.

At first Joachim merely preached repentance, the ways of austerity. On the prompting of Nikolaus, however, he soon began to lash out at the Church. He accused the local clergy of *Avaritia* and *Luxuria*, and foretold dire punishments in the coming holocaust.

The Bishop of Würzburg, he predicted, was going to catch the blackest roasting of the lot, at which the bishop was not best pleased, and ordered him arrested. But the drummer would not go easily. Through the summer of 1546 he continued to travel the Main valley, drumming and preaching as he went. Only when he returned to Mount Tabor did the bishop's men succeed in pinning him down. A fierce battle ensued, the streets ran with blood and dye, and in the end Joachim was captured, his drum destroyed.

Torture failed to make him recant. Incensed, above all, by the description of the Virgin's feet bound in rags, the Bishop of Würzburg used him so severely that the drummer was pronounced dead three times, and three times revived, until at last he was burnt at the stake, still declaiming his vision.

Nor did the story end there. The priest Nikolaus had written a full account of Joachim's crusade, and when he in turn was captured and burnt, the manuscript passed to Emico, who carried it back to Africa with him. For generations the tale remained in hiding, a thing of rumour and fantasy. The manuscript itself was lost or destroyed, and all traces of Emico himself disappeared. Yet somehow the tradition survived, and even spread, travelling from Tunis to Tiemcen and Meknes, Rabat and Mogador, and finally to the

Ivory Coast. From there, the slave ships brought Joachim's memory to the New World, and in that world's plantations it lingered, one small cult among many, yet indestructible.

It needed one Hosea Tichenor, a freed man of colour, to bring the wheel full circle. A Natchez barber by trade, ardent in the Negro cause, he'd grown up hearing the tale, and saw potential in it. So he wrote *The Deaths of Joachim*, a reference to the three resurrections from torture.

Privately published, its sales were not brisk, and soon afterwards the barber was found with his throat razor-slit. But his work was not forgotten. Frederick Douglass, for one, was familiar with the Deaths; later, Marcus Garvey was known to quote from them verbatim; and Hannah Bradenton, Luscious Maitland's godmother, kept a copy on her bedside table.

The volume had meant nothing to the Master then. It was just a storybook, and old-fashioned to boot, with its sacking cover and its scrunched-up type like spider tracks. The only thing that impressed him was the frontispiece – a woodcut of Joachim at the stake, with tongues of fire licking him all over, his legs and arms turned into charred logs. Even then, it was not the suffering that impressed him, or the stoicism with which the martyr endured, but the bunched muscles of his shoulders and neck, the puffy bags beneath his eyes. Put him in trunks and gloves, and you would have sworn he was Joe Louis, and the Brown Bomber, of all men living, was Luscious Maitland's God.

Only when he was railroaded into Attica, three decades later, did the text itself begin to make sense. Randall Gurdler, the Bishop of Würzburg – what were they, after all, but two faces of one coin? The deaths of Joachim were the deaths of every freed soul but enslaved body: 'Watch the story,' he said to Crouch, and joined the prison band on drums.

But there was more. On page 63, Tichenor had written: 'Beholt the man who bares the mark, he comes in HEAT, in splender he comes with mitie showting. By his BRAND in flesh then know him, my swans. By his coming make an END, and so be freed.'

It wasn't much to go on, of course. Tell the truth, when John Joe had tried to read the full text, he had found it tough sledding. All that sin and repentance, and contemplating your own worthlessness, it sounded downright Protestant.

But the Swans, God love them, were entranced. Every word that Joachim had spoken, they treated as holy writ.

His vision of Armageddon, above all. In one of his last sermons, the drummer had pictured The End as a wild party. Mount Tabor would be invaded by a plague of uninvited guests, bringing with them loud music and the gaudiest of finery, all manner of boisterous games. There would be jousting and tumbling, carousing, orgies of fornication. But this revelry would be sham. Underneath their fancy dress, the guests would bear deadly arms. Servants of the Antichrist, at a prearranged signal they would throw off their masks and unleash the fiery flood. Many freed souls would perish then, their leaders perhaps among them. But that was no cause for dismay. Dead or living, if they were worthy, all would be saved. Black swans, they would fly away.

So there it was, plain as plain. Any minute now Randall Gurdler would be making his move, throwing that switch, then Katy bar the door. *Many earthquakes will there be*, Master Maitland said, *and killings in the world, and the sky, the whole sky, will be red, and the blind rain will pour down on the desert, and in the East a star will come in the shape of a moon, and men will prance like racehorses, and women will bet them like men.*

Small wonder, in these conditions, that the Master's tongue

turned sharp at times. *And in those days shall men seek death, and shall not find it. And shall desire to die, and death shall flee from them.* That was no stroll in the park.

Still, John Joe felt no fear. Looking round the clubhouse in Mount Tabor, all he thought was home. What ease it would be to stay here, lost underground where no parakeets or cockatoos could reach. To sit watching the children playing Power Rangers, and the women hanging out their washing, and Jerzy Polacki fixing the waterbed. Even the sight of the Master's purple head bent over the Book of Job was solace to him. So was the whisky breath of Crouch.

That man was dancing up a ladder, creating the Seventh Angel from fragments of Mamie Van Doren. Slapping on papier-mâché for the body, Corn Flakes packets and toilet rolls for robes. Skimming up and down the rungs with that shuffle-footed lightness of his, and winking back across his shoulder. 'How's the patent portent?' he asked.

'Mustn't grumble,' said John Joe.

Master Maitland overheard that, and his head came up with a jerk. 'If we don't grumble, who will?' he said.

'Anna Crow,' John Joe replied.

Instantly guilt stabbed him like a hat pin. He'd promised to do some shopping for her. Pick up a rope she needed for a poetry reading tonight. She'd be waiting for him at Sheherazade, and he had clean forgot. *Never keep a lady waiting*, his mother had always said. Or Anna Crow, either. 'A woman's expecting,' he said.

'Let her expect,' said Master Maitland.

'I only wish I could,' said John Joe.

Out of doors, once he had clambered back up the five levels into daylight, he felt cast out. The man in the hardware store had a boozer's nose and a quizzical eye, you'd say he was a gobshite. 'Would you have a length of rope? Suitable for a noose?' John Joe asked him.

'Would that be for yourself?'

'A friend.'

The way the man cocked his eyebrow, you could tell he had his doubts. Reservations, even. 'A young lady,' John Joe explained.

'I see,' the man said. 'Will that be cash or charge?'

Sheherazade by afternoon, with the chairs upside down on the tables and Roach Motels in every corner, looked more forlorn than ever. Not even Bani Badpa was on hand. Only Anna Crow in leopard-print leotard and ballet slippers with her red hair hidden under a mop of yellow ringlets, standing with one arm held stiff against the bar for support, her left foot on point, her right leg pointed at the ceiling. 'Did you get it?' she asked.

'They had hemp just, no silk.'

'Hard times all over.' Breathing deep and regular, she thrust her leg upwards, once, and twice, and three times, then turned to catch John Joe staring. There was want betrayed in his eyes, he could feel that. 'What's up with you?' Anna Crow asked, not unkind.

'Could you manage a Starburst at all?'

Lordamercy that stricken look you'd have thought kidney stones or a hernia at the very least when all he wanted was a candy and not even a self-respecting chocolate bar like a Snicker or a Baby Ruth but a lousy Starburst at that. 'No, I couldn't,' Anna said, 'but you're welcome to some of my gum.'

At least he had brought the rope. She had felt squeamish somehow about walking in the store and up to Mister Man and asking for his best necktie herself. A bit like buying your first tampon, it was an embarrassment even if you knew it was only nature. Though nature could be a bitch, a stone killer. But that wasn't the point; what was the point?

*At least he'd brought the rope*, that was it.

Don't start her to talking, she had been going round in circles like this for days. A single dull thought would weasel its way inside her brain and set up housekeeping there. Settle into an armchair with its bunny slippers on and refuse to be budged. Like those godawful songs that drove you mad, flowerpots like *Feelings* or *Raindrops Keep Falling on My Head* or that cretinous jingle on TV, *Dr Pepper You're a Part of Me*, she was a martyr to that. Though what part would that be exactly? A muscle, a nerve, her sphincter maybe? Still she kept humming it in the shower, she couldn't seem to help herself, was she losing her mind?

Perhaps she was. Lord knows that mental frailty ran in the family. Look at her own brother Leon who worshipped Apollo. Or her cousin Driskill that became a mime. One of those whiteface loons that pretended to be a statue on Oglethorpe Square, made her puke, praise the Lord for pigeons. But that was not the point. The point was lunacy and the Crows, you could write a book. Remember her in Shalimar, after all. God help her, she sounded as bad as those flowerpots. *Remember me in Shalimar, Pale hands beside the cookie jar*, but that had been different, a breakdown with all the trimmings, howling at the moon. This time around, it didn't feel like barking madness, more like bone stupidity, and where was the cure for dumb? How could you go to a medical man and explain to him *I'm a moron, Doctor, a hopeless imbecile, can you give me some pills?* He would look at you funny.

But that was not the point.

The point was she had the rope, now, Shut up. Time to get her ankle out of her ear, and set about her business, dress up for the night ahead. *The Faking Boy* was a poem she'd never done before, and vernacular was never her strong suit, she needed a deep breath before she plunged. Especially after this morning's fiasco with *La Belle Dame sans Merci*.

She should have smelled a rat when Verse-o-Gram told her it was a birthday gift. What kind of friend or lover would send a poem like that, after all, only a dumped boyfriend trying to scare off his replacement. So she'd found herself reciting to a stud who looked like a young Marlon Brando, except without the fat ass, and a Lady in the Meads wrapped in a bed sheet, and by the smell they'd been at it like minks in heat, when in walked Miss Thing declaiming *I saw their starved lips in the gloam with horrid warnings gaped wide,* perfect timing, *Ah! Woe betide!* that rattle at the window was her tip flying out.

Of course, she should have known she was in trouble the moment she passed Kate Root on the stairs, that woman was doom in blue mules. If anything, her new schtick, this Chatty Kathy act, seemed more sinister than the basilisk eye of yore. At least when she'd put the whammy on you openly, you knew you had been zapped. But this morning was more sinister. Too much perkiness by half, the flushed face and that bird-bright gleam in her eye – Anna sniffed dirty work at the crossroads, a storm of fanshit brewing.

But that was not the point.

The point was, she had a gig to do, a costume to put on. Back through the kitchens she led John Joe, into the storage space with soiled tablecloths and canned chickpeas, and stripped off her leotard, and cooled her skin with a hairdryer, 'And how was your day?' she asked, stretching.

'The Master called me Ananias.'

'You poor lamb.' But she hadn't the patience to hear the gruesome details. Far as she was concerned, the Black Swans were a royal pain, good for nothing but grief. These sects and millennial cults, they always ended in tears if not worse. Just look at Leon, one day an investment broker, the next day handing out pamphlets with a scarlet sun stamped on his forehead in Oglethorpe Square right next to Cousin Driskill, and that was nothing compared to Jim Jones in Guinea, or was it Guyana, or that rock guitarist in Waco. Waiting in the subways until the Rapture hit, you couldn't call it healthy. Certainly not hygienic. What did they use for bathrooms, she'd like to know, though it might not seem a respectful question with The End so nigh, still you had to ask yourself, at least she did, or had their shit vaporized into spikenard and saffron, calamus and cinnamon, being freed souls and all?

She wouldn't have minded, only she worried for John Joe, which was odd to say the least, but it was a fact, the worm had wriggled under her skin.

Amazing when she thought of it. Considering her reaction the first time she'd clapped eyes on him in poor Godwin's room that night the roof caught fire, *look what the cat drug in* was putting it mildly, though even then he'd seemed restful. But what she'd never have imagined was how useful he would prove, the man was born to cater.

Some change from Willie fucking D. Strange, no make that bizarre, to think how she'd been lost in lust fathoms-deep for that creep. That preening five-timing carwashing piece of nothing, well, piece of ass, it was true, but nothing else, although his hair, of course, but absolutely nothing else, yet she'd bitten her nails down to the knuckles for him, she had climbed walls, *Anna wants a little kiss*, she'd said that night of the cockfight; had actually spoken those words in front of God and everyone, why the earth hadn't swallowed her up she would never know, couldn't stomach her she guessed.

*Want gave tongue, and at her howl, Sin awakened with a growl*, whose was that, not Longfellow, but someone with an L, maybe Lowell, anyhow it didn't matter. Not now, when all she wanted was clean sheets, and beauty rest eternal. Maybe this unending heat had sucked out all her hormones or the deadness in her head going round and round in circles, *what's the point, what's the fucking point*, had robbed her pussy blind, but the thought of sex made her yawn, and its image made her heave.

Of course the lull wouldn't last, it never did. In a day or a month or a year the curse would be on her again, but at this minute, in this storage cupboard, all she wanted was a Fig Newton and the comfort of John Joe watching.

He did that nicely, just sat on the floor with his knees raised to let the trails of ants pass by undisturbed and looked at her out of his burnt eye as if she was a slide show when she walked naked and stretched and touched her toes with their broken blood vessels from too much hoofing in borrowed slippers, then dressed heself for *The Faking Boy* in Verse-o-Gram's best Becky Sharp, an ankle-length white satin gown cut high at the waist and low in the bosom, with scarlet sash and white satin pumps, and pirouetted for his approval, thinking *Wonder what he sees*, which struck her as strange, normally she would have thought *Wonder how I look*, but that was typical, even the first-person pronoun was going south on her, so she simply stated without posing, *The faking boy to the trap is gone, At the nubbing chit you'll find him; The hempen cord they have girded on, And his elbows pinned behind him. 'Smash my glim!' cries the reg'lar card, 'Though the girl you love betrays you, Don't split, but die both game and hard, And grateful pals shall praise you!'*

The accent was the main problem, she didn't sound proper Cockney, more Birmingham England and Birmingham Alabama mixed, a bit like Kate Root in fact, and flat as a pancake to boot, '*Smash my glim, smash my glim,*' she said like an MC trying out a balky microphone, testing, testing, '*The nubbing chit.*'

'I like that one,' said John Joe. 'It rhymes.'

'Anon's always do.'

'Having nothing to hide? Or on a hiding to nothing?'

She really couldn't say. Those were the kind of remarks he made sometimes she wondered if he was a few inches shy of a first down, *not the full shilling* as Yeats would say, but that was not the point. Mr Sheridan was waiting, she had a job of work to do, so she put on a bicycle cape over the white gown, stuffed the rope up her sleeve, '*The bolt it fell,*' she said, '*A jerk, a strain! The sheriffs fell asunder; The faking boy ne'er spoke again, For they pulled his legs from under. And there he dangles on the tree, That soul of love and bravery,* bravery, bravery . . .'

'*Soul of love and bravery,*' said John Joe.

'*And bravery,* right,' she said, staring in his face. As if it might hold the answer. As if he carried the next line around with him like a spare toothbrush, that's how befuddled she was, how lost and then found again, '*Oh, that such men should victims be,*' she said, '*Of law, and law's vile knavery.*'

Brinsley Sheridan, if that be his true name, had an address in Alphabet City on one of those barren blocks not yet gentrified that looked like a bombsite, East Berlin or Vienna at the end of World War II in an old newsreel, but the name on his bell read Handelman, and he looked like a Handelman when he opened his door four floors up, a small grey man in grey corduroys and a patched grey sweater, rimless glasses, wispy hair, a librarian's look.

His room was a high loft, with a handsome traverse beam that looked like solid oak, but its air was stale, thick with flies alive and dead. Books were piled high on tables and chairs and the floorboards, old books and new, paperbacks and cloth, *The Anatomy of Melancholy* on top one pile, *The Good Soldier* another, *Stay Me, Oh Comfort Me* a third, and on top of *Scaramouche* an unwashed plate of sausages and congealed baked beans turning green and phosphoroid that caused Anna to shiver when she shucked her black cape. 'Are you *The Faking Boy*?' she enquired.

'I have that honour,' said Brinsley Sheridan.

He sucked his teeth, they were yellow, this was not at all what she'd had in mind. When Verse-o-Gram had called her with the booking, she'd pictured a dining club, some pack of young bloods from the Ivy League perhaps, Elis or Crimsons on a toot, celebrating the Great Cham's birthday or whatever with a champagne breakfast like Johnson and Boswell when they watched the hanging at Tyburn from a rented room. A table of wannabe Garricks and Oliver Goldsmiths in wigs and stockings and velvet coats, taking snuff and passing the port. Not this desiccated slice of limburger finicking over her cleavage and petulant with it, sniffing between sucks. 'You're out of period,' he whined. 'I clearly stated pre-Regency.'

'Would a beauty spot help?'

'Lydia Languish, I said.'

'Or a fucking fan?'

'That attitude will get you nowhere,' said Brinsley Sheridan. 'Absolutely nowhere.'

Well, he was right of course, it wouldn't, it never had, or not since Charleston when she'd told that cop on King Street to take his filthy hands off her or he'd be wearing his dick for a bow-tie. But she mustn't blow another tip, she really mustn't, so she reined herself back, she simpered and took instruction, meek as any miss in school while Sheridan posed her beside a window bleared and smeared with toil. 'Relax,' he said.

'How about the rope?'

'What rope? I know nothing of any rope.' His voice was a flinch and he snatched the hemp from her hand, he tossed it aside like a thing unclean. 'I never requested a rope, I never,' he said. 'Rope never entered my mind.'

So humour him. Touch his wrist with shy fingertips, and make little gurgling sounds, perhaps they'd pass for contrition or at least compliance as she looked down across the patch of wasteland full of smouldering bonfines between a

Chinese laundry and a gutted bodega, and the three men crouched in the rubble behind a burnt-out car, shielded from the street but not from overhead when they took turns to drag at the pipe, and she tried to picture the gallows, it wasn't so hard. 'Now,' said Brinsley Sheridan. 'Now.'

'*The faking boy to the trap is gone.*'

'Not so fast. Take it slow.'

'*At the nubbing chit you'll find him.*'

'More expression. Give it more emotion.'

'*The hempen cord they have girded on.*'

'Correct,' said Sheridan.

He was behind her now and seemed calmed, there was no noise but a couple of books toppling and a light creaking like a rowboat, no movement but the flies on the window-pane, *Though the girl you love betrays you, Don't split, but die both game and hard*, said Anna, and heard a sigh, could it be a muffled sob at her back in its white satin gown cut low, her shoulders too knobby she knew, still, a graceful neck, *And grateful pals shall praise*, she said, sneaking a peek at the sausages in their furry mittens although she knew she shouldn't, she really shouldn't, and the sobbing sounded louder, across the street one of the men was on his feet reeling, shaking his fist, *The bolt it fell*, she said, and heard a gasp, a palpable croak, that caused her to turn her head like Persephone against her better judgment and see Sheridan strung up from the oak traverse, the rope so deeply bitten into his throat that only the tag-ends showed, his head a puce balloon in rimless glasses about to go Bang, and thrusting from his corduroys a modest contribution that looked like a red-headed goldfish till it jerked. 'Well, honestly,' Anna said, and snatched up her slicker to cover herself. 'Cut me down,' said Brinsley Sheridan from inside the puce balloon, but she couldn't stay, she really couldn't.

On the street, where she was running and running with no direction, a woman on a doorstoop laughed, and a dog darted out of a basement to snap at her ankles, a Jack Russell she thought, and the reeling man by the burnt-out car yelled something about cats, or it might have been carts, she wouldn't have liked to say for sure, and then she was inside a bar, she was inside some bar, then she wasn't running.

The man behind the beer pumps was a beefhead, he looked like a Pole. There was a dartboard. The tube in the Bud sign was failing, its light kept flickering. Somebody was smoking a pipe.

That dog was a Skye terrier.

Not a Jack Russell at all. A Skye.

She was almost sure of it.

The bar was long and dark, the sunlight only touched the first two stools, its brightness slanting was full of motes. 'You look Polish,' she said to the barman. 'Are you married?'

'Three children.'

'What's their names?'

'Caithleen, Sinead, Sean Timothy.'

'Are they safe?'

The snapshot the man pushed across the bar showed three kids who looked just like kids posed on a beach somewhere. To judge by the state of the boardwalk and the two bikers loafing against the railing it might have been Coney Island. 'Are you sure they're safe?' Anna asked.

'Caithleen has a scholarship,' the barman said, and he said a whole lot more, only she didn't follow him. Padgett, when he was her husband and raged at her, always used to claim she didn't give a fuck for other people, she was only concerned with herself. Absolutely true, and who in his right mind would blame her? 'I shot my boyfriend. I killed my true love,' she said.

The man was a barman, he didn't ask how or why, just poured her another shot and went back to polishing glasses. She was drinking mescal, she liked the thought of the mummified worm in every bottle, she liked the motes drifting in the sunlight down the bar, she was happy to be here.

But that was not the point; the point was something else. At Camp Pocahontas one morning, or least she thought it was morning, inside that vat of feathers it was never easy to tell, Chase had been sleeping with his head cushioned on her belly, maybe even dreaming for all she knew. And when she bent to kiss behind his ear and make him surface, when his face turned towards her, he looked just like a drowned man washing up. Or being dragged up. And the sickness in his eyes then, hauled back to the light, she had thought he would never forgive her.

His flesh not tan but burnished, like something wild, maybe dangerous. 'What do I owe you?' Anna asked.

'What can you afford?' the barman replied.

Back on the street she walked with her head down, her eyes fixed on the sidewalk, and didn't see the length of rope lying there until she'd almost tripped on it. There was somebody's face in glasses at Sheridan's window, but the sun was too bright in her eyes, she couldn't tell who owned it. The rope beneath her shoe felt soft and squishy, degutted. What the fuck, it was a souvenir, she put it in her pocket.

Was this stealing? She hoped so.

On that day in Savannah after Chase woke up she'd lain in the feathers with their colours like tropical diseases, trying to rest but no such luck, some man who couldn't play the trombone was playing the trombone across the boating pond, her brother Leon probably, and some other man was felling trees with an electric saw. She could not sleep and she could not lie awake with those undrowned eyes accusing her, she couldn't do a thing in fact but throw her clothes on and haul ass, ride her bike downtown to the City Market and Franklin Square, where the longshoremen waited for work under the live oaks outside First African Baptist and she drank Stingers at an outdoor café, getting quietly but efficiently loaded while eavesdropping on the two women at the next table, two large and stately dames in Carmen Miranda hats who knew a girl called Sistra whose man had cheated on her with her own mother, then stolen her Bingo money, and when Sistra caught up with him he was shooting craps behind the Paradise Club, where she took her pistol and shot him till no bullets were left, *And that, gentlemen*, she'd said then, *concludes the entertainment for today.*

Anna's sentiments exactly. Rolling uptown on the Broadway Local in the rush hour she didn't know what she'd been doing, she only knew she was done. No more Verse-o-Gram, no more Zenaide from Zonguldak, no more faking boys of any stripe. *No more free lunch*, she thought, and let herself go limp, held upright by the crush of passengers, so that when the doors opened she was swept out like a rubber dinghy, borne away resistless on the tide.

This was easy, this was not so terrible. *On roars the flood* came to her mind, John Clare when he was in the asylum. *On roars the flood – all restless to be free*, she was carried up the stairway and over Broadway, *Like trouble wandering to eternity*, up the block and inside the Zoo where Kate Root sat, her bulldog's chin resting on her fist, staring out at nothing that Anna could see with that new pert and bird-eyed look of hers, and scratching her ankle with fingernails freshly painted, all moist and gleaming.

Fuchsia, no less.

Wearied, Anna looked for some place to sit and rest a while, but there was no free stool, that pearl-pied cockatiel was perched on one and a pair of flesh-pink tights was draped across the other, there seemed no room to rest her bones anywhere, so she started to head upstairs to her own room, though that seemed weak, that seemed like giving in.

The day she'd had, she couldn't stand just to crawl away whipped. Even if she was. And something else held her back as well, she couldn't think what. 'Is something different?' she asked. 'Did you move the cages around?'

'The TV is off.'

Of course it was. No *Macmillan and Wife*, or whatever was on at this hour, not a sound but the snakes and birds, it made the place seem unnatural. Spooked, almost. Then, looking at Kate, she had the oddest sensation, for a second she almost liked her, she felt a connection somehow.

This made no sense, it must have been after-shock, a form of whiplash. It wasn't what she wanted, God forbid, and she did her best to fight it down. But she was not able. Right at this minute, she lacked the strength. Some lunatic urge to share and give, fatal words, had got her by the throat, and she dug out the noosed rope, she tossed it on the counter, she spread her hands in abdication. 'Take it,' she said. 'It's yours.'

# Fourth

That last night in St Martinville when Mary said goodbye, Kate had been in the worst mood. For months
she and Charley Root had dragged the back roads of
Louisiana, peddling postcards and leftover scented candles
out of the back of a broken-down Plymouth. Business was
lousy, prospects were nil, and only this afternoon she'd
caught Charley Root mixing up a batch of Amarillo Virgin
Tears in the bathroom sink.

She had screamed out loud. Not at the act itself, which
seemed almost routine by now. But at the moment she'd
discovered him, he had looked back at her across his shoulder
with exactly the same expression he'd worn that first night
in Tarpon Springs, the time he'd got stuck zipping up his
corset. The look of an ancient tart surprised at her toilet, at
once sheepish and coquettish.

Kate could not endure this, not a second time. So she'd
screamed, and punched at him with closed fists, and in return
he had scratched her face with open claws. For a few seconds
they had struggled and thrashed together, two she-cats in a
hissy fit, and then Charley Root had broken free. Snatching
up his beaker of Virgin Tears, he made to throw it in her
face like acid. Then he stopped himself. It was money, after
all.

They were staying at the Acadia Motel, a mile outside city

limits, having driven in that afternoon from Eunice and Ville Platte. St Martinville was the small town where Evangeline had once met her lover at an oak tree in some poem, but now she manufactured hot sauce and the air was peppery with capsicum. It stung Kate's eyes, made them hot and red.

An old child's swing was strung between two locust trees in the motel yard, and she rode it till the stinging stopped. Warped and rotted as it was, with its rope half eaten away, the swing's motion was hopelessly skewed. Instead of a smooth pendulum, it described a broken circle, dragged Kate at every angle but true.

At one edge of the circle was a dusty bush with sharp red spikes, she never knew its name, but the branches were like chariot spokes wreathed in thorns, and each time that the swing's course brought Kate around, these thorns galled her legs, her bare knees.

At first she tried to keep away. She drew her legs up to her chest, she shrank back in modesty. But with each circuit her efforts slackened. Normally, pain was not her pleasure, that was the last thing she sought. This evening was not normal, though. The image of Charley Root's hips flirting, plus the pepper tormenting her, made her reckless, and she started to push herself forward. To offer herself, allowing the spikes to cut and lash at her, till her legs were riddled with puncture marks.

Blindly seeking, she let herself imagine how the blood would taste, salt and sweet at the same time, and how it would feel like balm on her burning eyelids. So then she swung harder, she bore down so fiercely that one thorn tore the flesh above her ankle. Her eyes flew open at the shock, and Mary was sitting in a live oak across the yard.

It was dusk, and the girl was wearing a dark dress the same colour as the light, so that only the whiteness of her face and hands was clearly visible, and the radiance of her eyes. That radiance was dimmed by grieving, however. For a flash Kate thought it was her own doing, and she was mortified. To be caught defiling a bush, it was obscene, she couldn't imagine what had possessed her. Then the pepper stopped burning her eyes, she could see clearly, and she realized that guilt was irrelevant, this sorrow went way past shame.

The girl had come to go, it was as simple as that. Out of the kindness of her heart, she hadn't wanted to leave Kate without a word or sign, just dump her, but the basic message boiled down to the same. The Virgin Tears had been the last straw, probably, or maybe she'd already made up her mind. Too much tackiness, one too many betrayals, she just couldn't stand the stench any more, and who could blame her? Not Kate.

The parting was not dramatic, that was never Mary's style. She simply sat in the branches of the great oak that was draped in Spanish moss, looking down across the yard at Kate now motionless on the swing, the dusty bush with its torn and ruined red spikes, the tufts of parched grey grass that surrounded it, a couple of chickens pecking in the dirt, and an old blind dog playing dead, its eyes milky-white with cataracts. And she spoke her mind. Though she rarely talked, preferred to listen, she started to tell Kate everything. *Don't fall in love with suffering, it is the deadliest disease*, she said, and that was just the start, there was plenty more where that came from, you could tell.

Only Kate was not fated to hear it. Before Mary had the chance to say another word, the jukebox started up inside the motel bar, an eruption of raw noise so violent that the chickens flew away squawking, even the blind dog raised his head.

It was Charley Root, of course. She didn't need to catch him in the act to recognize his touch, or feel the malice that made him punch up an Elvis, *Are You Lonesome Tonight?* Across the yard she could see Mary's lips moving, but the only words that reached her were *Does your memory stray To a bright, sunny day?*, and the dog rose up, began to waddle towards her where she still sat, as if paralysed in the swing. A repulsive, flea-ridden creature, it was, slobbering and snuffling with its white eyes staring at nothing, the furthest thing from Pompey, and it must have smelled the blood on Kate's legs, it stopped to sniff, then it started to lick. *Is your heart full of pain?* Elvis sang, and usually this was Kate's favourite song, she could listen to it all night, but right now it sounded foolish, it was ruining everything. With every line the girl's image in the oak tree got fainter, more translucent, till Kate could see clear through her dress and white hands to darkness. The dog's tongue was rough as sandpaper on her shins, it smelled like swamp, and its milk-white stare stung worse than pepper burning. *Will you come back again?* Elvis was singing, not knowing what he did, and Kate couldn't stand it, she shut her eyes. Just for an instant, hardly more than a blink, but when she looked again the girl was gone.

There was only the gathering dark then, and this useless apology for a swing. When the number ended, the jukebox went dead, the chickens resumed their pecking, the blind dog waddled out of sight, and Charley Root stood backlit in the bar-room doorway, glugging Dixie beer from the bottle. He had won.

Next morning Kate woke up sick. Glandular fever, the doctor said, and sent her to the hospital in Lafayette, where she hoped to decease but failed.

She stayed there seven weeks, which was a blessing, she

needed the rest, but nothing much happened until the night before her release. For supper she had mushroom cream soup and crackers and spam salad, creamed chicken with cream of spinach, lime jello with whipped cream and a cherry on top, then she fell fast asleep and when she woke, it was dead of night.

Somebody was rattling.

At first she thought it was the man in the next bed who was dying of something he couldn't pronounce, but he was peaceably snoring. Besides, the rattle didn't come from the west, it hung directly above her own bed. A crackling, a dry choking, that seemed to float in aimless circles like a plastic boat in a bath and whenever she tried to pin it down it bobbed away on a tide of ripples.

This disturbance kept her awake. She needed rest for her nerves, she wasn't feeling so good. Truth to tell, she might have eaten too much. All that cream lay on her stomach like dead weight, she felt bloated. Then she started to suffer cramps. Her guts were growling, she had to use the bathroom, but her bed was so cosy, so warm, it seemed ungrateful to leave it. To put her feet on the cold slick tiles and go walking in the dark. With that rattle on the loose.

For the longest time she lay with her eyes shut, willing both the cramps and the croak to leave her be, but it was no use, neither one of them would shift. So she set off down the ward, doubled over against the spasms. And the rattle travelled with her. It wafted above her head like a blasphemer's fake halo, chattering and choking, and no word Kate knew had the power to silence it.

Charley Root called bathrooms The Necessary, and just this once he wasn't wrong. Reaching safety, she opened the door a crack, squeezed in sideways and turned the lock double-quick, but the rattling passed through wood as easily as air, it never paused for breath. If anything, it sounded louder and more aggressive. In this enclosed space it seemed to echo, and the echo was mocking, deliberately offensive. So cocksure, in fact, that the cramps were intimidated and faded, and Kate was sick instead.

She shot her supper chapter and verse. Soup and salad, creamed chicken and spinach, lime jello and the cherry on top, until she was vacated, utterly forsaken, staring down into the bowl at what had once been part of herself, with the rattle peering over her shoulder. Kneeling beneath it, she could feel its breath hot with triumph crawling on her neck, its croak now almost a crow, and she knew its name.

Of course she did. She'd known it all along, only she hadn't liked to admit it, not even to herself. But now she spoke the name out loud, and laid a curse as she did so, rising out of her cowering to flush it away, the name and its rattle and her supper dispatched together in one great whoosh. So she was freed. She went back to her bed and slept the sleep of the purged for twelve hours, with no dreams, and the next day Charley Root came to collect her, he took her from this place.

They lived in Jeanerette then, no more travelling and no more huckstering, the Studebaker stayed in the driveway. Kate was not yet sixteen, she was just a schoolgirl. Elvis was in the army, and there was a boy called Acie Dotson that had the cutest smile, and the Club Why Not was a few miles up Highway 90. Only Charley Root wouldn't let her go there, and he fired an airgun at Acie Dotson when Acie hung over the garden fence too long. Even though he was a sick man these days, poor old Charley. The veins in his legs swole up and clotted, fungus sprouted in his lungs, and he couldn't catch his breath, he kept choking. Rattling, you might say, till one morning in The Necessary, reading the baseball box-scores, he reached behind him, flushed, and dropped down stiff as a board.

If that wasn't murder, nothing was.

Or manslaughter, anyway. But Kate had felt no guilt, and she felt none now, sitting in the Zoo in front of the Zenith and scratching idly at the spot above her ankle where the thorns had scarred her in St Martinville, it had been itching her all day.

Talk about rattling, Pearl kept shaking and twanging the bars of her cage like some wino in a drunk tank, and she'd stirred up the other birds, the whole Zoo was in uproar. When Kate walked the aisles, trying to restore order, she felt herself tumbled on a drowning tide. The sweating walls, the hanging plants wet against her face, the gas heaters grinning in their corners, the funeral scent of the orchids, the clamour of the macaws and conures, the hissing of the pinesnakes, and the slurp like swamp underfoot – this place was a nuthouse, she saw, and was surprised that she'd never noticed before.

The tumult was partly her own fault. All day she had been jangling, a bag of jump. Couldn't seem to settle to any task, up and down the aisles a dozen times an hour, frittering and futzing, sweating like a pig. Though pigs did not sweat, she didn't believe they knew how. But sweating bullets, say, or communion wine. She couldn't even sit still for Billie and Bo, the storyline made no sense. To tell the truth, these soaps were a little silly at times, they got on her nerves. Which got on the animals' nerves in turn. Then the air was full of knives.

She knew that she ought to calm herself, but where was calm to be found? Every place she looked, she found mere anarchy. Anna Crow in a wheelchair, wrapped in blankets and feathers. That boy Wilfred run through by a subway train. One customer with a gas leak in his basement, and a second with creeping mould in her silver fox, and a third stone-deaf inside a year. John Joe Maguire and a saucepan of boiling milk.

What staggered her most was the sheer profusion. After all these years in deep freeze, to be flooded by so many pictures, such a riot of images all at once, she simply couldn't keep up. Seeing was like any other sport, you needed to stay in shape. If you didn't, you wound up sun-blind.

There seemed no place to shelter, or even to catch her breath. When she snuck upstairs to Ferdousine's room for a slice of Dundee cake, she had not taken two bites before she saw the wedding feast again, the pomegranate trees and the peacocks, the aghound with his hennaed hair, those flabby yellow buttocks like weeping Dutch cheeses beneath their *shalwar kameez*, and the cake went down the wrong way, she started choking.

It wasn't decent, really. More to the point, it was not professional. If she'd had the least sense of responsibility, she would have been ashamed of herself. But she hadn't, and she wasn't. Somewhere down the line she seemed to have misplaced the gift of astonishment. Pictures that would have shocked her once, or left her stricken with guilt, now seemed like free entertainments.

She felt a sort of drunkenness. In the Zoo she sold a canary to a priest, and saw him naked except for his dog-collar, shackled to his bed at the ankles and wrists, while a lady in PVC thighboots tickled him with a feather duster. The vision was so spellbinding that she couldn't make change for watching, and she ended up blowing the sale.

Blew it to smithereens and back, and she didn't care. Two minutes after the priest walked out, a Rasta with waist-length dreadlocks took his place. Kate saw him tumbling in free fall from a stage into a mosh-pit, there to suffer a broken back. But all she could think was how beautiful he looked in flight, and how his dreadlocks, caught by the arc lights, shone like snakes.

What had she been fearing all these years? Why fight so hard to stay blind? By the time she closed the Zoo for the day she felt as though she'd run a marathon in concrete boots, she could hardly keep her head up or her seeing eyes open, she was lathered, dizzied, spent, and she couldn't stop humming *Stuck on You*.

*Don't fall in love with suffering*. That had been sound advice, she should have minded it. When she locked herself inside her bedroom, and started to prepare herself for Wilfred's lesson, she dug deep in her closet and brought out a Bird of Paradise. It wasn't the same costume she'd worn for Charley Root, of course, she had outgrown that long ago. But Charley Root was not the only blade she'd stood to in her time. Years after his death, she had found herself back in Florida again, adrift in Sarasota, and she had met a knife named Eddie.

He wasn't certified, only an apprentice, but he threw a nifty True-Bal bolo, 15-inch axe, handle-grip, you could see that he had potential.

And Kate had been negotiable. Since St Martinville and the Acadia Motel she had been marking time. A year in England with Fred Root to get her health back, more or less, and ever since she'd been aimless. Working in fields and factories, knocking down pay checks, nothing more. She kept drudging up and down the Gulf Coast. Canning peas in Pensacola, shucking oysters in Mobile, flea-marketing in Bay St Louis. Picking pepper out of flyshit. But she could find nowhere to settle and not a scrap of function. She had no skills, no value. No friends, and she wanted none. After Mary, all other girl-talk fell flat.

She took it for granted then that she would never see again. According to Monsignor Beebe, visions of the Virgin always came with an exclusive contract. You saw what you were given to see, for as long as you were found worthy. But once the engagement was over, the gift of sight withdrawn, you were retired for life.

It was an anticlimax. In Sarasota, when she wasn't busy waitressing, Kate either got drunk or got laid. But she wasn't much good at either. The cheap burn of alcohol that your body didn't want. And the cheaper burn of sex, ditto. So she took to loitering without intent near St Armand's Circle, on the way to Lido Beach, and that was where she saw the sign.

*The Sarasota School of Impalement*, it said, and when she stepped inside she found herself in a converted bowling alley, now operating as an academy for blades.

The walls were hung with portraits of the masters, past and present. Frank Dean and Paul LaCross, Sylvester Braun and the great Skeeter Vaughn. The Gibsons, who brought the first Wheel of Death to America. And Adolfo Rossi, the matchless Argentine, who used to split an apple or potato on the back of his wife's neck with a customized machete. So far so promising, but the operation proved sloppy. Target boards hung crooked where the bowling lanes had been, and the students threw unmatched knives. There was no sawdust to keep the grips dry, no alum or brine or even horsepiss like Charley Root had used, in case of cuts. *Amateurs*, was Kate's thought, and she was turning to leave when Eddie appeared.

He had good hands, nice and slow. Prehensile fingers, perfect balance, he had all the makings. They drank beer in a tavern on Orange Street, where the jukebox played Merle

Haggard. *It's Not Love (But It's Not Bad)*, the song was, and Kate always could take a hint.

He needed a partner, she needed exercise. So they had a new Bird of Paradise run up, and they started working a few shows locally, Nokomis and Gulfport, Zephyr Hills, even Tarpon Springs for sickness' sake. Strictly small potatoes, but it beat working. Until that night in Dade City when Eddie threw a triple-time combo from behind his back, *zip, Zip, ZIP*, and in the rush of blades Kate saw a cat on Main Street, not black but tabby, a tom, run over by a beer truck outside Sylvester's Saloon.

So much for Monsignor Beebe. In the morning she had a new business card printed, *Your Future Is Your Fortune, Kate Root Sees All. Strict Confidentiality, Competitive Fees*, and the Bird of Paradise went feet-first into her closet.

It looked a little sickly now, a bird off its feed. All these years out of daylight had given it a jailhouse pallor, and a few of its feathers had moulted, but the main body had held intact. Not that she was planning to work in costume tonight. Live targets on a first lesson were not recommended, even with padded knives. Even so, she had a yen to try it on. Just to see if it still fitted. Whether or not it would do.

Paradise came in thirteen sections, two each for elbows, shoulders, hips, flanks, breasts and throat and one last for the topknot, but throwing knives below the waist had been illegal in Kate's day, so the costume had no legs, only flesh-tan tights so riddled with ladders and bagged at the knees that she couldn't use them, she had to leave her legs nude.

One glance in the mirror, and she saw that wouldn't do. Her real flesh was too white and pink, much too torn to pass muster in any light. So she set to work with paint and brushes, powder and lotion, until she was sunset orange from ankle to crotch. Then she took a pair of eyebrow tweezers and plucked those long red hairs like weeds that were forever sprouting on the scar above her ankle. Though she knew it was a vanity. A little pathetic, really. Still, a girl had to be well-groomed.

Perhaps that would stop the itching, though nothing would stop the heat. Of all the broiling days in this killing field of a summer, today seemed the most brutal. The last day in creation that you'd choose to put on plumage. But then choice had nothing to do with this. It was an affair of honour.

Twenty pounds if not a ton the feathers seemed to weigh when she started to pin them in place. First an undercoat of dyed chicken and turkey, then blue jay and thrush at the hips, seagull in the flanks, and rising slowly, cardinal over the breasts, canary and greenfinch draped across the shoulders, peacock eyes of course for the headdress. And as the design took shape, the weight ceased to bother her. She no longer noticed the heat or the sweat rolling thick like sludge on her belly, down her spine. All that she felt was herself transformed. Age and hurt and damage wiped clean, and this high-flying bird in their place.

Orange-winged amazon at the elbows, white-eyed conure at the collarbones, and a spray of pied-pearl cockatiel, God forgive her, at the throat. Then she was completed, and she fluffed herself full, she flapped her wings, she took one look in the mirror.

She saw Mother Goose.

A stout party of undetermined sex, disguised as a woman with pantomime hips and a false bosom, disguised as an item of poultry.

Half an hour to get dressed, five seconds to strip. Birds flew helter-skelter through the bedroom, dashed themselves against the windows, such a fluttering and thrashing that the other birds downstairs in the Zoo took fright and started racketing again. The record player in Ferdousine's room was playing *Tea for Two*, and the figure inside the mirror now was a plucked chicken, a Purdue oven-stuffer with a few stray feathers still clinging to its pelt, a bit of fluff wafting from one ear.

God grant her strength.

Or failing God, brandy. She helped herself to a tot of Ferdousine's Courvoisier that she kept in an old bottle of Magie Noir for extremities. The burn of expensive alcohol didn't feel much better to her than cheap, but it settled the stomach, it was dynamite for gas. Fred Root had told her that, so it must be true. *Medicinal purposes*, she thought in his rusty voice, and she saw her horse Baloney Breath munching oats in his stall. His coat looked thick and glossy, his eyes were sharp. For an old hobbled nag, he looked in fine shape, she wouldn't have minded a ride.

Nothing too violent, no showing-off. Just an easy lope through woods or beside a stream perhaps, that would have set her up a treat. But this was not the right moment, of course. She didn't have any clothes on.

To work effectively with knives, she ought to be dressed, she needed to look like business. She brought out the green tweed skirt, the sensible shoes and starched blouse that she'd worn to poor Godwin's funeral, they made her look like a schoolmistress, a woman who didn't jangle. She popped a few Tums for safety. Left off her girdle. And crossed herself. When she went downstairs to the Zoo, transformed, none of the animals knew her. Or if they did, they gave no sign.

The boy Wilfred came dressed like a flamenco dancer in black matador pants with a silk sash, a frilly white shirt and black satin vest. 'You're late,' said Kate, though he wasn't, and led him through the velvet curtain into the barbershop. 'Let me see your hands,' she said.

As he held them straight out in front of him, palms down like a schoolboy being checked for dirty nails, Kate caught a whiff of Christian Brothers. Or Holy Martyrs, that was right. One of the sisters had big red hands, fit for a lumberjack. Which was more than you could say for these dainty items, hardly fit for a poodle-clipper. Slender girlish fingers, freshly manicured, and a pampered child's span. Skeeter Vaughn he wasn't. Not even Charley Root. 'Are these the best you've got?' she asked, but he only goggled at her, he seemed to be struck dumb.

Now that she took him in whole, she saw a village idiot. The flash of his costume had fooled her at first, also the fading light in the Zoo. But here, by the spinning light of the barber's pole, he looked a mess. The arrowhead on the bridge of his nose glowed livid; a nerve kept jumping at his temple. Bad posture and bloodshot eyes, dragging feet – he looked like a man on his way to get fried.

Best to take no notice, Kate thought. Just carry on with his lesson, as if nothing at all was amiss. She straightened his slumped shoulders, slapped at the bow of his spine. Then she pushed back the cowlick that drooped soft and glossy as a raven's wing above his smeary eyes. 'That hair'll have to go,' she said.

Her fingers rubbed harshly at Wilfred's scalp, roughing him up, while he suffered her. She'd never learned to cut hair properly, it was one of those courses she kept meaning to take but couldn't ever be bothered quite. In any case, improper cutting was more fulfilling. It left her free to let the scissors snip and hack as they liked, and not be distracted from the skull beneath.

Wilfred's was undersized but well-formed, deficient in Veneration, Sublimity, Mirthfulness and Conjugality, prodigal in Self-Esteem and Adhesiveness. No surprises there, but her true target like any phrenologist's lay lower, more protected, in the shallows behind his ears.

The moment that she touched it, she saw him stretched on a brass bed surrounded by duck hunters, his skin blue and green like a fish seen underwater.

Odd way to carry on; a little disturbing somehow. But she had no time to ponder. That itchy spot on her ankle was giving her gyp again. Without a thought for modesty, she raised her leg and gave such a scratch that she almost drew blood. As she did so, she felt the boy shudder, and an odour like burnt Melba toast, or maybe it was scones, came to her.

Mysteries, she hated them, they stole your soul. In her perplexity she had no taste to test him further. His Alimentiveness and Continuity could remain between him and his manufacturer, she'd seen enough.

Admitted, the boy's haircut was not her best work. One side had been cropped convict-short, while the other remained in tufts, carved seemingly at random. Better not to show him a mirror right off the bat, Kate judged, and laying down her scissors, she reached for the knives.

The shooting-gallery shape of the barbershop was ideal for the purpose. She had nailed the target to the far wall, with her spare mattress as a backdrop. In a perfected world, of course, the target would be custom-made by Crouch, something on the lines of Larry Cisewski's Devil's Doorway. But Crouch, as usual, was off gallivanting, so she'd had to make do with a toilet seat.

Consider it a horseshoe.

At least it was soft wood, absorbent. A worse problem was the spinning light, which created a whirlpool effect, a shifting pool of shadows. Still, this was only Lesson One. Subtleties of texture and lighting would keep. Right now, all that mattered was making a start.

Fifteen feet from the target, Kate placed the boy in throwing stance, the Address Position, with his left foot forward and his right drawn back, sunk into a half-crouch. Her hands moved briskly on his shoulders and spine, his butt, trying to set him correctly. But his body refused to be moulded. The harder she tugged and twisted him, the more he resisted her. Even gentleness failed to control him.

As a last resort, she gave her Introduction to Impalement speech. Back in Florida, when she used to give seminars, it had been considered a model of its kind. 'Any determined sportsman who truly wants to become proficient in the ancient art of impalement needs only to commence with the ability to throw a baseball, cast a fishing rod, crack a whip, or toss a playful dart,' she began. A few casual words that never failed to put novices at their ease. Only this time they failed utterly. The boy hardly even seemed to hear them. Just hung where she had placed him, tensed and rigid. Wound so tight that he couldn't have thrown his own shadow, never mind a Harvey McBurnette.

Impatience flailed at her; whirled her into dizziness. To think that she'd passed this whole day and the endless night before in delirium, climbing walls and spitting nails. Been bombarded by pomegranate trees and peacocks, weeping yellow buttocks, women in chains, Rastamen with dreadlocks like flying kingsnakes. Debased and flogged herself, let herself be turned into Mother Goose. And all for what? This shivering, snivelling turd on toast.

This apology for a blade.

Still, she would not admit defeat, surrender wasn't her style. 'The science of knife-throwing is constructed and predicated on one elementary physical act,' she continued, and when this too failed to get a response, she grabbed the boy by his shoulder. 'One elementary act,' she said, and gave him a shake. 'To wit?'

'Don't know.'

'Letting go,' said Kate.

In the morning Willie D had woken a healed man. As if he'd been sick with a fever and now the disease had left him. When the train pulled into his room at first light, it hadn't rolled and tumbled him, or crushed him under its wheels like it had in his affliction, but raised him up refreshed. He'd only slept a few hours, but he felt made new.

Not only did he feel primed to take on Kate Root, he was ready to conquer worlds. *Swallow a pound of pig iron and spit it out as razor blades*. Deacon Landry said that.

The same as any other sickness, now that he was freed of it, it seemed mostly fuss about nothing. He had been temporarily indisposed, that was all. Put it down to the heat.

That's not to say he wasn't nervous. Of course he was. Like any other performer before a major premiere, his stomach disputed him, and his mouth was sandpaper dry, there was a burning behind his eyes. Moving at random through Ivana's room, his balance felt wrong, and he had to watch himself every step, in case he veered off course, stumbled over a stray duck hunter.

But edginess was no bad thing; not as much. He had seen boxers in their dressing rooms before the Golden Gloves, and they were like men with St Vitus's dance. Twitching and jiggling, running to the bathroom, punching the walls. Anyone who didn't know better would have said they were terror-blind. So many pigs to slaughter. And anyone would have been dead wrong. Ready to rumble, that's all those fighters were. Hot to trot.

Likewise with Willie. The way he felt, everything that he had suffered in the past month had been down to training. Roadwork, sparring, getting whipped into shape. What was that dumb Jane Fonda phrase? *No pain, no gain.* Well, just maybe it wasn't so dumb after all. He had been subjected to hell on earth. Stripped naked, half-broken on the wheel. But he had come through. He was on the other side now, and if you wanted his humble opinion, not a thing alive could touch him.

What gave him such certainty? It was obvious. Everything that went down in the Zoo last night had been a dead giveaway. The style that snake had stared at him, challenging. And the way he had responded. Not cowed, in no way abashed, but rising up redoubled. Raw to conquer worlds. Take on any species of red hair that dared come at him, and bring it to order, to heel. And Kate Root, of course, she'd felt that. Sensed the change. The moment she came down the stairs and inside the room, brandishing that gun, she'd known him for another man. No pushover, no more. No shape or size of weak stuff, but a contender. A horse.

She hadn't even tried to face him down. What would have been the point, when they both knew the truth? The way her hand flew to her throat, clutching at her nightdress. Her face and throat all flushed, and the gun spinning from her fingers, you couldn't fake stuff like that. Nor the look she gave him when she ducked behind the counter, and handed him the knives. Not looking through him, no. Not as if she saw nothing, and there was nothing to see. But as if they were joined somehow. Allies, or partners in crime. 'Seven

207

o'clock,' she'd said. Or whispered, to be exact. And Willie was set free.

Looking back now, all the way from the morning after, it seemed almost humorous to think. To picture that a few hours ago he had lived and died over three red hairs, used, shopworn, not even clean. It just went to show.

Part of him was tempted to walk away. Leave the old trout flat, wham bam thank you ma'am. That would have been the percentage move, no question; not a man at Chez Stadium would have blamed him. Still, he didn't like to be discourteous. The true Man of Power did not run. Didn't even jog.

Besides, the story was unfinished. Not to be vindictive, but he had a score to settle. The image of Kate Root in pink tights and a whalebone corset, pinned helplessly against a wall while he buzzed knives like hornets round her ears, teased him still. It was the least he deserved.

Of course, he'd need new shoes.

Picture a black boot.

A black boot, calf-length, in Verona leather. A black Verona boot, matte finish, with stacked heel and a tapered toe of timeless elegance terminating in a blocked wedge and decorated with a strong yet tasteful motif. A classical black boot embossed with a silver blade.

Of course, it would take finance. This time around, he would need to earn his feets the old-fashioned way; anything less would be bad karma. So he sprinkled his toes with sandalwood talc. To lend him intestinal fortitude while he suffered Mrs Muhle.

This day she prepared a simple but nutritious lunch of Sauteed Chicken Livers with Blueberry Vinegar, the tart fruity sauce a perfect complement to the richness of the livers. 'One pound livers halved, trimmed and patted dry,

208

four tablespoons sweet butter, four scallions including green tops chopped, vinegar, crème fraîche, and a generous pinch each of ground ginger, allspice, mace, nutmeg and cloves,' said Mrs Muhle.

Her plateful cost her $300.

And afterwards, when Willie walked into A Shoe Like It, Mariella neither smiled nor flinched, merely bowed her head. Allowed the long black veil of her hair to shelter her. 'What do you have in the way of halfboots?' he asked.

'Would that be cash or theft?'

The exact design he had visioned was not in stock; no silver blades came to hand. Instead, he was forced to settle for a retro Beatle. The toes were too pointed, the heels too Cuban, and the leather was mere Padua, but at least they were not disfigured by buckles. Leaning forward to try them on, he smelled the bottled horses running wild in Mariella's hair, and he felt himself rise and swell, stiffen.

That was when he knew he was truly saved. But he did not take advantage. For this moment it was enough to feel Mariella's hands on him, her touch like answered prayers, and to breathe in that smell of virgin shoe leather which was the sweetest aroma in creation.

According to Deacon Landry, the dancer Bojangles had had his coffin lined with stage shoes that he didn't get around to wearing in life. They were his conception of eternity's scent; of paradise.

A thought like that, it brought you up short, forced you to take stock of deeper things. 'Do you want to wear those right now?' Mariella asked.

'Ask rather,' said Willie D, ' "Do they want to wear me?" '

The manner the girl looked at him then, you would have thought he had proposed a suicide pact. Position one, mouth open wide; position two, mouth open wider. Obviously, the spiritual plane was beyond her compass, she couldn't begin to follow him there.

'It's a concept,' he explained, off-hand. 'I get them all the time.'

Which was the truth. When he was firing on all cylinders, his brain was an 007, licensed to kill. Sister Teresa with the moustache had told him once, if he didn't slow his smartness down he would do someone an injury. Maybe even himself. 'If you be sick, your own thoughts make you sick,' she'd said. But that was just her ignorance. Being smart had a trick to it, same as anything else.

*Keep It Simple*, was all.

There was an old movie, he couldn't remember the title, but some of the lines had always stuck in his mind, they went right to the heart of everything. 'Just don't get too complicated,' this character said. 'When a man gets complicated, he gets unhappy. And when he gets unhappy, he runs out of luck.'

Someone should carve those words in marble someplace.

But enough philosophy. What signified here was practice; strictly business. His new boots in street action proved tough and rigorous, yet bracing; in a nutshell, hard but fair. There was a jut to their strut worlds away from the armadillo's languorous glide. It made him feel like a conquistador. A warrior born, and he carried the knives to prove it.

$73.26, after tax, still nestled in his hip pocket, but Willie didn't take a taxi uptown, he walked. To let the Beatles get used to him, and he to them. To work up a full partnership, with no dirty secrets, and nothing held back.

All the way up Broadway he felt rabid, scraped raw, but exulting; a thoroughbred on the muscle. Every bitch he passed, it seemed, had legs up to her armpits. *Long, lissome and luciferous* – what man had said that? With their hard butts and tip-tilted tits, creamed butter. And the pussies, oh those pussies; those sleek sugar slits. Jailbait jamming on the crosswalks, the green light meant Go.

At the corner of 42nd, a girl in cut-offs saw his boots, and she flashed him her scars. Razor slashes, they looked like, and maybe a cigarette burn or two.

If there was one thing that lit Willie's candle, always had done, it was a quality deformity, and these looked aces high. Still he kept on keeping on. Kept his mind on the blowfish, and nobody else. Because she was his. Yes, she was. Because.

Only when he came in sight of the Chemical Bank clock, and Sweeney's, and Blanco y Negro, did his guts start to lurch again. And what man would dare to downrate him for that? This was no easy riding, after all; it was his life's destination. *Kill or be killed*, as the saying said. Confidence was one thing, arrogance another. Like at the Golden Gloves. Any fighter who stepped in the ring, let himself go naked under those lights, and he wasn't aware that he might be carried out in a bodybag – that wasn't bravery; that was just bone ignorance.

Outside the OTB, he paused and tried to whistle, but only dead air came out. So he made a stab at a ditty. *We Are the World*, he tried to sing. Forget it.

Ten minutes to seven, five, he walked round the block, then round again. One word like a tin hammer kept jarring on the off-beat. *Love*, it sounded like. That could not be right.

Kate Root at the moment she opened the door reminded him of someone he couldn't place. Not Elvis, not George Washington. The Statue of Liberty, that was it. Which made no sense. Realistically, they didn't look blood related, not even second cousins. But there was something in her attitude.

Big shoulders squared, head high, a hint of a sneer. 'You're late,' she said.

And Willie D was powerless. Straight back to square one. Scrub all that stuff about the Golden Gloves, and warriors ready to rumble, he was paralysed. Never laid a glove on her, no contest. Under that flat, dead stare of hers, he was done before he'd begun.

At one glance, the night before was swept away. Maybe Osain's feast had drugged his senses, or maybe it had been a trick of light. Whatever, he'd been fooled. There was no partnership here, there never would be. *You're in thrall, that's all.* Sandman Ames said that.

Couldn't get his breath. His feet trapped in the retro-Beatles felt limp and slimy as slugs, and when he held his hands out for Kate to inspect he had the sickest hunger to be found wanting. Have his knuckles rapped with a ruler, collect red weals on his sweating palms. Get his ass kicked even.

Any excuse to weep.

But one thing he hadn't noticed before: the hollow at the pit of her throat. A smooth round like a shallow cup, and there was a smear of juice in it, looked like it would taste sweet. Snake out your tongue, take a lick, a man would be refreshed. 'That hair'll have to go,' Kate said, and he was laid sprawling in the barber's chair, she had the freedom of his head. The Harvey McBurnettes in their wine-red morocco case were sitting snug on his lap, a weight warm as a fat cat, he could almost hear the purring. 'Sublimity,' Kate Boot said.

Absolute surrender. In this place and time, it didn't feel disgraceful; if anything, it felt like a reprieve. Then she took a step backwards and propped her foot on the wrought-iron rest, she scratched her leg like a ten-dollar whore. And there was only skin. A white patch raked by scratches. Dead ground, where no hairs grew.

And after that? Willie couldn't say exactly. Could not have sworn on oath. For the moment he was too stunned to compute. Just sat enthroned as if stuffed and mounted, until the woman shunted him to the floor. The old trout.

Her hands were all over his body, moving him and turning him, kneading him like play-dough. Talking at him, words he heard clearly but had no power to obey. 'Constructed and predicated,' she said, and a knife was in his right hand, she was positioning his fingers along the handle. 'One elementary act,' she said, and she pushed his arm upsides his head, the blade pointed straight ahead.

Willie smelled Brasso.

Half the night he'd sat up with these knives, cleansing them of rust and grime, scouring them with steel wool, shining, buffing, honing; and now the sharp, goatish tang of metal polish acted on him like smelling salts. His mind crept back to him, he felt himself start to tremble. Then a solitary thought, quite distinct, detached itself from his fog. *I'll kill him*, it said.

It calmed him right down.

It gave him his sanity, a branch to cling to until the dark flood receded and he could think calmly, in rhythm, *I'll kill him, I will kill him*, rehearsing it like a jingle, *I will kill him, I'll kill him, I will decease him dead.*

How did he know it was a man? Stood to reason. No woman would do such a thing to herself. Those hairs had been Kate Root's uniqueness, she would never destroy them. But some man, spurned and jealous. Or no, not jealous, just possessive. The sort of dickless wonder who thought, if he couldn't own beauty himself, beauty had no right to exist.

And all this time Kate Root kept handling his body, she

213

did not stop talking. 'Grasp the handle firmly in the same natural manner as if you were picking up a household hammer, keeping the plane of the blade vertical with your thumb extended along the top edge, acting as a pointer,' she said, and he saw her stretched on a bed, you could call it a vision. It was night, a candle burned on the bedside table. Her face was buried in a pillow, her upper body covered by a sheet, but her left leg stuck out into the flickering light. Where the big thigh bulged, a man knelt by the bedside, his hands were fumbling with an open razor. The three red hairs looked bronze in the candlelight. A cross-draught ruffled them, and they swayed drowsily. The razor flicked, its blade glimmered, the three hairs vanished. Kate Root never stirred. Only mumbled in her sleep when the kneeling man rose, and revealed himself.

He was the colour of jaundice.

He wore a cutaway bartender's jacket, a stained bow-tie, and he looked like someone had whacked his eye with a branding-iron, his mama probably.

That rouge Irishman. The defective. JoJo, or whatever his name was. Sneaking in the shadows like creeping Jesus, never saying a word, you'd think he was a choirboy, a freaking eunuch. When all the time he'd been plotting, lying in wait. An unfaithful servant. 'The thrower should remember to avoid any wrist snap. The blade should be released as if it was hot butter,' Kate Root said. But Willie had no heart to follow her, he'd lost his driving wheel.

His first knife wobbled like a paper aeroplane, and his second rose almost vertically, stabbing at the barbershop ceiling. 'Fucking Ada,' Kate Root said, and slapped him. Smacked him right in the face with her open palm. He felt the sting distinctly, and heard a thwack of impact, though this seemed a long way away, it could have been in another room. 'Get a grip,' Kate Root said, and he did his best to obey her, he opened his eyes wide to concentrate. But all they saw was her shape stretched upon the bed, and this man JoJo hovering over her.

It was a different angle this time, he was watching from above. A far better view, that gave him access to every detail. And right away he saw that his first sighting had been incorrect. Kate Root's face was not buried in the pillow, after all, she was turned halfway to the light, looking down the length of the bed. Watching the razor glinting in the kneeling man's hand. Waiting on his move with an expression half nervous, half expectant.

In the shifting half-light her green eyes looked oceanic, and that gap between her front teeth seemed wide enough to snake a tongue through. Willie didn't have to watch the man's hands moving, he knew the moment that the razor flicked by the way Kate Root's mouth went slack. Her eyes went cloudy then like underwater when a diver hits bottom. 'Now try again. Now try again,' he was saying.

'Stand to me,' Willie said.

He didn't mean to; it spoke itself. Spilled out of his mouth like a gaffed fish and lay there flopping while Kate Root gaped. 'I'll pretend I didn't hear that,' she said.

'Just one knife.'

'You can't hit a dead president with a dollar bill, and you want to throw at me live?'

'One blade is all.'

'Not on your life.' The face she turned towards him was flushed and lumpy, her lips were flecked white with spittle. 'This is plain moronic,' she said. She brushed away the stray hairs that sweat had plastered to her cheeks, she wiped her wet mouth on the back of her hand. 'This takes the biscuit,' she said.

It was only when she had walked the length of the room and taken up position that Willie recognized the target he'd been aiming at so far and, when he did, he was glad that he had not laboured to hit it. That would not have been dignified, that would have been a travesty.

But talk about travesties. Now that Kate Root's hands were not fussing him, controlling his every move, and he was freestanding again, he felt something wrong with his hair. Put up his knifeless hand and found the massacre.

Ruin.

The spinning light from the barber's pole hit only one side of Kate Root's face, while the other was deep in shadow. 'The trajectory should be fast and flat, making sure that the plane of the knife remains vertical as it leaves the hand,' she said. The original target had been removed, and she now stood with her feet together and her arms held straight at her sides, her back pressed against the mattress that served as a backdrop. 'The follow-through is the continuation of the throwing movement after the knife has been released and is spinning towards its goal,' she said, and she froze in position, fixed her eyes on Willie's hand. 'Don't miss,' she said. 'You really must try not to miss.'

The fresh blade he selected from the leather case felt cool and grateful to his touch, slid into his hand as like home. So Willie wasted no time. Raising the knife to eye-level, he sighted along it like a gun barrel. Its coat of oil gleamed and dappled in his sight, and he looked at Kate Root direct.

Her body in its green tweed skirt and starched blouse was shapeless, hopelessly baggy. Give it the benefit of the doubt and call it sturdy, still he could find no target there.

Or in her face either, it seemed. The one half that was clearly visible, moving in and out of the spiralling light, looked all humps and potholes and ruts. You wouldn't drive a Spyder on a surface like that, never mind bury a blade. Straining for a clearer sighting, Willie squinted. He closed first one eye, then the other. Then he tried the opposite, and opened them as wide as they would go. He felt his eyebrows arch and stretch, his pupils flood with light. He felt a stinging like chlorine. But his sight was clear.

The face he saw then was quite close. In some place that didn't concern him he was aware that Kate Root remained across the room, fifteen foot away, but she seemed close enough to touch. To study and explore in peace, without even aiming.

The light spinning over her in waves lit up a different fragment at each turn. A broken vein at the temple, the wing-tip of a nostril, two chickenpox pits. A jagged circle of discoloration, acorn-brown over pink, on the jaw's curve beneath an ear. Freckles scattered at random, soiled confetti. A lower incisor with a steel filling. A bloodspot at the hairline.

The ear was finely made, it surprised him. He would not have imagined the shell to be so delicate and cleave so closely to the skull, or the lobe to let the light filter through like a rose. If he hadn't seen it for himself, he wouldn't have credited that.

Or the sweetness of the crescent line that skirted the corner of the mouth. It was a wrinkle, he guessed, but it looked like a sliver of moon. And the speck of matter that clung lopsided to her lower lip, caught in a vertical crack the same way that moss gets trapped in a crevice of rock. That would be grunge, some form of funk. It looked like spun glass.

And the shadow beneath the nose, faintly blue. And the socket of the eye, its hollow almost purple. And the gap in the front teeth, a black hole.

A man could drown here.

A man could fall in and never come up. He could travel his mortal span and not be done. Travel his life away, and still not arrive at the eye.

He should have been that man himself. If he'd had a lick of sense, he would have pitched his tent in some sheltered spot, the cleft of the chin maybe, or the soft fall beneath the mouth shaded by the overhang, and been satisfied. But not Willie D. No, not Willie. He couldn't leave well enough alone, he had to keep on pushing and stirring. So he risked the eye, that green sea.

It didn't look right. It looked bruised and raddled, it looked fearful. As if it had been something hideous. A vision too sick to be endured. An abomination.

But what was there to see? Only himself, and that made no sense. That could not be right, that was not possible. 'Do it for God's sake. Get it over with,' Kate Root cried, and Willie flung up his hand in self-defence. *I'll kill him*, he thought, and threw the knife; he let it go.

If only he hadn't worn rimless glasses, why did they have to be rimless? Not that a puce balloon wearing shades or tortoiseshells or even wire frames was a fashion statement or dressed for success exactly, but rimless was plain degenerate, the thought of them had poxed and plagued her all night, she couldn't close her eyes to take a nap in this room with the gilt mirrors and Chinese slippers without reliving them in living colour, how noxious, when all she asked was a little decorum, a touch of class, and what did she get? A rimless fuck.

The only thing in Sheridan's favour, he had concentrated her mind. Hangings did that to you, they put you on the spot, and ever since the Broadway Local the train rhythm in her mind had kept repeating *No more, no more, no more*, while the backbeat echoed *Now what, now what, now what?*

She had not the faintest or foggiest notion. In a movie she would have gone home to her family and its soggy bosom, but family values had always made her think of discount stores, Ace is the Place for trashcans and school prayers, and besides, most of her relations were in Bonaventure Cemetery with Chief Wigwam, and the rest should have been. She couldn't see herself handing out pamphlets for the Sun God with her brother Leon, or passing the tin cup for Cousin Driskill, and her sister Mignon had sworn to shoot her on sight, although that was honestly not Anna's fault, just the nature of husbands, you couldn't tell the difference once you got them in the dark. Or broad daylight, come to that.

So that disposed of blood, and maybe Savannah wasn't such a hot idea period, not after that little unpleasantness in Monterey Square with the drag queen and the gerbil, apart from anything else it would have smacked of defeat, hell no, she wouldn't go.

But what then? *Golden lads and girls all must as chimney sweepers come to dust*, and Anna was choking on the stuff. Couldn't make the rent or eat three squares, could hardly keep herself in clean nooses as it was, and here she was planning to deep-six the only lifelines left to her. Blow out Verse-o-Gram and Sheherazade, and what was she meant to fly on, a wing and a prayer, or go in the bucket like Stevie Smith's tigress Flo, *she fell, she whimpered, clawed in vain?* Well, it was a thought.

Make space in Bonaventure, always room for one more. But no. She did not have time for demise, not when Bani Badpa owed her a week's wages plus benefits. Innocence might be caged, that didn't make it half-witted, and besides, John Joe had bought her a brand-new veil, she hadn't even worn it yet.

The sensible plan was to do a Sarah Bernhardt, make one last, but positively my last and final appearance, virgin veil and all, then exit pursued by a bear.

Well, sensible she was, if there was one thing she was, it was sensible, and she was never going to get her nap anyway, not if she counted all the sheep in Shepherd's Bush. So she jumped out of bed, or propped herself on an elbow at least. And she would have got up at any moment she really would, the cheque was in the mail, only she was saved by a sudden hubbub on the stairs below, Kate Root shouting *Useless!*

*Bloody useless!* in that blowsy barmaid's singsong of hers like a tart with a heart in some old movie, more Australian it sounded than Texas or Louisiana or whatever dream state she claimed. *Call yourself a blade*, Ma Root yelled, and she sounded just roiling, Rumpelstiltskin wasn't in it. Though she might be faking at that, she was a tricky number, you needed to keep an eye on the silver spoons. But then came a thud like doom or a split melon, a door slammed across the hall, and before its echo had faded a knuckle tapped code on Anna's own door. 'Sanctuary,' said Willie D.

Or what was left of him, anyway. Which wasn't much, he would never have passed for a person. Shaking like an alky, with his shirt hanging out behind, the top of one shiny black boot pierced as if he had been stabbed by a passing dachshund, and his hair, his poor hair, instead of that glossy black mane just bare rock strewn with clumps and tussocks, he looked like an outcropping.

How could she refuse him? She couldn't. What would be the point? After all it was Willie D she'd wanted sopranoed, not this train wreck with the cancelled eyes. 'So come in if you're coming,' she said.

Her room was a mess, and what else was new, with stuffed pandas and Burmese scarves and one Charles Jourdan in the sink, Tarot cards scattered over the rug and that tattletale bottle of crème de cacao all too empty on the bedside table, well at least it wasn't Mother's Ruin, that was one good thing, though Willie didn't seem to notice or care, did not seem anything in fact but starved, driving her backwards across the floor to the bed, not touching her with his hands but angling her, nudging and encircling her like a sheepdog herding a stray, you couldn't call it coercion, nothing so gross as assault, even if she could not get away, not a chance, you would hardly call it force.

To begin with she was defenceless, and afterwards she put up no defence. Some fool in the street threw a firecracker, she saw its flare loop and spin, heard the report like a car backfiring, and a few lines from *Mad Tom's Song* jumped out at her, '*The moon's my constant mistress And the lovely owl my marrow The flaming drake and the night-crow make Me music to my sorrow*,' but Willie seemed not to hear her, he only kept her pushing back. 'Sanctuary,' he said again.

Anna heard him distinctly. Or not distinctly exactly, his mouth was pressed against her collarbone and elocution was never his strong suit, still she heard him. Mumbling, not quite moaning, and what other word could it be, *sanguinary* made no sense when his voice cried for mercy, not blood, and his fingers scrabbled at her breasts like Pepe LePew going off a cliff.

Even blurred and mottled it was the loveliest word, she couldn't pretend it wasn't, and the force of it carried her in a dying fall, as if weightless, to the bed. Knowing well it was not correct, she shouldn't go so easy, but she did anyway. And Willie came to her like a virgin. No, really. Like this was his first time and he was scared shitless, fumbling and thrusting blind, she had to help him enter, though she could have saved herself the bother, three strokes, a jerk, a strangled bleat like a sheep with its throat cut, and he never called her Mother.

Men and sex, how odd they were, how ill-matched, it never ceased to bewilder her. Like that restaurant in Augusta when she was travelling with Waycross Martin and the menu featured *bemused chicken*, she knew just how that chicken felt. Lying watching the firecrackers above the street while she stroked the rubble where Willie's hair had been, softly scratching as if he was one more stray mutt and herself the last stop before the pound, and then he started to fuck her again, deep and slow this time, robotic, it was like nursing almost.

Maybe that was her true calling. Maybe when day was done she wasn't intended for a wild child, not even a dirty dancer, but a starched angel of mercy in a white uniform with orthopaedic shoes, her heels flat as flat, and a thermometer in her breast pocket like they had in Shalimar. Stranger truths had been recorded, look at Nostradamus. And she always had had a knack for healing. Waycross Martin when first they'd hooked up had seemed as good as corpsed, two ODs in the book already, his arms and legs and even the soles of his feet trackmarked like an outhouse with termites and diabetic to boot. Yet today twelve years on you couldn't turn on the TV on Sunday mornings without hitting him all spruced and born-again, his hair trimmed solid as St Augustine grass, singing *Dropkick Me Jesus Through the Goalposts of Life* with that Barbie-doll blonde wife of his and their three kids, saints preserve us from saints, who ever would have thunk it?

Not her for one, on those nights in Athens and Valdosta, Milledgeville and Calvary, and certainly not at the Ramada Inn in Tuscaloosa, across from the Burger King with the giant neon hotdog and the sign that read *It Takes Two Hands to Handle a Whopper*. That night and the next morning when he lay sweating and heaving trying to perform, never mind a whopper, even a tiddler would have seemed like progress then, but the funny thing was she didn't mind, she had almost liked it. Cradling him and rocking him to rest, and later writing down the lyrics for a new song on a Snicker wrapper.

Waycross Martin and the Crosscut Saws. Hottest Southern band this side of the Allman Brothers, or so his manager said, and the song had been entitled *Dickhead World*, she

223

could still recite the first lines: *A dickhead world from my perspective, Like looking through a contraceptive*, so all right it wasn't Dante, still it rhymed, and she had inspired it, she'd been there.

And now she was here, talk about a coincidence, looking down the length of her chalky frame at this olive-coloured person who hovered above her impersonal as a rutting android though wet and warm to touch. Somebody down there with her nipples hard and hurting kept trying to distract her, trying to make her lose her train of thought, but forget it, she wasn't so easily ambushed. Freeing her arm where the bicep was getting squashed she held herself apart, time-frozen in the Ramada Inn, Room 202 if memory served, when Waycross ordered a dozen more Snickers for dessert, they were all he ever ate, and the tattoo of the Georgia Bulldog on his shoulder that snarled or slobbered according to which way he twitched, and the slick shiny socket of the pit in his stomach where a roadie had shot him, and his face after he had hit a vein, sleeping Jesus, laid out on the Sealey Posturepedic like a marble effigy on top a tomb while Anna kept vigil, had she been happy then?

Hard to say, and she didn't much care, the issue was not germane. She'd had a function at least, she hadn't just laid there futile like a paper sack impaled on a stabber, spying on her own body while it betrayed her for spite. 'Don't start me to talking,' she said, and she snatched her hand from Willie's ruined hair, she flung it up against the air, her knuckles jarred the windowpane, the glass cracked.

Willie, glancing up at the impact, seemed surprised to be here, a shade embarrassed. 'How you been?' he asked.

'I've been worse,' she said.

'Keeping busy?' he asked.

'Mustn't grumble,' she said.

'Glad to hear it,' he said, and soon he was smoke, she had the boudoir and the whole ball of wax to herself again. Just her and the vetivert-scented candles, the ivory spice-pots from Nagaland and the *fin de siècle* shoe lasts, the hand-blown Venetian glass slippers.

The things you picked up in thirty-plus years, not all of them diseases, though John Joe, of course, had reached the exact same age without acquiring anything beyond a faint smell of fish glue, still John Joes didn't count. 'So much baggage,' she said aloud, and it was the plain truth, you would like to think of them as possessions, accumulated treasures, the record of a life lived even, but baggage was all they were.

Not easy to recall now, glomming over the Claddagh rings, the sepia postcards and broken lighters, where she'd picked them all up, or why. Her whole life she seemed to have snatched up every dead thing that came her way, never asking what it was, what use it might be, or if she liked it even, so long as it cost money she had to have it regardless. And humans the same. Padgett, when they were still married, had used to call her a sexual microwave, but cement grinder was more like it, just throw her the bones, she'd chomp them down. Vanish them at a gulp, then call it love. Though all she meant was action. Something new and not hers to mess with. Someone to chew on and tear at, twist and ravage and burn, some other body to bear the brunt, what was that line in Philip Larkin, *Where's the sense in saying love but meaning interference?* He must have peeked.

In Shalimar she'd written a poem herself, or the first lines anyhow, *Whitemeat has no asshole*, it began, *You would notice if it did*. Dr Bone did not approve, he said it was juvenile, but Waycross Martin later on had liked it fine, he'd wanted to set it to music, though of course he never did, and

225

she'd never thought he would, now what was that to do with love?

Search her.

But you got tired, oh you did get tired, you got so very tired you couldn't imagine not being tired, you got so tired, 'Oh, shut the fuck up,' she said, and covered her nakedness. Pulled on tights and a Danceteria T-shirt, and the low-cut velvet dress that she'd been booked to wear tomorrow as *My Last Duchess* but that was BS, before Sheridan. No more dangling participles or any other dangling parts for her, she'd never rhyme again. Just pose in the mirror like so, *There she stands as if alive*, and eat Fig Newtons till she burst, *Notice Neptune, though*, she said, pocketing her new veil, *Thought a rarity*.

It was only the act of reaching for her shoes that made her think of Willie, his stabbed boot, and she remembered she had forgotten to wash.

This didn't seem possible. Still and all, it was a fact. Not a splash or sprinkle, not even a dab with a Kleenex, and her such a stickler for hygiene. Miss Dental Floss of Savannah, Miss Douche Tybee, yet she had been brought to this, awash and swilling in bodily fluids, it made her want to shoot her lunch.

So she did.

First she brought up the afternoon. The puce balloon and rimless glasses, the furred sausages, the man reeling by the burnt-out car, the dog leaping out of the basement to snap at her ankles, and then she brought up the night. Retched and spewed till not a thing was left, she was entirely vacated, as hollow as any hollow drum, and when she flushed, the last to go down was Willie's shorn hair, she saw it tossed and swirled, dragged under, rise up for a last gasp, then sucked down for the count and gone, goodbye, she was freed.

Or paroled, let's say. Given a ticket of leave, space enough at least to go out of this place. Take a final stiff belt from the crème de cacao and leave her room to its cracked window, its mirrors and its junk. Streel down the block to Sweeney's, and take a first stiff belt of mescal.

Further down the bar Crouch was drinking boilermakers, a beer and a shot, dancing without moving on his stool, '*For the great day of his wrath is come,*' he said. That John the Revelator shit again, it gave her the bends. If this man had been close to hand it would have been her pleasure to smite him severely, but he was out of range, there was nothing to do but simper. 'Bottoms up,' she said.

'Down the hatch,' he said.

'May the road rise up to greet you,' she said, gritting yet grinning with *Mad Tom's Song* still weaving through her head, *From the hag and hungry goblin That into rags would rend ye The spirit that stands by the naked man In the book of moons defend ye*, and she took one more hit of mescal, here's mud in your eye, chin-chin. 'Sanctuary,' she said.

What could he have meant by it? Was it losing his hair, or was there something that escaped her like the detective in that B-movie at the Carnegie, Dick Powell, she thought, or maybe Victor Mature. *Is this all about a homicidal maniac,* he'd said, *or are we dealing with something deeper here?*

The trouble was, she didn't really know the boy, he was not the type of boy you did know, his uses were strictly otherwise, so she had no context, no leads. Just his face blind at her door, and this one word: SANCTUARY.

A place of refuge and asylum.

Like Shalimar.

Where else? Again she travelled the white corridors, and heard the crackle of starch as the nurse bent to straighten the patient's blanket, only this time the nurse was her, she

227

could feel the fret of the white stockings with their seams dead straight, she could see the morning sunlight on the lawns beyond the high bright windows, *place of refuge and asylum*, she could smell the bedpans and the pine essence from here.

Anna Crow, RN.

So it was true. That feeling she'd had when Willie was stabbing her below, and the firecrackers flying above the street, while she scratched at him behind his ear like an injured pooch. Thinking, *This is me. For this I came.*

Nurse A. Crow.

She could see the name-tag on her bosom now. Just three syllables, count them, but so many echoes in back. The rooms full of light and fruit baskets, the clean white sheets, the balconies at night with the frogs croaking in chorus and the gardens by day all blossom, Confederate jasmine and oleander, black-eyed Susans and Cherokee roses, bougainvillea even. Though she'd probably need some training first, they didn't hand out the Smile buttons to just anyone. Still, Dr Bone had always been so understanding, so easily moved, no wonder they called him Doctor Goodbone, and there were so many ways she could help him out. Render service like that Russian woman who was Khrushchev's mistress for years and when he died on her she applied for a state pension and badge, the Grand Order of Soviet whatever, but not for herself, for her pussy, it just went to show. And not only sex, of course, there was healing and tending and nurturing as well, ministering and cherishing, even bringing flowers could work wonders at times, *There with fantastic garlands did she come, of crow-flowers, nettles, daisies, and long purples*, or wait, wasn't that Ophelia, *long purples that liberal shepherds give a grosser name*, Lordamercy, *but our maids do dead men's fingers call them*, her and her big mouth.

Not that *Hamlet* in itself was any cause for shame. Dr Bone had always placed great emphasis on the artistic impulse. Dramatic renditions and finger-painting, the Dance, you couldn't strike a match round Shalimar without setting fire to a Finer Thing, and if Anna was brutally brutal, maybe that was where her future lay, not so much in rubber walls and restraint, or even diagnostics, a wall full of diplomas, she always was useless at exams and what were they good for anyway, absolutely nothing, like war. No, her strength lay more in creativity. *The Art of Healing through the Healing of Art* perhaps, that sounded right on the money, not that money was her primary concern, of course, but paying the rent was no capital crime, those starch uniforms didn't grow on jacaranda trees.

So the Dance. Tell the truth, that had always been her dream. On and off, but mostly on, she'd been waiting for a chance like this ever since Mrs Sweetwater's. Long before Bani Badpa or spangled G-strings were dreamed of, when she'd danced *The Firebird* and *Giselle* under the twin chandeliers, or else Aurora in *Sleeping Beauty*, perhaps that had been her best. Or no, not quite, her best of all was *Swan Lake*, she was a rage in that. A flaming sensation.

Odette, the white swan, she'd bet she could still dance her today. Or else Odile, even better. It would take a lot of hard labour, admitted. Crucifixion for the thighs, boiling oil for the abs and pecs. But Odile, well, yes, why not?

The black swan.

For a moment the phrase just hung there noodling like a cartoon bubble above her head. Minding its own business, no bother to anyone. So Anna took another glug at her mescal, and she thought of the mummified worm, then the alcohol recoiled in her gut as if trampolining, leapt high in her throat, choking her, and in that flash the other shoe dropped.

And everything was made clear. The only wonder was that she hadn't seen it earlier. Too bottled up in her own concerns, she guessed, too hung up on Shalimar and the wild blue yonder, and all the time the answer she sought had been right under her feet, two hundred feet down.

*Black Swans*. Well, of course.

Funny thing, but she had never liked them before. Mole people, subterraneans, they sounded like bad science fiction. Just because they were on TV and all over the *New York Times* didn't mean she'd ask them into her home, if she'd had one, like the people you met in Shalimar, some of the best-born psychos in Chatham County, even barking like dogs they knew their forks. While these swans by contrast sounded nothing but unpleasantness and dirty fingernails, though who was she to talk, bitten to the quick and the varnish all chipped. Fie! For shame! Still, there was such a thing as breeding, not only polo ponies or backgammon, but something in the blood and bone. Not to be a snob, God forbid, but all that Antichrist and the End is Nigh, she hadn't much cared for their attitude. But that was before today and tonight, before her eyes had been opened and she'd realized that she hadn't been set on earth just to get laid then get old, she had a purpose, a gift, she was here to help.

What else was a nurse meant to do? Go down among the lost and hapless, the ugly, the dumb. Tend to them and feed them, soothe their hurts. Dance for them when requested, even make romance if that was required, it wasn't so much to ask, after all, and think of the happiness she'd bring, call it succour, call it ease, never mind the phraseology, what mattered was the burn. When she spread joy. And joy spread her.

Put like that it sounded sappy, of course, everything did when you said it from the heart, just look at love. Standing up she realized that the mescal had played her false, she was not fully mistress of her ambulatory organs, but that didn't mean she was out of order. Far from it, she was functioning perfectly, a well-oiled machine. Or no, not oiled, let's say finely balanced, equiponderant – she was a walking miracle of poise, born to nurse, and the first black swan she met, she was going to prove it, fuck the white uniform and the orthopaedic shoes, fuck the framed diploma, who needed them, and fuck the bougainvillea while you're at it. All that signified at day's end was the spirit, and her spirit would not be denied, just lead her to the sickos in question, and she'd help them, make them right. Because they were not really sick, only ill, and illness was nothing but a disease.

'*Nazdrovy!*' she said, but Crouch did not respond, he was not there, and neither was she, she was on Broadway instead, and the night was hot as any oven, not that she was complaining, when you had grown up on the Golden Coast you weren't fazed by a little summer sultriness or even a freaking inferno, still, this did feel a trifle torrid. There was something bullying and gross in the air, a lowering oppression, as if the whole last month had gathered to a fullness, everything was about to go bang, and what spelled dog days in one word, eight letters? *Canicule*. It did, it truly did, only that was not the point. The point was she was late again, and Bani Badpa had her money. But she didn't have Bani Badpa, he was miles away, still trying to fix the john, no doubt, but that john would never be fixed, not like the black swans, her swans. '*Khar Kosseh*,' Anna said, and flagged a cab.

When debouched at Sheherazade she was stone-cold sober,

don't ask her how, she just was, and even colder when she started to dance, Zenaide from Zonguldak had never swallowed a drop in her life, an ice-maiden, she was, in her nice new veil, a subtle shade of gold trimmed with crimson tongues that licked at her like flames when she rose up rippling, trapped in the caged circle with one dim spot for moonlight.

Performing, she felt strange, then stranger, every nerve in her seemed a humming wire, the little muscles up and down her inner thighs in their slit skirt darting like schools of silverfish, most disconcerting, and the jewelled headband pressing on her skull was a ring of steel, this didn't feel right, not right at all, even Bani Badpa and his money were not worth this jag like bad cocaine, twitch, twitch, another hanging, although she tried to stay slow and under control it was no use, her roseful bosom jibbed, her mouth gaped with lunging, then a crazed madness entered in, and where the fuck was she, back at Camp Pocahontas, the day of Chase's burying, standing inside the concrete pagoda on the balcony with the wrought-iron railing that circled above the vat of feathers, carnelian, gamboge, heliotrope, curcumine, azulene, far away in her mind when she placed one hand on the railing and vaulted off into space, spinning down all arms and legs in one simple line talking with no editing no petty interruptions no limits whatever saying, *I wish I was never born I wish I never was I wish I was I wish . . .*

'Illness is just a disease.'
    'What about a toothache?'
    'A toothache is an infection.'
'What about boils?'
'A boil is a curse.'

She looked dead white so she did. When she finished her dancing and came over to the bar where he was gainfully employed polishing glasses she looked fit for laying out. But she said it was all in your head: 'Sanity is only a syndrome,' she said. 'But dementia is a distemper.'

John Joe had seen her in these takings before, it would not pay him to comment. The wise approach, he'd found, was like a runaway horse: let her run. Drop the reins and close your eyes, just pray you didn't eat a tree. 'Not a bad crowd the night,' he said.

'Not a bad crowd? Two drunks and their dog? I've seen livelier crowds in a morgue, you should have been in Darien when Waycross Martin had his second OD, talk about a dickhead world, those clowns in the county hospital couldn't find a pulse not a flicker, let's face it, they couldn't find fleas on Fido, so they carted him off to the ice-house and me along with him, blubbing in buckets but giggly at the same time, full of dumb schoolgirl jokes, *I wouldn't be caught dead in a place like this*, nerves, I guess, and the smell of

233

formaldehyde. Thinking of the meat-racks inside the freezers, those slabs of raw beef, and meanwhile Waycross under his white sheet with one foot poking out, a lime-green sock with pink alligators for a pattern, you didn't know whether to laugh or cry when his toes twitched, then he sat up dreaming, *Every goodbye ain't gone*, he said, and started searching for his stash,' Anna said, sucking her teeth. 'Don't you think that was strange?'

'More odd than strange,' said John Joe.

She looked reassured. 'Oddity is not an ailment,' she said. But you could tell her mind was elsewhere, she was just rattling for camouflage. Her eyes kept roaming the room as if searching for rescue, John Wayne on a white horse, and she would not take a drink. 'Never touch the stuff,' she said. But that was not a true fact.

Sipping fruit juice, she stood in the pose that John Joe liked best, swaybacked with her toes pointed out. Still it was not the same if she didn't flex, and her head that should have been held swan-high, had the droops. 'I lied,' she said. 'I've never been in a morgue in my life, I never even smelled formaldehyde, I wouldn't know the smell from doublemint or dogshit, I just said it to say, the day I've had I needed to say something, such a day you wouldn't believe, if you read about it in a book you'd say I lied.'

'Mothballs,' said John Joe.

She looked at him sideways then, that way she had, as if he was God's misprint. 'The smell of formaldehyde,' he explained.

'I am a dead man,' Mr Badpa said.

He had sneaked up on them unawares, this man shaped like a pot-bellied stove in polyester carrying an Accounts book, and the moment he uttered, Anna whirled on him: 'Eat my dust, I'm leaving you dinner, I received a better offer,

Club Cleopatra wants me, the opportunity of a lifetime, my agent says, my managers too, I'd be mad to turn it down, simply mad, I'd be out of my tiny mind,' she said. 'Where's my money?'

'Lend me fifty,' Mr Badpa said to John Joe, which John Joe did, and Mr Badpa handed it to Anna Crow, who threw it on the floor, then swept away towards the kitchens and her dressing room, trailing her new veil behind her, old gold with crimson tongues, it matched her hair almost. But her own colour wasn't good, those fever spots like redcurrant stains were on her cheeks again: 'One word for you, Badpa,' she said. 'Boils.'

The storage space where she changed was John Joe's hiding place. His room at the Zoo didn't feel his own, it was too full of Godwin. Though that was a terrible way to go certainly. To drown head-down and unblessed in a vat of pizza dough, that was a tragic end. Many nights he could not shut an eye till dawn for picturing the final moments, your man's legs stuck in the air and thrashing, frantic at first, then slower and slower like a wasp trapped in a glass, and not a priest in sight. *He died as he'd lived*, Anna said, a thought to poison any room.

But this snug spot felt like home. He knew every label on every can, the robed woman crossing the desert on Demetrio's Hearts of Palm, the kneeling camel on Maravasti Pitted Olives, the veiled houri on Jalaver's Nectar. And the step-charts that papered the walls, the Oasis Floor Lift and Dervish Spin, the Turkish Travel and Pelvis Flutter and Double Hubble Bubble. And the verse tacked to the back of the door, *The Belly Dancer*, he could recite that by heart. *I can arch my back in pride, Contract my spine in humility, Sway my head in grief, Ripple my arms like a snake*, those were lines he would not forget. And the music keening in the club, the smashing of plates in the kitchen, and Bani Badpa cursing, his sisters squealing, the sound and smell of the jakes next door.

All of them together meant Anna Crow.

The rickety table where she made up was covered every inch with pots and vials and jars, and these too he had memorized. They seemed to hold the key to all mysteries, all secrets. In the long afternoon when everyone else was gone and he had Sheherazade to himself, he would speak their names out loud, and savour their descriptions: Princess Marcella Borghese diNott Complex; Mango Body Butter; *spectacular lashes that extend happily ever after*; *colours that won't kiss off, good riddance to fine lines, added shimmering reflectants*; Exclusive Triple AlphaHydroxy Fruit Acid.

Every one of these words was a wondermeat, but *exfoliates* was the best. God alone in his greatness knew what it meant, and even He might need to think twice, yet the sound of it, drawn out long and slow on a dying fall, breathed all the world's romance.

What were those words that Anna Crow loved? *The lapsing, unsoilable, whispering sea.* Those were good right enough, those were champions in their own time. But *exfoliates* had them hammered: 'Knocked into a cocked hat,' he said.

'Cocked hat is right, or a tin cup even,' said Anna, sweeping bottles of Velvet Cleansing Milk and Turnaround Cream from the table. 'Stick me out on a street corner in a Betty Boop costume doing the splits I'd pull down more than I do in this sweatshop, this fucking black hole of fucking Isfahan. When I think of what I sacrificed, I could have been a *première danseuse*, the toast of the Golden Coast, I could have had the world at my feet, sucking on my toes, and now look at them, there's a broken vein for every light on Broadway, I could weep, I could just howl.'

'Calcutta,' said John Joe. 'The black hole of Calcutta.'

Hair mousse, setting gels, skin toners and moisturizers flew off the quaking table, and smashed against the wall. John Joe had never seen her so violently disturbed, her bare breasts flapped like loose tent-flaps in a thunderstorm: 'Martha Graham wanted me,' she said. 'Wanted me in the worst way and no cheap cracks out of you, Merce Cunningham too, he said he'd never seen anyone like me.' Snatching up a tube of New Lash Out mascara, she aimed it at the Anatolian Shimmy, then changed her mind. 'I'm hungry,' she said.

'I have some peanuts just.'

The nuts were still in their shells, and Anna Crow, when she skinned them and nibbled, used only her front teeth, squirrel-style. 'Stevie Smith had a parrot once, called him Onan,' she said, moving through the room, stripping off her skirt and headband and gilt sandals, scattering peanuts in their shells. 'He spilled his seed on the ground,' she said, and she struck a pose, hand on hip, flaunting like one of the dirty pictures in that book Juice Shovlin brought back from England once.

Art it was called when John Joe was fifteen and Juice passed it round behind the bike shed. Most of the females displayed were old or blown enough to be your granny in their skins, and one of the Three Graces was the spit of Mrs Kinsella that ran the tripe shop in Killybegs, but there was one picture of a girl still fresh. A skinny French bit lying stretched across a white bedspread with her legs splayed and hanging, stiff as hurling sticks, her private part split open for all to see. 'Would you look at the quim on that one! It's a city in itself,' Juice Shovlin had said, and every man jack present had laughed, John Joe included. Only he had taken a moment to cross himself, too.

The painting's title was *La Maigre Adeline*. Juice Shovlin said that was French for a dose, and maybe it was the truth, but John Joe thought not. Instinct told him that, far from being a pro, the girl took in washing. The white bedspread with the squirls of green wallpaper behind and that scantling body laid sprawling with no defences, its legs stuck straight out towards you when you watched – for some reason he couldn't pin down, the whole set-up made him think of scrubbing, a ceaseless scouring. '*I wash my hands among the innocents,*' he said.

'*And I will compass thine altar, O Lord,*' Anna Crow answered him, and she stopped her pacing, she stared. 'Lord-amercy, where did that come from, St John the Baptist's maybe, the Washing of Hands, *O Lord, I have loved the beauty of your house, and the place where thy glory dwelleth*, the clutter that clings to your mind, *Take not away my soul, O God*, the worthless junk.' But she seemed calmed. At least she threw no more bottles. 'I could use more nuts,' she said.

Far from washed, her hand when she cupped it to cradle the shells was stained blue and camomile-pink with spilled lotions, and the state of her black nails John Joe could not describe. '*My soul, O God, with the wicked, nor my life with men of blood,*' she said, and put her mouth on his, her tongue lapped at his teeth.

She had never kissed him before, not even a peck on the cheek, and he sensed no lust in her now. The way her tongue probed and burrowed, it seemed to be searching just. Asking a question, it might be. A tongue not plump or sleek, but whippy as an iguana when it flicked against the roof of his mouth, then drew back and licked at air, seemed to be considering, then entered him again.

This time it didn't move, her tongue lay flat and dormant upon his own. He could feel it pulse with her breathing, quick and shallow like a dog's. It tasted salty of nuts and raw of spirits, it was coated in slime. A sleeping slug, it felt like, without sex or any nature of desire. 'Take me down,' Anna said.

'Down where?'

'The Black Swans.'

That was surprising to his ears. Times past when he had mentioned those chosen persons, she had responded with no great warmth. *Toxic waste* was one phrase he recalled, *loonytoons* another. But perhaps these stories in the papers and now on TV had helped soothe her doubts.

With each day that passed, it seemed, mole people were more the rage. Not only reporters and book-writers were swarming the subways now, but all manner of entertainments. A fashion shoot and rock videos, there was even talk of a film.

Along with the glitz came more and more guards. Randall Gurdler himself had been on the News, promising drastic action. These subway dwellers were no picturesque eccentrics, he said, but drug addicts, sociopaths, violent criminals; a menace to us all. As President of the MTA, he pledged himself to a purge.

The Black Swans were not mentioned by name, no more was Master Maitland. But no freed soul was fooled. All this blether of drugs and violence was just decoy work, a tactic to mask the true target. The packs of gun-toting mercenaries who roamed the tunnels on Gurdler's behalf were after one prize only, and his name was not Fu Manchu.

Not a place or situation for a young lady of refinement. John Joe wished she had not asked. Wished she'd left Mount Tabor as his own; his personal retreat. Everything he possessed, of course, was hers to share, no questions asked. Or simply hers to take. But the swans had been his life apart. The thought of exposing them to any outsider, even Anna Crow, made him raise his hand, trace the puckers and ruts around his trick eye.

No value to struggling, though. 'I need to go. I must,' Anna said, then she left him and started her pacing again, moving through the room in her nakedness with her scrawny boy's bum and those dimples on the back of her thighs like vaccination scars, he could never remember their name, and her failed breasts that would never hold a pencil clasped or even a cigar. A carrier bag was in her hand, and she was throwing in her possessions without looking. The Mango Body Butter, and the Exclusive Triple AlphaHydroxy Fruit Acid Complex, and the Exfoliating Gel. Exfoliate; *X-Foal-I-Ate*: 'Take me down,' she said again. So he did.

She put on a long velvet gown, and over it the slicker that she used for camouflage. Shiny black like a watchman's cape, the slicker's insides stank of a grey-faced monkey, of urine and rot, John Joe knew that for a fact.

As for her new gold veil with the crimson trim, she wore it coiled like a bracelet at her wrist but left both ends free to flutter, twin pennants as she sailed out of her dressing room and through the reeking kitchens to the club where the fat girl called Yasmin danced in see-through underwear, wriggling her appendix scar in a turquoise spotlight.

The alternate barman stood filing his nails, too bored to speak when Anna raided the cash register, scooping up banknotes in both hands and stuffing them down her cleavage; then departed.

The night as they walked crosstown towards Grand Central smelled like a storm, and the sidewalks were slick with wet, but no rain fell, there was only heat-mist. Outside the station the boys with their megaphones were still hard at it, they never gave up. 'Would you say I was black?' John Joe asked.

'Black is beautiful. You're yellow,' Anna said, and she drew him inside, across the grand concourse underneath the painted night sky and the electric stars flickering, into the subways, she brought him underground.

Never mind *Take me down*, it was herself that did all the taking. There was not a thing for any man to do, only trail three steps behind her and follow where she led, up steps and down ramps, along platforms to other platforms, past the workmen laying down red carpeting and the runway for tomorrow's fashion show, and the added guards with their bullet-proof vests, until they were good and lost. Only then did she pause for breath, take one look into his face. 'Well, call it jonquil. Or maybe saffron,' she said. She trailed his cheekbone with her veil, placed one fingertip in the socket of his eye, blew softly on the burns. 'A fetching shade of quince,' she said.

For some cause that no words fitted, John Joe felt guilty in her sight then. Unknowable she was to him, forever beyond his grasp, so he turned away in haste, let the tunnels swallow them.

Descending to Mount Tabor at this time of night was no easy task. Lawmen were prowling in posses, and fugitives running in packs, scurrying between the tracks and along the overhead ledges, smashing every source of light for secrecy. So that John Joe and Anna were forced to find their way by feel alone, groping at the tunnel walls, stumbling over garbage and sleeping bags and maybe fallen bodies, there was no means to know. 'This is fun, this is a delight,' Anna said in darkness, 'I always did like going down, I mean descending, *When the going was good, I got so good at going,*

Waycross Martin wrote that, *I got so good at going, I forgot how to come,* or plummeting by any other name like skiing or snorkelling or even bungee-jumping, or diving into a vat full of feathers come to that, my natural element so to speak, freefalling is what I do best, and why not, it's what I've done longest, my earliest memory, did I ever tell you that?'

'You did not.'

'Must have slipped my mind like I slipped through Chief Wigwam's fingers when he was pushing me on the swing out by the boating pond. I must have been five, and he kept driving me higher and higher with every push, clean over the treetops it seemed, till finally the rope snapped, and I was flung into the air. Flying then falling, I never was so scared, so thrilled, and when I tumbled back to earth, the instant before I crashed, guess what I thought, *I wish I could see me,* I thought.'

'Did it hurt?'

'Only when I landed,' Anna said. But when she hit bottom this time, it seemed the other way round. John Joe heard her gasp in relief, felt her hand soaking wet through his sleeve. 'My lips are sealed,' she said, and he tapped at the metal steampipe with his keys, received the two taps in reply, then held open the door in the rockface while she passed into Mount Tabor.

A few hours just had passed since John Joe had been here last, yet the mood was changed utterly. Instead of a clubhouse, it felt like a bunker now. No children played Power Rangers, no women hung washing, and rifles were piled high at the feet of Crouch's sculptures. Under the gas lanterns, Master Maitland sat surrounded by his troops, each man garlanded with an ammunition belt.

Seeing Anna Crow, a stranger, the Master did not rise to

greet her. Hunched massive in his black robes, he merely surveyed her, indifferent. 'What are you good for?' he asked.

'I can dance,' Anna said. 'Well, not just dance, I can sew and cook as well, nothing fancy you understand, just home-style Southern cooking, smothered pork chops, meatloaf, my chicken-fried steak has won golden opinions, and then I'm training for a nurse, I can heal, I can make you well.'

'*Good for*, I said.'

But Anna had no time to answer him afresh. Before she could compose her thoughts, there came a noise like a stampede, massed footsteps thundering in the tunnel outside, weights hurled against the walls, a shouting and blaspheming that sent the Black Swans scrambling and left her by herself, coiling and uncoiling the gold veil with the crimson tongues round her wrist.

John Joe made no move, merely stood against a wall among the three unclean spirits, watching Master Maitland, with his bull's head lowered as if to charge, and Luther Pratt and Jerzy Polacki and Joe Easter racing for the grenades, and Marvella Crabtree with her hand across her mouth to keep the screaming in when the door in the rockface exploded, when the first shot was fired.

He didn't see who fired it, couldn't tell you who it hit. There was no reality to this at all, so he felt no special alarm. When something shattered the third spirit, and the gas lamps blew out, and fat popping sounds like pellets of blood sausage dropped sizzling into the pan were all around his head, even when everyone started rushing outwards, he let himself be carried on the tide, not straining to resist or shelter, only searching for Anna's veil. And he found it. Right ahead of him, a few inches out of reach, the red tongues were drifting towards the broken doorway, out into the white light that flooded the tunnel beyond. For a second he almost had them, but then he slipped down. Something live was moving under his foot, it pulled at him. 'Don't start me to talking,' Anna Crow said, and her veil got away.

# Last

5 83: SOILED SHIRT: you are prey to remorse or regret; and sweating armpits meant shame. You sat in Chez Stadium, drinking apricot schnapps to forget, but your pits wouldn't let you. Every time you started to wriggle free, they snapped on the cuffs again.

He should have showered, only he could not stand to lay hands on himself. Just the thought of his own flesh returned him to that barbershop, sighting down his blade at Kate Root.

Even now he couldn't figure what had happened. Certain people had told him dreams were the same way, they made sense while you were in them, but when you woke everything was twisted. Bombo Garcia would know, but Bombo was not around. Nobody was.

How had it all gone so wrong? He'd come to the Zoo on such a high. Nervous, yes, but full of hopes. Thinking *Love*, even though it made no sense. Resigned in his mind to surrender. Let himself be taken over, swept away; let the fat bitch have her way, if that was what she needed, Willie D would not fight back.

And she had pissed on him. She'd taken the good faith he offered, and turned it to puke. Instead of giving him solace, she'd looked at him like the devil incarnate. So the knife had slipped from his grasp, and he had stabbed his own boot.

You couldn't call it fair play. Nobody could claim that was playing the game. The plain truth was, the woman had taken advantage. Like the Deacon was always telling him, Willie had been too soft with her, and she'd played him for a sucker. Too trusting, too big in heart.

Ivana all over again.

It just went to prove the thought that kept running and running like the Times Square tickertape through his head: *I am not my self*. If he had been, he would never have stood still for this jive. He would have marched her straight back to the target, handed her one of her own Camels for a last cigarette, even offered her a blindfold if she liked; then he wouldn't have stopped throwing till the lights went out. Not until he had pleased himself.

*Please myself, and pleasure her* – Mouse Williams had said that. Instead of which, he had raised his face the same way a boxer does when he's all through and secretly wants to be knocked out, he had abandoned ship.

But no more. *Don't get too complicated, Eddie. When a man gets complicated, he gets unhappy.* No more twisting in the wind, no more puzzling and theorizing, racking his brains for explanations that didn't exist. *And when he gets unhappy, he runs out of luck.* Sweaty armpits meant shame.

And the man with jaundice; JoJo, the dog-faced boy. How could he have allowed a freak like that go trampling on his patch? Giving him horns by candlelight? For a moment after he pulled the knife quivering from his stabbed boot, and Kate Root had pushed him out in the passageway, Willie thought he heard the fucker moving upstairs, messing with Anna Fucking Crow, and never mind the language, fucking Man of Power be fucked, if he'd got his hands on that fuck the fucker would have been fucking dogfood right then.

But JoJo had been too tricky. By the time Willie got up

the stairs in his crippled boot the man had already gone out the window or over the wall, whatever, and Anna was on her own.

Naturally, she acted innocent. Like she couldn't guess why he was there. Gave him that look dumb and dazed, shell-shocked almost, as if cum wouldn't melt in her mouth, and the next thing he knew, he didn't know a thing.

What had brought him round? The windowpane. He'd heard a blind, trapped sound like a bird makes when it blunders into glass, and he opened his eyes to see stars. Someone must have set off a skyrocket or maybe a Roman candle. It burst above the rooftops, shooting out flares of silver and gold, then tailed away in a shower of sparks, and as it faded, it darkened. Deep molten red, it turned to smoke, and the smoke turned to wisps. Within thirty seconds, the only traces left were three snaky plumes, faintly pink. They looked like uncut hairs.

More red than pink, on second look.

So there was no end to it. And never would be, it seemed. He was stuck with this disease till the fat lady sang. Sickness or possession or love, the terminology didn't matter. Bottom line, his number was up, and that number was 223: DEATHBED: if you witness your own death, you will experience melancholy.

In a way he was almost relieved. Knowing the worst, he could at least stop his struggling. No point in going back to Tia Guadalupe for another offering to Osain, or Sly Sy Stein for another blade. The cards were finally face-up, his position was plain. There was only one move left for him to make, and that was to take back his life; get equalized.

A stillness came over him then, a backhanded sense of peace. When he looked around him and noted that he was in bed with Anna Crow, he felt nothing but weariness. There were so many traps, the flimflams never ended. All these bimbos in limbo. But they no longer bothered him. Let her use him while she could. Milk him and drain him, haul his ashes, if it helped. Even play with his hair.

His hair!

Full recall returned at that, the whole nine yards. The barbershop and the knives and the toilet seat, the light from the spinning pole, that look in Kate Root's eye.

A frozen calm wrapped him, the same neutrality he'd felt once in a car wreck, flipping over the median barrier on the BQE, hanging upside down and barely moving, meanwhile thinking with perfect composure *I am going to die. Deacon Landry can have my shoes*; and as the car hit the wall broadside, slewing back against the traffic, *These Blazers have lousy shocks*, and finally, coming to rest, *The wing-tip Oxfords would look better on Sandman Ames.*

Same thing now. In freefall, his thoughts were *She got me. I'm done for.* But he would have his revenge. *Take the A Train, then change to the D at 125.* He would fix his hair, he would walk in new boots. If it killed him, he would be freed.

Get out at Tremont Avenue, walk across to Crotona, and he made it to Littles Fernando's. Fernando Littles, his name had been when he was playing shortstop for the Piscataway Pirates and Bombo Garcia was in rightfield. Now he was a certified hair artiste, the self-styled Michelangelo of Heads, whose sculpted designs graced some of the def skulls in New York. Bobby Bo wore his Manhattan skyline, Frankie Knuckles his fire-breathing dragon. 'What you got for a man on a mission?' Willie asked.

'The gryphon be boss,' Littles Fernando told him. So a gryphon it was. The razor sliced him, the tongs singed him, then the scissors remade him. The body and wings of an eagle, the head of a lion, etched black on olive like a wood-cut: 'That'll be forty bucks,' Littles Fernando said.

'Take a hundred,' said Willie. 'Just give me your shoes.'

Fernando's loafers were old and scuffed, down at heel, but at least they didn't have a knife in their ribs, they were not bleeding to death. Willie gave them a quick fix of plastic surgery. Amputated their tassels, fleshed out their instep with foam for a sleeker line, camouflaged their cracks and wrinkles with mascara. Then he turned his feet to the city again.

Even the sight of Ivana could not deflect him for long. He had thought he would drop in on Deacon Landry, share a cup of news, but when he reached the Deacon's apartment, the girl was strutting the front steps, head-to-toe in black leather, hot ice on every finger and a heart-shaped diamond stud in a brand-new nose. 'Hot-sour soup. Get your good soup here,' she said, daring him to hit her. But he would not grant her the honour. Why sully himself? All his force and will were reserved for one thing alone. Willie D's Last Stand.

By the time he reached Chez Stadium, and ordered his first apricot schnapps, he felt like the Man with No Name. He who rides alone, who trusts no man or woman born. Who needs nothing but need itself.

Mouse Williams and Warren White and Sandman Ames were drinking together in the corner booth, there was room for one more, but he chose not to join them, it would not be smart. One thing he'd learned, you could not change your act. Whatever it was you did in life, don't stop. You could either be possessed, or you could possess, but you could never switch hit, your public would not permit it.

Better wait till he'd finished his business, and his mind was back in its proper place. *Physician, heal thyself.* Anna Crow said that. *Mortician, embalm thyself*, she said that, too. Both were equally apropos, you'd hate to have to choose. What

251

he wanted right now was a mix of the two, and he would be dead to rights.

Finish his drink, then make his move. Wait till Kate Root would have shut up the Zoo and retired to her bedroom. Wait until there was no waiting left within him, only act. The deed itself.

Tilting his glass back to drain it, Willie glanced at the nylon butterflies dangling from the ceiling. The glitterdust was almost gone from their spread wings, he could see their plastic skeletons underneath. So he raised his empty glass to the ruins, and that was the moment the bomb went off.

It sounded like a bomb, anyway. A deep boom and shudder underground, you'd have said a mine caving in, except there were no mines around here. Willie's glass trembled on its coaster, and the last of the glitterdust came down in a dandruff cloud. But that was all. No breakage, no blood. 'Barry White burped,' somebody said, it might have been Warren White, and everybody started laughing, the way people did after false alarms. Mouse Williams called for a fresh round of drinks, and Willie started over to join the corner booth. Never mind his soiled shirt, forget his pits. Suddenly, he felt in the mood to celebrate.

Then the lights went dead.

The power blacked out, cut the jukebox and the ceiling fans, and there wasn't a sound. Silence so profound Willie thought for a moment the world had simply quit, Planet Earth was a wrap. Then he heard a siren wail outside. Some man started muttering, and a body jarred against his own. Something heavy went crashing, sounded like a table overturned. There was another siren, and another. A wet hand touched his cheek, and he dropped to all fours. Got down on his belly and started crawling. A foot stomped his arm. People were shouting and cursing now, glasses shattered. His hand gripped an ankle. From the fact that it didn't try to kick he would have guessed Shanda Lear. A shard of glass pierced his thigh, he felt a trickle of blood. 'Fuck oh fuck oh fuck oh fuck,' the woman with the ankle was saying. The sirens were wailing non-stop, too many to count. His knuckles bruised against wood, and the wood gave way, it was the door, he was out.

New York City was pitch-black, except for the cherries flashing on the roofs of the cop cars, but the street was already swarming, the sidewalks massed and spilling over. The surge of the crowd carried him downstream, scrambling along Eighth Avenue towards Port Authority, but when he reached 42nd Street it was like hitting a rubber wall. An unseen barrier bounced him back, and he was spun into the path of those rushing up behind, who flung him back again, and then again, a human pinball, slurping inside these shoes two sizes too big, thrashing out for balance, till at last his hand found something solid. A tube of metal, rising up, it could have been a street lamp, and there he clung, he would not be moved.

Between the blackout and the stampede, he couldn't see much. Just a narrow strip of floodlit kerb between two ambulances, and a plain-clothes law with a walkie-talkie. Willie raised himself on tiptoe, and a man started running in and out of his sightline. A raggedy black stringbean with a dark stain on his shirt, could be blood or soot, he was waving his hands and yelling, but you could not make out the words above the sirens' wail. *Shooting*, Willie heard, or was it *shitting*? And something like *fire alarm*, or it might have been *fiery brand*. Then a couple of cops got hold of the man, they wrestled him away, he was lost to view. 'Hear that?' a woman said, close behind Willie's head. 'They shot Farrakhan.'

The shouting and the cursing had almost stopped. Along the Deuce, unseen, someone was shouting through a bullhorn, repeating and repeating one short sequence of sounds, and those sounds were probably words, an order of some kind, nobody could be sure. Below the sirens, Willie could hear the herd breathing, hard and ragged at his back. Someone was weeping, saying, *Farrakhan, oh, not Farrakhan*, and someone else was groaning. All the rest stood still, hung fire.

Something smelled bad here.

Not flesh, or fear, but something chemical. A sharp and whippy smell that Willie did not recognize, but didn't like. His eyes stung suddenly, he put up his hand to wipe them, and then the crowd was running again, everyone was screaming the same words, and he was ripped bodily from his refuge. The street lamp's warm smoothness slid through his hands, and he was hurtled back where he'd come from, tossed and spun up Eighth. *A turd in the maelstrom*, Anna Crow said that. His shoulder was rammed into a wall or gate, felt like steel, and the shock of pain made him bite through his lower lip. Blood flushed his mouth, he punched the dark. Something pulpy splattered under his fist, a body went down, that felt good. *Don't get too complicated*. Willie D said that.

Three blocks, maybe four, and the crush began to ease, he could hold his ground. Candles and torches showed inside a few windows now, there was enough light to make out shapes. People were sitting on the kerb, moaning. A few had been caught by the tear gas, the others moaned to moan. A man in a doorway was swinging a metal club. Stepping out, he took two steps along the street and smashed a shop window. Flecks of glass showered Willie's face and throat, reminding him of his wounded thigh. His pants' leg was stiff and matted, he could feel stickiness down to his shoes. A man's stumbling shape brushed past him, bearing something big and square, might be a TV. Willie's shoulder ached, his whole arm was numb. A block uptown, guns began.

On the corner of 46th there was a fire in a garbage can, it glowed like a brazier. In this choking heat men gathered round it to warm themselves, chafing their hands. Other men, hurt maybe, lay or huddled nearby.

The dog-face boy, for one.

'Don't start me to talking,' she'd said. Her veil was gone, and she was somewhere beneath his hand, and then he was swept past her, she was gone as well. He tried to stop himself, turn back, but there was no chance of that, the force of flesh driving him was too great. The tunnel was blinded by white light, and a woman screamed. The most dreadful sound it was, worse than a boiled kettle.

When John Joe turned towards this scream, he saw Master Maitland framed in Mount Tabor's doorway, beating at his burning body with clenched fists, his black robes bright with flame. Then the Master rocked back, toppled slowly like a great tree felled, and disappeared from view.

Beyond the white light lay nothing. Men in uniforms and gas masks stood guard at the border, grabbing up each Black Swan who blundered into range and snapping them into handcuffs. Randall Gurdler's men, John Joe supposed. Ugly pieces of work they looked, best avoided, but what could he do? The parties shoving at his back were driving him straight into their clutches, he thought his goose was cooked for certain, when suddenly came an almighty bang. The biggest blast you heard or felt in your born life, and every man jack went down in a heap, Swans and guards and all living creatures together, you couldn't tell them apart.

At that there was great confusion, and all manner of hasty speech. A hand sharp as a steel claw kept digging at John Joe's ribs where he lay, trying to rob him he thought, but when he looked down it was only Crouch, hurting him for his own good.

One kick, a knee and a rabbit punch, then he was freed, and they were running up the tunnel, doubled over against the glare like Schwarzenegger or Stallone or any of those hard men. '*Receive not of her plagues*,' said Crouch, and the white light went out like a candle snuffed. Dark blackness cloaked them for safekeeping. Or black darkness, rather.

Crouch, being a caretaker by trade, had a pocket flashlight on his person. The beam it cast was faint and no fatter than a virgin's finger, but sufficient to lead them out of the main channel, through a chink in the tunnel wall, up a metal ladder to a concrete ledge, far distant from strife. The sounds of battle and pain came to them faintly, without reality. 'Don't mind if I do,' said Crouch, pulling a pint flask from his hip pocket. 'I thank you kindly,' he said.

But how could John Joe rest easy? The moment he ceased to run, his mind returned the feel of something live moving under his foot, and the sight of that gold veil, floating out of reach. 'I have to go back,' he said. 'My fiancée needs me.'

'Polk-salad Annie?'

'She asked me herself. *Marry me, you might as well*, she said, the very first night we met, and in my heart I answered *Yes, I will, yes*.'

'You shit me.'

'Of course, I know that she has her career and all, her public has the first claim, but the pressures of stardom can be cruel, it's a lonely life up there, and there's a B&B for sale in Croaghnacorcragh, I heard, just a hop and a skip from Meenadreen; we could do worse.' But his voice did not

257

sound right to himself. In this black hollow full of echoes, it sounded like the voice of a backslider. 'Don't worry yourself. Crows don't kill so easy,' said Crouch, tipping the flask back easy, but John Joe was already back down the ladder, it was his duty, he was running in mid-air.

Without the pencil light, he had only his senses to guide him, and they led him straight up the arsehole of nowhere. He tried to head towards the loudest noise of conflict, but whatever direction he turned, the war seemed always at his back. Groping his way by fingers and thumbs along the tunnel walls, he had not even a TV or any watching eyes to steer by, no break of any nature in this blackness like no blackness he had ever known, not sable or soot or raven, not nigger black, not carbon black, but black its very self, without end, black, black.

He had a desperate want of a bathroom. The strain of holding himself intact forced him to move crabwise, in baby steps, and drove all other thought from his mind. In Mount Tabor was a Port-o-San, there he would find relief. By his calculation, that place was below him now and somewhere to his left, so he travelled counter-clockwise, descending in spirals and loops. Sometimes the tunnel wall vanished and he felt empty space. Other times he missed his footing, stumbled over some dead thing. Certain creatures skittered against his legs, and flying objects that might be bats flurried in his face. The rasp and rattle of his own breathing lurched at every step. When he paused to listen, that breathing was all he could hear.

At last he found light. Not a radiance, but a glimmering at least. Where the tunnel bent a corner round he found a stalled train full of passengers. Trapped inside the carriages, they were burning matches and cigarette lighters. It looked like a vigil in there, a midnight mass. *And I will compass thine altar, O Lord,* John Joe remembered. But those eyes staring out at him unseeing were terrible in grief, he could not meet their gaze. A ship of the dead, it might have been. *Take not away my soul, O God,* he thought, and ran.

Dread had fixed his plumbing at least, he could move freely now, could work his path through the blackness as single-mindedly as any other animal. Circling still, he came upon other lights. A kerosene lamp inside an alcove showed him a man sleeping and a woman reading a magazine. This woman watched him pass by without interest, sucking at a chocolate bar, and John Joe was sore tempted to stop with her. But that would not be right. White light was in here somewhere, it was his job to track it down. He pushed on through another circuit, past a man with two candles, and a family eating under a bicycle lamp, and some youths standing over a fire, passing a strange class of pipe around, jiggling and laughing they were, their shadows thrown huge against the tunnel walls, as if this was any other night and black the natural colour of light. Soon after he reached a dead end.

Beside the tracks was an alcove where he rested. When his breathing quieted, and he could hear beyond himself, he tried again to locate the noises of battle, some trace of Randall Gurdler's men, but there was nothing, just water dripping, and the scurrying of the rats, and a faint quavering far above that might have been music, or more likely wind.

Anna Crow came to him then, moving through her dressing room, her breasts and scrawny boy's bum, the dimples on the backs of her thighs like vaccination scars, and her tongue inside his mouth, a sleeping slug. 'Exfoliate,' he said, and wept a space. Then he started retracing his steps.

Hand across hand, he moved himself back along the tunnel wall, only somehow it did not lead him to the same place. The black must have thrown his sense of direction out, or

259

perhaps it was just exhaustion. In this deep place he could not tell, but instead of the youths and their fire the next light he reached was a medical flare, three men in rubber suits ran at him and grappled him close, rushing him upwards, level after level, out onto the street.

The brightness up here dazzled him, though the people round him were blind. The sky was glowing, there were flickers and flashes of light up the block, a giant searchlight on a rooftop, and fires everywhere you looked. Hellfire could be no hotter.

To escape that heat he wandered away, trailing through side streets, turning and turning to his left till his feet would carry him no further. He felt himself begin to stagger and weave, and finding a fire to shelter him, he fell down.

How long he lay like a child in the street, he couldn't tell. All he knew was that the fire was warm, the fire was good. A hand gave him something to drink, and that was a good fire also. Then some foot kicked him. Whacked him in the ribs, but it hardly hurt. The foot wore a loafer with the tassels cut off, a shoe without heft. After it had kicked him, it drew back, seemed to be considering, then it moved away. A woman's face took its place. That face was streaked with soot and grime, displeasing to John Joe's eye. He thought he had better move somewhere elsewhere. Then he was asleep.

At the instant he woke, he glimpsed Anna Crow standing swaybacked in his bedroom doorway with her face invisible but the wild tangle of her red hair backlit from the landing beyond and her right foot turned out, its long shape wriggling and twitching like a stoat's snout. 'I might be wrong, I often am,' Anna said. 'But I think the roof's on fire.' Then John Joe was walking again, pushing back through the crowds, against the tide, working with his elbows and knees and even his fists where required, until he ran into a police cordon and a man with a gun made him stop.

The cross-street ahead was deserted but vivid with light, any number of torches and flares, a TV crew with kliegs, so that its emptiness seemed ceremonial, a sort of red carpet. All that was missing was the star of the show, and that star shortly appeared. Led down the aisle by a phalanx of motorbikes, a black limousine came into view, cruising slow and stately as an ocean liner. Its back window was rolled down, you could see a beefy red face inside. There was time to catch a glimpse just, and then the limo had moved on. But that one glimpse was enough. Juice Shovlin was in there.

In all this fuss and upset, John Joe had clean forgotten the man. The Shovlin Group, and the warehouse that needed a night manager, the whole shooting match had gone from his mind. But here was his chance to set matters straight. Calling out and gesturing, he struggled to reach the limousine, but the man with the gun mistook his intent, unkindly repelled him.

A few more yards, and the limo stopped anyway. The back door was opened wide, then the passenger stepped out into a mob of microphones and flashbulbs. A goodly figure of a man, he was, Juice Shovlin's height and size right enough. Only when he turned, John Joe saw he'd been misled. The high colour, the swagger, the cigar like a small torpedo, all the props were alike. But this person had another face. He'd had his teeth fixed, for a start, and his hair looked dyed. When you looked him over at leisure, you could see he was a slicker piece of goods altogether. A used-car salesman. And John Joe didn't have to see his doorstep smile, nor listen to his speech, to know him by his right name.

'There is no need to panic,' Randall Gurdler began. 'There is no need at all.'

She saw nothing. There was nothing to see. Looking down the length of the barbershop, she couldn't see zip, only space, and that red mark on the boy's nose.

Funny thing, she'd never studied it before. Then again, why would she? It wasn't much of a thing, hardly bigger than a zit. But curious in shape, it made her think of a coolie's hat or the punctuation mark above a French ô. How had he come by such a design? Concentrate, and she should be able to see. No use. She could see nothing.

She must be too tense, she had a lot on her mind. Well, she would have. Standing posed against this mattress like a coconut in a shy, about to be impaled by a total stranger. A lot on her mind? She must be out of it.

What the fuck, it made a change. As good as a rest, Fred Root would say. It livelied up the blood, rejuvenated the tripes. *Action*, that was always the loveliest word. Try to show her one finer, you never could. And what was a Harvey McBurnette in the small intestines, more or less? When every swirl of the barber's pole made those same intestines churn like riding a tilt-o-whirl when you plunge; when every part of her was melting. Feeling the rough ticking of the mattress fret and prickle her spine, and all the while trying not to breathe, seeing only that red mark, waiting on the knife.

And waiting. Dear God, would he never deliver? Babies

came quicker than this. Maybe he was teasing her, maybe he thought, if he kept her dangling long enough, she would flinch. Fat chance, she would see him dead first. Though she'd be the one that was dead, of course; be careful what you wish for. But throw the damn thing, anyway. *Roll me over in the clover.* Oh, Fred. Oh, Mary. Just throw.

If the red mark didn't fetch him, maybe the knife itself would. Shifting her sights a few inches, she drew a bead on the blade's tip, and willed it to fly. Of its own accord, if necessary. Make it jump out of the bastard's hand and wing its true way. To where? A hand would be nice. Split the uprights between a thumb and forefinger, so she could grasp the hilt without even moving. Just roll her fist over and pluck it out. Her very own blade. To have and to hold. Or throw back, if not satisfied.

She tried to stare the blade down. Narrowed her focus till there was no existence outside the knife's edge, the single bead of oil that had collected at its tip and now began to swell. Gathering to a greatness. Growing fatter and fuller until surely it must burst, it couldn't hold together a moment more, must shatter into atoms. So it did. It went splat like a cartoon bubble, and what was in it?

Not nothing, no, but nothingness.

Such a jolt. With no warning, not a clue. Her first impulse, typical, was simply to cover up. Bury dread in bluster, and blame it on the boy. Kick the shit out of him and into the street, then get herself to safekeeping, tucked in her bed. Try to ignore the feathers on the bedroom floor, this was no time for paradise or any other bird. Just shut the door, shut out the light, and pray. Except that no prayers came cleanly to her mind. *Agnus Dei, Agnus Dei.* Her mother in the back room dying, that sweetsick medicine smell of burning flowers. *Peccata mundi. Qui tollis peccata.* No use. *Miserere nobis. Dona nobis pacem.* A form of words, and what words could paper the void? *Yearning makes the heart deep*, but that was for love of God, not this gross hunger, for what? Not a thing. Not one damned thing that had a name.

Oh, but it was a desolation, an ache with no source and no end, she couldn't be doing with this. *God-buggering*, Fred Root had used to call it, he said it wasn't cricket. Not even rounders, he'd say, when he had sunk a few beers, and he held up his right hand to the light. Sausage fingers, scaly smooth, and his Charlie Chaplin feet. *Plates of meat*. When he showed her the grip for the googly, and she sucked on a Space Blaster. Or when he bowled tennis balls to her in the back garden, shambling in from the lobelia beds in his carpet slippers, that was peace, she could sleep then. But not tonight. Too many feathers, she couldn't focus; even the tennis balls had blades. Billie and Bo were getting married, the wedding was any day now, but she would not be attending. *No rest for the wicked*, Fred Root said. None, nought. Nothingness.

She lay undead in this place for hours or days. Then the earthquake came and rescued her. Or if not an earthquake, another convulsion that buckled the world. Its fathoms-deep shudder made the windows shake and the feathers swirl, the back copies of *Soap Digest* tumble off her bedside table. 'Shuffering shuccotash!' Kate said, grabbing at the bedclothes, and she was in another place, some other time.

Where would that be? Dade City, Highway 301. In a hot-sheet motel with Eddie the Blade, watching Tweety Pie and Sylvester on afternoon TV.

The Motel Malarkey, they'd called it, and were proud to sign themselves Smith. Drinking Coke and snacking on junkfood and fucking themselves bow-legged like regular persons, with a whole afternoon for their honeymoon before they had to get back on the road, make their evening show in Zephyrhills.

At this exact moment, they were between bouts; Kate was lying on her stomach, hanging off the end of the mattress with her head hung low; and Tweety Pie had just sent Sylvester crashing smack into a brick wall.

Picture it: the cat-shaped hole in the bricks, and the way his whiskers were bent at right angles like wires when he came crawling back into view, his eyes revolving in opposite directions. Spilled popcorn on the sheets, melted butterscotch sticking to her belly, and Eddie's good hands, a born blade's hands, cupping her. 'Sheesh!' Sylvester said, and when Kate looked down at the carpet below, a cockroach was watching her.

Waiting on its tea, she supposed; and meantime licking its chops. Quivering the long black tentacles that looped back in a horseshoe from its snout, she didn't know their names. Fact of the matter, she'd never really noticed how a roach was made before. Too squeamish, or she'd simply been in too much of a hurry. But there was no rush in Room 43, she had all day. Not a thing in the world to disrupt her studies when she wriggled down off the bed, propped her elbows on the floor for balance.

The roach was only inches away, and wondrous to see. The blunt triangle of its head like a Stone Age arrowhead; its antenna cocked like Pompey's trick ear, with that same sense of tireless vigilance; and the feathered hairs on its front legs, the faint flickering of its wings. 'Sweet Jesus, look at this,' she'd said, but Eddie wouldn't, he was not that kind. Loveliness escaped him, and he came tumbling down on top of her, rolled her on her back.

So then the cockroach was lost to sight, and by the time she was free to concentrate again, all there was to look at was Sylvester again, this time being shot into space from a home-made catapult. 'Shuffering shuccotash!' he'd said, then Kate was back again in her own bed, the room still dancing about her, and the earthquake's last aftershocks slowly dying.

The street lights had gone out, it seemed. Or maybe the fires were burning stronger. Either way, the birds downstairs in the Zoo weren't happy. Much yammering and squawking, no end of rattling cages.

Which reminded her, she must remember to talk to Maguire. Get him to fix Pearl's swing, it was hanging by a thread. Though, for all the good Maguire was likely to do, she might as well save her breath.

Search her why she suffered him. Soft-headedness, most likely. Plus that odd sense of knowing him from someplace. Not in another incarnation, nothing feeble-minded, but somewhere quite specific, she was sure she'd known him well. Either him, or his born double. Only she could never pin him down. Like smoke he bothered her eyes, she could never see him straight.

But why would she want to, anyhow? Why on earth was she fussing herself with Maguire? In the middle of an earthquake, too, with all those sireens downtown? She ought to get up, she ought to go see. But she was not in a seeing mood. Earthquakes, cyclones, cataclysms out the kazoo, they could take a running jump. Claim her if they wanted her, just don't leave a mess.

Let her be. Free to get back to Dade City and the Motel Malarkey, Room 43, and the cockroach.

When the cartoons were over, she had drifted into sleep, and afterwards they had packed, gone out to the car. Eddie liked to drive, and she let him. Squeezed in beside him, kissed his ear for luck, then suddenly she'd had a thought. Run back inside the motel room, the bag of buttered popcorn in

266

her hand. And she scattered it on the shag carpet. Left the roach a tip.

The stuff the computer cast up! Twenty-eight years, that must be, why ever would it kick back tonight? Never mind, she'd take it anyhow. It was not nothing, not nothingness either; she'd take it and no questions asked.

Keep her sights on that watching head with the blob eyes like a man from Mars, those praying-mantis legs, and maybe she'd be granted repose. An hour's respite, maybe two, staring black on white when first light broke. But the sound of the sirens crept closer. Noise shaped itself into a wave, gathering and rising. Not rolling in a straight line, but zigzag, a serpentine undulation, shimmying up Broadway, banging cans, breaking glass. She heard a gunshot, it seemed quite close, the birds were outraged, and she almost sat up. Then another shot, but this one muffled, somewhere underground she thought, and she subsided again.

Light was crawling on her feet, she felt peckish. Tell the truth, she could have done with some popcorn. Forget it; better that the cockroach had it. One good deed in a lifetime, it wouldn't look good to take it back. Not now, when fire alarms had started clanging up and down the block. Not right this moment, when she turned her head and that boy was back, Wilfredo, he was standing over her, and he wasn't wearing a stitch.

Should of, would of, could of. Maybe he should have offed the dummy where he lay, he would have been fully justified. Then he could have got some peace round here. But he didn't shoot fish in a barrel, that was not his concept of sport. And anyhow, his wants had evolved.

He had progressed to a higher plane, you might say. Even in the span of these few hours since the blades in the barbershop, he'd come to see things in their true perspective. Kate Root was his only target now; the one score that he must settle. What use was there in another dead mick, more or less? That man had only been a hired assassin, not the mastermind. Correction was all he required; a boot in the ribs to teach him respect. Only Littles Fernando's shoe had proved a weak sister. Too fat and too slow, no rhythm, no sense of balance. Like working with a limp dick, the only one you hurt was yourself.

At every minute more lights cut the darkness. Stare into the night, and it looked like a nigger with plague, a blue-black skin violated by numberless sores and blotches. Everywhere that Willie moved, people were talking about Farrakhan getting shot. They sounded mad, they were getting evil. Then the news spread that it wasn't Farrakhan after all, it was some other name that sounded the same, not Farrah Fawcett, but close, and then another name, not close at all.

'My baby. They killed my baby,' a woman started to screaming, you could hear her blocks away, and soon after that the stoning began.

Willie found himself caught up in a wolfpack then. Not by his conscious choosing, but he was standing on a corner when hooded marauders passed by, and their slipstream sucked him in, he was swept along. Not running flat out, only trotting for now, moving back and forth across the avenue in zigzags whenever cops loomed.

So the laws were powerless; all their weapons and riot shields meant zip. They could hardly shoot down the entire pack, it would have been bad for their image. Besides, the shifting darkness kept shuffling their targets. Truthfully, they couldn't do a thing but posture. Advance and retreat in a phalanx, point their guns in a meaningful manner, chew gum. While the pack rolled on unchecked, smashing every window it passed.

There was no fear, Willie didn't have the time. All his concentration was taken up with business. Keeping in step with the headless runners up front, a jump ahead of those behind him, not slipping down, not getting himself stampeded. Adrenalin surged through him, he felt the power. If the right brick had come his way, he would have grabbed it, and welcome.

Everywhere he moved, shop windows gaped open, full of stuff he could use. *Free*, that word was an uncut drug. The jagged edges of glass, caught by flashlights, looked as though they were winking. Luring him to cross the line. *One step*. There was a satin Yankees warm-up jacket in there. *Just take that step*. 7, that had been Mickey Mantle's number. *For free*.

But he did not cross, after all. He was just about to, his foot was on the threshold, his hand already reaching out.

269

'Step right up. Help yourself,' some voice said. Then he caught a flash of Kate Root; her eyes at the end of his knife. It hit him a clean shot, drove him backwards in the street. Almost floored him, so that he had to grab hold of a fire hydrant, steady himself against the crush. A moment later, the wolf pack had borne him on, he was back on track.

That was the moment of truth, right there. He had hung one step from falling by the wayside, losing sight of his true aim. His destination; his end. He wouldn't get waylaid again.

Sliding back in place, he let the waves carry him uptown. The darkness was less dense above the buildings now, it would soon be dawn. Already he could sense that there was no sky above him, only smoke. And smoke below him, too. Everywhere that light showed, he saw tendrils curling up through manholes and vents, snaking from cracks in the sidewalk. Hooded men with flame-throwers were setting fires, torching parked cars and abandoned stores, running, whooping, between the massed fire engines that couldn't stop them, only douse what they left behind.

Willie knew about fires; his Cousin Felix had fought them for his living. Black smoke meant conflagrations that were out of control, white smoke meant containment. But there was no white smoke in view, a nicotine yellow was the best deal going. A Foot Locker was blazing, and a Walgreen's was belching clouds of mucoid green. Why green? But green it was, and a Burger King was crumpling like blue touchpaper.

At Columbus Circle the wolf pack swung right, heading for the hotels to the east. Plush pickings inside the Essex House and the Plaza, pirate's treasure, but Willie refused to be tempted. Instead, pushing north, he travelled Broadway. Though his feet didn't climb, he felt himself rising up, out of a gulf to higher ground. The crowds were not so hard-packed here, and there were gaps between the fires, he was able to move almost freely. Now that the dark had given way to a murky brown, he could see his own feet in their clown shoes, see what and who they trod on. Next to a Shop Rite five bodies formed a ragged circle. A posse of horse thieves, they must have been, but they must have picked the wrong white mare to ride. One, a woman, sat propped upright in the doorway, the needle still stuck in its vein. A baby was on her lap, crying for the tit, but Willie could not stop, he was running late. Children were breaking in doors with hatchets and picks, cutting through metal gates with blowtorches, and a sufferhead in combat fatigues was brandishing an AK-47, and a burn victim lay stretched upon a pink blanket, black face roasted, no eyes. Ugly way to go, Willie thought, but he had moved beyond.

A late-model Mercedes that had rammed Nature's Nurture sat hissing. The driver was still making noises, but the tyres were slashed, the hubcaps already stripped. As Willie fumbled with Anna Crow's spare key, he heard the man gargle, go croak. Then Willie was inside, he was safe.

Down the passage and up the narrow steep stairway, sixteen steps; along, then he was in Kate Root's bedroom. Its floor felt spongy with feathers.

Straining against the dimness, he saw Kate's big shape bulging under a white sheet. She seemed to be breathing hard and ragged in there. For a moment he thought she might be crying, but the sound was not right, it was probably just fear. Or expectation, who knows? When she turned to see him standing in his skin, when she realized what he'd come for. But you couldn't guess from her expression; she looked at him dead flat. 'What is the meaning of this?' she said.

*The meaning of this?* She owed him, that's all. Her bill had come due, and he was here to collect. Blunt instruments

271

were hammering on the steel gates downstairs, baseball bats, by the sound of them, and Willie D whipped off the bed sheet, exposed her.

Splayed like a starfish, that heavy body inside its school-girl's pink nightie with the coy little flowers embroidered at the neck and the hem rucked up high around her hips, she showed him all she'd got. Didn't even try to cover herself, and what was to hide anyway? The three hairs were long gone, they would never grow back. Though he couldn't help but sneak a look. In case of a miracle, you never could tell. But the bone-white dime above her ankle was barren. Void.

By the time he raised his sights, the pink nightdress had been lowered, there was nothing left to see. But this absence only goaded him. One hand ripped at the woman's belly, the other turned her head. Her green eyes were inches below him, and the gap in her front teeth was almost his: 'Have some popcorn,' said Kate Root.

And he was dead meat.

It was the apathy that broke him. Scratching and spitting he could handle, he was no stranger to wildcats, but neutrality did him in. The steady way Kate Root was watching him, measuring. That same level look she'd used the first morning he had clapped eyes on her, playing with her para-keet or whatever on the sidewalk. It had paralysed him then, it killed him now. 'Put it away,' she said, and she didn't even sound mocking, you wouldn't hardly think she had triumphed. Almost conversational, she sounded, and she put her thick fingers to Willie's face, she touched the bridge of his nose.

The hammering downstairs was getting more frenzied, now it sounded like steel smashing steel. Still, her fingertips were unhurried, butter-soft. They felt him, shaped him to themselves. And all his rage slid away. All his hungers, and his vengeance. Ask him why he'd come here, he couldn't have said. To rest, probably. For a great weariness took him. Feeling these fat fingers mould and trace him, smelling Kate's warm-bread breath on his eyes. Sensing home. Though he had none.

Loudhailers and sirens were moving up the block. 'It's been a long night,' Willie said, and he'd started to slide down along the rumpled sheet, he was drifting away with his eyes open, when the gates of the Zoo went in with a mortal crash that made the bed buck and shudder like a startled horse, and a moment later the screaming began. 'My birds!' Kate Root cried, grabbing up her stun-gun. Then the screaming mingled with choking, an asthmatic gasping. 'My snakes!' Kate roared, and charged.

Never even stopped to put on her dressing gown. Willie carried it for her, just in case, and followed her spoor down the stairs. In this early light he was struck by the wallpaper. Three gilded petals on a creamy shield, was that what you called a fleur-de-lis? And he turned the blind corner into the Zoo; he walked into an abattoir.

Three or maybe four kids, dressed up in black as Ninjas and wielding machetes, were slashing at every living thing. The cages had all been opened, and the birds beheaded as they flew out. Their bodies littered the floor, hung from the trees, lay broken against the walls. Some still flurried in midair, headless clumps of feathers, jetting blood; others were piled in the doorway where they'd dashed at the light. And still the Ninjas whirled their machetes, cutting now at the wandering jews, now at the snakes crawling underfoot, now at birds that hadn't been killed cleanly, only maimed.

Kate Root kept rushing at them, howling with no words, and they kept taunting her, flirting their weapons in her eyes, slicing rips in her nightdress as she chased them. A blinded bear she seemed, striking out at air, slithering in the blood that lapped at her bare feet. Blood that the kids kicked up like surf, splashing her thighs and groin. They sported like Little Leaguers, tossing the severed heads of kingsnakes and whiptails back and forth across the Zoo; they might have been playing pepper. And Willie could not intrude. He knew it was expected, but he couldn't enter that lake of blood. Only stood on the outside gawking, when Kate, with a last despairing lunge, pinned one of the Ninjas in the wreckage of the steel gate and began to crash his skull against a buckled strut. Gouging flesh and matter, body-slamming him, still howling. Not to be prised loose even when one of the child's homeboys clutched her by the hair and wrenched, slid his blade against her throat.

Her teeth, white in red, looked like grinning when she looked at Willie in the doorway; then someone threw a dead snake. Twisting in air like a lasso, it flew at Willie's feet, and splattered Littles Fernando's loafers. And Willie snapped. Though they might be only borrowed, they were still shoes. Something heavy came in his hand, and he plunged. Swung his right arm once, swung twice, then again and again, feeling bones crack and flesh pulp, hearing screams that were no birds, till the blows hit only air.

The Ninjas had run off, nobody but Kate was left. She lay in twisted metal and shattered glass, no longer howling, not making any noise at all. Around her a few birds still twitched, one or two snakes lay coiled. Willie recognized the whiptail who'd teased him that night of Osain's grave. Its yellow-rimmed eye still measured him, ironic, but no body was attached.

The weight in his hand was dragging at Willie's arm. When he looked down to see his weapon of choice, it was the toilet seat from the barbershop, the one he'd aimed his blade at.

So all things were connected, even here, and he helped Kate to her feet, the two of them slipping a little in the mire, bodies bumping awkwardly at hip and knee.

When she grabbed at him for balance, her palm left its red double on his shirt front. A perfect imprint, the Line of Destiny, the Girdle of Venus; you could have read her fortune.

Stumblebums, they staggered as they moved, clasping tight to each other to keep their feet. The counter was a few steps away, it seemed a distant shore, and when they reached it they clung to it shuddering, gasping for breath.

Close beside the Zenith lay a cockatoo, pure white, its plumes fanned like an umbrella. At first glance it seemed unharmed. Only one drop of blood blemished it white breast, one drop its beak. And Kate Root at last began to weep. Hid herself in Willie, and he took her in. Harboured her, why not? She was an old woman, after all.

Afterwards she lit a Camel, then passed it to him, but the blood like smudged lipstick put him off. A time like this, smoke failed to satisfy. And Kate Root must have felt the same way. At any rate she wiped her eyes, she blew her nose. Blood, snot and tears: 'I need a drink,' she said.

'The need is mutual.'

'If it was mutual, it wouldn't be need.' But gently, not looking to start an argument. 'I have to powder my nose,' she said, and departed.

Willie D didn't care to stay in this place by himself. This boneyard. Bumblefooted in another man's shoes, he groped his way through the chasm where the Zoo's door had been, looked out into the street. Already the main body of looters had passed, only scavengers were left. The sirens and the mob's raging sounded a few blocks north, zigzagging towards Harlem. The Ansonia was burning, Willie saw, a wedding

275

cake with its candles blazing. A flock of black birds streamed from its blazing turrets. And one brighter colour among them. A flurry of vermilion over turquoise, it looked like a cockatoo.

The escape artist, it must be. Must have hit the door too swift and wild for the Ninjas to cut it down. The notion crossed Willie's mind to go out searching for other survivors, but he hadn't the strength left, or the will. Besides, he'd done enough. One true thing. It was all any man could deliver.

Through the velvet curtain in the barbershop, he perched on the high chair like a throne and rested himself, watching the striped pole spinning on the wall. The weariness was on him again, that same slow drifting he'd felt in Kate's bed. The sense of home, against all meaning.

It lulled him to sleep.

And at last he dreamed.

He was in church, it was dead of night, a black stormy night full of lies, and he'd come to the chapel to pray. But his prayers came out all jumbled, back to front, and he was too tired to set them straight. He felt spent, no flicker of energy left.

Sitting by himself in this empty church, with only a solitary priest for company. But this priest did not regard him. He was kneeling at the altar with his back turned, robed and cowled like a medieval monk in *Robin Hood*. From where Willie sat, the priest's face was hidden but he seemed to be making secret signs with his hands. Telling his beads, maybe, or casting a spell. Then Willie stood up, came close, and the priest turned. The light was bad and the angle of his hood covered up his eyes, but his attitude was stiff, intimidating, like somebody else's father.

When Willie looked closer, he saw that the priest had a bandit's moustache, he was dressed up like Zorro underneath his robes, and you could tell that he wasn't so harsh or cold after all, that was just his front. Willie snuck a glance beneath his cowl, and the priest's eyes were teasing, flirting. It was obvious that he hadn't been telling beads, not casting spells; what he'd been doing with his hands was creating a paper aeroplane. Exquisite workmanship, indescribably intricate. Willie bent close to inspect the details, and the priest spoke to him in a low voice.

The words could not be distinguished, but they altered everything. Instead of examining the paper plane, Willie was now riding inside it, first class, and the priest was drinking whiskey sour. A perfect gentleman, he asked Willie what he'd like for himself, and the way he smiled when he offered this, Willie knew he could ask for anything in existence. Just give it a name, it would be his. But no single word came to his mind; there seemed to be nothing he needed. Not now, not any more. So he shook his head, no, and a bowl of clear soup appeared. Then the priest raised Willie by his throat, not roughly or unkind but irresistible, and pushed his face beneath the surface.

Instantly, all his weariness washed away. He caught a glimpse of the priest reflected in the soup, and the priest had turned into a young girl, though he kept his bandit's moustache. Seeing Willie watching, he peeled down his monk's robe to show his breasts. His whole body was laid bare, offered up. Willie pillowed his face against the rounded hummock of the priest's pussy. The red hairs smelled wild like jungle flowers.

Waking, he felt rested but antsy; his business here was over. When he stepped out on the street, it had begun to rain. Nothing hard as yet, but you could smell a drenching on its way.

Broadway in daylight was no man's land. Huge tangles of

barbed wire rose at every corner, blocking off the side streets, and the areas between were minefields. Camouflaged manholes, smouldering trash-fires, unexploded tear-gas canisters. A garter snake and a gecko were lounging outside the Chemical Bank. The clock above them read 9.43, then 104°.

The late-model Mercedes had been removed from Sweeney's doorway. In its place was that man Anna Crow had told him about, the one who lived in the attic. Squat, he believed the name was. A dancing man, anyway, and he was dancing now. Reeling drunk, an open pint in his meat hand, he was doing a soft-shoe shuffle. Leaning way forward as if listening to something way downtown, he kept swaying, almost falling. Still his feet were light; you could see he knew the steps. A sand-drag, a pigeonwing, then a long slow rubber-legged spin, his arms flapping like a demented flamingo: '*Babylon the great is fallen, is fallen,*' he said.

It was a point of view. Made a ton of sense, when you took time to think. But Willie had no time, he could not afford that luxury. This was his day, he mustn't waste it.

Across the street a shoe store stood wide and gaping. The wolves had already gone through it, stripped it almost bare. But one pair had been overlooked. A pair of calfskin lace-ups, glossy nigger brown, absolutely plain. No armadillo or lizardskin, no ostrich trim or Spanish tonguing. Just a handful of lines, a few curves. Maybe that was why they'd been spared, they were so simple and understated that no one had noticed them. Only Willie. Who took one look, and stood rapt, too dazzled almost to claim them. Peering down at the label to see who the designer could be, Manzio or Berkeley Musser, Roscoe de Llama, Miami Mort Amity maybe, but it was none of those, the creator was not even listed. *Dark Brown*, was all the label said. *Man's Shoe*.

These were the titles of birds: *Calliope, Ariel, Frilled Coquette, Sainson's Doubtful Toucan, Red-capped Babbler, Turquoise-browed Motmot, Malachite Sunbird, Sappho Comet.*

The stairs were smothered with their feathers, her room was full of feathers, too. *Blue Creeper, Ant Tanager, White-footed Racket.* She couldn't stay here. She could never sleep in that bed again. A feather even stuck to Fred Root's portrait. *Crimson Topaz Hummingbird.* She swept it aside, but then it clung to her nightgown instead, as others clung to her arms and legs. *Abyssinian Ground Hornbill, Mexican Diglossa Honeycreeper*, she couldn't stay here.

Outside Ferdousine's door, instead of a Welcome mat, lay a tangle she could have used for a mop. *King Bird of Paradise: red head, white breast, and a ring of green throat ruffle; white and fawn wing feathers, green-rimmed, which can spread downwards like a fan; and two thread-like tail feathers which cross each other and possess green snail-like veins at the tips. Its call sounds like the mewing of a kitten.*

She had a thought to rap on that mahogany door, seek refuge in a cup of Earl Grey, but this was no morning for Melba toast, and anyhow Ferdousine would never hear her knock. These last days and nights he had been consumed by cricket, huddled over his short-wave radio, listening on earphones to the Test Match in London. England and Australia at Lords, in his mouth it sounded like a cathedral, and until play had ended, no earthquake or mere apocalypse would shift him.

No comfort there, not a hope, so she climbed more stairs, steep and strait, up above the feather-line, until she arrived at Anna Crow's.

She had not entered this room since Anna moved in. Why would she? A trifling piece of work, that one. Forever wheedling and twisting, slavering after a new pair of pants. *Needy*, it was the ugliest word. But what was she herself, after all? What else had brought her here, fumbling at the poor bitch's door, and when it gave way, sneaking in to snoop? Knowing well that Anna couldn't be home, she would never have stood her ground through such a night. A woman who screamed *Fire!* any time you struck a match. No more intestinal fortitude in that girl than would fuck a flea. Still, she had some nice things in here. God forgive her so many self-portraits, and that hand-tinted pink bridesmaid was obscene. But the ornaments looked well, ornamental. The spice pots and the Chinese slippers. A Claddagh ring, she hadn't seen one of those in years. A French shoe-last, that would fit well in her own room. And these silk scarves. And . . .

*God's holy trousers, forgive me.*

How could she be so crass? So perverse? These last weeks and months, she'd lost all sense of fittedness. *Gravitas*, that was the right word. Talk about trifling, she herself had taken out the patent. Self-defence, but no excuse. Spying on Anna Crow this way, she might have perished for shame. So she slid across the landing, and spied on Maguire instead.

This was another room she did not frequent; it was too full of Godwin. Poor boy, she felt responsible in a way, she never should have let him take that job, but how was she to know? Those were the days she was not seeing, she'd had no suspicion. And he had been so happy in his work, the long white apron, the chef's *toque* and all. How many midnights she'd spent in this same room, waiting for that little tubby body to trundle up the stairs with the evening's pie. Chicago deep-dish, Sicilian, she liked them both, but you couldn't beat straight Brooklyn, lean and mean, the crust slightly charred, with extra mushroom and anchovy. Plus some loose scraps in a bag for Pearl. *Foccaccia* for the bird, and hold it right there. No more waterworks. Or she'd never stop.

She scoured the room for distractions, there were none. Just the mattress on the iron bedside beside the barred window, a framed photograph of some broad ballroom dancing, one book.

The photo gave her the creeps. No particular reason, just the way the woman simpered in her backless blue gown, twirling on stiletto heels to show off her starched petticoats and all her scrawny legs. So she made do with the book.

*The Deaths of Joachim*, by Hosea Tichenor; she'd never heard of it. One of those mouldy second-hand jobs off a street barrow, or thrown out with the trash. Dust and mildew, it smelled of dirty secrets, and she opened a page at random:

'Fire being out & all Hands safe in the dye-works, 3 days before the final battel, noing now his Hours were numerd, Joachim led his faythful SWANS some mile outside the citie Gate, wher was a feeld of Clovr & Thyme. & there he recit his last sermon saying, O my swans weep not or wale. Tho dark Night ly in wait, even unto DEATH, by all means Keep good Heart & Cheer. For the false PREESTS shall tryumf here, but not hereafter, & their lude Mastres lykwys, a hollo show onlie, no Worth. But you, my swans, all eternitie will tast & sup. Tho bound in slavrie now & cruel usd, the END shall your great Fredom be, if onlie you endure. O BUT ENDURE, my swans. O BUT ENDURE.'

Not Kate's kind of stuff. Too much like hard work. But it helped fill her mind. Helped blot out the Zoo below. So she kept on flicking the pages. 'For I have speke agin to the VIRGIN, in the Night she coms to me saying, Fere not,' she read. '& I to her say in retern, I am not Fered, but qestiun Why must I dye. Why periss by BODDIE BURRENING, for saying The VIRGIN have feets. Because thou art blessed, she ansers me. Because thou SEE true. For my feets they mov so fast, no fals eye can hop to follow. & HERE alone is the deep of truth: my feets they VANISH if you BLINK.'

Strange, she'd never thought of that. All the hours she'd wasted arguing with Monsignor Beebe, struggling to explain, the answer had sat right there. *For my feets they mov so fast, no fals eye can hop to follow.* But she'd been too young, she couldn't see it. All that had counted then was Elvis, and painting her toenails, and stopping Pompey from slobbering on her blouse.

The book's frontispiece was a woodcut of Joachim at the stake, devoured by tongues of fire. But he was no average martyr. Instead of an anguished ascetic with his eyes upraised to heaven, he was built like a lumberjack, too hale and muscular by half.

Looked a bit like Fred Root, in fact. Only black.

The first chapter was titled *FALS HUNGERS OF THE FAYTHLES WORLD*. '& dreme I did of men chaned and lasht, SLAVES in theyr skyn but theyr SOLES flying,' Kate began, but that was the furthest she got. Somebody was standing in the door, she glanced up, and it was Maguire. 'I saw downstairs,' he said.

So she was dragged back. To find the floorboards littered

282

with Camel butts because there was no ashtray; and the rusted bars imprisoning the window, this glass was utterly filthy, she could hardly see herself reflected; and worst, Maguire himself. Looking like a deep-seam miner pulled half-dead from a cave-in, his clothes in tatters and his face caked with God knows what.

Tensed and hovering for instructions, straining to read her wish, his eyes on her were avid like some other eyes. Black eyes, one ringed, head crooked. And it came to her then whose eyes those were. They were Pompey's, of course. Waiting to be fed. So Kate closed her book. 'What happened to you?' she asked.

'There was a spot of bother.'

'What bother?'

'They killed Miss Crow.'

People, you could not trust them. And the dead ones were the worst. That morning they'd passed on the stairs. Yesterday morning it must have been, though that seemed unrealistic. When Anna was La Belle Dame sans Merci in her velvet robe and blonde wig, *I made her a garland for her head, and bracelets too, and fragrant zone*: 'She loved words,' said Kate.

She supposed she should ask for details. Hear the story out. But it was none of her business, after all, she had no call to pry. Far below, she heard something thrash, sounded like a broken wing flapping, and she clattered her feet to drown it. 'I have to go away,' she said.

'What about downstairs?'

'I'm sure you'll handle things just fine. You have a natural bent for this business, you know, I spotted that right off. Just remember the oil in the rape, two drops per dish, and don't forget the sunflower seeds.'

'But those creatures are all dead, they aren't eating.'

'Flake maize and pellets are best in the morning, save the peanut kernels for night.'

Now that she had determined to leave, there seemed no good cause to delay. 'Good book, I enjoyed it,' she said, '*O BUT ENDURE*, there's a lot of truth in that.'

The lies out of her mouth! How could she exist with herself? 'The lizards like live mealworms, you can mix them with wheat bran, or even termites if you like. Oh, and an occasional cabbage leaf or halved potato for variety. And mice for the whipsnakes on Sundays, please. The white ones are the sweetest, I always find,' she said. 'But snakes are versatile, they adapt. Any old mouse will do in a storm.'

'What about the iguanas?'

'Spam.'

Gingerly, as if testing her footing after a spill, she made her way down the stairway to her own room. She had a fleeting impression that poor Godwin was on the landing, pie in pudgy hand, but he was gone again before she could focus, and she knew he was a falsehood anyway. She was overstrained; she needed rest. Thirty-five acres, fresh air, loads of healthy walks. Maybe a few brisk swims in Lake George, there was nothing like a morning dip to perk you up. Of course, the buses might not be running today, what with this earthquake and all. Well, she'd wait.

Cross her bedroom without glancing down. Reach the closet and pack. The only luggage she possessed was an antique cricket bag. The straps had rotted, the zipper failed to zip, but this was no moment to quibble. She threw in a change of underwear, Fred Root's portrait, back copies of *Soap Digest*, her nightdress, her blue mules and dressing gown. Dressed herself in her flowered cotton dress, and left all other clothes be. Then threw out the *Soap Digests*, and left those behind as well.

284

Feathers coated her hands and feet, she had no time to pick them off. Only looked around for a belt or some tape to bind up the bag. Curled at the foot of her bedside table, where it must have fallen sometime in the long night's upheavals, was that length of rope Anna Crow had laid on her. It looked unclean, but never mind. The girl had had her uses.

Should she say goodbye to Ferdousine? Better not, on the whole. His Test Match might still be in play, she didn't like to intrude. Even if the game had finished, he would only weigh her down with macaroons and questions. A postcard from sunny Saratoga Springs would show more tact.

Maguire was behind her, still hovering, still waiting to be commanded. Should she kiss his cheek goodbye? Doubtful that he would enjoy that. Give him a hug?

They shook hands.

'Do you have everything you need?' asked Maguire. That fucking word again, it was a fucking contagion. *False Hungers of the Faithless World*. Well, the antidote to need was belief, any fool knew that. But she had so little to tap. All she believed on this morning for sure was that Baloney Breath was her horse's name, and a horse might lead to a hound, a hound at last to a sufferance. So grant her grace in small doses, roach by roach. Dog in the mirror make her whole.

He was a temporary man just. Nothing more than a stopgap while Miss Root took her holidays. The Adirondacks, she had said, and very nice too, though he himself favoured the seaside. Balmy breezes, shimmering strands, you couldn't beat the old bucket and spade.

Desperate peaky she'd looked as she said goodbye. Small wonder in it either, the horror she had lived through. Ten years' love and labour desolated, that would steal the roses from any woman's cheeks. And then as well, of course, she'd be grieving for Miss Crow.

It had been almost dawn before they'd brought Anna to the surface. Randall Gurdler had issued his statement and posed for his pictures, gone home to bed long since. Or back to headquarters, as he claimed himself, but John Joe would not believe one word out of that man's mouth. A born smarmy boots, you wouldn't buy a used fart from a tosser like that. Although some of the men under him seemed decent sorts. Master Maitland had said not to trust them an inch, they were the Antichrist's bumboys one and all. But those fire-fighters and ambulance men had plunged in the burning earth more times than you could count this night, bringing forth their dead.

Most were victims of smoke, it seemed. Two lawmen had expired from friendly fire, and one civilian from a heart attack. The majority, though, were still extant. Strapped onto stretchers, they were trundled under the klieg lights to the ambulance, their stunned faces caked thick with soot and oil. White and black alike, they looked like Mitchell's Minstrels down there. Strangers passed by in a breakless line. Then came Joe Easter, his chest stoved in. Then Burdette Merryweather and Marvella Crabtree, both smoke. Then a body in Jerzy Polacki's clothes, head bandaged like the Invisible Man. And Brulant Boniface, on foot, in handcuffs. 'What became of the Master?' John Joe called out.

'Vamoosed,' Brulant replied, then the lawmen took him away. The smoke pouring out of the subway exits was getting denser by the minute, you had to keep a handkerchief over your face, and even then you choked. The concrete underfoot kept gaining heat, it felt like hot coals. John Joe was forced to shuffle and hop, stay constantly on the shift, or else his rubber-soled Trudgett's might have got stuck to the sidewalk. And still the stretchers kept coming, the firemen's hoses kept sweeping their path, the kliegs kept drilling black holes in your eyes. Between the lights and smoke and weariness, he almost missed Anna Crow.

She did not seem damaged in any way. John Joe's first care was to search her for pain, but he found no trace. For a wonder, the worst soot had kept off her face. A few streaks and smudges on her forehead just, the rest of her was unblemished. As if the embalmer had done his work already, all fear and anger smoothed away. So this was not Anna. That person was elsewhere; vamoosed, like Master Maitland. While this waxwork lay in her place, borne in procession for all men to see.

All the ambulances were fully loaded, there was a logjam behind. Even as Anna Crow was being paraded, another great roar came from underground, and water rushed, foaming, from the earth. A burst main perhaps, or some other flood. Within a space of seconds, countless fountains erupted from fire hydrants and subway vents, unclassified holes in the ground. In the glare of lights, with the stretchers gliding slow and stately beneath, it was almost like the water-ballet in the *son et lumière* at Kilmullen Castle. John Joe had watched one summer night with Juice Shovlin, they had got in for half price.

Beautiful it had been then, and lovely now: the form of Anna still and white, the paramedics bent over her, tending. Better than the castle even, it might have been St Conall's stream, that night the stoats had buried their female. In silence they'd passed through the grove and over the stream, into the shelter of the bull, *Scaith-na-Tairbhe*. That was a burying proper, but Anna had shrugged when he told her. She wanted jazz, she'd said; she wanted cocktails with a cherry. But she got neither here, just one more blow-up underfoot, a gusher that sent the crowd floundering backwards, thrashing, and by the time John Joe could struggle into place again, the ambulance doors had shut, there was no more of Anna Crow.

He made his best way home then. Straggling through the lightening streets, water to his ankles and the fire above, and the sights he saw on his journey, the fornication and the drunkenness, the looting and burning, smoke-blindness would have been a blessing to him. And again when he passed that Black Maria outside the cop shop, and it was full of Swans. Valence Holt was one he recognized, and Gladstone Rivers too. Hilario Vargas and his wife Angelique, Clarence Codd, James Jeffries Word, and all of them in shackles, down by law. But still no sign of Master Maitland.

Where could he be hid? *Vamoosed* was not a word that told you much. Scrammed, skedaddled, he might be anywhere. Might have burrowed deeper yet in rock, found himself a fresh hiding place. Or been snatched away to heaven, just the way he had predicted. Risen with the raptured, enthroned at God's right hand. A Black Swan in glory, he might have the last laugh yet.

Well, strength to him, he might. But John Joe didn't feel confident. Regardless that they had been foretold, this night's affairs did not strike him as correct.

If only the Master had been at hand to explain. Maybe John Joe misunderstood the programme, and this was just a dress rehearsal. A test of faith, to see who truly believed, and who was expendable. Maybe the top Swans, those chosen as worthy to survive, would regroup at some later date and create another Mount Tabor. But it could never again be so snug. So companionable to his soul. Best of luck in their endeavours. Still and all, they'd have to make do without himself.

The moment he stepped inside the Zoo, anyhow, all thought of Black Swans fled his mind. Impossible, in this charnel house, to fret over Kingdom Come. He saw Barnabus the monkey pushed from the railway bridge, saw Rudkin scalded in boiling milk. He saw a white bull kneeling with its throat slit, its blood draining in black earth.

Who fathered such distress? What power of hurt could so betray a man? In their room above Duchess Gardens, his mother had pinned a poem to the wall one time. *Pain that cannot forget*, it read, *Falls drop by drop upon the heart Until in our despair comes wisdom Through the awful grace of God*. But no wisdom came to John Joe, or even a settled digestion.

It was the times that were in it. Sifting through the remains of these sliced creatures, shuffling them into plastic bags, he had to hold his breath so fiercely for so long, his skull filled with crackles and buzzings, and he failed to hear Mr Ferdousine descend the stairs.

John Joe hardly knew him to speak to, just a casual nod on the landing was all. Mornings when the old man stepped out to fetch his English newspaper, or Friday nights when he went to his chess club. Otherwise, they were strangers. But Mr Ferdousine appeared nothing shy. He stepped out crisp and keen through the Zoo, cast a cold eye on the carnage, picked his way through the body parts to the counter, and there he perched on a high stool. Though it was his own living that lay in its blood, he only nibbled at a flat tablet, it looked like caramel. 'Great tidings from London,' he said. 'England is destroyed.'

Taking inventory was no easy task. Every time John Joe had one animal reassembled, so he thought, one piece would still be missing, or an alien piece crept in. 'A most notable trouncing,' said Mr Ferdousine, nibbling, bibbling. 'At play's commencement, the English seemed home and dry, the Ashes were theirs. And now they are not merely defeated, but utterly prostrated. Perfidious Albion brought to dust.'

One hopeful sign, there were more cages than corpses. Two skinks and a chuckwalla turned up alive behind the velvet curtain, then John Joe found the Lutino Cockatiel huddled under a macaranga, sorely carved but breathing still. No other survivors, however, were reported at this time. 'Lambasted, lathered, skinned alive,' said Mr Ferdousine, then he glanced up sharply, as if caught short. 'Where is Miss Root?' he enquired.

'She stepped out for a breath of air.'

'I see.' And the old man started on a fresh caramel. 'A most remarkable woman, that; I met her great-uncle once. Fred Root, the famed Leg Theorist. Late in his career, he came one evening to Westminster School, to proffer a few coaching tips. He had been representing Worcestershire against Surrey at The Oval, and made his appearance at the close of the day's play. Hot and perspiring from his toils, he had not even time to change his flannels, but appeared in full working fig. Alas, I myself was not cricketer enough to qualify for his attentions. However, I took up a position behind his arm as he bowled, and I will never forget the splendour of his action. Two short walking steps, six accelerating strides, then the body rocked easily back. The left arm was thrown up as a pivot, the ball held in the back-slung right hand. Then, with a final leap, came the full rhythmic swing of those heavy shoulders. Root delivered at the acme, and as he followed through, his hand seemed to press down heavily on the air. His left foot plunged into the ground, and his arm swept on after the delivery, describing a wide circle. Such beauty it was. The mastery of the thing.'

From the holy-Joe tone that Mr Ferdousine employed, you could tell this story was meant to matter. But cricket was not John Joe's idea of a game. The GAA did not approve it, and Juice Shovlin had always said that only nancy boys played, a bunch of Fifi la Plumes scared to get their togs mucked.

'And afterwards,' said Mr Ferdousine, sprinking crumbs of caramel down his bottle-green velvet waistcoat, 'and afterwards, I walked home by myself. An alien, I was never popular with the other boys. Their ceaseless ragging and bullying were a deep bitterness to me, so that, when Root concluded his demonstration, I was glad to escape my confreres' unwanted attentions, and wend my way in solitude. The evening light was all but gone, the night came on apace. Lost in thoughts of the peerless exhibition that I had so recently witnessed, I walked oblivious to my surroundings. Thus, it came as a complete surprise when suddenly a car horn blared in my ear, and I looked up to see Root's smiling face at the window of his Morris Minor. It was not a handsome countenance; no amount of hero worship could make it so. Gnarled and lumpen, it was the face of a gargoyle rather. But humorous, warm, infinitely kind. And now he smiled on me. Something in my posture may have apprised him of my loneliness, for, without a word, he reached inside his cricket bag and brought out a cherry-red ball, as yet untouched by willow. A moment he paused to rub it on his flannels for luck, then tossed it to me. But the light was poor, and I was ever a duffer at catch. Slipping through my fingers, the ball fell to the pavement with a thud, then rolled away. When I retrieved it, its perfection was scuffed and marred, my humiliation complete. In desperation, I tried to blame the gathering dusk. *It was the dark*, I protested. But Root only laughed. *It always is*, he said, and drove on.'

Was that all? Surely this couldn't be the punchline? But Ferdousine said no word further. Merely waggled his birdy head sideways, staring at John Joe out of those yellow eyes, then he brushed the last crumbs from his hands, descended from his perch and, with one brisk nod of farewell, he went back upstairs to his quarters. Leaving John Joe with his broom and pail, and ten plastic bags filled to bursting.

Perhaps he'd missed something. Perhaps there was some hidden clue to that tall story he'd been too tired to catch. Or perhaps the old man had simply been gaming with him. Pretending to share a confidence, only to leave him dangle. In any case, there was disrespect involved, and he would not stand still for mockery. To slave and suffer as he did now, up to his udders in innards, and then be made a sport, he could get all that from Juice Shovlin, he didn't need it from any man else.

A minute there, resting on his broom, he was tempted to

sling his hook. Walk out on the whole damned set. But where was he to go? Not back to Scath, his room would be rented by now. Nor off to London either; England was destroyed. The sore truth was, he had no spot he fitted. On TV sometimes he'd hear some politician or golfer in polyster pants speak highly of patriotism. 'How must that feel?' he'd ask himself then. 'To hear the words *My Country* in your mouth?' But he had no way of knowing, and no likelihood of finding out.

If he didn't lie, the Zoo was his best offer. His only offer, why pretend? So he went back to his sifting and bagging. It was turned one o'clock, *Days of Our Lives* must be on. Billie looked smashing in her bridal gown, but, as for Bo, he wouldn't trust that man with Randall Gurdler's mother.

Outdoors beyond the ruins, when he looked, it was pissing down rain. No, tell a lie, it was snivelling more than pissing. On Broadway the last of the looters were making their way home. A child and his mother passed, they were bearing a toaster-oven, a microwave and a CD player, their arms hung heavy with new clothes. The same child it was that John Joe had seen on the street that day, the first time ever he'd met Miss Root.

A golden boy, he'd been, curled up on his side with his one hand stretched out in the light, the fingers bent as if begging. And his mother at the door of Blanco y Negro, her fat fingers clustered with rings. And the way he rose like a whistled greyhound at Miss Root's call. So now they went home with their spoils. Back to their fifth-floor apartment. Two rooms, John Joe saw, with a connecting corridor, the bathroom off to one side. He saw a portrait of the Virgin over a bed, an altar. Scented candles, Lucky Kentucky glasses full of pink water, green water and blue, a necklace made out of horse's teeth, hanks of hair, a sequined crucifix, and one spent bullet, ringed by fairy lights. But there was no cause to hurry, they might as well save their shoe-leather. That place was up in flames.

The image exhausted him finally. He had to use his broom like a crutch, or he might have fallen out of his standing again, the way he'd fallen after Miss Root shaved him.

Suspended between sleep and waking, he let his eyelids close. Then he felt as though he was sliding. *I always did like going down*, Anna Crow had said, descending the ladder. There was some joke in that, you could tell by her voice, but he was no good at jokes. *A fetching shade of quince*, she'd said, and he saw her by the boating pond. Her Da was swinging her higher and higher, then the rope broke, and she was flung into air, she was spinning, then falling and falling, oh love, on my love. *I wish I could see me*, she'd said. Five levels underground, in that lost land.

The dust and filth his broom had raised settled on his hands and in his hair, he tasted at its scum that coated his lips. Her tongue a sleeping slug. Some thief was playing a boombox in the street, the heavy bass thudding the beat like punches, and John Joe in his weariness began to move his feet in time.

He couldn't dance, still he shuffled. Let the broom fall, and he moved through the Zoo. His hands came up, curled into fists; his elbows tucked in against his ribs. The man on the boombox was singing an angry song. *Never hesitate to put a nigger on his back* was its refrain, and John Joe began to circle. Letting his fists travel as they would. A jab, a hook, a jab off the hook. A right cross, an uppercut, jab, jab, jab. A bolo, another left hook, and he saw his own person plain, a man of colours whirling, arms pistoning, the dust flying off him like silver spray, and a gold sword in flames.

A sudden flurrying behind him made him wheel. It was a

bird returning; the bird was Pearl. Not a scratch on her it seemed, or any feather ruffled. She hopped aboard the counter, she started watching Billie and Bo. Of course, she must be half-starved. Having missed her breakfast and all. So John Joe began to measure out her feed. Nectar paste and pellets, a slice of cuttlefish bone. Then he brought her the filled bowl, he served her.

It was his duty, after all.

# Acknowledgments

All of the characters in this book are my own invention, with one exception. There was indeed a famous cricketer named Fred Root, who played for Worcestershire and England between the World Wars. The facts of his career, to the best of my knowledge, are as given here; many of them have been taken from his autobiography, *A Cricket Pro's Lot*. But everything else that I have written about him – his life after cricket, his sweet shop in Wolverhampton, his drinking habits and, above all, his relationship to Kate – is fictional. As for Ferdousine's description of his bowling action, that is in large part derived from the late John Arlott's portrait of Maurice Tate, one of Fred Root's contemporaries.

During the writing of *Need*, I have built up a small library of reference books. From some of these I have borrowed; from others, shamelessly stolen. My thanks are due to them all, and so I list them in full:

*A Cricket Pro's Lot* – Fred Root

*The Who's Who of Cricketers*

*The Serena Technique of Belly Dancing* – Serena

*The Mole People* – Jennifer Toth

*Revelation Visualized* – Dr Gary Cohen and Salem Kirban

*The Santeria Experience* – Migene Gonzalez-Wippler

*Knife Throwing: A Practical Guide* – Harry K. McEvoy

*King Mob* – Christopher Hibbert

*The Success Dream Book* – Prof. De Herbert

*The Pursuit of the Millennium* – Norman Cohn
*Western Reptiles and Amphibians* – Robert C. Stebbins
*Pet Birds for Home and Garden* – Don Harper
*The Book of the Sacred Magic of Abra-Melin the Mage*
*The Prophecy Handbook* – William E. Beiderwolf
*The Rattle Bag* – eds. Seamus Heaney and Ted Hughes
*Cockfighter* – Charles Willeford
*Nineteen Acres* – John Healey
*The Barber of Natchez* – Edwin Davis and William
   Hogan
*Shah of Shahs* – Ryszard Kapuscinski
*In Conall's Footsteps* – Lochlann McGill
*Powers of Darkness, Powers of Light* – John Cornwell
*Fast One* – Paul Cain